RIALLARO

The Archipelago of Exiles

RIALLARO

The Archipelago of Exiles

GODFREY SWEVEN

Originally published in 1901.

Published by Wildside Press.

Visit us online at wildsidepress.com.

GODFREY SWEVEN AND THE SATIFICAL DYSTOPIAN TRADITION
KARL WURF

John Macmillan Brown (1845–1935), a Scottish-born scholar who emigrated to New Zealand, made his name as a pioneering academic and university administrator. Late in life, he turned to speculative fiction under the pseudonym Godfrey Sweven. His two novels—*Riallaro: The Archipelago of Exiles* (1901) and *Limanora: The Island of Progress* (1903)—are among the more unusual contributions to early twentieth-century utopian and dystopian writing. (teara.govt.nz)

Riallaro depicts a South Pacific archipelago of isolated islands, each one inhabited by groups cast out from a central utopian society. The book's framing device—an adventurer arriving after being shot from the skies with artificial wings—sets the stage for a satirical voyage. Each island becomes a case study in social distortion: a society driven to absurdity by one dominant vice, obsession, or ideology. (sf-encyclopedia.com)

This structure places *Riallaro* in a direct line with the British satirical tradition of imagined voyages. Like Swift's *Gulliver's Travels*, it uses geography as a moral mirror, exaggerating tendencies in politics, religion, and society until they reveal their dangers. Sweven's prose is less playful than Swift's, more earnest and philosophical, but the underlying technique—exposing folly through fantastical lands—remains consistent.

The sequel, *Limanora*, reveals the utopia that created these islands of exile: a tightly ordered society based on eugenics, technocracy, and long-term planning. This pairing underscores a theme that would resonate in later dystopian literature: the tension between progress and control. Brown anticipates concerns later developed by Aldous Huxley in *Brave New World* and George Orwell in *Nineteen Eighty-Four*. Both later writers would show how societies striving for perfection through science or ideology end up producing repression. Sweven's work, though less polished, reveals a similar anxiety. (depauw.edu)

Where Huxley satirized the pursuit of pleasure and Orwell dissected the cult of political power, Sweven critiqued the moral hazards of exclusion and the hidden costs of utopian engineering. His exiled islands become dystopias in miniature, each a warning about what happens when a single principle dominates unchecked. These themes situate *Riallaro* as a precursor to twentieth-century dystopian fiction, even if it remained little read outside specialist circles.

At the same time, *Riallaro* can be seen as a work of early science fantasy. Its devices—artificial wings, hidden archipelagos, speculative technologies—blend invention with moral allegory. This hybrid quality places it alongside other proto-science fiction texts of the fin de siècle, which often fused scientific speculation with satirical or philosophical intent.

In the history of speculative literature, *Riallaro* thus stands as an important transitional work: rooted in British satire, anticipating modern dystopias, and experimenting with the imaginative possibilities of science fantasy. Though obscure today, it marks a point where moral allegory, utopian thought, and speculative invention converged at the dawn of the twentieth century.

INTRODUCTION
THE MYSTERIOUS SHOT

"DEAD, FOR A DUCAT, dead," roared Somm, as he shouldered his gun and rushed to the beach. Nothing had come within reach of shot all afternoon till, in the thickening twilight, a flash of broad wings in the distance awakened our camp. "A wounded albatross," shouted both my companions, as they peered through the shuttling grey of the evening, and watched the south wind, still wild with the force of storm, shepherd some baffled creature of wings up towards our nestling-place. "Some still stranger bird," I thought, as we seized our guns and ran to the edge of the cliff. The sudden descent of night checked further question; and as the winged thing gleamed along the face of the precipice, three shots echoed across the sound, and, in a lull of the fitful gusts, we heard a dull plunge in the water far below.

It seemed but a few minutes till we met Somm in the rocky hollow that was the harbour for our boat; he had rowed out and back, and was leaning over some dark object that lay in the stern. Not a sign of feather or anything that gleamed was there about it. It was the form of a human being, apparently dead. We bore it up through the bush with the tender care that diggers are wont to give to the corpse of a comrade. Our burden was so light that we expected to look upon a thin, emaciated body. But, as we laid it in the flicker of our hut fire, we were amazed to see the rounded form and ruddy cheeks of the dead stranger.

We stripped him of his wrapping,—a strange muslin-like transparent toga,—and searched for the gunshot wound. Except for one broad bruise, there was no mark on the body. And then it began to dawn upon us that this had nothing to do with the flashing wings, or our shots, that we were guiltless of human blood. It was a case of drowning, but not yet dead. And we set to work to draw the clogging water from his heart and lungs. Slowly the breath began to come and the blood to circulate. The bosom heaved and we felt ourselves in the presence of another and a stranger human soul. What he was, whence he came, whirled through our minds in silence. Faint and in need of rest he manifestly was. We poured some stimulant down his throat and laid him on one of our rude beds of manuka and fern. We saw him fall into a deep and healthy sleep. And dawn was already threatening the east with flickering light when we went into the open and drew a long, sweet breath.

We consulted together over the strange occurrence, and determined to search the fiord for traces of the winged thing that flashed out at our shots. Before we had gone far, we found a pair of huge fans that had drifted into one of the frequent channels amongst the rocks. They were not of feathers, but of some strong, transparent, and almost weightless material that did not wilt in the sun or the wet. We lifted them, and there hung by them dragging in the water filmy strings like the long tentacles of a medusa. We cut them adrift, and bore the strange wing-like floats up to our cliff. Each of them seemed to move on a pivot with ease, and almost rose on the gentle breeze into which the storm had now died. After full examination of them, we laid them far back in the cavern, which we used as our storehouse and larder, and thought no more about them.

We cooked and ate our morning meal, and then spread out over the bush that overlooked the waters of the sound, forgetful of the stranger whom we had left in one of our huts. We were in search of gold, and, having found faint traces of it on the small, fan-like beaches that intervalled the sheer precipices on our side, we had been prospecting several months for the alluvial pocket or the reef from which the glittering specks had wandered down. The following week we were rewarded with success; but, as we have no desire to have our noble solitude disturbed by the noise of a frenzied, gambling crowd,—we are but woodmen and sealers and photographers to the outside world when it intrudes in the shape of tourists,—I shall not mention at present the name of the New Zealand fiord in which we live.

I was working up a watercourse, panning the sand and dirt that lay in the crevices and occasional levels, at times startled by a weka that impudently slid through the undergrowth and eyed me close at hand, or by the harsh call of the kea, as it flew from some resting-place and circled in the air. Rudely awakened from my absorption, I looked out on the marvellous scene that lay at my feet; precipice towered over precipice, often forest-clad from base to summit. Almost sheer below me slept the waters of the sound, landlocked as if it were a lake. Only the indignant cry of the kea, or the weka's raucous whistle, or the echo of a distant avalanche ever broke the silence of this solitary land. Never did it cease to throw its shadow on my thoughts or stir their sense of beauty or their sadness.

Absorbed in contemplation of its sublimity, I sat for a moment on a rock that rose out of the bush. I almost leapt from it, startled; a voice, unheralded, fell "like a falling star" through the soundless air. I had heard no footstep, no snap of trodden twig or rustle of reluctant branch. My senses were so thrilled with the sound that its purport shot past them. There at the base of the rock stood the strangest figure that ever met my eyes.

It was the sea-trove we had left sleeping in the hut—a small, well-knit frame like that of a north-country Englishman; but folded though it was in the slender gauzy garment we had unwound from it the night before, I felt conscious of a radiance that seemed to rid it of its opaque substantiality; it was as if lit from within; the face was luminous and clear, like the star-limpid waters of the fiord at night. My eyes were drawn to search the depths; yet the veil of flesh and blood still hid all but the aurora-like flashings of thought and feeling that swept in and out across the features. There was the play of some strong inward tumult, the revival, I soon found, of long-dead memories. I sat dumb as a stone, too much moved to break the silence, too much awed by the face to know what to say. It seems that my face too, with its weather-beaten vigour of northern life, had stirred the nature of the stranger to its depths; a long-forgotten existence had surged up in him from the darkness of the past, and he was recovering it feature by feature. I have often watched the conflict of cloud and wind, of light and gloom, across the torn azure of night's infinity before the coming of a tempest; but the sight did not approach in intense magnetism the dizzy chase of shadow and gleam across this singular countenance.

At last the turmoil had passed its crisis. The memories had fallen into array. And, in slow but passionate northern English strangely shot with silvery rhythm, I was asked what country this was and whether I was not an Englishman. My palsy of speech vanished. And the familiar words, uttered though they were in new accents, led me back into the common world of question and answer. I found it was the Britain of a generation ago he knew, before the colonies of the Pacific had focussed her new spirit of enterprise, or transmuted their golden dreams. He remembered the mining fever of Australia, but it was news that it had smitten New Zealand too.

As I spoke with him, he seemed to be dragging his language out of the depths of sleep. His words and recognition of my meaning came half reluctantly. And through them wove fitfully hints and after-gleams of some intervening existence that had reached a higher plane than that of his youth. The ethereal ring would come into his voice, the translucent look into his face, and then vanish before the touch of those lower terrene reminiscences. Yet even amidst them there would appear at times the tremulous appeal of human pathos. As our words approached the memories of his childhood, they sounded from his lips like the funeral bells of a village folded in mist. The grosser humanity that seemed to come back to him from a buried past grew shadowed and mournful with piteous thoughts. There sighed out of his lost youth a winter wind that sounded through the crevices of ruined cities and over uncounted graves.

It took weeks for us to reach more familiar intercourse; and this alternation of a common and ethereal humanity in him continued to break the magnetism that often seemed about to bind us. We came from the same district of the North, although he evaded all questions as to the locality; and I came to know by instinct the topics to avoid with him. He would listen by the hour to stories and descriptions of the dales and hills; but he never permitted a reference that would fix his native place or time. One serious difficulty at first was his refusal of all our ordinary food; he would not touch the flesh of animal in any form, and we had to give up to him all our meal and flour and lentils. But, as we saw him at times grow faint, we introduced some of our animal soups into his food—for he refused all food that needed the use of teeth. A singular change seemed to come over him from this time; he began to grow more like our muscular, carnal humanity, and his moods of limpid ethereality were rarer and briefer. Thereafter he seemed to lower himself more to our plane of thought and life, though even then he rose long flights above us. Why he stayed with rough miners like us so long, when he might have shone in the most brilliant circles of Europe, was a mystery; but it became clear at a later stage. He worked with me and had a marvellous power of revealing the secrets of the rocks and the crust of the earth; like the fabulous divining rod he knew what metal lay below, and how far we should have to seek for it; and ten thousand times over he repaid all that his living cost. We offered him his share of our partnership; but our proposal was ever smiled aside as if it came from children in some childish play. He seemed to look years beyond our point of view.

How deep the debt we owe him when we think of all he taught us! Beside it all else sinks into nothingness. And there is no way in which we can vent our gratitude to him but by telling his story to other men as he told it to us. We could have spent all our days as well as all our nights in listening to him. But it was only now and then he fell into the mood of reminiscence. And so great a value did we attach to his every word that after each conversation or monologue we retired into our storehouse cave and wrote it down. We did our best to give his own language and form, but memory is treacherous, and we felt at each attempt that we had marred the beauty or nobleness of his utterances by phrases of our own or by the tinge of our personalities. He followed no sequence of time or circumstance; for he spoke as his own spirit or our themes moved him. But out of our rough jottings we have pieced together the following narrative, most of it our representation at the moment of his speech, some of it from the distant memory of incidental talks with him in the bush, when we were far from paper or pen. It is as close an approach to his very words as our love and reverence have been able to achieve.

Godfrey Sweven,
Theodore Somm,
Christian Trowm.

CHAPTER I
RESURRECTIONS

GOD, GOD! HOW THY past clings to us like shadows, turn we as we may forever to the sunrise! Out of the night and from beyond it come forms that seem buried below the reach of grave-desecrating memory; they plead with us and claim us as their kin, and all the nobleness we have laboured after succumbs to the witchery of their piteous appeals.

> It was indeed pathetic to see his face as he struggled with a past that had been dead for a generation. He thrust it from him and it would return. He reached out for dim features of it he had loved, and they eluded him. At last came out of the wreckage of dreams the solidarity of life and law.

How tyrannous the bond of nature is! What love my mother bore me, and how the memory of it wells over the desert of my youth! Had she lived, I never could have broken with my European life. It is maternal love that binds age to age. A torrent of inborn feeling wakes in me for the old graveyard where she lies overlooking the sea. I know she is not there, and yet I could kiss the dear earth that covers her ashes. From her I drew all that was best in me; to her, only a fisherman's daughter, I looked for every thought that controlled me in boyhood. My father, the earl's son, disowned for his lowly love and marriage, was only a phantom to me, honoured but unreal; for he died soon after I was born. Nor could I ever own the churlish stock that thrust him forth for loyalty to a peasant. Often did the crabbed old grandsire try to woo me from the sea-smelling hut to his great castle; as often was his pride wounded by refusal. What had I to do with a race still savage in its adherence to caste, and incapable of seeing the beauty of a character apart from position? All my being belonged to the gentler, more civilised nature of my mother; I was obstinately democratic in my sympathies, hating even the shadow of primeval aristocracy that rests upon childhood and youth.

One thing he succeeded in doing. He drove my mother, by dint of threats, expostulations, and reasonings, to send me for a few years to one of the large English public schools. And this period was the purgatory of my life, such despotisms and persecutions demonised over the unconforming nucleus of my character. And, when summer came, her love, the uncouth sympathy of the fishermen, the rhythmic sea, and the steadfast foreheads of the cliffs cooled the fever of my wronged spirit. Only the persistence of the old fire-eater with his instinctive valuation of the still savage virtues of his caste could keep her from yielding to my never-ending entreaties. Not till palsy shut the gates of his expression did she take courage to resist his influence, and let me remain with her and solitude as my teachers.

A few years more and his iron spirit left its long-dead tenement. His title and mansion and great estates were thrust upon me. But I refused to acknowledge the position except so far as to divide the revenue amongst the poor. What did I or my mother need more than we had? Why should we leave our lowly friends, and our comradeship with the sea? What good purpose could it serve to spend these vast sums every year on personal enjoyment that would be none to us? We stayed in our little dwelling perched in a nook of the cliffs, and I followed my ancestral calling over the ever-moving element that had nursed me. Courage and lowliness and love of mankind sank deeper and deeper into my system. Books and thought and the ever-changeful waves tutored my spirit and widened the issues of life. I began to feel strangely dissatisfied with all that was called civilisation, seeing how far it fell short of justice and truth and liberty. I was harassed with my own destiny and even more with that of mankind. How could I better my thoughts by heaping the responsibilities of lucre upon them? The everlasting antagonism between our longing for rest and our need of labour goaded me as it did all others. And how was change of sphere or multiplication of financial cares to effect a truce? No; it seemed to me, in my youthful romancing, that the possibility of cure lay not in increasing the desires and their means of satisfaction, but in reducing the needs. The denominator in this poor fraction of the universe called human life was more plastic than the numerator. What was the acquisition of wealth and influence but the insertion of ciphers in our little decimal of existence? What could the world do for the inborn sickness of the human spirit?

If the rest was to be found, it was in primitive conditions of life, perhaps in some obscure tribe that lived close to nature and had never heard an echo of our western world. With the restless nomadic instincts of boyhood and youth passionate within me, I longed to set forth on a voyage of discovery into seas untraversed. The sea-ferment stirred my Scandinavian blood. To rove untrammelled, to meet sudden storms and dangers, to hold intercourse with pure human souls fresh from God's hand and unstained with the duplicities of luxurious grasping races—this was the dream of my early years. But my mother would not stir from the loved shore of her girlhood or the grave of the husband who had died too young to shatter her romance. And she was a comrade from whom I could not part. Year after year had bound us closer together, and, before manhood had unloosed the reins of my will, her forty years and locality—a stronger influence in her sex—had riveted down their fetters upon her spirit.

But ah, God! there came a time——

The surge of memory was too great for him. He would not let the tears come and he fled out into the woods. We saw no more of him for days. Nor could he approach the subject but with wild resurgence of sorrow that choked up speech. But by hint and inference we were able to mosaic together the history of this tempest that swept through his life. His mother had died not long after he had attained his majority, and his grief palsied his energies for almost a year. But driven to the net and the sea again by sheer fatigue of brooding, youth reflooded his veins with the old passions and ideals, and the flame in his blood mastered grief. Then came the thought that the wealth he had repelled so long might enable him to fulfil the dream of his boyhood, and to reach some land untainted by the vices of Europe. And the discovery that part of his heritage was a yacht driven by the marvellous new power of steam, that laughed at wind, and wave, and current, made him as one possessed. Everything bent to his new idea. He gathered his old comrades and playmates together, and he went with them to master the whole craft of the steam-engine and the screw; they learned every item of the marine engineer's trade; and each he set to gain skill in some special part. He travelled himself from university to university, from laboratory to laboratory in order to master the best that was known in the physical sciences. He fitted out his yacht with the apparatus and material that would be needed for repairing any part of her, furnished her with everything that would enable him to pass years away from civilisation and to gain influence over the wild races he might encounter. Nor did he fail to collect for her a library of the finest books, not only imaginative and scientific, but pertaining to the arts. And, when all was ready and his machinery and crew had been tested in

brief voyages north and west across the winter and summer
Atlantic, he bade farewell to his hut upon the shore and the
loved graveyard on the hill and set out to seek adventure and
a land of primitive simplicity in untravelled seas.

How our blood surged with delight as we swept away to the south under
full sail and head of steam! The ridged currents of the main, the wind-curled
summits of the great billows only made our hearts to tingle. We were out
free with God's elements, our friends; no rumour of cruelty or injustice or
bitter grief to harass our spirits. Young, bold, well-mated, bound by the ties
of common tastes and common traditions, nothing seemed to us too difficult
to attempt.

Round the old cape of storms, down into the latitude of icebergs, we easted
till we hailed the coasts of Australia. In her towns and cities we learned from
traders and sailors all we could of the islands that lay in the Pacific. Much
of romance, much of dim rumour based on fact vitiated their tales and yet
drew us on with magnetic power. Past New Zealand with her sombre fiords
and the argent glory of her mountains we swept, gleaning from her sealers
and whalers still more of the mysteries of the dim Pacific world we were
about to see. Our blood coursed quicker in our veins as we touched the first
palm-fringed atolls of the coral belt. And every new island we reached we
seemed to get closer and closer to the centre of the primitive world we desired
to visit.

For through the narratives that we heard of the wonders of the great Pacific
archipelago there ran an undercurrent of reference to some mystic region that
had deeply impressed the imaginations of all frequenters of this tropical sea,
whether natives or foreigners. The islanders would scarcely speak of it and
a curtain of superstition hung round it unlifted. Even Europeans spoke of it
with bated breath.

But the more they evaded my questions, the more was I roused to get at
some definite knowledge. From island to island we sailed in quest of the direction of this strange mirage of the sea. At times I concluded that it was but a
religious myth, a hades invented by the priests or by the crude imagination of
early worshippers to account for the misery of man and to define the destiny
of his wilder nature. Then would come some hint that pointed to physical fact
as its basis.

After weary, half-baffled investigation, I seemed to find a certain nucleus of
reality. There lay away to the south-east of Oceania, out of the track of ships,
an enormous region of the Pacific sealed by a ring of fog that had never lifted
in the memory of man. Ships had sailed into it and never come out again;

canoes that had ventured too near had been sucked in by the eddies that circled round it, and never been seen again. Above it there flashed strange lights that dimmed the stars and the play of gleaming wings seemed at times to rise far above it and vanish. To some islanders it was the refuge of the souls of their dead; to others it was the home of the demons who issued half-seen, half-unseen to torture them with plague and storm and disaster.

When I had discovered the direction in which it lay and defined its position on my chart, we ran back to the coast of New Zealand for coal and other supplies that would last me months, if not years. All ready, I summoned my staunch comrades who formed the crew and told them the bent of my enterprise, laying stress upon its dangers and uncertainty. Not one flinched, perhaps because their lives lay all in the future; none had left wife or sweetheart behind, none was old enough to have fixed ambition or a desire of settled existence. The sea had bred in them through their long ancestry a love of its mystery and its many-voiced dreams. None but imaginative natures had attached themselves to me in youth. And on board, during their long periods of rest, it was romance, and poetry, and other books of imagination they read. Not one of them had escaped the lotus-breathing air of these dreamy archipelagoes. Not one of them but loathed the thought of western life with its mean ambitions and falsities. Anything was better than the labyrinth of disease and wrong and crime wherein they must lose their way in old Europe. Even without such considerations, there was enough loyalty to their old comrade and leader to make them follow him wherever he would go. A cheer ended our conference, and we weighed anchor to a new chant with the refrain "Heave ho! let's seek the secret of Riallaro."

CHAPTER II
RIALLARO

SUCH WAS THE NAME that one group of islands gave to this mystic region of the sea; and it meant "the ring of mist." A sense of awe fell on me as I listened to the chorus. Whither was I dragging these young spirits with me? What would be the end of our expedition? Would we ever come forth alive from this misty sphere? It held within it, I felt, some of the most momentous secrets of existence; but whether these would be baneful or gracious no one could tell. It was only after I had felt everything ready for my venture that I became tremulous as to the result. The energy of my nature, that had been absorbed in definite search for knowledge, and definite preparation, was now set free for brooding; and I passed daily in thought from hope to despair, from despair to hope. All the delight of outlook was now lost in the uncertainty. The few shreds of fact, that I had been able to pick out of hint and tradition and religious fear, seemed in the immediate presence of the mystery to be ridiculous and inadequate for any definite step. I became the prey of trepidation and self-upbraiding. Dreams of failure and disaster haunted me day and night. I thought over the stories of Ulysses, and Æneas, of Orpheus, and Dante as the prototypes of our enterprise; they had returned from the lower world; might not we too return from this nebulous hades? But alas! no consolation came from such tales; they were but the shadows of dreams; whilst we were about to face an impossible geographical problem in the midst of a sceptical scientific generation. How could I close my eyes to the insane hardihood of our venture?

Before I could recover from the truculent despotism of such thoughts, this sphinx of mist stared me in the face, and no retreat was left for us. Long and silent meditations and pacings of the deck had left me exhausted, and one breathless and moonless night I sank into a profound sleep that fettered me down long after sunrise. My officers could not waken me, and it was only at last sheer necessity that drove them to rouse me by main force. I stared about me dazed; but one word from them—"Riallaro"—set every nerve a-quiver. I rushed on deck and saw close on us a mist that blurred the whole eastern side of the sky. I stopped the engines and then reversed them. But on came the mist; on flew the ship into it. I looked over the bulwarks, and saw that we were borne along by a current like a mill-race. My men stared blankly at me. The engines had little effect in stemming the force of the water. And before we could think what to do the fog had closed in upon us, and we could not see above a ship's length in any direction.

Away we rushed, whither we knew not, for the compass spun wildly back and forward on its pivot. Every piece of iron on the ship seemed to be turned into a magnet. And what was worse, my signals to the engine-room were unheeded; and on looking down, we found the engineers lying stiff upon its floor. I sent two down to take their place; and as soon as they had stopped the engines, they too succumbed and fell into a trance. Even the man at the wheel felt drowsy and incapable, only violent self-control and movement resisting the somnolence that seemed to creep over him. I remembered that the house in which he stood was iron, and that around there was more iron than anywhere else on the ship, except in the engine-room. I determined to husband my crew till I had understood our position, and was ready for a supreme effort at escape.

Amazement passed into terror, as there swept out of the mist and slowly passed us an old Spanish caravel, with rotting sails and yards, and shrivelled mummies in antique Spanish costume lying on the poop and at various points of the deck, in the attitude of sleep. We could have almost leapt on board this ship of death, so close was it to us. The horror paralysed us, and out of sight it vanished, taking giant proportions to it in the mist. Not many yards behind it moved another apparition of the past, a canoe with mummied natives fallen at the oar as in a trance. And still another in the ghostly funeral train, a Malay proa with motionless crew that seemed just fallen asleep, loomed spectral in our rear. Was this awful procession never to cease? Were we to fall into its line and sail on for ages? The last apparition was right in our wake, and had it moved nearer to us would have struck us on the stern; but it swept on after a brief interval aft. And then I had time to think that it was the impulse of the reversed engines that had thus brought us within sight of three different craft in this ghastly pageant.

The native superstition that nests in every seafarer's heart began to leaven my crew and master even their courage and their loyalty to me. A curse seemed to rest on all that were drawn into this mist-bearing current. Whither it was to take us and what would be our fate weighed heavily on my own mind. A drowsy feeling crept over me as I stood and meditated; only when I moved about could I drive off the lethargy. If once we went to sleep, there was clearly no awaking. Action was needed; and yet how to act was a puzzle; in which direction to steer we knew not.

Out of my reverie was I startled by a new and appalling danger. There rose gigantic out of the mist upon our starboard bow a great ship as still and silent as the reef into which it was wedged. My men rushed with a wild cry to the bulwarks to fend off our yacht; but we grazed past her unhurt; and on her decks we saw the forms of English sailors stretched in sleep at least if not in death. The sight dispelled the creeping torpor from our minds. I saw that swift action must be taken. I sent a volunteer down into the engine-room; and, before the iron drowse overcame him, he managed to fasten two ropes, that we let down from the skylights, in such a way that we could start or stop the engines from the deck. We must get steering way upon the ship in order to avoid these reefs and their wrecks. We moved gently ahead and passed along the ghostly procession; every generation for centuries past, every seafaring race upon earth seemed to contribute one ship of death, or more, to this long funeral train; ghastly lay their crew, sometimes shrivelled by long ages of rest, often seeming to have just fallen asleep.

My newly stirred thought now grasped the meaning of this sepulchral pageant. The movement of these hurrying graves must be in a circle round some centre that lay on the starboard; round and round they had wheeled for years, many of them for centuries. If I were to fulfil the purpose of my voyage, our way lay to the right; for from the larboard side we had been sucked into this whirlpool.

I took the wheel myself and steered the ship across the floating funeral train. Once we grazed the bow of an East Indiaman; again we cut in two a war canoe of the islanders; out of the mist they swept appallingly upon us. Nor could we pause to see what became of the shattered craft. A half an hour and we sailed in freer waters; for several minutes not one circling apparition loomed through the mist; the set of the current grew less impetuous; and the fog seemed to rarefy. Before long a luminous warmth mingled with the nebulous atmosphere; we could see denser masses move and break above us; and at last a corona of light shone hazily through the gloom. Our hearts leapt within us; and yet we repressed the cry of joy that rose spontaneously to our lips, for we might only be passing across from one circle of eclipse to another. The glimmer of light grew into intermittent gleams and then broke into the resplendence of full day. The repressed cheer burst forth at the sight, and our comrades stirred in their trance at the sound. They rubbed their eyes and awoke. They marvelled at our jubilance, and thought that they had fainted but the minute before. It had been an hour or so after daybreak that we entered the circle of death and now the sun was westering towards its set. The long hours of fast and terror and anxious thought had exhausted those of us who had been awake. And after instructions to those who had but risen from sleep to stop the ship and watch, we succumbed to our fatigue.

We lay inert for almost twenty-four hours, and our comrades, after stopping the engines, had again fallen into their trance. It was more than mere exhaustion that held us so imprisoned in unconsciousness; it was the magnetic power of the ring of mist through which we had passed.

I learned afterwards the causes of this strange phenomenon, though for years it remained a mystery to me. Thousands of ages before a submerged continent had left an irregular oval like a broken ring close to the surface of the water; and this annular reef consisted chiefly of magnetic iron molten from the adjacent rocks by the heat of the great central volcano that formed the nucleus of the gigantic atoll; on this adamantine ellipse the coral insects had raised their lace-like ridge. Upon the north and south sides of it respectively two great currents impinged, one from the tropics and one from the antarctic regions. The warmer rush of waters was bent round the eastern side of the circular wall of iron, the colder broke round the western side; and instead of losing all their impetus, or neutralising each other, they ran parallel most of their watery orbit before they mingled; and this continuous proximity of hot and cold generated the circle of steam that sealed the waters of this mighty unknown atoll. Into the swift circle of death ships were sucked both from north and south, and the magnetic force of the iron foundations of the reef caught their life in the trammels of sleep and then of death. Never before had a power that could master these subtle forces entered the sphere of their influence. Steam had broken the seal of this annular exhalation. And good fortune had led me to steer our new craft through the only opening left unpiled by the little coral workers. A feeble branch of the elliptic current found its way into the quieter waters within; and upon this we chanced in our efforts to get clear of the ships of death that swept on in funeral procession.

So gentle was this current that I had not noticed it before I fell asleep; and when I awoke under the stroke of the noon's rays I found that we were drifting rapidly upon a precipitous coast.

With the swiftness of alarm I wakened my men and sent her spinning astern at full speed. As we stood out from the land, I could see it was a low island or promontory, for the water beyond gleamed across it. And far in the distance were the dim outlines of two or three islands that broke the horizon line; and like an iceberg rose, at a still greater distance, the snow-capped peak of some great mountain that seemed companion to the clouds of fleece in the sky. Behind us lay the wall of mist through which we had broken; the eastern curve of the ellipse was too far off to show the slightest fleck of mist above the rim of sky.

CHAPTER III
LANDING

AT LAST, I WAS sure, we were about to know a people that had not blurred the features of primeval virtue. And yet I laughed at the thought. What was there in human nature to insure material advance without contamination of the spirit? How were the ages to whip the old Adam out of us but by new vices? Never had the world known exception. But here were lands fenced off from contagion for uncounted ages. Perchance the strange conditions had evolved a simpler civilisation; perchance the strange quarantine in human history had checked the influx of all common spiritual disease.

And there was a strange ethereal beauty misted over the parts that we could see. A thin veil, as of gossamer, withdrew and yet revealed the features of the scenery; and our imaginations were stirred to know the reality we could but dimly see. It excited us like a dream but half-remembered. Our natures tingled with curiosity and eagerness; and every nerve was braced to find our way beneath the veil.

We made for a beautiful landlocked harbour that seemed to promise shelter of the fairest; but it was only a mirage and faded into a long shelving beach of sand. We tried to anchor, but we could find no bottom. And as there was perfect calm we rowed towards the shore with a hawser, hoping to find some rock or tree on which to tie it. The sandy slope was but an illusion, too, and when we came to solid features we found there was nothing but a sheer wall of rock, rising to hundreds of feet above us, that laughed at our toil. Chance after chance, point of vantage after point of vantage led us on, eager, expectant, only to sicken us with illusion. It seemed to be the land of phantasms.

At length, weary with chilled eagerness, we saw the coast slope downwards to the mouth of a river. Our labours were about to be crowned with success. We found an anchorage and rowed towards the shore. But no landing-place offered; every piece of seeming solid shore turned out a quicksand when we touched it with our feet; only the watchful care of our comrades in the boat saved us from disaster. And the breakers on the bar of the river churned to white warned us off. We risked the entrance at last, and were capsized. I swam for a jutting rock that near the bank stemmed the outrunning current. Exhausted with the long effort I reached out and caught the weedy tangle that clung to its sides; I dragged myself up its jagged, wounding slope, and fell into a hollow that held me as I lay in swoon.

Annihilation thawed into consciousness of the blue sky in my eyes and of the flinty rock on which I was stretched. I rose, torn and bleeding, and looked out for my comrades. I could see only the keel of the boat floating out to sea; no yacht, no sign of life. In my hunger, exhaustion, and abandonment I could think of nothing but to make for land and the nearest habitations. I ate some of the shell-fish on the rock, stanched my wounds, and then threw myself into the inflowing tide. I easily breasted the current that divided my solitary crag from the bank, yet it bore me in its swiftness many miles inland before I could reach a landing-point; for broad spaces of glistening mud, in which I sank and floundered, divided me from the green fields beyond. The tide swept me towards a grassy point; I seized an overhanging branch of a tree and sprang upon the firm ground.

A sight of marvellous beauty held me rigid for a moment. Marble palaces, margined with gleaming gardens, flecked the length of the river as far as my eye could reach, and rose, nested in trees, terrace above terrace, up the slopes on either side. Boats with brilliant coloured awnings plied from bank to bank, like swarms of tropical butterflies, or lay moored to flights of snow-pure steps that flanked the water at intervals. Great temples and public buildings broke the outline with their sky-pricking spires. For an instant I doubted my eyes and thought illusion was playing them false, such a dream of beauty lay before them.

I dared not approach such noble purity so begrimed as I then was. I sought the outskirts of the city, for I knew that every town, however beautiful and rich, draggles off in some direction into meanness and filth and penury. I marvelled at the extent of the squalor here. When I reached the highest point of view I saw every gully and level teeming with the evidence of indigent myriads. A reeking human quagmire stretched for miles over the flood-soaked borders of this noble city, like a rich robe of lace that has dragged its train through liquid filth. Groves of trees failed to conceal the squalor and destitution of these low-lying suburbs.

Yet there I felt must be my resting-place till I had found a footing in the land. I had enough precious stones in my possession to serve me as money for months, if not for years. Most of them I buried in a secret place, which I marked well; and I traced a map of its position from the chief features of the city, and from north and west by aid of a small compass I had. With two or three rubies I made for the centre of the city's pauperism, and by means of gestures managed to change them in a mean pawnshop for the coin of the country.

CHAPTER IV
THE LANGUAGE

IN ORDER TO AVOID too much observation, I got housed in an obscure hostelry that often accommodated foreigners. But none of the occupants knew my language, nor did I any of theirs. Gesture and mimicry supplied the defect for a time, and a few weeks sufficed to give me command of the vocabulary and syntax needed for the common intercourse of life, so easy seemed the tongue and so clear the articulation.

But the difficulty came at a later stage. I found I could not advance far without a teacher, and a man of the purer blood was procured to act as my tutor. I put on the dress of the marble city, and went daily to him for my lesson. What a revelation I had of the subtlety of language! It was like learning to skate; everything seemed to contribute to make me stumble or fall; and the effort to recover was more dangerous than collapse. Every word and phrase and idiom had countless variations of meaning dependent on the intonation of the voice and the peculiar gesture or facial expression adopted. There was a grammar and vocabulary of tone as well as of actual speech. And, besides this, gesture and grimace contributed their own shadings to every expression. The twitching of an eyebrow would turn "God bless you" into "God damn you." A peculiar curl of the upper lip would change an inquiry into the state of a man's health into a doubt as to the morality of his ancestors. A shrug of the left shoulder would make out of a fervid "I love you" as fervid an "I hate you"; whilst a shrug of the right shoulder would change it into "I despise you." The eye had to be on the alert as well as the ear in finding out what a man meant; and every limb had to be watched as well as every feature of the face.

The dropping of the lid of the eye, left or right, could impart to a sentence, or even to a whole conversation, meanings so radically different that I became nervously conscious of every involuntary twitching as I talked; it might imply sinister intention, or confidence partial or complete; it might convey compliment or insult. It depended on the amount of the eye left uncovered, on the rapidity or slowness of the motion, and on the eye in which it took place. But, most bewildering of all, every depression of the optic shade varied in meaning according to the sex of the person addressed and the person addressing, and the presence of both sexes, or only one. The raising of the eyebrow had, similarly, a whole grammar and dictionary to itself.

But perhaps the most difficult and dangerous of all the sections of their language was the use of the nose in conversation. For both piety and lewdness had seized upon this obtrusive organ as their own. If a phrase or word was snuffled up through the nasal channel, it might express either gathering devotion or rising passion; only a member of the inner social circle could tell to a nicety which it meant, for the former was not often accompanied with the elevation of the eye to heaven, nor the latter with obscene gesture.

I would have abandoned the task of mastering the various grammars and dictionaries but for the enthusiasm of my tutor. He believed that nothing ever existed so much worth learning—except what were called the rotten tongues. These were two languages that had been spoken centuries before by a race now despised, if not extinct; it was a hotly discussed question who were its descendants, and, in order to avoid the awkward necessity of seeming to follow the lead of a now debased people, the usual course was to deny their existence or their connection with the sacred or rotten tongues—Thribbaty and Slapyak. The great books of their religion were studied in these; for, although it was quite a different language in which they were supposed to have been originally communicated to men, the missionaries who had established the faith in this country had spoken in either Thribbaty or Slapyak, and the ritual had been for ages written in these. A great political revolution had changed all this generations before, and the holy writings were read and the prayers and public functions performed in the vernacular. But it had become the custom for orators, wits, and men of the world to adorn their speech with words and phrases and quotations from the rotten or interred tongues, though all their best wisdom and thought had been incorporated in the native literature, and the stage of civilisation and especially ethics that they represented had long been antiquated. They had come to be the most valued shibboleth of the privileged classes, the barrier which none but the most nimble and daring wits of the mob could overleap. On them, therefore, was based all education; to their acquisition were attached all the great prizes of state. On an apt quotation from them some of the greatest reputations had been founded. By a dissertation on some obscure point of their grammar the ablest statesmen had leapt into office. They were spoken of as the highroads to greatness and power.

Recently doubt had arisen as to their sacredness, their supremacy, and their monopoly of wisdom and thought, culture and education. For many of the youth of the poor and unprivileged had begun to show great aptitude for them, whilst the gilded youth groaned under the burden of their acquisition.

But the intellect of the nation was on their side, and still more the conservatism of official life, hating, as it does, to learn some new routine. So it was shown how noble they were, how fit they alone were to be true instruments of education, and how a real knowledge of the vernacular could be acquired only through them. As I read the numerous philippics against the advocates of the new learning, I felt that it would be well-nigh profanity to neglect these marvellous rotten tongues.

Once I knew how much depended on them, I entered on their acquisition with great zeal, and found it an easier task than learning the grammars and dictionaries of tone, and gesture, and facial expression. I had been bilingual in my youth, speaking in the dialect of my mother and writing literary English; and thus new languages came easily to me. My teacher swelled with pride over my progress, though I think he had little to do with it. But my success in this lessened his labours in teaching me the shadings of his own tongue, for it minimised my despair.

And something, indeed, was needed to overcome my aversion to the subtleties of their overspeech. Cautious as my pedagogue was in introducing me to new sections of it, I was almost daily stumbling into them. One day, thinking to put him into good humour, I had referred to him as a great scholar; I was startled to find him grow red as if at an insult; and he had to show me that the attitude I had been in (I had been leaning my forehead on my forefinger) had turned the word into "addlehead." Another day I spoke of him as "well-bred," with the same result; and he had to explain to me that, blowing my nose as I had been at the time, I had made the word mean "nincompoop." And he had to initiate me into the whole by-play of the handkerchief; it took me days to master the infinite variety of meaning conveyed by its varied manipulation. By ladies it was not so frequently used; the scent-bottle took its place. And by its aid the gentler sex could woo, propose, and win with as great ease as the other and with far less indiscretion in word.

There was not an ornament or free appendage about fashionable dress but was brought to bear in the expression of shades of thought and emotion—the eyeglass, the key-ring, the chatelaine, the fan, the shoe-tie, the garter; the slightest motion of each of these was pregnant with meaning, and a mistake in their use might lead to serious consequences; for almost every word contained in germ senses that were often contradictory. The word for "good" also meant "feeble" or "silly," that for "vice" also meant "pleasure." The same word stood for "heaven" and "the purgatory of fools," another for "well-born" and "idiot," another for "gentlemanly" and "inconsiderate," another for "well-mannered" and "apish," and still another for "genius" and "lunatic." So love and lust, fashion and gas, insult and courage, fornication and marriage, harlot and messenger of the deity, deception and artistic power, impudence and prayer, bankruptcy and good luck, illegitimacy and the legal profession, beautiful woman and hag, sage and pedant, murder and nobility, candour and credulity, sword and stigma, infallible utterance and absurd error, wise saying and despicable thing, universal religion and bigotry, worship and play the hypocrite, to please and to conjure, to knock down and to co-operate, wit and vanity, to prepare food and to embezzle, courtier and pimp, sacred rite and vexation—each of these pairs had but one expression for both.

I characterised the language that could be so double in its meaning as insincere and barbarous. My school-master argued that the two meanings were in each case naturally connected and that nothing so subtle or refined had ever existed; he hesitated and added, "except Thribbaty and Slapyak. It is the highest stage of social development to have a language so ambiguous and difficult that it takes the greatest wits to manage it. Look at the common people; they have but one meaning, the more concrete and physical, for each word; and the result is boorish and superficial." I called his attention to the simple and direct signification of the words in the admired rotten tongues. He assured me that I was mistaken; great scholars had shown how there were depths beyond depths of reflected and refracted meaning in every word of the great Thribs and Slaps. "And was it natural that two peoples such as these, ignoring, as they did, nay despising, truthfulness as a virtue, should leave their language so unrefined, superficial, and straightforward as they seemed to untrained eyes? To tell the truth in clear and unambiguous language is the mark of barbarity. It is their very example that has led us to hide truth like a precious treasure in wrappings of subtlety. We shrink from exhibiting her to vulgar eyes. It would be but sacrilege. And our greatest investigators have shown *a priori* that nations like the Thribs and Slaps could not have existed without overspeech like ours to express the subtle shades of emotion and thought."

There still lingered in me grave doubts whether, if this were the contribution of the rotten tongues, they had been of any great service to the nation. It had already puzzled me to think that a people who glorified truth (calling their land Aleofane, as they often explained to me, "the gem of truth") should take as their model two ancient nations that held this virtue but lightly, that it should almost deify purity of life and modesty, and yet bring up its youth on two literatures that laughed at these. The moral ideals of this people had been the scorn of the Thribs and Slaps.

But I had not command enough of the language to express these thoughts, and I had to accept his apology for the rotten tongues. I was soon able to adorn my conversation with fragments of them and roll Thribbaty and Slapyak words and phrases off with unctuous gusto, as if they settled every question. It was a great satisfaction to feel that without intellectual effort one could knock down his opponent in argument by a quotation, however little one understood it. And it gave one a blessed sense of superiority to rattle off a long word or phrase that others could not understand.

After I had gained skill in the use of the speech and the overspeech and the rotten tongues I thought my task was done. But I found there was almost as much to learn before I could enter into their highest social life. Assisted by a posture-master, he initiated me into all the niceties of fashionable conduct. I had to learn the methods of address to every caste in society and to every rank in official life. The most reverential terms were employed very freely: "Your noblest highness in the universe," "Your most serene godship," "Your most beautiful ladyship upon earth," "Your most reverent of all sages." I protested against the indiscriminate use of such fulsome flattery. But it was explained to me that all this was neutralised in the next section of deportment. I was taught to reverse or cancel every compliment I was paying by a peculiar use of the facial features as I bowed. I could even turn the flattery into a curse when I had become skilled enough in the practice of oaths and oath-making gestures. I wondered how it was possible to conceal from the person addressed such reversal of compliments paid to him. And here the posture-master stepped in. He told me I must be ignorant of the barest elements of deportment, when I did not know how to bear the body in addressing high social functionaries. He laughed at my innocence in thinking that we should turn face to face and bow or shake hands. That had been the custom in ancient and barbarous times, before the great period of King Kallipyges and his queen. But for generations the proper method had been to turn back to back and bow gracefully; and if the two wished to show special fervour, they then ran butt at each other. This monarch had had a most repulsive face, whilst both he and his queen looked magnificent from behind. Hence the change. I did not dare to laugh. But it was a hard task to conceal my amusement when he explained that one of the most delicate attentions a superior could pay to an inferior was to face round after the preliminary posterior bow and raise the point of the right shoe to his nether garments. It took me several weeks to acquire ease in all these details of deportment.

And it was well that I had learned them and reduced them to commonplace by familiarity. For when my old pedagogue and cicerone led me into society, the sight of the posterior bowings and scrapings was almost too much for me.

CHAPTER V
ALEOFANIAN SOCIETY AND RELIGION

LIKE THEIR LANGUAGE, THEIR social fabric was an intricate work of art, and it took me months to understand even its elementary lessons and principles. It had the qualities of all great products of nature or human industry; its structure at the first glance was simple and clear; but it would have taken the lifetime of Methuselah to study out its meanings and principles. Those who belonged to the inner circles, of course, knew the whole code of conduct; but they kept a judicious silence on disputed points, and nearly all points were disputed. It was perfectly simple, they said; in fact, they would not condescend to explain the obvious. I was perpetually meeting difficulties, but they smiled a superior smile and let me flounder. Even my old tutor threw mystery round the topic and indulged in smiling silence over my bewilderment. I have little doubt that what seemed paradox and contradiction to me was to them clear and harmonious.

The first principle of their life was, I was assured on all sides, devotion to truth. The name of their country, Aleofane, meant, they insisted, the gem of truth. Every statement they made was prefaced with an appeal to truth in the abstract, and ended, if it were of any length, with an apostrophe to the deity as the god of truth. Their favourite oaths had reference to the virtue of truthfulness. Their greatest heroes never told a lie, as the tombstones and biographies showed in letters of gold. Their commonest form of asseveration was, "May all the spirits of dead truth-speakers testify," or "In the name of all who have been great and truthful." And in every one of their courts of law and witnessing-places there was a copy of their sacred books; and this had grown greasy with the kisses of myriads of these Aleofanians, swearing upon it to the truth of what they said. Nay, the expletive that entered into every second phrase of conversation—"dyoos"—was the popular remains of a prayer that perdition might catch their souls if they did not speak the truth.

I had found an ideal people. This was my reflection as I discovered how deep was their reverence for truth—so candid were they, and yet so courteous. With my own crude knowledge of their language and conventions, I was ever stumbling into some too candid statement that my tutor advised me to withdraw. That was but a small check to my great joy in finding a people so sincere, so removed from all falsity. Wherever I went I found statues of Truth or of the heroes of truthfulness; there were temples and shrines specially devoted to Her worship; and the sacred books of the people were the embodiment of absolute truth concerning the universe. Some, if not most, of the historical statements in these and all of their representations of the laws and processes of nature had been challenged by latter-day investigators as contrary to fact. But the priests and theologians had amply shown how these writers had, with their eyes blinded and uninspired, taken the crude superficial sense and failed to penetrate beneath the veil under which the truth sheltered itself from the profane gaze. Daily they prelected on the hidden meaning of their inspired literature; but the people were so convinced of the greatness of truth and the safeness of the hands to which absolute truth had been intrusted, that few or none ever listened to these prelections, for if any went to hear them, they fell promptly asleep in order to show how unquestioning was their faith. It was one of the most convincing testimonies, I was assured, to the inspiration of their sacred books and the supremacy of Aleofanian worship—this child-like trust of the people; nay, I have heard priests declare that, as they read or spoke their defences of the absolute truth of their religion, the nasal confession of implicit faith that rang through the temple seemed to them like the trumpets of heaven proclaiming theirs the only true creed on earth. Ah! the devotion of these men to truth! Nothing could stand in its way. Their predecessors in former ages had tortured with the greatest ingenuity, disembowelled, roasted alive the deniers or questioners of the truth of their tenets, so much did they love that truth. And these guardians of it would have done the same but for the sweetness and nobleness of their courtesy and forbearance. They went so far as to hold that even the precepts, if not the spirit, of their absolute truth must be disregarded at times, when dealing with those who would throw doubt upon it. What was there to compensate for its loss in life, if once it were allowed to be questioned? "Truth first and all the world after" was a favourite saying. And they considered that they might violate all the temporal and local laws and forms of truth in order to preserve intact and undoubted truth absolute, seeing that they had it amongst them in written form. It was all for the good of the race and the creed, *i.e.*, the ultimate good of the whole universe. Little wonder that the Aleofanians, whether dead or alive, could sleep at peace within the temple walls! "The truth must be believed in by all even at the cost of truth"; this was the motto of these noble guardians of the faith.

CHAPTER VI
ALEOFANIAN DEVOTION TO TRUTH

MY ADMIRATION GREW AS I gradually discovered how everything in this wonderful country gave way before this great virtue. It was the first lesson taught the child; it was the last injunction of the dying Aleofanian to his friends as they stood round his death-bed. Every other book that was published had this as a moral, that truth would prevail; all their biography and history had this as their ultimate teaching; the schoolbooks were compiled with this in view; the copy-books had as their headlines the favourite proverbs on the theme, such as "Tell the truth and shame the fiends," "Nothing but truth will butter your bread," "The root of all evil is untruth," "Truth is the good man's friend, the sinner's foe," "Truth is her own reward." The popular songs and lyrics had this virtue as their chief stock-in-trade, for embellishments and even for topics. "True, true, love" was the parrot note of all the songsters. Beauty was but the other side of truth, truth the only claim to beauty. All sentiment played round the loyalty and candour of friends. On the tombstones were the headlines from the copy-books and the texts from the sacred writings that dealt with eulogy of the virtue. The graveyard was a perfect school of the prophets. So, too, was every hoarding and blank wall; for every seller of goods lavishly advertised their "truth."

I had grave embarrassments when I came to look at the practice of the people in this light that beat upon their lives. But these were owing to my ignorance of the language and the conventions. At every new paradox I felt I was a mere novice.

I had changed my place of residence to a public hostelry in the marble city as soon as my tutor thought I was sufficiently instructed not to shock people by my alien speech or ways. I had found no difficulty in negotiating and paying when I lived in the district of the poor. Now I misunderstood every week some term of the agreement, and the mistake always turned out to my disadvantage. It showed the selfishness of my European human nature that I should always have interpreted the words to my own benefit. And the correction was made with such courtesy, and so many and so profuse apologies that I rejoiced at the mistake as an opportunity of revealing the noble natures of the hosts. They never lost their good temper and suavity, however often they had to correct these financial blunders on my part. I began to feel that the ambiguity of their language was a wise provision of nature for bringing out the perfection of their manners in dealing with strangers and for allowing them to compensate themselves financially for their forbearance. My bills were generally double what I expected them to be; but I considered myself amply repaid by the gracious manner in which I was set right. The geometrical progression of my cost of living compelled me reluctantly to change my hostelry from time to time, and bid farewell to numerous suave and apologetic hosts.

I could have, if I had desired, spent all my sojourn after the first few weeks in private houses, so profuse was the offer of hospitality. It was a grievous thing to each host, as he proffered me the kindness, that just at that moment his house was in disorder; in fact it was in process of getting renewed and prepared for my reception, and he would not dishonour me by asking me to come during such a period of confusion. At last the invitations were so many that I dared not accept any one lest I should have to accept all; and it would have taken the lifetime of a Methuselah to fulfil the engagements. How deeply they grieved over this, they kept reminding me. And their grief was ever driving them to my hostelry and rooms that they might pour it out over my well-laden table. I shall not soon forget the fervour with which they shared in my victuals for my sake and performed the dorsal salutation. I never had such a multitude of true friends in my life. Each would deal with me as if we were the only two beings in the whole world worth a thought, and as if nothing could untie the knot of friendship. What looks of admiration they dealt me! At the close of every interview I felt how great and good we both were, what a genius I was, what a noble fellow he was. And so devoted did many of them become to me as a friend that they overcame their sense of dignity so far as to borrow from me. I was weighed down with the great burden of honour that was heaped upon me.

The greatest embarrassment from the wealth of their friendship was the number of those that claimed it. Each social circle, each member of it, came to daggers drawn with every other over me. And I began to feel myself one of the most unfortunate of beings, to have introduced such internecine strife amongst so peaceful and noble a people. I thought at times that the whole of the upper classes were on the verge of civil war over me, and that there would soon be universal bloodshed and annihilation. But the gentleness of their natures and the ambiguity of their tongue again stood them in good stead. They went so far as charging one another with the sin that was unpardonable amongst them, that of lying. But it turned out to be only a misunderstanding in each case; the double meaning of their words was a special provision of nature for keeping the peace. They fell on each other's neck and wept. Oh, how blessed was the equivocalness of the Aleofanian tongue! When everything had been settled amicably, most of them, to prove their friendship and devotion to me, took another loan from me. And I was fully compensated by the grace with which they conferred the favour.

As great generosity did they show in dealing with the reputations of their neighbours and fellow-citizens. It was cheering, indeed, to my feeling of human kindness to hear them eulogise each other. Even the marvellous riches of their vocabulary were found scant in the expression of their mutual love and admiration. Their ancestors had laid out much of their great talent for eulogy on the manufacture of language for it, and especially of titles of address. They had, as it were, established out of their linguistic wealth a great national bank of panegyric; and any one of the people of the marble city might draw upon it at any moment and to any extent, so nearly boundless were its resources. I have now none of that false modesty which is encouraged in your civilisation to shrink from the estimation or statement of one's own merits, because I have ceased to have any egotism or over-consciousness of myself; and yet to this day I hesitate to quote some of the methods of address used to me and the encomiums passed upon me. It was only their profanity that prevented me from bursting into laughter at their exaggeration. I was classed with the divinities; the attributes of godhead were applied to me. "O celestial person," "O propitiable refuge of the world," were amongst the least offensive. But I am bound to say that, when I went into the higher ranks of society, especially into the court, I found them most impartially peppered over the company. And it was in the same lavish spirit that the fixed titles of the nobility and other ranks had been measured out. They seemed to be proportionate to the acreage of the lands from which the nucleus of each was drawn. There was a law that superiors were to be allowed to reduce them to one thousandth part of their usual size, and equals to one hundredth part, except on ceremonial occasions. It was passed after a great social upheaval in which the political faction called The Economisers of Time won the day. It would never have succeeded but for a new king who by the death of many intermediate claimants to the throne had been raised out of comparative obscurity, and who delighted in outraging the proprieties. Moreover, he was somewhat asthmatic, and royal interviews had often to be postponed indefinitely because the royal lungs broke down in the middle of some official's name. Even after so many generations it was keen agony for most of the nobility to hear the monarch address the Serene Superintendent of the Royal Vaults as Nip, or the Grand Deputy Supervisor of the Royal Laundry Women as Tubby, the mere preliminary syllables of their acre-broad names. It was occasionally a relief to get into the lower ranks of this noble society, for then the difficulty of remembering and uttering the names of the people I met was complicated only by a few hyphens.

But here, too, hosannas rang in every term of address and every opening sentence. And thus having handsomely credited their neighbours and friends with so much, they felt that the debit side of life's account was all the larger. It was a sharp agony, they each told me, to lay bare the faults of those whom they so much loved and admired; but it was their painful duty so to do. How could the state be cured of its evils if this was not done? How could spiritual pride be subdued if the faults of men were not laid bare? It was a world of sorrow and care, and they had their full share of it in thus serving their friends and fellows. I had therefore the character of every man and woman whom I came to know faithfully analysed from a hundred different points of view. And though at times my critical friends seemed to enjoy the anatomy of others, it was, I was assured, only as the surgeon enjoys his own skill when he works with his knife in cutting out malignant growths. They were indeed most skilful anatomists of character. But it was all in the way of discipline; they had to disparage those who were praised too much, and sow scandal about those who had too good reputation lest that vile contagion of pride should fall on the community. It was an agonising duty to perform, but they had performed it without flinching; and they had already poured balm upon the coming wounds by preliminary eulogies drawn from the ancestral stock of curative panegyric.

Most of their social institutions and conduct had some disciplinary purpose. I often saw men and women meet their friends with a frown or pass them by with gloom on their faces. On asking, I found it was generally to cure the spiritual pride or some other defect in these friends that this sadness was assumed. I wondered, too, at the minute division into social circles that professed to be rigidly exclusive, but really overlapped, and at the haughty scorn with which a member of one a step higher in the scale would treat some other citizen who seemed to me infinitely his superior in both morals and manners, if not also in intellect and capacity. I found that all this was based on the same principle. The spirits of men and women had to be preserved from defect that the state might remain secure. This was the true scheme of nature that each man should be his brother's keeper; and by these fences and folds they kept their brothers apart so that they might be draughted up or down. And in order to keep these fences ungapped they had to exercise their hauteur and scorn. How many unhappy hours they gave themselves thus for the good of their brethren and the state! What brotherly love, what patriotism shone behind the frown upon their brow or the curl of the lip or the effort to point their long noses heavenward! It was especially evident in all large gatherings of the purest blood of the marble city; for then the moral spread, the lesson had its fullest effect.

The minute gradations of social life represented in the shades of this mutual discipline puzzled me even more than their dictionaries of overspeech. I could never reach solid ground in them. Once I thought I had found the very innermost social circle, where none could curl the lip at another. It included the family of the king and the monarch himself. I was speaking with some intimacy to the highest noble of this grade, and remarked to him in a confident tone that I supposed the king and he were the noblest efflorescence of this world's aristocracy. "Ay, if only that blot had not smirched the royal pedigree a thousand years ago," slid out of the curling lips. What a giddy pinnacle he seemed to stand on, this king-scorning aristocrat! He must have longed for other worlds to scorn and patronise and discipline. Mere human insignificance was too far beneath him to exercise his nasal elevation upon. I dared not affront him by revealing my ignorance of his ancestry. But I at once assumed that it was divine, when it could produce such sublimity of social solitude and noble blood.

It was a height which must have intoxicated him to think of. For he had only to turn to the literature of his nation to see it assumed that not only had there never been a nobler people upon earth, but that according to reasoning from first principles there could not be another to surpass it. This fundamental axiom was never overtly stated except in controversial pamphlets that had been issued against the contemptible claims of nations in other islets of the archipelago. But in their science and philosophy it was the tacit foundation of all reasonings and conclusions. Every scientist in making observations of nature or basing a law upon them had in his mind as an undisputed truth that this world was the only world that was worth considering, and that Aleofanian nature was nature absolute; what other peoples did or saw differently was abnormal, a mere departure from the scheme of creation. Every economist, much as he might disagree with others, ever agreed with them in this: that the system of industry and wealth and classes that then existed in Aleofane was the final economical system of human society; it might be and must be modified in details, but its great central principle was the only one that could keep mankind in proper gradation and subordination. Philosophy investigated Aleofanian humanity and systems and analysed the Aleofanian mind that it might show forth the divine plan of the universe. As for art, what else was worth admiring than what the Aleofanians admired? And by the Aleofanians was meant those of them who were in society. The philosophers had only to get at the abstract principle that lay behind Aleofanian music and architecture, painting and sculpture, and they would have the final secret of beauty, the ultimate principle of all art.

The only thing that shocked me almost past recovery was the application of this axiom to the sphere of religion. Brought up as I had been, a Christian amongst Christians, I felt that I had only to state to them the great and undisputed doctrines and the practical precepts of Christianity to make them turn from their idolatry of other gods, and their crude ideas of worship. What was my surprise and anguish to find even the most vulgar and least educated amongst them turn on me with a patronising smile and deal with me as if I were a child or a mild lunatic who had got adrift and had to be shepherded! They would not condescend to argue with me, and as I reiterated or argued, they only laughed louder at my simplicity. I had at last to cease speaking of my own religion and suffer my agony in silence. It was true that they were split up into innumerable sects, and many utterly denied the existence of their gods; but the sectarians were winked at or perhaps loftily scorned; for they at least accepted the fundamental tenets; whilst the atheists were endured, inasmuch as it was the Aleofanian gods they denied and thus made superior to the false gods of other races. Some two thirds of the population never entered the doors of the great temples; but there was much satisfaction in feeling that they entered the temples of no other gods, and that all their incomes gave evidence of their devotion to the Aleofanian worship by contributing one tenth each year for its support through the state treasury. The other third of the population were directly or indirectly interested in the temple revenues; every family had one member at least drawing a large salary from it by honouring it with his presence once or twice a year as superintendent when its worship was proceeding.

The principle of the religion was self-denial; but as one of their soundest philosophers had shown that all the world was practically included in the self or ego, inasmuch as thought was the perpetual creator of the world, and the chief element of the ego was thought, the inconveniences of the principle were avoided without sacrificing any of its glory or integrity. Their desires and appetites formed but an infinitesimal fraction of a self that included the whole planet, and an act of devotion once a year was more than enough to fulfil the duty of self-denial. The other and larger portion of the self, consisting chiefly of other people, they gladly mortified and denied and sacrificed; such incense was ever rising from the altars of their gods. The priests who performed the services and inculcated the precepts and explained the tenets showed in their emaciated frames and starved families how great the sacrifice of the deputy-self. Forgers, embezzlers, debtors who could not pay their debts, and in short all financial criminals were allowed to expiate their sins by devoting themselves for life to the service of a temple for little or nothing, generally the latter. Thus no people in the world did so much for the central principle of religion, that of self-sacrifice.

Not that the gilded race delegated all the duty. They lavished their wealth upon the art of the temples. The altars shone with precious marbles and stones; brilliant mosaics covered the floors and the walls; the domes were frescoed by the greatest painters and niched by the best sculptors. Some of their temples were so noble and spacious and adorned that the value of an empire seemed spent on them, and the poor human voice of the priest as he prayed or prelected sounded like the buzzing of a fly on a distant window-pane. And the robes that hung upon the framework of the skeleton-officiator were stiff with jewelry and brocade. It happened occasionally that one of the wealthy superintendents of religion had a gift of oratory, and then you would find his well-fed outlines filling the gorgeous vestments and his luxurious voice filling his temple and drawing crowds. And there again the self-sacrifice came in; every follower of his, especially of the opposite sex, gave up time and money to his welfare; and great fortunes were spent on this act of worship. The garments of the worshippers displayed as gorgeous art as the temple itself that all might be in unison in pleasing the gods.

But most of all were the gods supposed to be pleased by efforts to persuade the outer world to their creed. The zealous were greatly troubled at the obstinacy of the peoples of the other islets, who refused to turn from their own shade of piety and belief; I was assured that they were sunk in depravity and sin; for millions had been spent on their conversion, and in the long years only a few had been gathered into the fold. But these few were so well-kept and prosperous that they became shining examples to their infidel brethren. Ah, the fervour, the devotion, the self-sacrifice, the millions lavished upon these aliens! One must have been valued as much by the gods as a thousand Aleofanians brought up to the Aleofane worship. For tens of thousands huddled together in the fold, heedless of their own spiritual welfare, ignoring the existence of the temples, starving, unkempt, and ragged. Never were the grimy mob permitted to soil the precincts of the holy places, or to mar the beauty of the art displayed in them by the inhabitants of the marble city. To see the squalor of the labouring horde, I was told, would have cancelled the noblest acts of their artistic worship, would have made the gods to faint.

I have spoken of their gods; but they would have held it profanity so to speak. They had been polytheists in prehistoric times, and the missionaries who had introduced monotheism had been astute enough to take the best of their deities and find them in the qualities of the one. The generations of subtle divines that came between had solved all the difficulties of having

many deities rolled into one, so that the Aleofanian mind found it no sacrilege
to deify a dead hero or erect a shrine to one of their prehistoric deities, whilst
they persecuted to the death anyone who dared to deny the unity of godhead.
Just as there were myriads of stars and but one cosmos, so, they said, there
were innumerable manifestations of the deity and but one god. They were
ashamed of the polytheism of their ancestors, and as converts to the true faith
would have no slur upon it. Men might have no creed if they pleased; but if
they had a creed, it must be in one god and his religion. Their theologians had
discussed for centuries the manner in which the various old gods and new
saints coalesced into one; but none of them had the folly to deny the unity.
There had been and still existed a score or more of theological schools, each
of which agonised over the stupidity and unreasonableness of the rest in their
explanation of the unification. The dominant school used to roast or rack their
heresies out of their opponents; they still roasted and racked, but only socially
and politically; the spirit was as true to zeal for the one faith, only the method
had changed. And their library shelves groaned with volumes of anathemas
reasoned or unreasoned.

They prided themselves on their perfect command of reason; they could
adapt it to any purpose, so skilled had they become in its use. And they
assumed as a first principle of conduct that they had reached the final truth
on all things in earth or heaven. Only reason could teach truth; and they
alone of all people in the world had mastery of reasoning. The common beliefs
of the nation were therefore absolute truth; and each acted on the maxim
that what he persuaded himself of was unconditioned truth. Amongst a less
subtle people this would have meant continual quarrel; but with them the
ambiguity of their language stepped in as peacemaker. A disagreement never
came to anything serious; it was always found to be a misunderstanding of
words.

They had no need to state this syllogism to themselves; it was at the foundation of their conduct and beliefs. They scorned the art, the literature, the
philosophy of all other peoples as poor trivial monstrosities, permissible, of
course, in a world of variety like ours, but ridiculous in the extreme. It was
useless for a stranger like myself to criticise them and their civilisation; I
was only wasting my breath and affording them occasion for laughing at my
inordinate vanity.

CHAPTER VII
SOCIAL CUSTOMS

THE FIRST TIME THAT I went to a high-rank social entertainment of theirs, I broke into a hearty laugh at the spectacle as I entered; but I came to regret my imprudence. There were the select of the marble city, including the royal family, turning Catherine-wheels round the room in pairs to the sound of quick music; even fat old dowagers with bombasted breeches on kept up the frantic exercise, the perspiration pouring from their brows. It was a large room lit with hundreds of lamps, and round it again and again each pair had to roll, and as I looked at the stately nobles and dames head downwards my thoughts turned back to the street arabs of my native land and their cry, "Stand on my head for a penny," and I burst again into a laugh. My guide and introducer ignored the first; but at the second he turned round on me with questioning surprise. I was soon sobered, and turned away to smother my amusement. Another friend came up to greet me, and he at once burst into loud admiration of the scene. "Was it not noble? It was the finest flower of all art to see the most beautiful and high-blooded of men and women letting their souls forth in harmony, glowing with colour and life; surely this was the sight of sights; it was the very poetry of motion; what grace! what beauty and roundedness of calf! was it not joy to see the fair twinkling feet in the air, and in a moment so the solid floor again, pair with pair? It was indeed the music of the spheres, this revolution of the extremities round the centre of gravity; it was a copy of the motion of the great universe, sex with sex in unison pointing alternate head and feet to the zenith. Where else in the world could such a spectacle be seen?"

I acknowledged with as much gravity as I could command that I had never seen anything like it. And I must concede that after a time the whirl of bodies, as the music quickened, half intoxicated my judgment and made me almost long to join in the general somersault; the rhythm of so many feet and heads flying through the air fired my blood to fever heat, and as I looked on, my sense of the absurdity of the scene entirely disappeared; I became a partisan of the exercise and could see nothing but grace and harmony in it. I felt almost ashamed of my burst of laughter, though afterwards, when I retired to my hostelry and cooled down, the sense of incongruity returned, and I laughed heartily at the memory of haughty aristocrats standing on their heads, and the legs of shrivelled dowagers revolving like spokes of a wheel.

I found on inquiry that a considerable portion of their youth was spent in acquiring ease at this indoor exercise. Women especially gave the best of their days and nights to "fallallaroo," the name by which they called this art of rhythmical gyration, for they found it was their best means of ingratiating themselves with the promising young men; and most of the resolves to marry were formed in the meetings for fallallaroo. It was said by some physicians to produce certain common diseases, but the gilded society held that it was productive of health; they knew so from their own experience. Even the old men and women with grey hair and shrunken shanks kept up the exhausting exercise, for to leave it off was universally considered the sign of approaching age. It had been introduced by a monarch who had suffered from vertigo and St. Vitus's dance, but tradition had hallowed it and poetry had surrounded it with romance. And now it would have been like tearing up the roots of society to abolish it.

Another custom that was considered almost sacred tried my nerves still more. The men usually wore a bamboo behind their right ear, and whenever they were at leisure, and as often when they were not, they would take it out and fill one end with the dried leaves of a vile plant called kooannoo, not un-like a coprosma, and in smell pure assafœtida, and lighting it, stick the other end into one of their nostrils. Every expiration of breath sent forth a cloud of smoke and every inspiration drew some of it in; but they had grown so expert in the practice that they could always prevent it getting into the mouth or the throat, even when they were talking vigorously. The smell was something intolerable, and reminded me of burning heaps of rubbish and manure. In their more candid moods and when they were not themselves engaged in the practice, they acknowledged the likeness, especially on going into the lower quarters of the city; for there, in order to produce the fashionable flavour and smell, the kooannoo-sellers were accustomed to steep broad leaves in mire for a time, and drying them make them up as kooannoo; nay, some of the poor, when they could not afford to buy the leaf, openly stuck pieces of dried earth into their bamboos and lit them, and many of them adhered to the practice when they were better off, preferring the flavour and smell to those of the fashionable leaf.

I was surprised at the agonies the young men underwent in learning the loathsome habit, such nausea and pallor and misery overspread their whole frame; and it was only by the loss of all delicacy of smell and taste that they at last mastered the loathing and qualms; no refined senses could live within reach of the smoke. It was undoubtedly one of the acts of heroic stoicism on the part of the nation; they assured me that it was one of their disciplines for the subjugation of the body. But it acted, as most of their disciplines did, in an altruistic way; it had destroyed the fine sensations of the kooannooers themselves; but their neighbours, who had not learned, and especially women, suffered daily the agonies of disgust. And the agonies were undergone without a murmur, nay, with a smile upon the face, for the practice was almost universal amongst the highest class and in the royal family.

The origin was difficult to get at. But it seems that in some past age a number of the younger sons of aristocratic families had gone out in search of adventure; and during a period of great straits they had learned from a tribe of savages to eat and burn kooannoo in order to subdue the pangs of hunger. When they got food at last, they felt proud of an accomplishment that they had learned with so much agony, and, as they had ceased to suffer from it, they brought it home with them amongst other practices copied from the wild men. Their wonderful adventures made them the fashion; and all the youths set themselves to copy this, the most striking of their habits, counting it as the truest mark of manliness and courage. Having acquired it with so much suffering and difficulty, they would not easily give it up when it had ceased to disgust them. When kooannooing, they could sit silent with dignity whilst others talked; and it gave them a certain semblance of superiority to others, as they kept the red in their cheeks whilst others around who did not use the bamboo grew pale and sick. They felt masterful and heroic as they kooannooed, like the voyager who can resist the approach of sea-sickness when his fellows succumb. So the habit carried with it a certain overbearing rudeness and want of consideration for others. Generation after generation of youth had come to count it as the distinctive mark of manhood; and having learned the practice with great suffering they could not forego the sense of triumph over those who had not learned it; they were the braves of the nation; not to bamboo was a sign of womanliness and delicacy of feeling; and men who indulged such refinement and weakness ought to be disciplined along with the women; they were intolerant with their fine sensations; the world would not be worth living in if they had their way; it was time something was done to bring them into order. And these kooannooers felt most heroic and manly as they followed their loathsome practice. And most of the women endured their stinking breath and clothes and the agonies of nausea and headache in silence, or rather with the pretence that the habit was most delightful. There was something in what they said, that it soothed the men and put them into better humour; for when a kooannooer had a bamboo in his nose he wore a self-complacent smile; he felt manly and superior without the expenditure of any effort; his vanity was flattered. Of course a number who did not bamboo showed that the leaf acted as a poison and slowly sapped the health. But scientific kooannooers replied that small doses of the poison killed nothing but the germs of disease. They bambooed for the good of the public; they were the national sanitarians and fumigators. It showed how patriotic they were, when they persevered in the practice, though they knew that it tended to destroy the germ of manners as well as of diseases. These kooannooers were the most self-denying of philanthropists.

CHAPTER VIII
ABSTINENCE

"WHY SHOULD THEY REFRAIN from the gifts that God in His goodness had bestowed on them?" Thus argued a party of gilded youth with me as they polecatted the air of a gorgeous room with their bamboos. My senses had so far resisted the paralysing fume and its nausea that they were able to fumble about amongst arguments. And I tried to break their backs with their own rod. "Why did the Aleofanians abstain so rigidly from God's good gift, the juice of the grape?" "You have got the stick by the wrong end," they laughed. And the bell-wether of them took up the tale. "God's gift is transformed into poison by fermentation—" "And so is kooannoo by fire," I broke in. "But pyranniddee" (so they called their intoxicating spirit) "is seductive; kooannoo is repulsive; the one will master the strongest man; the other has to be mastered." I acknowledged the correctness of his distinction, but urged that all pleasures and pains in time suffer transmutation into their opposites; a habit, that in its nascence is pleasing, becomes loathsome in its supremacy, and one that is hard to learn gratifies the vanity, if not the senses, when mastered; the stoic rampant revels in his stoicism and goes to all lengths with it; the epicurean has soon skimmed the cream of his luxuries and has to suppress all his other natural needs and desires like a stoic that he may still the violence of his overgrown appetites or give them some hard-won novelty; I envied the stoic his epicurean enjoyment of his victory over life and passion; I pitied the epicurean wallowing in the world, that sty of desire, all its best and most luscious things trampled under foot. "But we have chosen a plant to bear whose fumes must ever demand resolution—" I unhinged his sentence with, "Yes, in those who cannot indulge in it." "You speak truly," he said, "and therein lies the nobleness of the choice; it is the great philanthropic plant; it is for the discipline and maturation of others that kooannooers sacrifice their finer sensations." This discussion would have fallen into a scramble of wits; for it was hard by any means to get the better of the subtlety of this people. So I held my peace. And as I listened, I learned and admired. They were too wise and virtuous to tope and guzzle and carouse. They would not steep their senses in sottish oblivion. They would have no dealings with a poison that sapped the will and made the human system all throat and liquid fire. Who would turn his inwards into a chemist's alembic, his skull into a vat?

I had heard eloquence like this in my own country and cowered before the tornado; I knew there could be no safety but in flight.

They were indeed a most ascetic people in all but the use of words. I tried in the first two or three hostelries to obtain a little wine; but the attempt had such a paralysing effect on mine hosts that I had to refrain. Anything that even smelt of fermentation was a horror. It is true I had seen many wine-presses and distilleries in the lower part of the town. But, it was explained, their products were meant for the shops of chemists and for use in the preservation of fruit and museum specimens. No freeman was allowed to touch the accursed thing; only criminals and bondsmen were permitted within the walls of these factories of the Stygian fluid, and then only under superintendence of government agents, who commanded the position from smell-proof view-points afar, lest even a whiff of the Tartarean brew should reach their nostrils.

I now understood why these Aleofanians when analysing the character of their neighbours always introduced, as the climax of the latter or depreciatory part of their analysis, devotion to museums and to fruit-preserving; and in the nearest approach I had seen two make to a quarrel, the one hurled at the other the epithet "Olekloman," or museumist, and got in reply, "Poolp," or fruit-preserver, whilst both reddened as if stung. No house in the marble city was without a large room devoted to natural history; every man was an enthusiastic collector of biological specimens, and in this room there were long rows of shelves of scarabæan bottles, each filled with some clear liquid in which floated a bug or centipede or some small parasite. They were as enthusiastic orchardists, and generally spent a third of the year in bottling the fruits of their trees. Autumn was the time of their most uproarious festivals and maddest junketings. This sober, staid, and abstinent people broke loose like bacchanals. The fruit they indulged in, they explained, fermented within them.

It was almost a painful spectacle for me after the admiration I had felt for their self-abnegation. They had such a horror for all fermented liquor that they called their devil and it by the same name, pyrannidee. And one of the wise men philosophising over the annual outbreak of high spirits said that, according to their own proverbial philosophy, the best way to confine a devil was to swallow him and to keep him down; he might pester the man who formed his prison-house, but he would be kept from all other wickedness. Thus the autumn revel of merriment was perhaps but another instance of the great virtue of the people, their eagerness to save their neighbours from evil.

They annually swallowed the devil to prevent him, for a short time at least, from going about like a roaring lion seeking whom he might devour.

At other times of the year I often found them, men as well as women, sitting in their houses and shedding copious tears over the sadness of this mortal state; so overwhelmed were they with the thought that their words jostled one another in strange confusion; and if they rose to bid me farewell, they fell upon my neck and wept, or collapsed in the greatness of their grief upon the couch or floor. This tenderness of heart was widespread amongst the upper classes; for days would they weep thus over the woes of existence. And still more unmanning was their sorrow for the death of friends; they would sit stupefied by the blow for hours together, unable to speak articulately; and a whole week or month of sickness and silent confinement to their bedroom would follow the stroke. How sorely stricken this people were I could not have realised but by my experience; the death of a dear friend occurred on an average once a month in the life of some fashionable Aleofanians at certain periods of the year, but especially during the severe season, winter. And when they rose from bed and appeared in public, their haggard, woebegone faces told the agony through which they had passed. Surely fate was too hard upon this much-bereaved nation. As hard was it upon their teeth; for the loss of a tooth under ether or stupefying gas was equally frequent; one friend, whom I had to see often, suffered grievously. I counted during my acquaintance with him forty-five losses of a tooth under ether. But nature was strangely beneficent to the Aleofanian jaw; she seemed to compensate for the losses almost immediately: my friend had as many teeth when I left as when I saw him first.

And with all these recurrent bereavements and the illnesses that followed, you may imagine how important a functionary was the physician in so-cial life. He was the father-confessor of the household. He was generally a soft-voiced, stooping-shouldered, silent-footed man. He condescended and yet he flattered; he insinuated himself into a man's confidence, and still more into a woman's, by veiled compliments; he mastered by seeming to accept his patient's opinions; he prescribed what suited the appetites and desires; the subtlety of the race rose to its highest in his profession, so skilfully had he to adapt himself to the weaknesses of his clients; he knew all the secrets of the household and built his omnipotence upon them; he had a feminine manner and a feminine vein in his character, judgment and action through instinct, and a passion for the minutenesses of life; and yet he piloted his way into the mastery of the family through the women, who, in spite of his womanliness, adored him; for he had learned by long tradition and training how to make them abandon themselves body and soul to his direction; their pains he knew how to soothe by anodynes; their troubles and sorrows he made them forget by either spiritual or physical consolation; he surrounded them with an atmosphere of belief in themselves and him as the two select of the world; he quarantined them from all other influences by flattery or pyrannidee; he dosed them with well-sweetened gossip made powerful by being communicated in confidential whispers and with oaths to secrecy; for he had command of all the inner workings of the private life of a neighbour-hood; and it was one of the wonders of his power that most of the families which he confessionalled were not on speaking terms with one another; he was always sacrificing himself to bring about peace, and each of them trusted him entirely; yet human nature is so prone to jealousy that they refused his mediation and only listened to his soft-voiced details of the inner life of their foes. What would the higher social life have been in Aleofane without this silent-footed intermediary!

The chemist fulfilled the same important function for the poorer classes. He sold the pyrannidee that the government factories made; but he was restricted to using it for the cure of disease and the assuagement of pain. And most of the grown-up population had a disease to be cured and a pain to be assuaged every day, so sorely smitten were they by fate, so long-suffering were they. It was one of the sights of the city to see the kolako or the warehouses of the chemists at night; crowds pressed into them by one door with agony depicted on their faces, whilst out from the other sauntered patient after patient with a wandering, nerveless smile upon his face, a jaunty, loose-gaited fashion of throwing his limbs, and a whiff of pyrannidee in his breath; for if it was not the medicine itself it was the medium of it, and he had left his pain behind him in the store. Little wonder that the chemist was a man of such power in Aleofane; he was generally of strong build and swaggering gait and showed his masterfulness in every gesture; for he had often severe muscular duties to perform; it seems that some of his patients of the most abandoned and criminal classes, after being cured of their pain or sickness, refused to leave his warehouse; seized by an evil spirit, I was told, they would foam at the mouth, kick, and bite; and it took great strength to tie them hand and foot and eject them. Some of my friends in the marble city mourned over this possession by wandering demons of the air; but they said it was only the degraded whose bodies they entered.

The profession was one of the most lucrative in Aleofane, for one of its essentials was great physical strength, and this was rarely to be found in the gilded classes. I could pick out chemists in a crowd by their brawny frame, bold gait, and short, well-knit stature. Their faces were as a rule strong and corrugated with muscle and tense self-control; they looked with an open and almost arrogant light in their eyes. Most of them, I was told, were descendants of a few survivors from a wreck on the coast, and there was occasionally a lurking fear that, with their great influence over the lower part of the city, their strong will, and their powerful squat frame, they might seize the reins of government; but this was prevented by dividing their interests and sowing dissensions and jealousies amongst them; the very largeness of the incomes they made lowered their ambitions towards money-making; and this made them fly asunder like globules of quicksilver.

But the contrast between them and the rest of the upper classes in physical appearance was very striking. The Aleofanians proper stooped in the shoulders of their long, thin bodies like bulrushes before the wind; not for weight of the head they bore; for it was small though well proportioned, and by various fashions and contrivances they managed to convey a false impression of its size; of their eyes it was impossible to make out the shape or colour; for they peeped through a thin slit between the eyelids, doubtless afraid of the glare of the sun; their nose ran like a sharp promontory down towards the middle of their upper lip, as if to help in covering the enormous aperture of the mouth and its thick, sensuous lips; these last I could see in the women, but the men concealed them by all the hair they could grow on their long-drawn faces; and their hair inclined as a rule to red. Their gait formed perhaps the deepest contrast to that of the chemists; they walked like ghosts, with a feline, scarcely perceptible footfall; and nothing could take them unawares or startle them out of it; yet ever and again some of them would pull themselves up and put on a bustling gait and bluff demeanour that completely belied their personal appearance; it was like a cat masquerading as a lion.

But they conducted themselves with great dignity in all the relations of their life. They would have no part in the gross candour of the chemists. Their whole demeanour and language were ordered with full regard to decency and decorum. They shrank with horror from lewdness and intrigue, and refused to acknowledge the existence of libertines amongst them. I never heard so much solemn and devout feeling expressed as on this topic; and at the corner of every street the attention of the passer-by was arrested by placards quoting in huge letters from their sacred books the noblest maxims on the sweetness of a chaste life. I could find no one to confess that there was such a thing in the island as a man who was libidinous, but every girl who broke this rule of morality was thrust forth from house and home. Scores of such outcasts I saw flaunting in brilliant robes along the streets. They had all the appearance of living in great luxury. But I was assured they were supported by secret funds sent by the inhabitants of a vicious island close at hand. And I could believe it. For no one ever spoke to them, and ladies as they passed drew their skirts in, whilst gentlemen after brushing past them would rub their coatsleeves as if from contamination. It was only the great chastity of the people that permitted these creatures to remain in their island. Nothing could surpass the horror and loathing which the Aleofanians exhibited towards them. It was painful indeed to see the agony the notables had to endure in suffering them to remain.

How devoted they were to charity! It was, I felt, their life, their all. They refused to do half the mischief that there was opportunity of doing to others. Every moment, every energy, was spent in restricting it to this fraction. So much destructive force was latent in them, so much destructive opportunity lay to hand, that they might have annihilated the reputation and peace of mind of all their fellow-citizens. How proud they were of their fraternal love in sowing only a few slanders and dissensions per day, and these, too, only to discipline the haughty and too fortunate, or to keep their own faculties from rusting! It was the same with their benevolence; nothing could surpass the nobleness and care with which they dispensed it. Half their revenues they gave away, but not in reckless alms; they were too wise and self-controlling for that; they knew too much of the economic laws of life, and respected them too well to violate even the least of them. So they never forgot discipline in giving to those who needed; they carefully exacted as much work from them as would pay the principal, and, lest the kindness should lapse from memory and leave no impression on the life and conduct, half as much again. To what infinite trouble they put themselves to see that these laws of nature should never be outraged by them! Great troops of the lower classes were fed and clothed and cared for by each of them for years, whilst they were trying to repay those noble eleemosynary gifts, and satisfying the laws of economics.

Nor must it be held an inconsistency in them that they thought money the root of all evil as against those very laws. They despised it and hated it. And lest it should do to their neighbours the harm for which they feared it and loathed it, they gathered as much of it into their hands as they could. "They swallowed the devil" again, according to their own proverbial phrase, as the best means of preventing the mischief he might do to others. It was one of the most altruistic of their principles, they considered, this accumulation of wealth in the hands of a few, lest the many should suffer. They could hedge the monster round and narrow his sphere of operations. And every provision had been made by the state for centuries that he should not approach the masses with his foul influence. It was the gilded classes of the marble city that could alone withstand the evils he worked, and amongst them therefore was he imprisoned. They were, so to speak, the turnkeys of this vampire of commercial races; and in their duties they were all vigilant lest he should escape and work irremediable havoc amongst the rest of the nation.

CHAPTER IX
THE ORGANISATION OF REPUTE

THESE ITEMS OF INFORMATION concerning the virtues of the race I learned not so much from the dwellers in the marble city themselves—they were too modest for that—as from public prints and the placards on hoardings and in public places. From the same sources I gathered innumerable details about the life of the monarch and the nobles and the wealthiest citizens, and these were always to their credit. Had I been as much in the habit of frequenting their temples or consulting the physicians as the gilded were, I would clearly have gathered still more, for I never heard a sermon or prayer or piece of medical advice in Aleofane but it contained or was accompanied by an elaborate eulogy of some one or more of the marble citizens besides a general exaltation of all of them.

I was also struck with the singular unobtrusiveness and even modesty of their public men; the more they were called for at public meetings, the less frequently they appeared; the more they were eulogised and fêted, the less eager did they seem to be spoken of. Their names were blazoned abroad in newspapers and on hoardings, yet they shrank from showing themselves. It was a game of hide-and-seek between them and the people. Crowds shouted for them; they ran off. Banquets and processions were held in their honour; they were the only men that withdrew from sight.

After a time I noticed that it was only a certain round of names that was kept persistently before the public. Occasionally a new one appeared and another vanished. But with them all, as long as they were in the line, it was a sort of file-firing of reputation signals.

I was at last eager to know what it meant, for it differed from any other social phenomenon I had ever observed. I soon discovered the secret of it. There was a department of state called the Bureau of Fame. At one time reputation had been allowed to look after itself, although men valued it even more than money. Private enterprise traded in it and juggled with it and made a monopoly of its growth, although it should have moved as freely as the air or water. For a time it had been in the hands of vendors of quack medicines and soaps; there were none so well known throughout the nation as they; there were none whose names would carry so much weight with the uneducated people. Simmity, the proprietor of a popular purgative, Hones, who owned the most widely advertised soap, and Bulunu, who sold the strongest kooan-noo, might have divided the monarchy amongst them, had they been able to come to an agreement, and thought it worth while to rouse and lead the mob for such a mere bauble; as it was they were both richer and more famous than the king; and what did they require? Their descendants were now the most powerful nobles in the land.

The next stage in the organisation of fame was to grant to a company the monopoly of all advertising opportunities in the realm. It had long been a scandal that men with little brains, less conscience, and still less education had got their names fixed in the popular mind more firmly and more widely than the ablest or wealthiest or noblest. It needed little persuasion then on the part of the company to precipitate the grant. And it set itself at once to organise all the methods it could invent for increasing reputation. It hired the best poets and prose writers in the kingdom; its artists were the most talent-ed painters and draughtsmen; whenever any boys or girls showed musical talent, it bound them to it by pecuniary and other chains; every demagogue with power of lung and command over words, every entertainer who could amuse the people, every jester who could make them laugh, every contriver of ingenious methods of attracting attention it had in its pay and ready at its beck. The newspapers and journals with their writers took instructions from it; for they knew there was no such good paymaster to be found. It had emissaries and claqueurs through all grades of the nation, mingling with their society, leading their thoughts, and touching their emotions.

A man could go into its office and get a quotation for any kind or extent of fame. He could have as little as a sixpenny-worth, a tanna, it was called; this consisted in a whisper set agoing in his favour within his own private circle. If he wished his name spread in a grade or locality that knew nothing of him, it would cost him a pownee, about ten pounds in our money, per month; for there was ever a time-element in these bargains. The price of keeping up a reputation increased till it was firmly established; then it lessened till the man passed his vigour of faculty; after the grand climacteric it increased again, but more gradually than before; for the mystery of retirement and the tradition of a reputation passing into the mouths of a second generation gave a man's story almost the vogue of a myth, and thus made it easier for the company to keep up the name. On death and for a week after, its charges were lower, as the funeral and obituary notices and the dark dresses and long faces of the relatives kept the memory green for about that length of time and relieved the servants of fame of much of their onerous duty. Thereafter the price rose till at a hundred years after death it became enormous, and at a thousand it became fabulous. Only one had ever had fortune large enough to buy up his fame for that posthumous period; and I still heard his name on all sides although he had been dead for twelve hundred years. The company had made large profits out of this bargain; for the uniqueness of the transaction had made the name a traditional topic in hours of leisure and a commonplace in literature; the natural channels of fame had become its unpaid auxiliaries.

Every kind of reputation had its own price per day or month or year, though the price varied from time to time according to the rise or fall of a particular virtue or line of life in public estimation. One item in the old price-list that amazed me was the money value of a reputation for truthfulness; it was by far the most costly, and next to it came the reputation for generosity, and that for purity of life. Surely it should have been easy to acquire the name of truthful or generous or pure in a community that paid such devotion to these virtues, and cultivated them so much. But, it was explained, there was of course greater competition for fame in them; men were especially eager to gain it, for it gave them full return even in money. It struck me that, where truth and charity and chastity were so widespread, it should have been very easy to get and keep the name for them; high charges meant special rarity in the commodity or special difficulty in obtaining it; and either seemed to argue widespread scepticism as to the possession of these virtues. But I was silenced with the argument that, where all or most had a virtue, it was difficult to win a reputation for special excellence in it.

The charges for fame in each of the virtues varied too with the employment and social grade. A journalist had to pay one hundred times more than a peasant or artisan for the reputation of truthfulness. The poet and preacher and vendor of quack medicines had to pay only one half as much as a news-paper-man for it; for, it was told me, they with their clients were perfectly well aware that their profession was to deal in fiction, and they tried in un-professional life to get clear of the taint of their trade, and took delight in blurting out the most candid truths. The highest price for reputed sobriety was demanded of the temperance reformer and the lecturer on the evils of drunkenness. The poor man and the spendthrift were charged next to nothing for the name of generous; the wealthy had to pay for the same, enormous sums in proportion to their wealth and social position. The reputation for wit was one of their cheapest commodities, being only a little higher than that for being not a bad sort of a fellow and that for being good but dull. And yet it was one of the dearest for ambitious young conversationalists and writers and orators and men of the world. It was almost as dear as a reputation for humour when professional jesters wished to buy it. The price-list indeed was one of the most striking comments on the past social history of the people.

What led to the overthrow of this strange company was a very natural extension of their business. They opened a branch for the destruction of fame, or, as they called it, for negative reputation. They found that they had continual demands made for this natural complement to their other function. At last they yielded to the pressure, and tried to use their old staff in the new service; but it was found that it destroyed their eulogistic talents; they rapidly developed into such accomplished slanderers and backbiters and defamers that they found it difficult to say a word in favour of anyone. In order to save the best of their old employees, the company had to hire a new set for the new business. They had intended to keep it an absolutely secret service. But, as the story of the new employment leaked out, their offices were daily mobbed by applicants for posts. They were of all sorts and sizes; but those who brought the most glowing testimonials to their capacity as traducers were tall and lank, long-nosed and large-mouthed, red-haired and small-skulled—as fine a crowd of Judases, it was said, as could have been picked out of living creatures. It was impossible to hire them all; half the nation would have been in the pay of the company. But those whom they rejected set themselves so vigorously to traducing the company that a yell of execration rose against it.

Such an outcry might have been ignored, but that their other department, which had been in full working order for several generations, had excited the hostility of many of the most respectable families. For the passion for posthumous fame had eaten into their fortunes. Men of wealth had taken the money that they should have left to their relatives and posterity, and willed it to the company in the purchase of as much immortality as it would buy. Some of the noblest houses were impoverished by this itch for keeping a name alive. And still more would have been reduced to poverty, but that they had a large pecuniary interest in the business, or had most of their members salaried in its employ.

It had come to be a great scandal and had roused the attention of the state; added to the outcry of the disappointed Judases, this supplied the opportunity for the reformers. And, on looking into the matter, they found that the company was growing too powerful for any government to stand up against it. It was absorbing most of the wealth and all the real influence over the Aleofanians. It had such vast and disciplined forces as no nation could bring into the field. The longing for reputation or fame had made one half the people its clients, and the necessities of fortune and the love of slander had made the other half into its servants. The king's ministers had to move with great caution, for they would have to meet all the talking, puffing, amusing, slandering power of the race organised into a subtle impalpable phalanx; the discipline was more imperturbable than that of the strongest army; there was no breaking the ranks whilst the influence penetrated everywhere like an atmosphere. In fact for generations they had not dared to move against their own creation. And even now that there was a strong set of the current of public opinion against it, its abolition could be brought about only by a secret and sudden blow. They met in dark conclave and took their measures without any item of the secret oozing out. The company was caught unawares and surrendered. Its business was appropriated and placed under the administration of a new department. A royal proclamation, accepting all its servants as employees of the new bureau, and all its obligations as state obligations, prevented panic; and the transference was made without the slightest public commotion.

The revolutionary measure left the directors of the company wealthy but powerless. And it gave to the government a prestige no ministry had ever had. The Bureau of Fame became a tower of strength that grew at last impregnable; and the direction of it was the main object of a statesman's ambition. It gave him the subtlest of influences over the desires of men. Before him even the greatest and proudest cringed; for he could make or annihilate that upon which their existence hung. They lived in the breath of others; to have all speak ill of them or, still worse, speak nothing of them was more bitter than death. What were wealth, huge estates, great fortune, unlimited power over luxuries, compared with the ballooning of their name whilst they lived and the surety that it would still be raised aloft when they were dead? Their present heaven consisted in the favouring winds of fame; the salvation of their souls lay in immortal reputation. One of their philosophers indeed had with much applause defined the soul as the breath not of a man's own body, but of his neighbours and his public. To be no more talked of was real death. The disanimation of the body was not the true end of life; many died long before that; whilst some few outlived the dissolution of the dust.

CHAPTER X
THE CHURCH AND JOURNALISM

THE Bureau of Fame had come to be the real shrine of religion. For it had the power of heaven and hell beyond as well as on this side of the grave. And one of the most significant changes in the government of Aleofane in recent times had been the amalgamation of the ministry of public worship with the department of fame. The church had of course from the earliest times been a state institution; and in spite of new-fangled philosophers was likely to continue so. For how could so subtle a force in human nature as religion be allowed to straggle lawlessly throughout a nation? Above all things it needed the most skilful piloting. A church apart from the state, an independent power, meant the spirit against the body, a divorce unnatural, if not monstrous. This was the philosophy of the position. And so convinced of it were the rulers that they allowed less independence of action in the ecclesiastical than in any other department. The head of the church was a minister responsible to the government, and they thought it illogical and feeble to let such an organisation legislate for itself. It was according to nature, it was the true primitive law, that the state and the church should be completely one. The idea of their separation was the result of degeneracy from the golden age. And what anarchy would ensue from an attempt to realise such a scheme or rather no scheme!

To speak of the separation of church and state in Aleofane was to speak of human life without breath, of the noon sky without the sun. The religion had grown to be the inner spirit of government. Never had there existed so religious a state. It could accomplish nothing except through its ecclesiastical organisation. It could affect the spirits of all the nation in any direction it pleased. It is true the people jealously guarded the traditional creed. But by gradual and impalpable change in the teachings of the priests or in the ceremonies the national mind could be bent in any way to suit the governors.

One of the first and most effective changes in the spiritual scheme of the state had been the gradual degradation of all the great posts in the church. The princely salaries attached to them were from tenure to tenure reduced till at last the chief ecclesiastical officers had to rely on charity for subsistence. The great spiritual influence that obstinately clung to them drew occasionally men of rank and ability. But all the common priesthoods fell so low in estimation that at last the state had to fill them with the milder type of higher-class criminals. No one would enter voluntarily into what was practically mental slavery to the government of the time. So, if any marble citizen fell into habitual and transparent falsehood, or failed before the eyes of all in some dishonest scheme, or let his fortune imperceptibly leak away and ceased to conceal the financial minus on which he luxuriously lived, he was promptly given the choice of the church or journalism; though for that matter the two had been for centuries amalgamated; they were but two branches of ecclesiastical business.

For it would have been foolish on the part of so successful a government to stop one intellectual leak in the nation and leave a wider one unguarded. It had been always a matter of course that those who could teach or influence the people with any talent should be the servants of the state. It came about, therefore, that, as a literature developed, the church was but journalism through speech and ceremony, journalism was but the church in writing. They were but two phases of the same function of the state. And the governors laughed as I told them of the position of affairs in Europe, where the state was supposed to rule the church, but had allowed the press complete independence. And they told me as a close analogy the story of one of their citizens who had soon drifted into idiocy; a bird of great beauty had flown into his house, and he resolved to catch it; and to make sure of it he planted a ring of servants all round the house and shut his doors and locked them, and opened his windows wide. For some time afterwards, if any one of them met me, he would with a twinkle of the eye ask me whether the governments of "Yullup" had ever caught their bird.

There was, I inwardly confessed, a logical thoroughness about leashing in the service of the state the twin spiritual powers of the church and the press. But I was pained in my European vanity to find the most cherished features of our modern civilisation so productive of mirth. They showed me that the only two logical positions were complete independence of both the great spiritual powers or complete control of both; nothing could justify the release of one and the bondage of the other.

As retaliation for their laughter at our civilisation and its hard-won fruits I smiled at their employment of criminals as priests and journalists, and asked them how they could expect to have religion well taught or truth well disseminated by such characters. They were not to be beaten—those subtle reasoners; I felt this in the smile of superiority with which they met mine. They asked me how I could expect priests who were by their positions and incomes independent of the state, and bound only by their own caprices or by those of the locality or circle to which they ministered, to teach the creed of the nation aright? To secure their salaries or to win reputation, they would launch into originalities, nay, into absurdities: they would pander to the predominant passions of their flocks, whilst keeping up the appearance of teaching the creed. The very contradictoriness of human nature would drive them in different directions from one another. With the journalists this would be still more the case, bound as they would be by no definite creed or set of rules or kind of emotions. How could they be expected to spread truth when there was no guide or master for them, no book of truth to appeal to? Nothing could be so productive of mental chaos as a class of men who without training or guidance or common consent or a common set of beliefs or principles should be allowed to pour their vagaries into the minds of the people. Would the nation ever advance, or keep from degeneracy, if these were to be its daily teachers, men who would pander to the commonest of popular passions and tastes, heedless of right or truth or even policy?

And when the state had both religion and journalism in its hands, how was it to secure the dissemination of what it considered absolute truth except by complete abeyance of the wills and characters of the disseminators? Centuries ago they had had a church whose priesthood was filled by men of the purest life and highest principle and then no one knew what the creed was; it was torn into shreds; and over its remains the preachers and theologians trampled like wild colts; there were a hundred schools and sects within the church, and each claimed for itself divine authority and divine truth; the people could find no guidance in faith or in morality; nor dare the state interfere with the extreme preachings or practices of any division, or even of any individual priest, for his followers, seeing the nobleness of his life and believing therefore that he had reached ultimate truth, would gladly die at the stake for him; and the high-salaried ecclesiastics having once got into their posts lived a free life without regard for God or man or government; they became fountains of immorality and discontent; by their example on the one hand and their luxury on the other, the spiritual head of the church was powerless; he dared not interfere with the privileges of his subordinates or even their beliefs; everything was indeed chaos, and that a chaos of religious enthusiasm.

It was the birth and growth of journalism that taught the state the true cure for such a diseased condition. Some of the most abandoned but able men in the nation had sunk so low that no one would trust them; in order to get something to live on they were driven to take advantage of an invention that had been recently made; the use of free types had cheapened printing, and with this and some other means of cheaply multiplying written productions, they determined to sell at a price sheets that would amuse the people. They were successful; and the more they invented lies and filled their sheets with fiction, the more lucrative it became. All the most accomplished liars of the nation crowded into it, and it was generally spoken of as the new profession of lying for the amusement of the people. The fortunes that had begun to be gained in it and the various attacks made upon men in authority called the attention of the ministry to the nascent power. And they were only just in time; a few more years and it would have been too strong for any state to cope with. They manipulated it with caution; they bought up the poorest and most unscrupulous of the journalists into what was practically lifelong servitude to the state, and turned the whole force of their talents in fabricating untruth against the few that had made fortunes in the trade; it was not long before these latter were ruined and had to sell their services to the government. But after a time it was found that the ablest of the state journalists grew vain of their powers and showed signs of striking out for themselves. Wages was not a strong enough lien over the talents of men who had grown conscious of their hold on the people. The trade was therefore proclaimed a state monopoly, and all the conceited journalists were weeded out; and into their places were put the most capable of the marble criminals who had been condemned to state servitude for life. It was made one of the rewards of good behaviour amongst convicts; for as journalists they were allowed to live in some degree of luxury; they had full scope for their craving for falsehood and dishonesty, and made of these a fine art. The only condition they had to fulfil was obedience to orders; all their productions were based on ideas supplied to them by the department and had to undergo criticism or revision by its officers. The state had them absolutely in its power; and yet the average of literary talent amongst them was far higher than when journalism had been free and independent; in fact a literature of some power, a pure state literature, had resulted. It was universally acknowledged that genius is essentially immoral on one or more rules of the moral code and sometimes on all; it has ever a vein of eccentricity or even madness in it that makes it leap over the pales of convention or principle or law; and hence in previous ages it had always been a pariah. At its first escapade it was now hurried into the fetters of the state, and was soon glad to accept the comparative freedom of state journalism. Thus the government had gathered into its service the greatest imaginations of the people, and through them could mould the nation to what purpose it would.

The success of this conquest of a new-born power and domestication of the wild spirits of the race pointed out the true secret for remedying the evils of religion and the church. Eccentricity was rampant in them; they were ever producing discontent and riot and rebellion; they were the homes of all that threatened the existence of the state. And yet the state dared not remove the offending priests, lest it should inflame the disloyalty of the people who followed them. The most astute of their statesmen saw the lesson of the conquest of journalism and applied it. He gradually reduced the salaries of the clergy, basing the policy chiefly on the ground that those who served God should be humble and free from the temptations of luxury; another and minor reason was that during a time of scarcity and depression economy was needed in the departments of the state. His successors carried out his craft with as much system and success, and, when the lower clergy had been reduced to a pittance, crusaded through the journals against the princes of the church and their luxury. By this time the marble citizens had ceased to send their children into the ordinary priesthoods, which gave no more the chance of a career, and all the clergy now belonged to the poorer classes. The higher posts were in the gift of the government; and it stripped them one by one of their great revenues and bestowed them thus lowered upon the common priests who showed themselves obsequious and obedient. And at last the very headship of the church was surrendered by the aristocracy, when it had lost its enormous salary and influence. The state at once created a department of public worship to absorb its functions. But, without journalism in its hands, it would never have been able to accomplish so complete a revolution; against it and its power over the people the church dignitaries were pithless; whilst the common clergy were too much torn by sectarian opinions to offer a united front. The later steps of this clever statecraft were easy and rapid.

But religion was not yet turned to its final purpose. Even the poor priests had their eccentricities, and broke away from state leading-strings. The unity of church and government was merely nominal, if this could occur. To make any function of the state real, perfect discipline is needed. A national army would succumb to the first foe, if regiments of it, or individual generals, were to follow their own caprice. And a national church, if it is to be a true engine of the state, has still more need of exceptionless discipline, inasmuch as it has to master the spirits of men.

Generation after generation of Aleofanian statesmen turned their best energies to this problem. Experiment after experiment was tried, but none succeeded till the policy of government journalism was adopted. Criminals with a turn for piety—and very few were without it—were offered the choice of incarceration for life or careers as priests. Already the people had been inoculated by the journals with the belief that the stream of divine unction had poured down through the ages quite irrespective of the channels along which it flowed; it would have been a hard thing indeed if the evil characters and lives of so many priests in the past had stopped their transmission of the favour of heaven to their flocks; long ago would true religion have failed them had it depended on the officiating ministers of the deity; it would have shown limitation of God's omnipotence if He had been supposed unable to send His inspiration through any person or character. The journalists had indeed found it easy to press home this doctrine, for the great church dignitaries, being often men of evil life, had been forced to inculcate it for many ages, and, being not seldom feeble in intellect, had reduced their duties down to the mere performance of ceremonies and the reading of prayers and portions of the sacred books. It was only amongst the poorest sectaries that the clergy had to use their brains in the way of reasoning out abstract doctrine into practical precept, or in rousing their flocks to religious fervour. Their light it was easy to extinguish or ignore. And all the marble city and its society readily accepted the change from the dull, uninterested performances of the old dignitaries to the smart elocution and brilliant histrionic attainments of the criminals. The state chose these not only for their piety, a common and superabundant commodity amongst them, but for their grace of speech and action, and sent them for several years to a great dramatic college, where every one of the arts of the stage was taught to perfection.

The long-talked-of reamalgamation of the theatre and the church was at last silently accomplished. What was the use of paying to see a poor performance in the theatre or concert-room, when they could enter any church for nothing and see a far more brilliant ceremonial enacted, and hear far more talented elocution? The minister of public worship encouraged by rewards the clever rogues, whom he had selected for the church, to invent new and more interesting modes of conducting the services, and new and more fascinating ways of chaining the attention of a crowd. The dramatic companies and public entertainers had to close their doors and seek employment under the state, and especially in the Bureau of Fame. The old revenues of the church were spent on magnificent choirs and instrumental bands, on the training of the musical talent of the nation for its services, as well as on the training of the criminals for its priesthood. As a rule the best histrionic ability straggled off into prison, for it delighted in outraging first convention and then law; it had a great taste, so my guide informed me, for extravagance and show, and soon developed a tendency to lying and hypocrisy. And such a truthful and sincere people had elaborate laws, of course, for the punishment and constraint of such vices. Thus the state got all the actor-talent of the marble city into its power. But it had to hire the musical talents, for they were too vain to have any vice but quarrelling; they had to be caught by other nets, the nets of gain; it secured from childhood all who had fine voices or great and original talent for melodious composition, or the management of musical instruments, and it trained them elaborately for the service of the church; the only certain employer was the state, and thus it had a monopoly of everything musical in the nation.

Elaborate and attractive though the church services in the hands of the state had grown, they still repelled or sent to sleep a considerable proportion of the worshippers; for the prelections and sermons had been left unreformed; they were as old and tedious and uninteresting as they had been centuries before in the hands of the incapable scions of the marble citizens. A reforming statesman had recently turned his attention to this defect; he had founded a great college of oratory, and selected the best of the cultivated and able criminals to be trained there. It was found an easier task than had been anticipated. For great gifts of speech and great powers of moralising were found to run frequently with immoral and criminal tendencies. And now it was remembered that, under the freer *régime* of an olden time, it had been men of the loosest life who had gained greatest influence over the people and the popular assemblies; popular orator and scoundrel had in the older language been synonymous terms; whilst even orator had had a flavour of dishonesty and untruthfulness, if not libertinism, about it. So the prison officials saw that it was generally the most untrustworthy of their wards who were most persuasive in speech, and had to be isolated lest they should incite to riots and rebellions.

Thus it was found necessary to choose all the future preachers of the church from the criminals classified as dangerous. But once their passion for oratory was allowed a safety-valve, once they began their training in the college, they became comparatively harmless; provided nothing was left in their way to steal, and no one sufficiently off his guard for them to deceive or corrupt. When I arrived in Aleofane, the first batch of oratorical criminals was being draughted into the service of the church. And I found great commotion amongst the older worshippers against the innovation; they complained that they and their ancestors had furnished their sections in the churches as dormitories; and now they claimed damages from the state as this expenditure had been rendered useless; just as the music had induced somnolence, they were roused by the bellowing appeals of these loud-lunged miscreants to conscience and the loftiest principles of morality; their ancestors had not thus been disturbed, nor were they going to be; they removed to the older-fashioned churches where the droning old sermonisers still buzzed; there they would have peace on holy days to rest; they would be gone to the final sleep before the ranting crowd had followed them. The younger set of worshippers were delighted at the change; for they listened now to lively declamation and vivid and picturesque oratory. Nothing could surpass the electric effect of some of those preachers on their audiences; you could hear strong men weep, and women that were usually marvels of silence cry out in wild ecstasy; thousands would sway as one soul to the passion of the speaker, or again a ripple of laughter would freshen over the throng, to be followed by a shadow of pathos like a summer cloud over corn-fields. I have seen men and women who had entered the building with smiling faces fall prostrate on the marble floors in an agony of repentance. It was one of their greatest luxuries in religion to have those strong emotions. They came to the church purposely to be moved out of their sluggish routine of feeling; and, having suffered the wild ecstasy, they had all the enjoyment of convalescence from the spiritual stroke of paralysis. The hysterical passions that were often lit by the flame of church oratory were like strong drink to them amid the level conventions of their daily life.

Nor did the state permit any preacher to pall upon his audience. As soon as the enthusiasm began to slacken, he was removed to another locality and church, and another brawny young orator fresh from the collegiate hulks was launched on his career of appeal to the emotions. The only danger was that in abandoning himself to the stream of his eloquence he might depart too far from the written sermon that had been revised by the state critics and utter something that might clash with state formulæ. But there were always in his audience guardians who kept their eye on him and by a threatening look pulled him up. And if he persisted, his promising career was broken off, for a time at least. The fear of this was generally sufficient to deter these oratorical and pious criminals from indulging in unlawful flights. For it was a terrible punishment for those who had the talent of persuasive talk to be shut up and have their speech throttled for ever in silent and repulsive cells. Indeed it was whispered that there had been attempts at suicide on the part of some budding orators who had so far transgressed as to be condemned to lifelong absence from the rostrum; whilst some who could not get their oratorical passions slaked or even recognised have been known to commit a serious crime and then stir up disturbance in prison in order to get scope for their power of influencing the emotions of others.

And it was marvellous to see the fervour of these convict-priests; they were most eloquent and convincing on the evils of the vice to which they were most addicted; they knew its subtlety and its fascinations; they could describe with the most picturesque realism its insidious progress and its resultant misery; they would enact the scenes of its various stages and phases with a truth and histrionic power that made the worshippers shudder. And then the appeals they made to repentance were really addressed to their own ideal selves; and so fervid and sincere were they, so full of pathos and melting prayer, that none could resist. I have heard a vast crowd of Aleofanians of the most righteous lives cry out in response, as if they had been the most abandoned of sinners.

What could not the state do with its people, when it had command of such channels into their very hearts! Whatever new purpose it had it subtly introduced into the sermons and church services, either didactically or dramatically; songs and hymns and ceremonies were manufactured for it; gorgeous spectacles were invented and drew crowds to the churches for months. But never was the purpose allowed to show itself obtrusively; it penetrated the spirit of these like a delicate perfume. And the people could not help being fascinated by it, so subtly did it ally itself with all the sweetest anodynes of care and pain and all the most tempting delights of the senses. Sweet savours, delicious perfumes, melodious sounds, the most artistic and beautiful sights soon made the new state policy the very atmosphere of the inner shrine of memory. And the priests and church orators touched the springs of emotion with hidden but concrete presentments of it; they were handsomely rewarded for every new and successful method they invented of getting it interwoven with the most popular feelings and the most sacred passions and memories.

But there was an ecclesiastical engine of state that promised to be more effective than any of these. For ages there had been in the church an institution that had somewhat fallen into neglect except with morbid women of the upper classes. They were accustomed to go at stated times into a box like a horse-stall and whisper the secrets that burdened them into an aperture like an ear; from this the sound passed by a tube into the secret chamber of the priests of the church; and there came back to the ear of the client spiritual advice that would console her in her difficulties or help her out of them. Neither priest nor worshipper was supposed to see or know the other; the act and communication were purely impersonal.

This custom the state revived and expanded, after it had begun to see what a powerful engine the church could be made. And it grafted it on to one of its few failures. When it had discovered how useful it might make criminals, one of its most ingenious and ambitious ministers determined to annex it to the medical profession. He saw its subtle and secret power in detail, and thought that, if he could weld this into a unity and make it an engine of state, it would be almost omnipotent; for the physician had complete command of his patients, and could make them believe what he would. He had their spirits and imaginations at a time when, at the lowest ebb of life's tide, they were most the prey of superstition. Whether hypochondriac or really sick, they were at his mercy, and what he prescribed or even loosely remarked sank deeply into them. Was not this the very vantage the state needed for riveting its chains upon the spirits of its subjects? The invalid periods of a man's life, and still more those of a woman's, and the invalid members of a household, are the very fulcra of the levers of existence. Such points of spiritual omnipotence should not be in the hands of private bunglers. The only thing that kept the physicians from ruling the nation was their mutual jealousy and perpetual disunion.

As a fact it was the state that supported the colleges of medicine and guaranteed the ability of the licentiates sent out by them. What could be easier than to go a step farther and make the physicians servants of the state? Some of the most astute convicts who had tastes in that direction were selected and trained in the full course of the medical schools, and sent out to practise with instructions to use their opportunities for the state. But there could be no check upon their proceedings as there was over the convict-priests. They revelled in doing evil, and a most obnoxious practice grew up amongst them. It was soon noticed that they became most luxurious in their style of living, and at last the death of several of their patients along with a new codicil to their wills bequeathing to the convict-doctor large legacies aroused suspicion and confirmed the long-unheeded outcry that the professional physicians had raised against them. It was found on close inquiry that they had milked their richest patients of most of their fortune, and the more alert and obstinate of them they had drugged into subservience to their will and then given them euthanasia. No custom could live in the midst of the odium that this revelation stirred. And the great statesman had to swallow his ingenious invention and policy.

But he was not content to remain passive under this recoil. He adapted his contrivance to the ecclesiastical organisation of the state, and turned his convict-physicians into confessors. They had been chosen to some extent for their soft, low voices, their refined and feminine manners, and their insinuating and confidential air. A little more training in the arts of sophistry and in the subtle distinctions and precepts of theology would fit them exactly to be spiritual advisers in the church. To warn them from the use of their posts for purposes of extortion, their brethren who had gone astray in medicine were severely punished. And to hold check on their conduct and advice, the confessional chambers of all the churches were connected by auditory tubes with the central office of public worship, and every confession and every consolation could be heard by the minister or his officials if he liked.

The practice of consultation in the auricular stalls of the church grew with amazing rapidity. The insinuating young voices, the subtle consolation, the efficient advice so soothed the perturbed spirits of the mentally sick that on the slightest commotion in the atmosphere of their life they rushed again to the ecclesiastical ear. Even the men began, at first in a shamefaced way, to await a vacancy in the stalls, afterwards most boldly and as a habit of fashionable life they indulged in the practice.

It reduced the revenues of the physicians by more than half; and they could make no outcry against it, for it was more powerful than they. At last one great financial minister of public worship organised the new departure; he had all the auricular stalls of all the churches of the nation connected directly with his central office; and in his presence all the spiritual advisers sat and received confessions and gave consolations. He had an army of clerks to insert in the secret doomsday-book opposite the name of each citizen anything in his or her confession that seemed of importance, whilst every morning he gave out the general policy and tone of the advices to be communicated; on exceptional cases he had always to be consulted at once.

He also offered a percentage on the legacies left by any worshipper to the church; this was given to the criminal on whose advice it was left. The department of public worship was coming to be the wealthiest in the state; for he fitted up the auricular boxes of the church as the most luxurious boudoirs, where a lady could lounge in the midst of the sweetest perfumes and music and the most beautiful paintings and statuary. He even allowed at a large rental auricular stalls to be let by the month or year to single individuals or families. Hither could the invalid or convalescent come in her moods of despair or depression and pour her sorrows into the ear of the soft-voiced comforter who shed, by his casuistries and gentle persuasiveness, balm upon her spiritual wounds. At last he permitted auricular tubes to be laid to the private chambers of confirmed invalids and of the dying, at a large premium. And this added such enormous sums to the revenue in the shape of legacies that he reduced the rate. Yet he left it as a policy of the office that it should never be so far lowered as to bring the privilege within the reach of those who had but moderate incomes.

Never had such a powerful engine come into the hands of the state; and every precaution was taken that it should not be abused and that no secret of this great confession bureau should leak out. But, whenever any citizen grew restive or obstreperous, an appeal was made to the pages of the dooms-day-book, and some secret found there was applied to him with the effect that he curled up into unobtrusive silence. The convict-confessors were, of course, all locked up at night in a well-sentried building, and by day every action of theirs was under unseen surveillance.

They still continued their medical studies and duties, and were able to prescribe through the auditory tubes to whatever patient could give a clear account of his symptoms. If anyone had symptoms that did not permit of a clear diagnosis of his disease, he was encouraged to come into the consult-ing-room of the office of public worship, and there the various convict-physi-cians questioned him and examined him unseen; the diseased organ or part was placed under powerful microscopes into which they looked; then the whole staff consulted on his case and gave him advice accordingly. But these were rare instances; as a rule, the patients were satisfied with the impersonal advice and acted upon it. Half the diseases had their source in the mind and only needed spiritual advice; and most were both mental and physical; none but felt great benefit from unburdening their spirits and receiving sympathy and consolation.

Half the confessor-physicians were on duty by night and half by day; and the former section consisted of the ablest and the most subtle and persuasive; for it was found that night patients and worshippers needed more spiritual consolation than day clients. It was during the sleepless hours of the dark that the soul sank into the abyss of morbid weakness and often into the paralysis of terror. It was then that it seemed to absorb the functions of the body and infect them with its own diseases. It was then that most succumbed to the assaults of sickness, the life ebbed farthest away and left the sensitive nerves naked to the irritations of thought and passion. It was then that the great harvest of bequests was reaped; seized by superstitious fears, by the terrors of the darkness around and to come, the spirit was ready to abandon the mere dross of life for a little support on the threshold of the grave, for a little religion. And the office of public worship never hesitated to promise all they asked for beyond the final darkness, provided they paid well for the boon. It was then that the most hideous secrets of life were whispered into the ear of the church, then that terror drove the soul into the refuge of complete disburthenment. Even when death was years off, the feebleness of the morbid or invalid or convalescent spirit during hours when sleep would not approach laid it open to assault; for the footfall of the awful destroyer seemed to be heard in the dread silence. It was then that it sought the consolations of the auditory tube and opened the flood-gates of repentance into the ear of the confessor-physician. The morning brought regret for the rash candour, but the secret was recorded; the office of public worship had undying power over the fate of the unburthened soul.

By the time I arrived in the island, the physicians felt that their profession was doomed, that the wily statesman had outwitted them; and doubtless before many generations most of them would plead to be admitted into the service of the state. When that occurred they would have to resign themselves body and soul to it; it would receive none but those who were completely in its power. Of course there was still much scope for them in families that would not trust mere impersonal advice or feared to resign their independence of spirit into the power of an office of state. They were also much employed in seeing the treatment recommended by the convict-physicians carried out; and in this they often retaliated upon the state by contradicting the advice and sowing doubt of its soundness in the minds of the patients. Doubtless the next move of the department of public worship would be to blow through pneumatic tubes into the auricular stalls of the churches, or into the chambers of the sick the drugs and medical requisites that were recommended.

By means of these three uses of the talents of convicts the state church had become a reality and was far more powerful than the press. Journalism poured suggestion into the public mind; but it was into the healthy, wide-awake, often recoiling public mind; its reasonings, eloquence, or imaginative schemes and suggestions were not always accepted; they had often to lie ungerminated in the soil of the national spirit for years, till they were forgotten and some new occasion laid them bare and made them seem to spring up spontaneously. The personality of the writers though not unfelt was unseen, and so far had the potence of that which is mysterious; but they could not, like the ecclesiastical convicts, use the shadowy distance of the world to come in the way of threats and promises; they could not stir the soil of the present to immediate harvest with the plough of the future. They had to depend on the weapons and tools of the average man; they had to reason and persuade, explain, or appeal to the emotions, as neighbour to neighbour, except that they had the impersonality and anonymity of confessors and could gag their opponents in any attempt at reply.

Their power would have seemed enormous, had it not been put into comparison with the complete state organisation of the church and been overshadowed by it. They were used as the dogs of war, gathering as they did into the hands of a minister the loose fangs of irresponsible gossip, leashed as they were to one purpose and one spirit or policy. They knew that they had but one master to please, one master who had their liberty and still more their luxury in his power; and him they served with all their faculties and especially their faculties of invention, personal venom, and vituperation. They had no principle, no scruple except towards him and the government he embodied. If they entertained the majority, they did not care who suffered. Their first object was to strengthen the roots of the state, and especially of the minister of the department; their next was to make the largest number possible read their articles and paragraphs. If any one of their victims turned upon them and denied the news about him as a slander, they were at once made by the head of the department to apologise and explain that by some mistake the paragraph had slipped out of the pure fiction column into that of news, and that the name of the citizen had strayed out of the column of eulogies in transferring type. Where this was impossible as an explanation, the minister could easily appease the wrath of his victim by showing him how an especially unscrupulous convict had been introduced new into the office and had acted on his own responsibility and ignorance of the rules of revision.

I wondered at so great and virtuous a people enduring such an institution in their midst. They marvelled at my wonder, and thought of it as based on the very laws of nature. How could any marble citizen indulge in such work and retain his self-respect, and how could a state be accountable for the vagaries of irresponsible writers, whose dignity and self-respect were lost? The only means of producing a united and vigorous literature was to make the writers bond to the state. The only means of keeping it pure and free from attacks on the nation and the national spirit was to put the journalists body and soul into the hands of a department, and to make the department responsible for their productions. This was a provision of nature as soon as such an institution arose.

CHAPTER XI
THE BUREAU OF FAME

I WAS EVIDENTLY AS far astray on this point as I had been on the employment of convicts in the church. And when the full significance of the functions of state had been laid before me, I had to acknowledge that there was much in their prejudice in favour of the enslavement of genius and talent—the most capricious of human things.

As soon as the organisation of fame became a function of government, it was an essential that national genius and talent, the arbiters of fame, should be robbed of their caprice and yoked to the will of a single responsible man. What would be the use of spreading one rumour if the press and the church, which could creep into the very heart of the nation, were able to contradict it or render it fangless? What would all other means avail for planting a reputation, if the reasoning, imaginative, and rhetorical ability of the nation were not bound to water and foster it?

It seemed to them as natural as breathing that the literary and oratorical power of the nation should be fenced in to the service of the nation. And no one ever thought of complaining that it was entrapped as early in life as possible into lifelong slavery to the state. Where would the reputations of all of them be if this were not done? They would be as safe as the lives of their children with a jungle of wild beasts let loose amongst them. Who could control these irresponsible madmen we call geniuses if it were not the representative of the force of the nation—the state?

Trained from youth by the strong hand, they might be of great service in moulding the national future; but if left from the first to follow their own caprice, nothing could result but the wildest confusion of principles and beliefs, and the sacrifice of the reputation of every average citizen to their unslakable thirst for fame. There was indeed no alternative left for any self-respecting community but the enslavement of all the capricious power of imagination born in its midst. They might train it to do their behests and serve their destiny; if left uncaged, they would have to do its behests and serve its destiny.

The amalgamation of the Bureau of Fame with the department of public worship and public opinion was a policy of self-preservation. The church made ready the soil, the press sowed the seed, and the bureau watered and weeded and reaped. It would have been a national folly to allow any disagreement or collision amongst these processes. Better almost to have left the national genius to its old internecine conflict.

Now the Bureau of Fame was the pivot of the government; and it was the greatest ambition of an Aleofanian to rise to its administration. Its minister for the time being was arbiter of all for which the ablest men lived; he could make or mar careers; he could raise whom he would to immortality, or damn him to everlasting execration, or, what was worse, oblivion; he was far more powerful than any pope and any monarch combined could be; it was indeed the chance of heaven or hell he could deal out.

There was, of course, a price-list for various kinds and periods of reputation; and a citizen with a large fortune could buy what was for human life immortality. But the chief business of the office was political, to enforce the privileges and enhance the fame of the marble citizens, and especially of those in power—a great noble, a child of the monarch, or one whom the court and the minister delighted to honour.

If the new protégé of fame was a commoner, the first proceeding of the bureau was to confer on him one of the noble titles which it had within its prerogative; for it was the guardian and creator of all orders and titles. Next it set one or more of its most imaginative criminals to invent an ancestry for him and a life-history; a few well-known dates and facts were supplied as the skeleton; but round the skeleton grew a living form that no one would have recognised who knew the original, so romantic, so striking, so sublime did it become. Into every historical event a progenitor was thrust and a large share was assigned to him. Marvellous incidents were interwoven with historical facts and the new name introduced as the centre of them. Back to the heroes the family story went until it was lost in the mists of the origin of all things. There was not a link left broken or weak, not an opening left for destructive criticism; for the most hypercritical of the journalistic criminals were let loose upon the result of the heraldic fictionists' work; they found every weak spot and tore the art to pieces. With this analysis and criticism attached to it, it was returned to the original authors for repairs. Again and again it went through the criticism factory, and again and again, after submitting to every test that could be thought of, it returned to the hands of the regenerators. Having reached the final form that withstood the scepticism of the subtlest critics, it was intermingled with the annals of the country and, being printed in a form that could easily be read, it was distributed amongst a section of the people

who were unlearned yet not uninterested in the national history. If they failed
to find the seams of the patchwork and accepted the newly intruded portions
as genuine, the work was finally passed as ready for the second process of the
bureau.

A staff of poets—epic, lyric, and dramatic—were turned on to the new
episodes, and, being left to their individual tastes, picked out one this and
another that. They each worked their theme into brilliant verse. The result in
one case would be a long romance fit for recitation during the nights of the
dimmer half of the year; in another it would be a rattling ballad or song that
would, when sung through the streets or villages, catch the ear of the people;
in a third it would be a dramatic scene or complete play that could be staged
either by the church or by the bands of strolling actors who perambulated the
country districts in the pay of the state.

Having thus got a brand-new literature manufactured for its protégé's life
and ancestry, the office set its staff of musicians to work on the legend and its
poetry, and gorgeous pieces were composed for the ecclesiastical and other
orchestras and choirs upon its various themes; and short catches and glees
and songs were composed for the common people and their ballad-singers.
These were sent out through the length and breadth of the island on the fingers and lips of itinerant players and singers and in the mechanical automata
that were manufactured by the hundred to repeat any tune of a fixed number.
The whole country was soon jigging and singing to the popular chorus that
enshrined the new name and the new deed or that by a new genealogy linked
the name with the gods or the national history. And all the marble citizens
and the people of the city were trying to whistle or hum or reproduce on their
private tinkling instruments the more melodious passages or the orchestral
or choral celebration of the new fame.

Meantime the journals had been playing battledore with the topic and
the various sections of it; they introduced it in paragraphs, in articles, in
verses, in romances; there was mysterious gossip about the new name and
loud, brazen-voiced eulogy; there were subtle inquiries about its fame and
as subtle answers. And these were all adapted in method and tone to the
two great kinds of journals. For there were journals for the common people
and journals for the marble city. The one inculcated due regard to the station into which a man was born and reverence for all notabilities. The other
fitted the idiosyncrasies of high-born society, describing its splendours, its
wit, its genius, its lofty origin, its generosity. The one was didactic, the other
descriptive and eulogistic. The one was tedious and thoroughgoing; the other
was imaginative and sparkling. And by each the topic was treated in its own
peculiar way.

The church did its duty too. It never failed to inculcate the fatalism of class and birth, even when it was floating some new man into fame, although he had but recently changed his class and had his ancestry manufactured. "Each man to the station God has given him," was the watchword of its prayers and its prelections. How pathetically the preachers dwelt on the fearful results of attempts to reverse the commands of nature! They could point to their own cases as the ruin of ill-weaved ambition. What could be a better proof of the evil of contravening the divine arrangement of classes than their own career? They had tried to rise above their fellows and the place God had given them, and, to accomplish this, had been impelled to break the laws; the consequences their hearers might see with their own eyes. And often the tears would roll down the orator's cheeks, and the audience would weep with him, as he painted the horrors of transgressing the divine order of society, and appealed to them to abstain from all such transgression and to be content with the station God had assigned them.

Yet the next part of the service would be a recitation of the mythical ancestry of some new man and of their great deeds, or a dramatic representation of his heroic efforts for the state, or a hymn in his honour with full choral or orchestral effects. Once the transgression of the divine order of the universe was accomplished, it was accepted as a portion of that order. However obscure the birth of the favourite, however base his nature, it was at once transfigured by his successful breach of the social laws of nature. And, when the Bureau of Fame adopted him as protégé, he was within less than a generation washed pure as snow, the noblest of the noble in personality, in ancestry, in posterity; all his life and character and origin were consecrated in the national consciousness; and it would have been treason, nay sacrilege, to doubt the divine sanction or the truth of the story or to give a hint of the poor facts that had been buried in oblivion. The name was interwoven with the holiest feelings of reverence; the splendid fiction in song and drama, in prayer and pulpit oration, stirred the deepest enthusiasm of worship, and wound itself into the most sacred memories. And the whole process had begun and gone on so impalpably, so subtly, that it was accomplished before anyone could awaken himself to criticism; and then it was past remedy. It was the great act of regeneration. The character and manners and morality of the man and his family might be as unclean and repulsive as before; his name—the true living principle of a man according to this people—was raised to the level of heroes and gods, was launched upon the career of immortality.

Alas! there were conditions and limits, as there are to everything human. The negative business of the bureau, though kept in subordination, still existed. If any man offended the minister or his patrons or satellites, then was his name first dropped, "quick as a falling star," from the heaven of all public services and performances; the literature and music and art that enshrined his deeds and the performances of his ancestry vanished no one knew how. For a time vague and derogatory rumours concerning him crept through the journals; they hinted at something base, if not criminal, and yet the hints could not be charged with any definite meaning. At last there was complete and unbroken silence. The man was buried better than if he were dead without tombstone or memorial.

I marvelled that a nation that so worshipped reputation could have allowed the concentration of this power in the hands of any man. But I was assured that it was used with great wisdom and caution. The negative function was rarely set to work, and then in the most underground manner; it was felt but never seen. The bureau employed no organised band of slanderers as the company had attempted to do. In fact it doubted the prudence or effectiveness of such a course. Continual and open-mouthed detraction of any man would probably produce the opposite effect; it would make the neutral suspect some plot against him and stir their innate sympathy for the oppressed. Nay, many would court the notoriety of organised criticism and derogation as a cheap method of keeping their names in the mouths of the nation. What the bureau did in the negative way was truly negative. Its policy was the inculcation of complete silence; and oblivion was the result—a result so telling amongst the Aleofanians that the marble citizens almost grovelled before the court and the minister of fame, and even before their parasites.

With the common people the bureau and its power of heaven and hell had no influence; to condemn to everlasting oblivion was no threat for them; to raise them to immortality was no reward. It was the main engine of discipline in the marble city. And never was there so effective a discipline amongst an aristocracy. A frown from the minister was enough to cow the boldest spirit. Never was a nobility so meek, so free from turbulence and rebellious self-seeking; they were willing to take whatever colour the court delighted in; they changed their opinions, their manners, their principles, their morality, their life to the subtlest changes in the court and the bureau; human chameleons, they would change their hue even from hour to hour, as the court changed. No group of beings in heaven or earth surpassed the discipline of these Aleofanians.

CHAPTER XII
FREEDOM AND REVOLUTION

YET THEY GLORIED IN their freedom and their love of freedom. No people could be freer than they. Daily in their temples were there songs and hymns chanted in honour of liberty. It was a truism of the journals that liberty and liberty alone could be the true spiritual atmosphere of a nation. They loved to worship superiors and reverence especially the vicegerent of God upon earth—the head of the Bureau of Fame. They bowed to him and did him every obeisance because he was the head of the church and worthy of all manner of worshipful obedience. But he had no control over their actions except the moral and religious control which they willingly acknowledged.

As an instance of their complete freedom of action they pointed to the way in which the government allowed them to do as they liked with the peasants and artisans and the lower classes generally who were in their service. In the discipline of these they were untrammelled. They acknowledged that they were responsible to the state for the good conduct of their servants; but on the other hand the state passed over to them the power of life and death over these so that their authority should be no mere nominal thing. Ah, freedom was indeed the noblest feature of life; they might as well pass into the grave at once as give it up or allow it to be interfered with.

I was afraid to suggest to them the information I had received from a foreigner in the lower city about a large part of the country people. All the former inhabitants of the island and most of the artisans were in semi-slavery. They saw the hesitation in my face and guessed its purport. And one of my eulogists of liberty launched into a prelection on the necessity of a stage of servitude in the history of all ascensions to civilisation. A people that had not long issued from the animal stage could never become anything better than half-brutes but through bondage to a more advanced race. It was indeed a noble mission of theirs thus to spend ages on the task of assisting a tribe of half-savages to subdue their foul passions. The peasantry would be nothing but wild beasts without such restraint. The process had been going on for centuries, and it showed the great patience and love of the Aleofanians that they persisted in such a repulsive and fruitless task. The artisans were those of them who had improved under the discipline, and so they had been partially freed. But even they were still somewhat savage in their natures; even they needed to be treated with great long-suffering. The marble Aleofanians were as patient with these degraded beings as a mother with her child, never sparing the rod when it was needed, although it lacerated their finer feelings to use such a means of discipline. He compared their conduct in this matter with their treatment of monetary relations. They were equally generous and self-denying and protective of the good of all the other people of the nation in dealing with money; they held it the root of all evil, and to prevent its working havoc widespread they concentrated it in the hands of a few,—the marble citizens,—who could not so easily be harmed by it.

I called his attention to the numerous interferences with liberty of action in the various laws that fenced them in from the indulgence of certain passions. Ah, that was one of the noblest instances of their worship of freedom; so devoted were they to it that they prohibited everything that would lead to a breach of it; no man could be allowed to circumscribe his own liberty; and all vice circumscribed liberty; hence all vice had to be checked. It was only in the interest of liberty that liberty was ever interfered with.

He slid into another eulogy of freedom and instanced the devotion of the Aleofanians to it in their conversation. No one was checked in his criticism of a neighbour or fellow-citizen; their city was indeed a mutual fellowship society in which the freest censure of each other was allowed for mutual benefit. The keen contest of wits moulded their characters and intellects. No one dared be absent from any social or conversational fête, lest he should suffer in reputation from becoming the topic of the meeting. Never would they descend to vulgar depreciation; they were masters of refined insinuation and veiled malignity. They could whisper away a reputation with the grace of a duellist; and at the climax of a mortal combat of wits their serenity remained unruffled. Oh, the grace and beauty of their social life! They were never done admiring it. But without this freedom of criticism it would be nothing. Ah, life in Aleofane was indeed a noble thing, so happy and free were all classes of the people, from monarch to peasant, from the bureaucrat of fame to the poorest artisan!

"Even the criminals were happy" was the climax of his eloquence. I asked him for an explanation. He proceeded to show me how it was failure that constituted crime. To deceive successfully was the highest art of life; for the essence of art was to conceal itself. And to be discovered was to fail in this. Whoever suffered this indignity was convicted of the special vice he had been concealing and sent to the hulks, that is, was turned into a journalist or priest. In these professions they were perfectly happy, for they were allowed in them to revel in their own special vices. The journalists manufactured their news whenever they found events fail them, and the priests manufactured their myths and creed whenever the sacred books failed them. So their capacity of fiction was exercised daily and hourly. And provided it was exercised in accordance with the purpose of the bureau, no one interfered with their enjoyment. The newspapers and the church were the home of fiction; and when truth was told there, it passed unrecognised. In order to keep up the interest of readers the journalists manufactured sensational news one day and contradicted it the next; and in order to draw crowds one priest would preach a most heterodox interpretation of the sacred books in his sermon and another would reply to him in his and contradict him. This neutralised the evil that might arise from journalism and its personalities and from sermons and their heterodoxies. It would never have done to put ordinary citizens or successful deceivers and slanderers into such posts; they would be too astute in deceiving the people; their fictions would not be so palpable and gross or so mutually contradictory that the simplest reader or hearer would discover them. So much had the Aleofanian palate become accustomed to such journalism and pulpit oratory that if the writers ever described facts or indulged in truths, they had to give them the flavour of fiction; and if ever the priests indulged in orthodox doctrines they had to give them the tinge of the heterodox. Ah, surely the whole people were happy, for all were so free as to be able to indulge their special appetites and likings!

I was scarcely convinced by this subtle and eloquent eulogy of Aleofanian life and liberty, and I determined to visit the common people and see for my-self. I had already examined the journals intended for them and seen how different they were from the fashionable literature of the marble city. They were generally presented to strangers and must have greatly impressed them, for they were full of noble sentiments and moralisations subtly interwoven with eulogies of the Aleofanian leaders of state and fashion for their great virtues and goodness. It was most edifying to read these sermonised news-sheets, saturated as they were with the highest ethics and deepest piety, and especially the doctrine that it was the duty of every man to adhere to the station in which God had placed him. But I was struck after I came into the marble city with the tone adopted towards them by the citizens of the higher class; they spoke of them with a patronising smile and disinterested approval, as if they were talking of children's Sunday-school literature or fairy tales. And about all the fiction in these popular journals there was the atmosphere of a child's fairyland; everything was happy and beautiful and as it should be. After reading a series of them I could easily have concluded that Aleofane was another paradise for the unambitious and lowly, and that death must be looked upon by the common people as an overwhelming catastrophe in that it put a stop to this full current of joy and happiness.

My curiosity was greatly piqued. I wished to see this other Eden upon earth. So with letters and passports and a guide, one of the journalists, I set out. And for the first few days everything was idyllic. But drunkenness, the special vice of my cicerone, got hold of him, and he collapsed by the way. Thereafter I found the whole scene change. It was now nothing but squalor and gloom and the lash of the whip.

A stranger from a neighbouring island, whom I had met in my first hostelry, explained to me the histrionic character of the first few days' experience and the reality of the last. He took me in hand, and under his guidance I visited one of their provincial cities. Here I saw men and women of the same race as the marble citizens crawling in filth and starvation, prostrate in a magnificent temple before the sleight-of-hand and the mesmerism of the priests. They were bound in the chains of superstition and ignorance, and they were encouraged to do little else than procreate and multiply; for to pauperise by religion was the first rule of the Aleofanian government, and to enslave the soul by pauperism and ignorance was its corollary.

Yet in a cave outside of the town we witnessed from our hiding-place awful and mysterious rites of a revolutionary propaganda proceeding. We saw thousands of the ignorant peasants and artisans getting initiated. And when the ceremony was finished we almost burst into laughter over the pathos as the agitators gathered round a fire and gorged. My guide had evidently something to do with this rising revolution; and he was so enraged to find that an agent from the communistic island of Tirralaria had crept in amongst the revolutionists. The heavens confound his impudence and cant! What he and his beggarly crew from the isle of thieves wanted was to divide the plunder of another island. They had communised Tirralaria into a cipher. Of the wealth that they had counted by thousands, when they landed there, naught remained but the nothings. The growth of the dummy citizen or cipher in the denominator had made Tirralarian property a vanishing point. The game of this Garrulesi was not to establish socialism in Aleofane, but to socialise its property into Tirralaria.

After his burst of anger I tried to elicit more about this socialistic community. Tirralaria was a large island, I got to know, into which had been tumbled some centuries ago a few thousand socialists with considerable wealth to their share. They had increased to tens of thousands, and their wealth had gone down to little more than a shirt to each back. After the besom of a tornado or a famine or a plague had swept the island the population soon reached high-water mark again; every square yard of the soil was littered

with a stronger and lazier humanity. The island stank of humanity miles to
leeward. There was scarcely room enough for graves, let alone beds. The lub-
berly and oleaginous let themselves out as mattresses; and so the space was
economised, and another increase was possible. The unclean rogues, they
never washed, unless they chanced to get hustled off the edge of the island
into the sea. The description contrasted so strongly with the rose-coloured
picture that I had heard drawn by the socialist agent in the cave that I determined to see for myself.

As we wandered through the forests of the island my guide told me of two
saviours that had landed on the coasts of Aleofane and become the protectors
of the poor. One refused to resort to the tricks of the charlatan, and, deserted
by his followers, perished at the hands of the aristocracy, who then adopted
his tenets and worked them into an elaborate hypocrisy. The other, learning
by his fate and bettering the jugglery of the marble citizens, put heart and drill
into the poor who flocked to his standards, and led them to victory. He seized
the throne, but, flattered by the old aristocracy into belief in his own divinity
and into desertion of the cause of the poor, he vanished in pomp, luxury, and
corruption.

By dint of persistent inquiry I got him to explain his hints about the island
from which the ancestors of all of them had come. It was called Faddalesa,
or the isle of devils, because of the appalling phenomena they encountered
whenever they attempted to return to it. It had, he acknowledged, been called
Limanora, or the island of progress; but for thousands of years that name
had lapsed. And on the shores of now one island and again another strangers
had landed. But as they were wealthy, and taciturn, no questions were asked,
and their descendants had vanished into the ranks of the aristocracy. It was
many centuries since any had come, though it was generally supposed in the
archipelago that I had come from the central island with my fireship. I saw
the mistake that they had made would serve my new resolve to make for this
mother isle; and I left it unchallenged in their minds.

In the great northern harbour of Aleofane I came across the same filth
and a similar rich temple; but I also found clearer evidence of underground
revolution approaching consummation. And for the sake of my fireship and
its powers of helping on the movement I was initiated into the mysteries of
one of their societies. The socialistic agent, Garrulesi, insinuated himself into
my acquaintanceship; and for the sake of being able to return with him to his
home I endured his eloquence on the perfection of the altruistic life. Competition was the bane of the human race; and its only products were poverty
and disease and unhappiness. It was responsible for property, and the only
crime was property. Was it not monstrous that one man should taboo what

another man needed! Obliterate property, and you wipe out crime too. How gentle and amenable and humane was the true commonweal, where neither property nor class existed! No law was needed, no law could persist. Every natural instinct and passion of the human breast was allowed the fullest scope. There was indeed no further stage to reach; need of progress, of effort was passed. Man under such a rule had become all that he might be, and he felt that whatever is is right. Evil and darkness had fled before the light of primitive happiness, and existence had become the throne of God.

As he dilated on the nobleness of Tirralarian civilisation I saw his eye flicker and his colour change. A stranger had passed. He told me that we were being watched. He wished me to take refuge in Tirralaria with my fireship if anything occurred. But I had promised it to my guide and fellow-traveller. He showed one flash of anger. But it vanished at once. He led me to the shore and pointed out his falla or ship. In it he would hang round the coasts for me, and he indicated an unfrequented point, whither I could flee and find safety on board his ship. He offered to take off to my crew any message that I desired to send; I might instruct it to come to Tirralaria for me after it had been to the isle of dogs. I wrote in English, and sent my orders to my comrades, knowing that the language would be safe from his prying.

CHAPTER XIII
IMPRISONMENT AND ESCAPE

HE WENT ON BOARD and I returned to my guide, whom I found greatly disturbed. An official spy had come down from the marble city; and this meant that a whole army of them in covered armour were in the neighbourhood and on the alert. He had scarcely ears for an account of my interview with Garrulesi till I reached the story of his blanching at the sight of a stranger. His alarm grew, and he was concocting a scheme for getting to my fireship, though he knew it would be almost impossible to pass through the cordon of state guards that was, he was certain, drawn round us. Just as dusk shuttled into dark he had matured his scheme, and we were about to put it into effect when the door of our room in the hostelry opened and a missive was delivered to each of us. We were invited by the monarch to return to the marble city and sojourn with him in his palace. Nothing could be clearer than that the bureaus had received information of our movements and suspected that we were engaged in stirring the artisans and peasants to revolution. And this was a pleasant invitation to euthanasia. Our doom was fixed if we could find no other way out of the noose.

Early in the morning a car of triumphal proportions drew up at our door and we were bowed by the town officials with great ceremony into it. It went off at funereal pace by a coast road to the marble city, accompanied by an escort of royal guards. It was plain from the faces of the wayfarers of the ruling class that there was something portentous in our procession, for they looked back at us with glances full of pity. My guide, who came to be more self-controlling in his manner and more confidential and intimate in his tone, told me how often he had feared such a result; but they had followed their own diabolical style of letting him have complete freedom till he had become reckless, and now they had pounced upon him. He asked me, if I escaped, to make for Broolyi, his native country, and inform the authorities of his fate; they would give me full protection and treat me with the greatest hospitality, I might be sure. He told me his own name—Blastemo—and said that the mention of it would turn all his relatives into my friends. But lest the devils should, with their usual pharisaic inhumanity, make their refined methods of torture take the place of euthanasia, he gave me a small nutful of a most potent drug, a pinch of which, small enough to be hidden under the nails, would launch me in a few seconds into the tide of unconsciousness that leads to death. In the palace we would be watched by a hundred eyes that we could never see. Unseen, unguessed-at espionage was one of the secrets of the mysterious power that the bureaus had over all. They seemed to know almost what was transacted in the depths of the soul in the darkness of midnight. The only safeguard in the Isle of Liars (thus he translated the name) was the universal suspicion that tortured the marble citizens. None of them felt sure of even his nearest relative or closest friend. And if any chance of escape came to us, it would be through some official of the palace who was getting uneasy about his own fate.

We were welcomed at our destination with great and effusive ceremonies as if we were about to be enthroned. And for days we seemed to be the centre of all its hospitalities; we were fêted and banqueted and amused in the most elaborate style. And through the whole series of festivity and pomp we were without any apparent caution kept strictly apart, so that we were not able to pass even a word.

The monarch showed himself greatly interested in me and asked me innumerable questions about my people and country, being especially amused at my description of the use of steam in doing work, and of the use of firearms. His little six-year-old boy was even more entranced by my pictures of the steam-engine and of our warfare. He was the one weakness of his father. He clung to my side, especially when in disgrace, and that was very often. It was he who told me that my fireship was off the mouth of the estuary where I had landed. I stimulated his curiosity to the utmost, seeing a possible way of escape. He kept begging the king to let him go to it. But clearly the bureaus were against such a venture.

At last the child fell ill. The physicians declared the illness to be one of the heart, and after a time warned his father of its dangerous character if the boy were in any way thwarted. He whined every day his old request that he might be taken on board my fireship. The king pleaded with the heads of the bureaus to let him go; and they at last grew alarmed too, for he was the only heir to the throne, and the father's life was by no means certified by the physicians as likely to be long. They saw the risk of getting thrown out of power. And they consented to the expedition, but under the most stringent conditions. I was to remain on shore whilst Blastemo and the little prince should go on board with his father and a royal escort.

We set out, and after much floundering in the mud and grappling with the current they swept over the bar under the guidance of a fisherman who knew every sand-bank and could prevent such a mishap as befell me when I landed. I had sent a note with them, and I could see that the three were received on board with every sign of friendliness. But the boats containing the escort drew out to a distance from the steamer.

Everything seemed to go well for a time; the sea was calm, with a slight breath and ripple off the shore. Suddenly I saw a whiff of smoke shoot out from the bow of my yacht, and with a loud report reverberating from the cliffs behind, a ball landed in the midst of a troop of guards that was stationed to cut off my retreat towards the north, the only possible way of escape; on the other side was the river with its acres of mud, and behind was the road to the city, well guarded at all points. The result was as sudden as the shot. I had just time to collect my senses and look round; and away on the highway I could see the tails of the guard in the wind. Another shot and another ploughed the earth or flapped into the mud, and cleared the lowlands of every Aleofanian.

I soon realised the situation and quietly walked off to the north over a long spit. I made no attempt to run as if I were escaping. But as I moved higher and higher on the rising ground I could see the shot strike the flat I had left. When I reached the highest part of the promontory I found the reason for the demonstration. A falla lay in the offing, sheltered from sight of the retreating troops by the high bluff in which the spit terminated. Garrulesi's instructions flashed into my mind; and I remembered that this was the point he had indicated for my safety if ever I needed to escape.

I got over the ridge, and as I looked back I could see the sand occasionally pirouetting in the air and I could hear a reverberation sound in the rear. I then ran as quickly as legs would carry me towards the shore. In a sheltered nook of quiet water lay a native boat, with the men sitting paddles in hand. They gave me the signal agreed upon, and I readily jumped on board. The canoe shot out from the rocks. And it was not too soon. For a troop, recovering from their panic, were making down the sheltered side of the spit, unnoticed by the yacht. And we were not out of reach when the first arrows sliced the water. The men redoubled their efforts, and only half a dozen missiles struck the boat before we were safe on board Garrulesi's falla.

CHAPTER XIV
THE VOYAGE TO TIRRALARIA

I ASKED HIM TO sail round the bluff and communicate with my yacht. But he would not hear of it. He said that this would endanger the safety of all, for the Aleofanian king would see at once how elaborate had been the conspiracy and how treacherous we had been, and he would take every means to frustrate our departure, or, if we got safely off, to avenge the insult. I had to accept his reasons, for I was in his power. But I was sure that there were others; he was afraid that if I got on board my own ship, Blastemo would persuade me to go off with him to Broolyi; on the other hand, if he secured me for his island, my fireship would soon be in Tirralaria too.

I found out afterwards from my sailors that the king had fallen into great consternation at the firing of the guns, especially when the boats with his guards made off towards the shore. One of the shot had opportunely ploughed up the sea not far from their station and had evidently filled them with panic. My men knew that Garrulesi was waiting for me on the other side of the point, and they kept firing towards the beach till they thought that I should be on board. Then, in order to quiet the fears of the king, they put him and his boy into the yawl, and pulled him on shore. In his excitement he had forgotten all about Blastemo, and, before he had regained the upper reaches of the road and joined his troops, the yacht had lifted anchor, picked up her boat, and steamed out to sea. They saw my signal on board the falla, and knew that I was safe. So they followed my instructions and made for Broolyi, whilst the wind bore us in the opposite direction.

But the shadows thickened, and before night fell we had run into the shelter of some high land and anchored. The men hung a dirty guttering lamp in the main room of the high poop, and by its light I could see how slovenly and foul was the whole cabin. It smelt of fish-oil and of unnumbered meals past. The floor was littered with garbage, so that I had to clear a path through it to prevent slipping. I could find no convenient ledge to sit on that was not embossed with grease and oil. I was glad to reach the night air again, for it at least helped to deodorise the deck. I got them to hang me a hammock in the shrouds, resolved to keep out of the cabin as long as I could.

I was awakened at early dawn by the movements of the seamen, and through the grey light I saw that we were lying off the bleak, rocky shore of an islet. We hoisted sail and were off before a whistling wind that sang violence to come. They had considerable skill in handling the falla, and we left a long scar behind us across the crests of the emulous waves. Swift though the current and surge ran with us, we outstripped them, rising like a sea-bird to the full impulse of the wind. I could tell at a glance that the ancestors of these seamen had been accustomed to rough waters through countless ages.

My host came on deck after we were fully under way and at once joined me. He launched again into eulogies of the socialistic community. I was at the mercy of his eloquence, and resigned myself to my fate. Yet before the voyage closed and we ran into port I was rewarded for my talent of listening. He got weary of tempting my admiration by his praises, and soon slipped into what looked like fact. He gave me a picturesque description of the island when its rude outline began to sierra the horizon. There were miles and miles of lawns and orchards that terraced the lowlands from the lapping water on the beach to the roots of the mountains that I saw dim white against the sky rim. Gleaming rivers streaked the meadows with their silver, or hid beneath the blossoming or fruiting trees. Here and there they swelled into sylvan lakes whose surface was spidered into moving gossamer by flocks of tame sea-birds and by canvas bent on pleasure and ease. Towering above the tallest trees stood vast temples that seemed in their shining marbles to outstrip the snowy giants that were every hour revealing to me more and more of their stupendous proportions.

I piloted him by judicious admiration and questions into a description of their faith. It seemed to be a polytheism that was practically a pantheism. Every spirit that existed in the universe apart from body was equal to every other spirit. As soon as a man died his soul became a god, as worthy of worship as any other god that had existed from the beginning. Through the whole of space, and even permeating matter invisibly, impalpably, gods lived and moved and had their being. They needed no sustenance, no addition of energy, no extension of space to live in. The universe was full of them, immortal generators of other spirits, other gods. It was indeed an Olympus that was so united, so free from all jealousy and enmity that it formed but one god, just as the living cells of the human body, though each having its own individuality, made but one human life. And there was still infinity to fill. Worlds died every hour, having fulfilled their purpose of producing all the divine life whereof they were capable. Every hour worlds were born evolving energy and at last life, which rose by stages up to the human that dying might be divine. The stellar system is but a great god-factory. Not an atom that lives is wasted. Everything that comes into existence rises up and into the nobly human; then the physical sequence ceases and the divine begins. Death deifies all men; evil falls away from them with their bodies; and, winged through the vault, the souls flit, rid of passion and whatsoever clogs pure thought. They have no desire to materialise again; they have no desires at all. They can interpenetrate and unite and disunite without the sense of disunion. They are one with existence that is not bound to what is matter or has senses. They make the final all; and yet this all increases every moment with transcendent growth. Its one imperfection is that it cannot fill the whole of space; its one aspiration is to colonise infinity. Life is too poor to satisfy it. It must grow for ever and for ever through new systems and oceans of worlds that evolve myriads of new gods ready to people the still unmastered regions beyond its ken. Its energy is not diminished by the stupendous labour at the unceasing birth of worlds. Every new effort means increased possibility of energy. It is of the nature of pure spirit to develop its potence of energy by energising. Once freed of cumbering matter, its life grows fuller and freer the more it operates on the atoms of the ether to raise them nearer and nearer to its own nature and being. Nor can it work except through this laborious ascent; this is the only hierarchy of life, the only altar-stairs in the universe, whereon being of lower grade clambers up to godhead. Once the altar is reached there is nothing but equality. There is only imperfection and perfection in existence. Of imperfection there are as many gradations as there are kinds of being; in perfection or godhead there is no differentiation; there degree, class, distinction cease. For all gods are one in the all. In the stage just precedent to godhead, in humanity, gradation has begun to vanish. It is only the adulterate nature that still keeps distinction. The higher the range of the men the less the difference between them; and at last death obliterates it; they are perfect in freedom from the long-obstructive matter, perfect in godhead, united to the all.

This outline of the socialistic religion came on me with the surprise of one who should see wine flowing in the bed of a torrent instead of water. I began to have a certain respect for this eternal talker whose verbal bubbles had suddenly turned to pearls. He stopped just when I had wished him to go on; and, to tap the same vein, I asked him how his countrymen worshipped their god.

He came dangerously near to winding up his eloquence clockwork, for he pointed to the sky and then to the snowy bulwark that loomed along the horizon; and he straightened himself out and cleared his throat. I feared the complacent glitter of his eye, and I rushed to the water-vat and drank. The interruption seemed to switch off his energy from his almost automatic word machine. He had grown meditative and rested his head on his hands as he looked over the rail into the sea.

I approached him when I saw his new attitude, and he began in a soft, reluctant voice: "We are all priests as we are all kings in our community. To have a hierarchy or even an intermediary who should be supposed to be in more direct sympathy and communication with the gods than the rest is the worst of insults to the divine energy of the soul. To make a special profession of that which is the aim of embodied life is but to commercialise the divine and embrute the human. The priests place their feet on the necks of the ignorant, and it is their interest to reduce all to ignorance. Instead of the equality, which is the true principle of life, we should have a double tyranny; we should grovel before our gods, whose superstitions would weigh us to the ground; and we should have their professional agents introducing the caprice and imperfection of the human into their yoke. I know not which is the worse: the purely spiritual slavery of timid, startled worship, or the mingled slavery of priestcraft that makes the divine mysterious and terrible in order that the worshippers may bow before it body and soul.

"It was a question with our ancestors when they were apportioning the wealth they had brought with them to general purposes, whether they should build temples to their new and universal god or take the dome of immensity as his shrine. They had brought with them a love of art devoted to divine service, and a traditionary love of temples as the symbols of the divine dwelling-place. And yet temples would imply attendants who would soon raise themselves into a spiritual tyranny. Whilst there around them was the free ether wherein dwelt members of the godhead; there above them was the marvellous roof of night frescoed with worlds. Surely it was better that the chrysalids of gods should live in the same temple as the gods. There was no sanctuary like that which the divine had chosen and made for itself. To set apart any portion of it as a holy of holies would sully the nobleness of its workmanship. Fane there was none but the universe; and any poor chantry erected by man, however stupendous it seemed to him with his span of life to build it in, would be a mockery of the Infinite. How pigmean it would seem beneath the vault of night, wherein distance was fenced by the penetrative impotence of human eyes, how atomic when gauged by thought, the true instrument of worship!

"At first schism threatened over this burning question. But at last yon steaming censer of the mountains gave the solution. The first night fell, and they saw a strange glow above the ranges as if it were a fire amongst the clouds. Superficial thought would fain explain it as the after-sheen of sunset. But the hours advanced and still the radiance flushed and faded, flushed and faded, and often with fuliginous and lurid glare. At times a pillar as of smoke and flame seemed to unite earth and heaven. Every eye was fixed on the turbid glimmer as it enhaloed the sombre beauty of the night. The still lingering superstitions that lurked in the graveyards of many minds took it as a sign from the world beyond death. In the dusky aisles of night, as they discussed the theme in low and reverent voices, there spread the magnetic power of resurgent superstition in a crowd touched with the mystery of the universe; and before the dawn suffused the sky or flooded the ancestral recesses of the mind, it was resolved to take this fiery peak as the altar of their worship.

"But the elements had decided otherwise; the searing, blinding power of its everlasting snows, the torrid ebullience of its great cup, and the ruthless fury of the clouds that so often blotted out its heaven, drove the worshippers to the lowlands; and there the frequent austerity of the elements, aided by the old love of art, compelled the erection of the temples you see beginning to fleck the dusky background of the rocks and forests. But the more progressive section of the community, who favoured no temple but the open heaven, had their fears as to the future allayed by a written agreement signed by all that it should be a penal offence to propose a priesthood or a service for them. Everyone may worship where he pleases, within these tabernacles made with hands or without in the pantheon of all men and all gods, in the star-vaulted minster of infinity."

It was indeed an impressive sight as we approached and the dim sierra grew into a stupendous range that overshadowed us; in its midst rose gigantic the gleaming peak of their fiery monarch dominating all. Above him hung, as if to shade him from the rude fire of the sun, a great tree of smoke whose leafage touched the heaven, and majestically swung in the wind. At its roots the forests and marble fanes were dwarfed. No eloquence of gesture or of word could make me turn my gaze from him to them; but a lower bastion of mountains in front moved upwards and blotted out his serenity. Then I saw the magnitude of the temples, dwarfing as they did the loftiest trees of the forest.

I asked him where the houses were, and with some reluctance he pointed off to the right, where nothing could be distinguished. Then my mind ran on to the symbols of civilised life, and I inquired for the schools and other educational institutions.

"There are none," he said. "They are only symbols and nurses of inequality. After we had abolished caste and class and social distinctions, we soon came to see that the most offensive of all was culture, and especially scholarship and learning. Who contemns his neighbour so much as the pedagogue that knows a language or a series of facts more than other men? Academic snobbery is the most pernicious, most galling; for it can immediately put in its proofs of the superiority it claims; it can rout all but its equal and rival. It is the most exclusive, most presuming, most irritating. We started with universities and academies and technical schools, under the impression that, by making them free to all, we should give all equal privileges. Before we were through a generation of our new history the fallacy became transparent. We were rapidly manufacturing a class of intellectual peacocks, or at least men and women who sneered at the vulgar herd. By our constitution every citizen was entitled to a certain minimum of food and clothing in the year. The scholar could always live on less than this, and, by offering the surplus as payment, he could get others to perform the mechanical duties of his life. He had what he wanted in free libraries and laboratories and lectures. So he came to have an inordinate share of happiness; and in many cases he had an inordinate scorn for the bulk of the people, who took no advantage of these privileges. A yearning for books and for exercise of the mind is anything but natural to most men, and the nation was rapidly sorting itself out into a small class who were happy and prided themselves on having everything they wanted, and a majority who envied these their content and grumbled at the enormous wealth they had accumulated in their minds. It was true that these men wrote books and made discoveries and inventions; but what good were their books and facts and machines to any but themselves? Nobody else used them or wished to use them. They might talk of the advances of science and the nobleness of art and the glories of literature. But their talk was unreal to all but their own narrow circle; for the rest of the people it was like descanting on colours to the blind.

"The worst was to come; there afterwards grew up a class of sham scholars and æsthetes and critics who learned the shibboleths of the scientists and artists and writers, and used these shibboleths as instruments of offence against what they called outsiders. There were two primitive languages that had, in earlier ages before the migration and before the growth of a native literature, taken deep root in education. These were treated as the marks and symbols of culture; and their rudiments were laboriously shuffled through and promptly forgotten by a large section, who thereupon assumed great airs of superiority to their neighbours. These counterfeit scholars and critics made the two languages into a fence and stockade that would defy the assaults of the mob; within it they fell down and worshipped as the gods of the earth the few who did know them well and could speak them. Most of them had learned by rote some passages from one or two of the favourite books in them; and they were accustomed, when they were worsted in any conversation or discussion, to roll off, relevantly or irrelevantly, one or the other of these, and thus silence their opponents. Only the mock scholars ever did this; the real scholars knew too much of these languages and had too much to occupy their minds otherwise to resort to such trivial weapons. The contemptuous manners of the charlatans of culture became insufferable. You would have thought that there was something divine in these tongues, so fiercely did these bastard scholars bridle up at any disparagement of them or any comparison of them with the vernacular.

"The growth of this charlatanism became a serious danger to our socialistic community, and it was thought that by its removal the danger would be over. Accordingly it was resolved, only the scholars and their mimics dissenting, that the study and use of these primitive languages should be interdicted. The books written in them were burnt,—to the great joy of the boys and girls in the seminaries,—and it was made a penal offence to write or speak any word of them. There was much sophistry used to get round the law, as a good deal of Tirralarian phraseology was derived from them. But this difficulty was surmounted by a clearer and more detailed definition, and the cultured hung their heads defeated.

"It was not for long. Before another generation had passed, the scholars had invented other claims to pre-eminence, other shibboleths. Now it was the laws of nature and the laws of beauty that supplied the platform for scorn of neighbours. The scientists and artists and critics of art became the small privileged class, who had more than their fair share of happiness and content. They produced something that seemed to be of more value than the musty books of the scholars written in languages that none but themselves could read. And their humours and superiority were borne with at first for the sake of their discoveries and useful contrivances and beautiful works. It was they who built the temples and decorated them with such splendour and filled them with such machines and expedients for the use and comfort of the citizens. They were few, and not very obtrusive in their contempt for the multitude, and their superior airs were counterbalanced by their usefulness.

"This tolerance was a mistake. The idea of having exclusiveness without detriment to the socialistic principle was only a dream. There sprang up the fringe of insolent make-believe again. Herds of pretenders to art or science or criticism flocked into the universities and technical schools. They gabbled of genius and talent, of principles and laws, of elements and atoms, of cells and tissues, and of ideals and the spirit of beauty. The trick was more transparent than the other, for they had to use the vernacular in their patter; and a good deal of it was manifest nonsense to the simplest mind, whilst the astuter amongst the uneducated stripped even their most high-sounding maxims and laws into the nakedest of truisms. But the empiric scientists and artists and æsthetes shifted their ground every year and manufactured other and more mystic phraseology. It was difficult to follow them through their thickets and labyrinths of gibberish by which they kept off those whom they were pleased to call the rabble. They became almost as stupidly contemptuous and insolent as the possession of the rudiments of the most unintelligible languages could have made them.

"It came to be clear that the old danger to equality had only taken a new form. The mass of the nation clamoured against the new pretensions of culture. They would hear of nothing but the abolition of its factories, as they called the universities and schools of art. What would come of the principle of socialism if this aristocracy of genius and talent, brummagem or real, was to be let alone with its capacity to blow itself out with its limitless vanity about its own importance? No sane man would answer for the consequences if the wild rage of the uneducated was allowed to vent itself on this superficial pretence and shallow scorn. Scholars, scientists, artists, critics, and the parasitic crew that battened on their results and used them offensively against the multitude would fall in one great welter of blood. The gentler section of the community could not look on this risk to their ideal of society without a shudder. They convened the whole nation, and by an overwhelming majority it was resolved to abolish the institutions that fostered science and art, learning and criticism; it became high treason to establish a library or university, or a school of art or science, or a seminary of literature or criticism. There were the same attempts as before to elude the provisions of the law and get round it by quibble and sophism; but this led only to greater stringency and detail in its clauses. It was made penal to write a book, or make a scientific discovery, or invent any contrivance, or produce any work of art; and you may be quite sure that, with the bulk of the people acting policeman and spy for the law, it was soon carried into force, and pictures and statues and books and machines ceased to be made. The insolence and contempt of the intellectual parasites had no soil to fatten on, and ultimately vanished from the state."

He stopped with a snap of the jaw that said plainly: "There now; are you satisfied? If not, you are a most unreasonable being. Where will you find a civilisation grander than ours on the face of the earth?"

I was by no means satisfied. He had left one of the main branches of my question unanswered. He had explained the history of the higher institutions and the fate of the sciences and art and literature; but I had asked him about the schools. I still pressed the question.

"Ay, that was another danger to the social constitution. The energy of talent and genius, and the sham intellectualism chased from one post of vantage took refuge in another. A pedagogic class sprang up that would have grown into a most contemptuous and insolent aristocracy. The loud and haughty arrogance and overbearing dogmatism of the charlatan fringe of the profession were beginning to impress the bulk of the nation with disgust and alarm, when there arose a fierce rebellion among the scholars. The hundreds of mean-spirited empirics that had crept into the ranks of teachers for the sake of the emoluments in the shape of prestige and opportunity for the scorn of neighbours had had to resort to the most tyrannical and cruel methods in order to keep discipline. A few genuine instructors there were, who were able to cope with the knavishness of the worst of pupils by means of their strength of character and power of sympathy and imagination; they always elicited what was best in the embryo humanity that came into their hands to be moulded; they could use the laughter and sympathy of the majority to whip the offensive disposition and will out of the laggards and would-be rebels; and the latter were cowed and disciplined without any sense of unfair treatment. But the closing of the channels of science and art and criticism to the aristocratic quackery, that flows, if unchecked, from the corrupt fountains of human nature, flooded the profession with supercilious pretenders. Their scholars easily measured their intelligence and sincerity, and turned the school-rooms into pandemonium. The high-flying charlatans conferred together and invented new and cruel modes of punishment. They introduced a reign of terror into the schools. The boys and girls formed secret societies which combined into one great brotherhood all over the island. They drilled in darkness and armed every member with a catapult and pea-shooter. They wrote the agreement and signed it in their own blood, and managed to keep the proposed rebellion shrouded in mystery for five whole days, for it was strictly confined to those above the age of twelve. But the fear that it would leak out precipitated the rising; and they drove the schoolmasters and schoolmistresses out under a fierce fire of peas and pebbles, till wounded and bleeding the charlatans took refuge up the mountains amid the snow, or in the waves of the beach, ducking to avoid the missiles. The rout was most ignominious, and the scholars were able to dictate their own terms. It was agreed that they should be exempted from school and family discipline and be admitted to the full citizenship. For it was seen that the exclusion of children above the age of twelve from the schools would so reduce the numbers of the insolent parasites and shams in the profession as to remove the forefront of the offence.

"But it was found that twelve was a mere artificial limit. Inspired by the example of their predecessors, the ten-year-olds made a successful revolution and had the minimum age of citizenship reduced to ten. Still the pedants were felt to be a most offensively arrogant class; the smaller their numbers grew, the more they plumed themselves on their superiority. And every new rebellion against their authority was aided and abetted by the multitude, who huzzaed as the catapults of the pigmy forces swept the field and the volleys from their pea-shooters told with deadly effect, and after the defeat of the pedagogues granted citizenship to every child of a certain age. Victory followed victory till at last it seemed a farce to have schools at all. They were turned into playhouses for stormy or wet weather, and the limit of age was removed from citizenship. Every child, as soon as his legs would carry him and his tongue would wag, could come to the conventions of the people and record his vote. It greatly encouraged marriage and the increase of families, for a man or woman with a dozen or score of children had become a power in the state. Thus the last vestige of privilege disappeared, and with it the last chance of intellectual charlatanism forming an aristocracy. Every man was like his neighbour, and for that matter so was every child. Sex, age, genius, talent, profession, trade had ceased to form the basis of caste. Equality within the nation had at last been reached."

There was unspeakable complacence on his face; and yet my look of inter-rogation broke it up. I had heard much about the professions and their history in Tirralaria. I had heard nothing of the medical profession. I wondered how they guaranteed the healing art.

"Oh, as for that, it disappeared in the earliest jetsam of the community. Of the charlatans and nose-elevators the privileged doctors were the worst. They blundered and buried their blunders, and wildly resented every question. They kept up a mysterious patter that was of the very essence of aristocracy and privilege. The atmosphere of superstition that they threw round their old-wives' remedies imposed upon men when they were sick; but as soon as they were well their fear vanished, and they determined to be clear of the empiricism and mummery of the profession. And at last, after a great plague had laughed at their charms and talismans and skill, and swept half the nation down to the worms, their quackery had become too apparent. One third of them had taken boat and migrated to other islands of the archipel-ago. Another third had died of their own plague-nostrums and salves. The remainder had lost their self-confidence and dogmatism and were willing to acknowledge that they knew little if any but the simplest diseases, and to these they applied the herbs and salves that every old woman tried. The nation took them in their mood of humility and destroyed the fences round the profession. Everyone was left free to use his own remedies. In a fit of gen-erosity they handed over the secrets of their trade to the public, and salves and medicaments and pills and powders were manufactured wholesale by the state chemists and issued free with instructions for their use. Whether it was the abolition of the caste or not, the death-rate has, if anything, decreased, and plagues are no more frequent than they were before. Everyone who treats another and kills him is liable to punishment by the state. So, few undertake to prescribe, and every citizen is responsible for his own treatment. In times of privilege a doctor was licensed to kill with impunity; he and his brethren could always throw dust in the eyes of any inquiry by technical terms and abracadabra. We are rid of that chicanery, and in health and death-rate we are no worse off than before. So much for physic."

CHAPTER XV
TIRRALARIA

I HAD OTHER QUESTIONS; but we had run into a basin that had once been a harbour. Every bastion and rampart had been pounded and bruised by the billows till the débris lay scattered along the beach. Every house and building stood in dilapidation. Yet to look upwards over the terraced slopes of the lower hills was still to think of paradise. Magnificent temples, pure with marbles and broken in outline with minarets and towers and niched statues, dwarfed the forest trees or the cliff over which they stood. There was not a meaner building to be seen. It looked as if only the gods dwelt here amid blossoming or fruited trees; and streams flashed at intervals athwart the verdant slopes; and over a precipice or down a ravine they smote the dark rock with the noise of their silver sword; and at every impulse from the capricious fan of the wind the emerald face of the cliff shone faintly through the silver veil of water that twisted back into a single thread again. Up for hundreds of feet the great stairs of the hills mounted, each step crowned with a gleaming fane and enriched with meadow and orchard. And Time, the supreme artist, had been there with his brush. I could see the moss and ivy and other coloured creepers brocade the human architecture and soften the gleam of the marble with their cool tracery. Beneath the warm passion of the setting sun the picture was most entrancing. Nothing was too new. There was a quaint tone from the centuries even about the motley garments that clothed the throng of beggars in the roads and lanes; for there were no streets and no comfortable looking citizens and burghers to be seen, unless the loungers that crowded the arcades and piazzas of the temples and leaned against the pillars up the hill were of that class. I supposed that some convulsion of nature had wrecked the edifices of the flat by the beach and the piers of the harbour, and that there had been no time or purpose for rebuilding them, and as the sun flared up from beneath the turban of clouds that hid his disk, the softened colours stole into the rents and crevices of the ruins and raised them into beauty. The dim suffusion of rose lent a picturesque warmth even to the rags and patches of the lazzaroni that smeared with unctuous indolence every available resting-place.

I was glad to get on shore; for the rancid food of the falla had not been to my taste, and the foul odour and sluttishness of the cabin were alone enough to close the pores of appetite. There was at least power to move away from these on land.

Yet the change was not altogether for the better. Dry though the roads and earth underfoot were from long absence of rain, the nose was still assailed by something that seemed to strike out from all quarters. A whiff of the sea wind would now and again beat it down only to make it more obtrusive. The whole putrescence of the earth seemed to have found here a lay-stall. Garrulesi looked quite unconscious of it. We hurried along over prostrate bodies that as the shadows clotted into night often tripped me up. They might have been logs, so irresponsive were they even to the impact of my toes. I soon learned to jump over everything that seemed to gather more darkness to it, and after a time we began to ascend, and the streaks of moveless humanity lay along instead of athwart our path. An occasional snore or groan or sigh told us of layers of it beneath the trees to right and left. One consolation was our gradual escape from the purgatory of stenches as we rose. What surrounded us I could not see, but it seemed heaven to all the senses, so keenly did they sympathise with that of smell in its new freedom.

We wound and zigzagged ever upwards till at last we reached the portico and arcade of one of the great edifices I had seen from the sea. Time and the seasons, I could perceive, even in the underlight of the stars, had carved and wrought its walls with eccentric design. And no human hand, as far as I could see, had interfered with their workmanship. They had been analytic more than synthetic architects, for, when we went inside, the stars peered down on us through chinks and rents with impudent curiosity.

It was indeed a strange building. A great torch flared over what had once been the altar, and moved and guttered in the baffling draughts. As the eyes focussed themselves to the sandwiched light and gloom, I saw a great tablet of marble with a raised map of some mountainous country upon it in spent grease and resin; and the huge fagot of pine splinters and pitch that was stuck into a rent in it was still at its work of mapping in relief. I followed the flicker of the lambent flame upwards and was amazed by the height of the roof or dome above the pillared nave and aisles. Even yet beneath the grime and smoke of ages and the litter of myriads of birds I could see carved woodwork of graceful or fantastic shape and an occasional dim relic of some gigantic fresco. The windows were choked with logs and branches of trees and débris of all kinds, and yet they showed how marvellous they were in their grace and magnitude. How the architects could have raised that stupendous mass of stone to resist the centuries, how they could have hung that sea of stone foliage and flower in mid-air, were bewildering questions. I could see the graceful floral shapes even underneath the guano of ages.

It was the scurviest sight I had seen for many a day; but the worst was to come. The crowd of rather noble-featured beggars that jostled each other on all sides were evidently preparing for rest. Mats of tree bark or dried leaves of a tough texture were being slung like hammocks from every corner of vantage. Garrulesi handed me one from a niche in the wall and some cordage, and led me to a space between two pillars that was still unoccupied. Dozens came in afterwards and hung their mats above me and below me and on both sides of me till I felt stifled by the slung and snoring humanity that festooned me round. He also pitched into my hammock some hard fruits and dried meats, which I munched till I fell asleep with the fatigue of the unwonted exercise. When I awoke in the morning this great ecclesiastical dormitory was unslinging itself. Unfledged deities were sitting in their hammocks as far up into the clustering darkness of the dome as my eye could reach, and yawning and rubbing their grimy eyelids with their grimy hands. They did not seem to notice the stercoraceous volley from the restless birds as the winged multitude flashed and screamed athwart the shadows or rustled and tore through the withered branches that filled the windows. Some of these callow gods descended the pillars or the festoons of sleeping mats by finger and toe as nimbly as monkeys. Others were gathered round a great fire by the altar roasting grains or kernels of fruit, whilst in corners lounged groups munching ugly viands that they held in their hands.

I was marvelling over this stupendous rookery, watching its antics as it unrolled itself out of the coil of dreams and descended with its mats by ledges out into the foliated and clustered pillars, when Garrulesi appeared. I scarcely recognised him, so transformed was he by his change of dress. Instead of the spruce garments of Aleofane that added such neatness to his oratory, he had clothed himself in a motley collection of rags of varied colour and texture. His beard hung in smeary locks, his hair was a mop, and by some process that was almost artistic he had begrimed his features and hands. He did not leave me time to question or reflect on the transformation of the divine demagogue into the beggar, for he threw into my mat a bundle of choice antiquities that might perhaps have brought twopence in any rag market. He assisted me to disentangle the foul and rent miscellany and to tack them together over my nakedness. My other garments he took from me, and, bidding me follow, hid them, I alone present, in a secret crevice of a vault under the edifice; he rolled a huge stone in order to conceal the aperture.

He explained to me that I must adopt in paradise the primitive clothing of paradise, and that to appear in other guise would offend the humility and sense of symmetry of his people. The greatest sages had preferred beggardom and a crust to wealth and luxury, and what could any nation do better than to follow their example? And at this point it flashed upon me that the crowds whom I had taken for beggars the night before were representatives of the nation.

When we returned to the temple above, we found all the pillars and niches and roofs free from their chaplets and festoons of sleeping mats, and the whole frippery stowed away in holes and crevices of the walls. The birds had the upper ranges all to themselves and were evidently satisfied with the division of the space, for they had ceased their screaming and uneasy flight. The marble floor was covered with groups standing, or sitting, or lying, engaged in easy conversation or in cooking or eating food. Most of the night's occupants had evidently gone outside. I now began to see that most of those who cooked were beardless, and although the rags of the two sexes were indistinguishable, I could separate them by the different outlines of the forms and faces. There was little respect or honour paid to the gentler sex; they were jostled and pushed about; they had to look after themselves and their interests. The men had clearly all cooked their morning meal before; the women had to be content with the remains of the fire and the remains of the heap of food that had been piled in one of the corners of the edifice. There was undoubtedly equality of the sexes; gallantry and chivalry had been banished as an insult to their common humanity.

After a time I could see that the women were struggling to seize a share of the food, not for themselves, but for others who were sick or weak or deformed. The stronger men would have had it all but for this, and the helpless would have gone unbreakfasted. The women were most of them as brawny and tanned by the weather as the other sex, and they had come by long struggle and heredity to be able almost to hold their own. They hustled the crowd that stood in their way and gave tit for tat with as lusty a muscle as if they had navvied from infancy. But it was interesting to see in them the survival of their old tenderness for the sick and feeble. It was doubtless their maternal functions that had saved this relic from the general wreck of femininity.

CHAPTER XVI
SNEEKAPE

THERE WAS ONE EXCEPTION to the rule of masculine indifference. I had been watching the figure for some time amongst the women before I discovered it to be that of a man. He had a small, well-proportioned head, even smaller than that of most of the women; and it was poised on his long neck like a bird's; it had such rapidity and variety and ease of motion as if it were on a universal joint; it wiggled and bobbed, it danced and undulated to every emotion that came into his breast, while the little bead eyes twinkled and leered and winked; no head other than a sparrow's ever pirouetted and jerked and quivered with such manifest enjoyment and self-admiration. He thought himself a humourist too, for some of the younger women smirked and giggled as he stretched his wide mouth and curved the corners of his eyes and shook and wagged his little head. His themes were evidently the men around, but his voice was too low and his gusto over his own jests too great for any of them to reach beyond his immediate circle; like all wits of the shallow type, he was his own best audience, though I could see he needed a feminine smile somewhere about. At first I had admired his gallantry and kindness, for he was the only man who sided with the women in their struggle for food. But afterwards I hesitated, for I began to see that it was only the women of handsome, stalwart form and finely moulded face, the women who needed no help, that he fidgeted and bustled about; if ever he helped any who could not help themselves, I saw that they had graceful forms and the hectic beauty of the delicate. Another feature of his chivalry that lowered my first opinion of him was that, nimble and sedulous though he was in his attentions, what he did was superfluous; even the women who most smirked at his jokes and innuendoes could not conceal a lurking contempt for his officiousness and feminine vigilance about trifling minutiæ.

Tall and graceful though he was, with an air of brisk intelligence and dapper education, I began to take an inexplicable dislike to him. He seemed to have some magnetic sense of this, for, after appearing unconscious of my glance for a long time, he sidled up to me and with a purring, confidential tone in his voice and a wise wag of his little head and self-appreciative twinkle of his little eyes, he apologised in the Aleofanian tongue for addressing me; but he heard from my accents that I was a stranger, and felt drawn to me, as he was an alien, too, in a strange land. If he felt any recoil against my somewhat brusque rejection of his sympathy, he did not betray it. He wheedled himself by abject subservience and subtle self-abasement into what he thought my confidence. He artfully fished about for topics on which he could agree with me, and ostentatiously paraded a yearning to know my opinions on them; he looked transports of admiration and enthusiasm for them when uttered; and the whole piece of acting was done with such an appearance of candour and amiability that I began to feel myself discourteous and unjust in being so surly to him. His urbanity and sweetness of temper were never for an instant ruffled. He wore his most fascinating smile as if to the manner born. He was bent on being the good Samaritan to my spiritual wounds; he would not probe a single sore; he would apply balm to all my sorrows if only he could get at them, if only I would admit him to my heart of hearts. The kindness, the brotherly love he displayed for all men at last won me over from my thorny silence, although I still inwardly wished the fellow would insult me in order that I might have the pleasure of kicking him. With all his suavity and cooing benignancy and hearty assumption of good-fellowship, he stirred up in me the savage irascibility that lies still in the heart of even the most civilised; and I did not thank him for it.

He had much of the wisdom of the serpent, too, or at least a certain magnetic instinct that stood for it; for he did not follow up what he manifestly thought his victory over my churlishness with any use of it; he went off to his group of feminine worshippers. I could see from the eyes of some of them that his witchery had taken effect.

Garrulesi had been outside, and his return withdrew my observation from the stranger's sinuous wiles. We went outside, and my thoughts were caught up by the sight. We stood on a platform that overlooked the tranquil ocean. Not a breath disturbed the morning air. The sun from behind us had not attained his tropic strength; his level shafts still flung colour over the land and sky, and shot the silken fabric of the slope before us with fretted shadow. The great edifice out of which we had come threw a dark and cool sierra out upon the sea; its lofty towers and pinnacles and domes lengthening out in silhouette into gigantic peaks. Above us rose the alabaster cone of Klimarol, the smoke-haloed mountain, along the shoulder of which the great disk of the morning wove his web of shimmering light. Our temple rose from the plateau of the front range, the highest of all that broke the emerald wave of foliage between the sky line and the sea.

He was silent before my delight in the scene. Then we moved out into the forests of palms and fruited trees. I ventured on asking him about the scene inside the temple. He told me that, when the religion had crystallised into the socialism of gods and men, it was felt that the mere difference of a material shell should not exclude the human-divine from the privileges of the divine. Into these great edifices the artist caste, so long as it had existed, had put all their genius and time and all the wealth that they could extract from the people as a whole or from individuals; in fact, half the wealth of the nation had disappeared in them. And, as by universal agreement there was no service or ceremony performed in them, it became obvious in time that they were a monstrous waste, thus unutilised, when half the people or embryo gods slept during the wet season in the open air and suffered from the inclemency of the nights, whilst the other half had only roofless or dilapidated huts, or caves or holes in the rocks to sleep in. It seemed a gratuitous insult to the slumbering divinity within the people to exclude them from the shelter of these great domes built for divinity. The birds of the air with their excrementitious filth were allowed to nest there from year's end to year's end; and the gods in human form, only because they were still unfledged and wingless, were fenced off from the use of this buried wealth. Nothing seemed more irrational to the Tirralarians of a former age than such an elevation of the mere beasts and the disembodied gods into a special caste that were to be sheltered and roofed from the weather with the noblest architecture. They shrank in horror from such a violation of their constitution, and thereafter they ranged men with gods and winged beasts. Some of the temples have been set apart for the women and children, who may, however, penetrate by day into any of the others they please. This that we have left is specially occupied by those who are the council of advisers of the people, though others may in emergency set up their sleeping mats in it, and the strangers who are not feared or suspected are housed here. It is called the council-and-guest temple. But guests are excluded during important deliberations.

He had mentioned a council of advisers, and I asked him if this were the government that they had. He looked furtively round, and, seeing some rag-poles lying near under the shade of some trees and others approaching, though at some distance, he struck an oratorical attitude and launched forth on the enormities of all governments. He was wound up for hours, and I saw no chance of rescue; for lazzaroni citizens littered every corner with their slouching, rag-patched fat. I could gather from the loud voice and the rhetorical touches that he was addressing every ear within reach, and giving unctuous vent to the official creed. The gist of what he larded with eloquence was this: government was an insult to full-grown humanity; where reason ruled, every man was a law unto himself; all that was needed was a committee selected from time to time for the distribution of the fruits of the soil and the gifts of nature; there was no labour, and therefore no need of organising labour; there were no lawyers, no police, no professions; for every man attended to his own needs; whilst all worked as they wished for all; nature dealt with the weak and sickly and gave them brief life and swift euthanasia. It was indeed a perfect life, where all were equal and serene in perfect content, and health, and strength.

I was almost glad when the red-haired bewitcher of women approached and rescued me from the declamatory clockwork and his inexorable pendulum of rhetoric. A look of disgust swept like a cloud over the broad self-complacence of the orator's face; whether it was at the untimely interruption of his speech or at the personality of the intruder I could not tell at the time; afterwards I saw that it was the latter.

The amorous stranger was profuse in apologetic flatteries, and did his best to soothe the injured dignity of the people's adviser. He resorted to his confidential trick, and sidling up whispered in his ear what seemed some important secret, at the same time throwing me from his agile little eyes a smile that was intended to take me into still deeper strata of his confidence. He succeeded in neither project, and was yet well satisfied with his nimble diplomacy. There was always an air about him as if he were dealing with toy humanity that might be broken by rough usage; he had doubtless acquired it by long handling of the merely amorous elements of life. He moved with such a familiar and confidential superiority even amongst strangers, and such an interlarding of egregious flattery and subtle assumption of special and intimate friendship as implied lifelong engagement in intrigue and the lowest estimate of the intelligence of the women he dealt with.

My gorge rose before he spoke a word to me, and the peddlingly confidential manner had evidently the same effect on Garrulesi, for he abruptly turned his back and walked off. Unabashed, the lath-like diplomat laid his little head close to mine, under the assumption that he had made another conquest. He poured into my ear faint praise of the fast disappearing orator and subtly slid into a faint disparagement. As I held my peace he passed rapidly into the elevation of himself and me into a category by ourselves against all the world. He fixed his bead eyes on me with a bewitching look as if he sought the inmost depths of the spirit and would rest there. I lowered my glance with a certain scorn and loathing that was scarcely full-formed. He clearly assumed the change to mean humble submission to his advances; and he slyly entered on a most abusive and captious analysis of Tirralarian civilisation, wording it in velvet that, lest he should be mistaken in me, he could cover his retreat or involve me in the consequences of his strictures. He was an adept in white lies and ambiguous calumnies that seemed to do honour to the victim.

As far as I could gather from his insinuations, the island was nothing but an organisation of thieves, who, when they could not get any foreigner to steal from, had to pass their time in enforced but delightful idleness. There was nothing to steal amongst themselves. That was the meaning of the rags they wore. He always landed in a dress that was a harmony of worthless fragments. His first few visits had been a painful experience; piece by piece his garments and possessions had vanished no one knew whither till he was left naked on his sleeping mat, and only the vanity of a Tirralarian buck, who wished to show him his skill in pilfering, gave him shreds enough to make a loin-cloth. No one of them cared to have anything above rags and a bare subsistence, for he knew that if he had, it would disappear mysteriously. Their skill in purloining seemed like a magician's. It was the only talent that had remained from their old civilisation; into this their inherited cleverness had run; and any one of them would make a fortune either as a juggler or as a thief in any other nation; but none of the other islands of the archipelago would admit them, knowing well which of the two professions would be the more lucrative and fascinating for a Tirralarian. So their wonderful gift was hidden under a bushel.

Of course I knew the principle of the constitution—that there should be no private property. Property, they held, is theft; and so to abolish theft they abolished property, and law with it. Everything that anybody got or made or produced was anybody's, and they were magpies at concealment. The first trick Garrulesi taught me was to stow away my valuables; he saw Sneekape lead me off, and I might be quite sure that for further safety he had bestowed it in another crevice that he alone would know. Work had ceased generations ago, for no one could secure what he produced unless he were as sharp in pilfering and concealing as his neighbours; and he had not time to learn the secrets or the skill of these arts when he was busy with other things. Every trade and craft vanished into legerdemain and light-fingeredness. Their existence was only hand-to-mouth; and winter or a hurricane or any blight on the fruits of nature sent all who had not an extra store of fat on their bodies into the grave. They had now grown too indolent to fish or make raids on the wealth of their neighbours. An occasional atavistic survival like Garrulesi, with a gift of talk and a restless energy, went out secretly and tried a mission on other islands that the converts might bring their goods with them and help to stave off the ever-recurrent evil day. It was supposed to be the duty of the advisers of the people like him to supply everyone with food and clothing and roofage. But it was difficult to divide nothing. Not long after the abolition of private property, all property vanished that could be stolen or could retain its value only by labour. They could not tax, they could not compel the labour that everyone was supposed voluntarily to contribute to the community; and their position had become no enviable one. In fact it was difficult to find advisers; a few revealed in their green youth, before they knew the relationships of things, a talent for glib talk, or for governing, or muddling, and were thrust into the position; and they found it no easy task to relinquish it, hard and slavish though they came to count it. When they grew older and wiser they were eager to get out of it, but flattery or persecution kept them at the helm till they dropped from old age or disease. They were the real martyrs of Tirralaria, though many of them, like Garrulesi, enjoyed their martyrdom for a time, as long, in fact, as the atavistic energy burned brightly in their veins. A few were so goaded by the slavery of the position that they feigned paralysis of the tongue in order to be clear of it, and they remained dumb till death; and one or two had been driven to the extraordinary activity of suicide.

What made the duty particularly difficult and offensive was that where there was no law every man was his own policeman. Of course they declared and proved that there was no crime amongst them. But it depended on the meaning of crime; crime was a breach of the law; and where there was no law there could be no breach of the law. Instead of wiping out the old outrages against human nature, their socialism had greatly increased them, and they called them peccadilloes. I would see the ragged savages fight like wild beasts over any accidental find, or even what one had failed to steal from another; and when they had come to blows, one of the combatants had to die unless a crowd was near and could separate them. Each knew that the other, if beaten, could not live and leave the insult unavenged; indolence might postpone the day of revenge for a time, but it was sure to come. For his own protection he had to wipe out his opponent, and if he buried the body there would never be any question. For there was no family life or family love. The unions were only temporary. The fundamental principle of their society was that they lived by love. But they more often died by it. The most fertile source of fatal quarrels was the appropriation of members of the opposite sex. The women had their combats, and counted their scalps as well as the men, for the two sexes were supposed to be on an equality.

For many generations after they had socialised property, they kept up households and family life and monogamy. But idleness produced libertinism, and libertinism became concubinage, and then gave place to polygamy and polyandry. A great rebellion of the younger and unprivileged in matrimony, both male and female, against the older who monopolised the best and fairest of the other sex swept away the last traces of marriage. It had always been felt to be an inconsistency that there should be allowed in their state the private possession of affection or of children. Children were now common property after they could run without their mothers. They had to look after themselves if maternal care deserted them, and that generally occurred after the first year. The female advisers were supposed to attend to them; but when they had no common stock they had little to give; they had enough to do to keep an eye on their own and to keep the life in.

As for the royal roads to education which Garrulesi would descant on by the day, they amounted to imitative skill in picking up the tricks of a conjurer and thief. The education that the royal roads led to was about as much as would exist amongst a community of monkeys or magpies. They had no arts, no learning, no literature; for these had, when they existed amongst them, stirred envy and jealousy, and they were voted by the majority to be disturbers of peace and of true socialistic civilisation. How could anyone have what others could not share in without breeding uneasiness and strife? So there was nothing then to learn except the supreme art of the whole nation—skill in pilfering. Their education in this proceeded every moment of their lives, unless during a famine, when no strangers approached the island, and there was food only for the strong who could seize it and keep it. Then force alone was able to sustain life by clutching the coarse remains of the summer's produce. A famine was often prayed for by those who had the best interests of the nation at heart, for it checked the overflow of the people and strengthened the generations by leaving only vigorous survivors to propagate the race. Every ten or a dozen years the numbers became too great for what unaided nature within the limits of the island could supply, in spite of the ravages of neglect amongst the children and the effectual obliteration of so many by quarrels over treasure-trove, thefts, and amours; and then, even without the aid of a hurricane, or an epidemic or blight, the shortage of food made brief work of the surplus population. Amongst the survivors the skeleton frames soon swelled with fat; for after a famine year, nature, having lain fallow for a season, lavished all her powers in superabundance of fruits, like a mother after the punishment of her child, exhibiting her treasures of love to it.

If there were anything worth ruling in the island, it would be the easiest thing in the world with a few faithful troops and a few cart-loads of luxuries to master it in a day or two, the whole people were so lazy and such klepto-maniacs. All the conqueror would have to do would be to pretend to conceal a cart-load of goods in one part of the forest and another in another part. Within half an hour after the concealment the whole population would be busy over them as flies over pots of treacle; a few dozen men would trap them clogged with spoil, or absorbed in hiding it or pilfering it when hidden. Their fingers were always itching for goods to steal; it was the only channel for their great talents. But what would be the use of them after being trapped unless you could distribute them through some wealthy community like Aleofane, and be sure that you could make them disgorge their plunder? They had nothing to rule, nothing to steal, nothing to divide.

Yes, yes, they had once had lofty purposes and ideals. They were going to recreate the world when they settled here. But there were perpetual oscillations for many ages from despotism to revolution. The chiefs had little thanks for their work. Their distribution of labour and its products was a continual source of discontent that rose recurrently into emeute. They had to apply the strong hand and suppress the journals and journalists that encouraged the rebellion. Reign of terror followed reign of terror, for the people were never satisfied; whatever arrangements were made, some large section of them found them unjust, whilst some other section cunningly learned to make more than their due share out of them. Money had been abolished, but everything that was substituted for it—labour ticket, token, bread, fruit—came to suffer the abuses of money; professions that traded in the substitute sprang up, and attempts to suppress them only made them secret and virulent. None would take to the offensive trades that had to do with stenches and corrupt matter. The burying of the dead, the shifting of refuse and manure, the obliteration of filth, the uncleaner domestic services, were left to themselves, and plagues became common till the advisers of the people kidnapped men from outlying islands, put them in chains, and set them to these foul employments.

And at this point he began to whisper mysteriously in my ear. "I shall take you some night, when all in our temple are asleep, to see how they respect liberty and equality. They have slaves who never leave the crater of Klimarol except under the whip. You have seen its glow on the sky of night. It comes from the burning of the dead and of the refuse of the temples and huts of Tirralaria. During the night a detachment of slaves descends the mountain under the lash of the whip; a section of the council superintends the work by turns; they gather the débris of the previous day's Tirralarian civilisation, and by the morning they have drawn it on sleds up the snow-cone; and during the next day and night it is thrown into the boiling lake of lava. The stench is past endurance for any who have not been brought up in it. Within the crater are raised and made the produce and the articles that those below are too idle or too refined in senses to have anything to do with. If it were not for the great slave factory within Klimarol the country would soon be without an inhabitant, for they have always been too proud to keep themselves or their land clean, and now they are too indolent to do it if it were needed; and plagues of the most virulent intensity would sweep the island.

"Not long after they landed here and abolished differentiation of reward for labour, except a slight one for special employments and professions and for special skill, medicine was deserted. The night work and the offensive or cruel tasks of surgery and the constant intercourse with the weakly and sick and dying were not sufficiently rewarded to be attractive. The chiefs attempted to coerce the clever young men and women into the profession. But their cleverness always enabled them to evade the order; they were perpetually feigning sickness or paralysis of the arms and hands. At first they thought of teaching their Klimarol slaves the secret of the art, but they shrank from putting the lives of themselves and their fellow-citizens into such hands. So the cure and care of the sick and dying have been left to chance, which means nobody.

"This page of their history has been torn out and a fiction substituted for it. So, too, is the introduction of slavery hidden under the pall of night, for it is an outrage on the foundation of their community, the dignity of man's nature. They count it treason for any stranger to meddle with or inquire into these secrets of their prison-house.

"They are keenly sensitive to any mention of their gradual lapse from the great ideals with which they began. All were to work voluntarily for the whole community; there was abundance of everything to be produced for the use of every citizen. It soon turned out that no one was to work; for it is always more pleasant for average human nature to play or idle than to work. The talking professions were flooded; orators and logicians and lecturers and preachers and writers soon came to form more than one half of the population. The other half began to feel themselves slaves, and threw up their spades and mattocks and the tools of their trades. Nothing was produced but what nature and the slaves of Klimarol gave them. And as soon as any compulsion is applied the cry of tyranny arises, and threatened rebellion puts an end to the reform. Where there is no force, no stimulus, no motives, it is not difficult to see what human nature will do. To work for the community is too shadowy to be effective; it implies the almost perfect humanity to begin with, which all human social systems set up as their aim and goal.

"At the beginning there were many who were willing to toil for the sake of the ideal, especially the cultured and artistic. They could live on imagination and its products. And it was they who erected these marvellous temples that are now the abode of the bat and the owl and the Tirralarian. The real difficulty came when the measure of remuneration had to be fixed. How were the various trades and professions to have their relative values estimated? That was the first rock on which the new socialistic community split. At first a rough time-standard was adopted, the number of hours of work per day, with some little differentiation for the various trades and professions, according as they were more or less offensive or more or less intellectual. But this attempt at comparison of kinds of work was only arbitrary and could never be based on any principle. It had to be readjusted every year. And as there was a continual outcry against an aristocracy of mind and one of stench, the intellectual and offensive employments being fixed at a smaller number of hours per day, the whole system was at last abolished, and all had to work the same number of hours. It soon became apparent that this was as unjust a standard as the differentiation of kinds of work. Some dawdled away their hours of labour, whilst others wore out their energies and shortened their lives at their toil. For a time they discussed a true and scientific standard of measurement. A few of the thinkers saw that the only possible approach to it would be to gauge the amount of tissue used up in the act of labour. Some scientists thought that they might discover a method of doing this; but the shadow of the old difficulty fell over them again. Tissues differed in delicacy and in the value and refinement of the nutriment they each required. How could they weigh brain tissue against muscular tissue? And it took geological ages to make an infinitesimal advance in the organisation or amount of the one, whilst the other would palpably change in a few days or weeks. Here crept in another of the prime difficulties in measuring remuneration or punishment—the contribution of ancestry either negative or positive. The whole attempt was felt to be doctrinaire and impossible. And it was only those who argued for it that gave any prominence to the only true and fundamental standard of wages—payment according to the real results, that is, the advance secured for the race, or for humanity at large, by the act of labour.

"The final interpretation of their maxim, 'To every man according to his works,' was 'To every man according to his hours of work.' A fixed amount of food and clothing was to be doled out to each, and every citizen was to work so many hours a day, whatever might be the nature of the employment.

"When this was secured, the amount produced for the state and by the community grew less and less, till it became utterly inadequate for anything but the barest subsistence in rags. One by one the citizens fell into the feeblest way of filling up the required tale of hours; and at last nature had to produce unaided what was necessary for life. All but the artists were idler during the supposed hours of work than during the hours of leisure. And the cry against an aristocracy of art and culture grew to be the daily occupation of the unoccupied national tongue, and at last swelled into a revolution that destroyed art and educated employments. The whole nation became an aristocracy of lazzaroni."

I had become deeply interested in the story in spite of myself. And, without noticing the distance we had travelled through the groves and orchards, I found before he stopped that we had rounded a great promontory and come suddenly upon a large settlement; for crowds moved or lay about the shores and under the fruit trees. I could see no temples or houses. But before long we came upon a succession of holes in the earth roofed with fallen trees and withered branches, or fragments dragged from the ruins of a former temple that we found afterwards in the forest. The race was again becoming troglodytic; and with my fine, sparrow-headed guide, I could see no fate before it but a complete though gradual return to aboriginal barbarism. The only things that stemmed the downward current were two: the retention of slave labour in Klimarol, and the periodical famines that cleared out the weaklings. But the survivors were ever becoming feebler and idler, and it was growing more and more difficult to fill up the gaps in the ranks of the slaves.

As we returned, the critic had by talking and explaining and slandering so worked himself into full confidence that I was now deeply attached to him. I knew that he had no more affection or loyalty to me or to any other human being than a cat. But, as he purred and made himself comfortable over the débris of his criticism of others, he gave out a certain amount of magnetism that seemed to make the intercourse close and fervid. It is the substitute in the amorous for friendship or love, and can be turned on or off with almost mechanical precision. The only safeguard against it amongst its victims is the vanity that accompanies it and makes it a desultory wanderer in its desire for further conquests.

He assumed that I was now a devoted admirer of him and his powers; and perhaps he put down my silence to moroseness or scant acquaintance with the language. At any rate he needed no key-word or question to start him on a new track. He had in fact now come to the subject for which he had been all along preparing the way; and it was amusing to see the ambushes and underground works by which he attacked it. Long before his mines reached the ramparts of the subject I saw his aim. He evidently knew that I was the owner of the new marine monster that had appeared in the waters of the archipelago, and he was anxious to secure my help for a great seraglio raid that he had planned for the repopulation of his island—which he let me indirectly know was called Figlefia, or the island of love. It was their efforts in the cause of humanity that had thinned their numbers, and a noble race would soon vanish unless some means were devised for introducing new blood. It had a great mission in the world: to leaven mankind with mutual affection and a lofty ideal of human rapture. Only by such a stock, inoculated with the nobleness of passion, could the world be turned from its evil ways.

Preaching could not do it; propagandism was barren of permanent effect; absorption by conquest was a chimera. The only way to save the world was by stocking it with new blood. This was taking advantage of the path of nature. She worked by generation and crossing of breeds in order to get at the hardier race that would withstand the new conditions of new times. Figlefia was a great experimental nursery. Scions were introduced from all the races and stocks of the world and grafted on the Figlefian race. The finest women that could be found were brought to the island, experiments were made, and the finest results were carefully preserved and nurtured to plant out in other regions of the earth. They were trained in the noblest doctrines of love and sent forth to propagate them through the nations and to introduce amongst them a newer and better breed that might make the race of man advance at an ever accelerated rate. The Figlefians had struck on the only true method of improving mankind and of covering the planet with the finest human stock it could support; and perhaps in some future age, when they had renovated all the nations of the earth, they would send out new breeds to the other planets and systems. It was indeed the noblest scheme that this orb had ever experienced.

Meantime their efforts for the good of the species had stinted their numbers, and new grafts were needed for their experiments in cross-breeding. The nursery of mankind needed replenishing. It was useless introducing sires, for the Figlefians were the finest on the globe. All that was needed was new dams that the great experimental method for the conversion of the world might proceed. There was no religion like that of the improvement of the human race; and no such improvement could there be as by the Figlefian scheme of cross-breeding and defertilising the failures. Did not my heart burn within me as I listened to the mighty creed? Did not I feel that the world, if not the universe, was getting reborn? Did I not desire to join in the great experimental method of progress?

I felt that he was coming close to his chief object, for he blinked his beady eyes and wagged his sage little head and looked unutterable things at me; he tried his strongest hypnotism on me and would hedge me round with him as the two select of the world; he shot his most magnetic influence into his words; he was bent on finally and completely chaining me to him by his fascinations. The upshot of it was that I would be serving the whole human race if I should lend him my wind-compelling or wind-defying ship to run half a dozen voyages through the islands in order to recruit the great nursery of mankind. He had the women selected and persuaded to leave with him if only he had the rapid means of conveying them. He had his own ship lying off the coast of Tirralaria awaiting his orders; but it was slow and wind-obeying, and it might be years before he restocked Figlefia by her means.

I professed that I did not know where the *Daydream* was; I had come in Garrulesi's falla, and whether she would follow or not I could not tell; but if she did I might be able to accommodate him for a voyage or two. I was not deeply impressed with his scheme, for the sufficient reason that I should be sorry to propagate the great Figlefian species, if this were a specimen of the stud. The world would soon be full of a race of feline hypocrites if he and his like were to repopulate it. And, though I had been cornered by the courtesies of the situation into promising my yacht, I prayed that she might keep far out of his reach.

He managed to close the negotiations just as we got back to the temple of the advisers of the people. The bulk of the food that had been run down by the slaves into one corner of it was gone; but Garrulesi had hidden a portion for me, and one of the inamoratas of the Figlefian sparrow had done the same for him. So we fared not ill. Our share consisted of fruits that were not unpalatable and of the flesh of some wild animal that abounded on the slopes of Klimarol. I cooked and ate and was satisfied.

I left my amorous instructor absorbed in his old occupation amongst the women, and stepped out again into the sunshine. I found Garrulesi waiting for me on the platform that overlooked the ocean. He gazed at me sadly as if at a lost sinner. He thought me wholly given over to the popinjay.

A few words put him into his most rhetorical humour. He understood my estimate of the man by the very tone of my answers to his first remarks. So he made no attack on the guest of his temple. With all his loose-jointed character and morality, he would not take advantage of my sympathy to slander one whom I plainly despised. He was too good-natured to trouble himself much about the designs or the petty gallantries of the creature. He merely scorned the unmanliness of this trifler with women, and fought shy of even speaking of him, as he would of a dunghill. In conversation with others of his countrymen who knew the Aleofanian tongue I found out what good cause he and his whole nation had to hate and persecute this Sneekape, as, they told me he was called. He was nothing but a pander for his island. The Figlefians were voluptuaries, and had been so for untold generations. They still retained something of the boldness that enabled them to subdue the aboriginal inhabitants of their island; and with this they enslaved them and kidnapped others from other portions of the archipelago. The hard fare, the brutal treatment, the stoical life of toil that these had to bear kept up their numbers and gave, in what they produced, great luxury to their masters. But the day was not far off when the slaves, hardened and emboldened by their mode of existence, would throw off the yoke of the sybarites and resume their long-lost freedom. A few of the aristocratic Figlefians had, like Sneekape, retained some of the energy and courage of their forefathers, the subjugators of the island, and either managed the work of the slaves by means of the lash or sailed out in search of new occupants of the harems. The rest were the vilest of debauchees, spending most of their time in cheating their neighbours out of the loyalty of their wives. And the whole race was ulcerous with disease, puny, though tall in frame, and periodically on the verge of madness. Its stamina was exhausted by concupiscence and debauchery. The skull was of the smallest, and most of its capacity lay in the back of it; it was like a cocoanut trying to force its way into a lemon. And the hair that covered it, as a rule, was of a dirty yellow merging into red.

They were not unhandsome, these Figlefians, with all their corrupt blood and the gleam of incipient madness in their eyes, for most of them had come from some of the finest women who could be entrapped by their emissaries throughout the archipelago. But they knew it so well that they were intoxi-cated with vanity; they bore themselves like coquettes, smirking and caper-ing and continually expectant of adoration. They kept, most of them, huge seraglios to which they were ever adding. Yet their greatest rapture was to get into a neighbour's, and especially a friend's enclosure and decoy his most faithful or most beautiful concubine. Six days out of seven were occupied in maturing or revenging some such intrigue. They had a code of honour based upon this feature of their life, and they counted the honours of their pedigree by the number of handsome women their ancestors and they had been able to cajole; and all the women they fascinated were, in the annals of their families, handsome. The other side of their roll of honour was the number of men they had slain in these amorous adventures. To add a sharp savour to this their chief employment and amusement, they upheld monogamy to be the true and divine form of the relations of the sexes; and their preachers almost daily prelected to them on the nobleness of purity of life. Half the taste of their erotic enterprises would vanish if they were allowed to follow them up without check or secrecy. Their whole polite literature would fall to dust at a stroke if either polygamy or libertinism were made legal, customary, and religious. A legislator who passed such a law amongst them and accom-plished such a reform would obliterate all the traditional wit and humour, all the smart stories they had to tell, all the gusto of their grotesque and often lewd art; life would become so vapid that there would occur an epidemic of suicide. To legalise these irregular unions that filled their seraglios would be to annihilate the purpose of their civilisation.

In some islands Sneekape and his fellow-panders were publicly proclaimed as enemies of the state, and, if at any time they were discovered there, were liable to be hunted down like vermin. In Tirralaria their offence was not felt so deeply. For the leisurely, pleasure-loving life precipitated a larger proportion of female children than of males. The freedom of intercourse between the sexes removed all special premiums on the passion; there could be nothing illicit in love; there was no bond and no law to dare or break. And thus they held there was nothing of intoxication in amorous intercourse; there was no more stimulus to it than there was to eating; it had become commonplace; and lasciviousness was as rare as gluttony, if not as miserliness in a state that had no money. As a rule, though there were no bonds, no state authorisations of permanency in the unions, they were more constant than in a monogamous community; and as there was in most years plenty of food to be got for nothing and parents could at their option retain their children or hand them over to the temple of female advisers, there was no check on the growth of the population. They were not sorry then that some of the women should elope with the Figlefian emissaries; in fact it relieved the drain on the supply of food and left fewer to suffer from any famine that might occur. There was indeed no compulsion on their women any more than on their men to stay on the island. And those who did follow Sneekape or any other of his libertines went with their eyes open; they now knew the capricious fate of a Figlefian seraglio. It was only the young fools amongst them that now allowed themselves to be decoyed. As a rule, they were handsome women who were flabby from adulation, and most of them had only the hectic beauty of weakness and ill-health; and these soon died off amid the rigours of Figlefian prostitution. Few ever returned from their escapade.

It was clear that they winked at Sneekape's mission, and rendered it as easy as possible, whilst he hoodwinked himself into the belief that it was his personal attractions that removed its difficulty. The high value that he placed on his face and figure, and especially on the hypnotism of his eyes and tongue, laid him open to any trap that an astute schemer would set for him; his vanity rendered him as foolish as a coot, whilst it at the same time made him think that he was a heaven-born diplomat and intriguer. For the morbid natures of the sickly and weak-willed he had manifest attractions; he could practically mesmerise these feebleminded beauties and make them follow him wherever he would, and he prided himself on these conquests with bantam-like gestures and crow. The strong-willed women were too wholesome in mind and too astute to be influenced by his flatteries or his hypnotising glances. They entertained a certain amused scorn of his vanity, his amorous advances, and his adulation.

During the day Garrulesi and his friends showed me great attention and descanted on the glories of their state. Whilst other communities had elevated the means towards happiness into an end they were already at the goal; they did not trouble themselves about the future, but enjoyed the present; they did not fidget 364 days that they might rest on the 365th, with the chance of dying before it came; they loved the bird in the hand better than ten thousand in the bush. The fools of the world, the most of men, chased the elusive to-morrow or wailed the vanished yesterday, till to-day had run its sands. Between two phantom worlds, the one dead, the other to be born, they let the present run, a rosary of tears or prayers. The moment was the only capital that men could be sure of; what folly to hide it in a stocking for that which may never be, to lose the reality in grasping at the shadow! The Tirralarians had based their whole life and civilisation on the maxim that neither the past nor the future is theirs to deal in. Time is but the flight of a moment between two midnights; all else is a dream; out of a dream we issue; into a dream we vanish; how vain to spend our only sleepless present as a lethargic past or an uncreated future!

And, as I walked about with them, I felt that there was something strikingly ephemeral in their existence. The only members of the community that thought of anything but the immediate hour were the advisers of the people; and even they were satisfied with but the outlook of a season; they tried to secure nature a chance of repairing the ravages a dislawed people might do her in gratifying their appetites with her products; they saw that the trees and bushes were not so broken down or pillaged of seed that they could not restore their vital powers; they watched over the recuperative faculty of a climate that though sub-tropical yet needed the husbanding of the trees and other growths.

It was indeed like talking with children from a cross between the barbaric past and the coming millennium, as I encountered and conversed with these ragged philosophers. In the opportunities of their civilisation they were not one step in advance of the savage of ten thousand years ago; in their mental and lingual outfit they were the equals of the subtlest and most advanced of nations. All day their life through, they sharpened their wits in argument, or discussion, or dream. They had had nothing to do but talk for centuries; and their power of rhetoric or argumentation was the accumulated legacy of a hundred generations. They had no books or art, for they had deliberately destroyed or abolished the professions that worked in them. But they had almost overcome the results of such a defect by the keenness of their memory and the potency of their imagination. Though they professed to live in the moment, their minds swept through all time and space. Without infinity of

past and future, of stars above and beyond, the present would have been
an intolerable prison-house. The energy that was no longer used in muscle
and framework and the processes of digestion concentrated in the brain.
They counted it no blemish on the perfection of idleness to dream for ever
waking dreams or keep the tongue in perpetual motion. They did not harass
themselves with imaginary cares and thus waste the tissue that went to
the enjoyment of complete living. If disease or famine came, why then they
died and there was an end of it. But what could it profit them to anticipate
such evils? They could not by thinking and acting and forerunning sorrow
and harassment add a moment to their years or postpone the arrival of the
inevitable end.

They acknowledge that records might have aided them in enhancing the
happiness they had, but writing them was too much like the old chase of
the mirage, the search for happiness. Who could be expected to postpone
the enjoyment of a brilliant fancy or noble image for the purpose of giving it
written expression? If they had had from the nervous energy of their old and
futile civilisation some automatic means of having their words or thoughts
recorded, then would they now have books enough to let a generation amuse
and instruct those that followed. But, before many generations had gone,
books would become a burden to the race; the necessity of having to read
them and know them would sit like a nightmare upon every man who wished
to be up to his age. Libraries crush the souls of men till they become all eyes
and comment on the past; their heads are twisted on their necks till they can
see only behind. The worst books contaminate the future like a foul stream.
The best books become gods that tyrannise over the ages to come and bind
the human spirit in irrefragable chains of minute devotion. They preserve the
past only to be a fetish and slave-driver of souls. Through them the generations can lay dead fingers upon the hearts of men and frighten courage out
with their stony stare and grasp. The noblest of them when deified by time
grow an evil dream. Books, they found, had become the high-priests of the
human spirit, and ultimately claimed communion with omniscience. Why
should they, when they had abolished all privilege in earth and heaven, as
far as they were concerned, leave a privileged race of human creations that
would episcopate over every nascent thought or imagination or element of
faith? The past was too much with them even as it was. Through heredity
it fettered and lamed the footsteps of mankind. What we have done, still
more what our ancestors have done, lays mortmain on what we do or have
still to do. And books give the grip of a vice to this dead hand of the past.
The Tirralarians grew weary of perpetuating outworn elements, and made a
bonfire of their libraries. Theirs was thoroughgoing socialism that would not

permit inequality of voice and influence even among the dead. Every man had his chance of moulding the future through his children and friends. Heredity gave him as strong a power of flight through the spaces of time and over the barriers of death as socialism or nature could allow. In all nations and races it needed far more strength to fight the dead past and throw off its yoke than to climb up the steep of progress. Tradition aiding heredity gave it almost omnipotence. Books, completing the yoke, gave such organisation and order and permanence to the power that it had no limit, and the young generations and young talents and thoughts were hopeless in the struggle. Through them tradition became like the snake-haired head of fable that turned all it stared at into stone; orally it is liquid or at least malleable, if not plastic; but in record it is the petrifaction of the past. Half of every life is a struggle with this gorgon, this sphinx, even when it has only the diaphanous texture of myth; but when it gathers to it the worship of past ages, it has the mystic fascination of destiny in its eyes, and there is no evading it in our threescore years and ten. We are born with the tentacles of this octopus round us, and with our growth they grow; and if they have in them the strength of past ages that literature gives, there is no spirit, however herculean, but must succumb to them; for every snaky arm that we unwind from our souls, a myriad retwine themselves about us. It is an unequal combat, this of the human present with its past; we arm the latter with weapons of such might, we are such traitors to our own happiness and our own future. The history of civilisation in any nation is but a record of the struggle of man to disentangle the coils of his past from his soul; and what makes it so tragic is that in his folly he is ever feeding the monster with his own vitals, his devotion, worship, reverence. Oh, the cruel laceration of his heart in times of revolution, when he rises to superhuman passion and resolves that he will be rid of the snaky coils! But, as the great mood begins to burn low, he finds that the hydra has only crept down on him with renewed life. To enjoy the present we must not multiply the terrors of the past by eternalising them, or brood over the dangers of the future till they become nightmares.

The rest of my day in Tirralaria had the sharp savour of epigram in it; so mean were the externals of life, so easy and opulent the thought and phraseology. Low living and high thinking was the rule amongst those whom I came to know. But I had the suspicion that these were but the floating remains of a great intellectual past come down the stream of heredity, for I saw gleam out of the eyes of most that I did not speak to the spirit of a wolf or of a sloth. Envy, malice, hatred, the passionate soul of Cain, had not vanished with the destruction of property, class, profession, literature, art. Low living without any thinking was the rule of the majority perforce; and it was these embruted elements of the nation that usually survived a famine or plague. I could see savagery loom at no distant date on the horizon of this people, for it had no means of conserving its higher elements or natures. High thinking cannot live in the sty of Epicurus; even in the higher natures it must drown in the deluge of talk.

I slung my mat with these melancholy thoughts dominating my mind and with the resolve to investigate the civilisation of the island more minutely before I left it.

I could not have slept long when a movement of my hammock awoke me to the hoarse chaos of a hundred nasal trumpets. I sat up in consternation, and through the darkness I could discern the figure of my Figlefian critic erect beside me. He waited a few seconds to let me master the situation, and then whispered in my ear: "It is time to set out if we wish to see Klimarol." I remembered our tacit agreement, and rose after donning my rags. On getting into the starlight my wits returned to me, and I began to think how dangerous was the enterprise, especially with such an untrustworthy guide. I pleaded that I had forgotten something, and, picking up a bright shell that gleamed upon the earth, I returned to my mat and wrote upon it, as well as the darkness would allow, a brief message in English for my men, telling them to beware of Figlefia, although they might find me there should I have left Tirralaria; they should take a guide and follow me with caution. On its outer surface I scratched a word or two in Aleofanian to Garrulesi.

CHAPTER XVII
THE MIDNIGHT ASCENT AND FLIGHT

THE DARKNESS AT FIRST set the whole sense of touch on the alert; it seemed black and solid as a prison wall. But the eyes soon focussed the sparse rays of starlight and massed objects into clots of night. The shadow of dreams still hung about my senses, as if sleep had not wholly fled. The trees and rocks we passed seemed rather to move past me. I was weary and languid, and every object and motion took feverish proportions. It was a world as strange and gruesome as if I had followed Dante into hell.

On I stumbled after my guide. I scarcely knew how or whither we went, nor cared I much. It was a life drugged with night that I was living. Between thick walls of darkness faintly parted overhead by a dim line of starshot grey we filed; ghosts we might have been but for the clang of stones beneath our feet, or the screech of some night-bird startled from his nest. There was little underlife in these islands to fear lurking in the shadows or thickets; they had too recently purged themselves of monstrous or snaky traces of the earlier features of the world in the all-cleansing bosom of the ocean. Only winged existence or human with its trans-elemental powers had found its way into these secluded survivals of an ancient world baptised and rebaptised in the obliterative sea.

Thoughts like these chased from sense to sense the dreamy fears of shapes and noises that formed and vanished in the night. Monsters crept back and forth out of the caverns of the blackness. Low yells and shrieks and groans just eluded the power of hearing; echoes of them faintly haunted the silences. Dim foreshadowings of horrors about to be born struck my senses with obscene wing; ghostly adumbrations of forms I had seen in dreams floated round me. Phantoms of the dead and of the unborn filled the hollows of my brain. I had no safety but in madly rushing on in the footsteps of my guide.

He doubtless heard the ringing echo of my advance, for he never turned to look, athirst though I was for a human word or the glance of an eye. He seemed to know every step of the labyrinthian path. Upwards did it climb at last; I grew giddy as it snaked and twisted and spiralled athwart the face of former landslips, along the edge of cliffs, beneath it Avernian gloom yawning, up the rugged bed of hissing streams, across the bouldered blackness of still pools, or the shifting gleam of a hoarse torrent, ever up with forests here and there or great walls of rock shouldering the starlight from them.

Sneekape never rested or stayed; ahead of me he darkened or vanished like a spirit of the night. My imaginary fears gave me speed and endurance and a lightning-swift instinct to shun real dangers. By day I should have been drunk with the dizzy steeps or black-hearted chasms we skirted.

Hours must have passed in this terror-goaded ascent, when suddenly we stood on a broad platform that overhung the sea. Far below us as it pulsed I could see the phosphoric shimmer of its discontent. In the shadow of a clump of trees we sat down to rest on a fallen giant of the woods. I was conscious of human life upon the level; the air was restless with sounds and motion it but half absorbed; and, when the eyes grew accustomed to the half-light of the stars hoarded between sea and sky, they discerned dark masses shift, and vanish against the stellar distance.

We had our backs to the cone of Klimarol, and by degrees I came to feel that there was other light in the air than that of the sky or sea. I looked up and saw the stars blotted out above the peak and in their place a lurid gleam that threw the unearthly glimmer, which I had been conscious of for some time, into the interjacent night. And up the slope between the broad ledge we sat on and the cloud reflector, there rushed like a funeral car a gloomy mass lit with the murky wind-sucked flame of a torch. I saw it reach the lip of the broken cone and disappear. This was the nocturnal incineration of Tirralarian débris and dead.

Sneekape gave a long, low, strident note thrice repeated, different only in the interval between the sounds from a night-bird's cry I had heard. Again he gave it. And before long I could hear a step rustle in the fallen leaves and dead herbage; a short grace note as of another bird, and my companion darted forward under the shadow. A moment's peering into the darkness, and I saw a human figure, half-naked, but with head enveloped in some helmet that looked like a diver's. The two disappeared together through the gloom-clus- tered foliage. And I had time to look aloft at the gleaming slopes of the great cone, scarred with dark zones and the track of the cinerative sleds. Fire and frost were the artists that carved this wonder of sheen and gloom. And even as I gazed the lustre of the overhanging pall flashed, and a light dust fell upon my hands and face. Another dark encaustic lay along the slope of the argent cone. The cloud that canopied the peak was rent with fulminant volley and a thin veil suffused the landscape for a moment; again the stars etched the darkness with their keen light, and the upper slopes of Klimarol were coagulate gloom. Its pall rose after a time and revealed the alabaster of the cone sloping to the stars unblemished. The tesselation and veining of the snow had vanished into spotless marble.

My companion returned, and, to overcome my fear of the volcanic showers, he told me that never was there so good an opportunity of seeing behind the scenes. The overseers had taken refuge in some caves lower down the slopes; the outburst had alarmed them, and the slaves had encouraged their fears, though they knew from long experience of the mountain that such an ejection relieved the tension of its heart, and none would follow for at least twenty-four hours. Thus they got rid of their repulsive work and the lash for a few brief breathing-spaces. He was in league with them and could get them to throw off the yoke at any time. They would lay down their lives for him; he alone gave them a consolatory future.

I rose and followed him, and our feet were clogged with the fresh mud of the mingled ash dust and rain. A few moments more and we were seated in a sled full of fallen branches and leaves and shooting over the snow at great speed, a pine torch flaring at our rear and bronzing the unsmirched gleam on either side of our track. To look down into the snow-lit gloom of the abyss we were deepening every moment appalled me. I crept to the front of the car and found a great chain attached that cut by the fire of its swiftness a black line through the pallor of the slope. Half-way up there shot out of the gloom and into it again a sled like our own laden to the lip and guided by half-naked cresset-headed slaves; and behind it in the snow-gleam I could trace a dark line parallel to that made by our chain.

Almost before I could withdraw my thoughts from the new subject, we had surmounted the edge of the mountain cup and in a few minutes were landed on the sulphurous platform that fringed it within. A foul stench was in our nostrils that gave Avernian shapings to my inward fears. Down into the pit of everlasting fire I seemed to look; a breath of wind fitfully lifted the turban of steam and smoke that hid the central furnace, and I could catch suggestive glimpses of a molten lake clogged with ever-thickening ever-cracking congelation of liquid rock. Only for a moment, and then all was grey steam again lit from within with fire that seemed to threaten conflagration.

It was long before my eyes could find their way amid the mingled gloom and flash and twilight. But at last I could discern inside the lips of the fiery mouth the desolation of a great city. The cyclopean blocks of lava that made its walls were heaved and split as if they had been the missiles of giants. Yet amid their rupture and dissilience and beneath the sulphurous spume that streaked and sicklied their sombre outlines with lichened yellow, I could discern the features of the magnificent past. Here and there the fragments of great domes still stood propped by their own ruins or soldered by new

streams of molten rock. Mighty walls rose up above the now solid torrents
of lava that had flowed along their base. It was the strangest sight; vast
sculptured figures standing to their necks in new rock, like mammoths from
their graves of century-vanishing ice. Mythic animals or monsters from a
long-buried past, some with half-human faces, looked out untroubled from
their bed of stone upon the seething hell beneath them, whence had issued
sea on sea of terrene fire to curd in massy base around their feet. Tall columns
lay imbedded in sulphurous ash; others stood broken and vitrified by the dash
of some fiery billow. Statues rested half sunk in a shallow inlet of once-molten
stone. Great temples still showed the tracery of their mullioned windows and
the marvellous fretwork of their walls and roof beneath the glassy yellow of
their incrustation. It was as if a city of noble giants had been crushed into
fragments and then preserved in amber. Even beside the tremendous forces
of this mighty vent of subterraneous passion the ruins showed immense.

Amid them skulked large-headed human figures that with their oily
nakedness gleamed bronze at times in the palpitant light of the central furnace. But for these I could have wished to explore the cyclopean fragments of
a great civilisation of the past. But I feared the iron-barred eyes that flashed
so savagely from beneath the huge visors. I knew that these headpieces were
to protect the eyes and tender parts of the slaves from the fall of ashes and
other red-hot ejections from the bowels of the mountain. Yet in the darkness
and lurid gleamings they showed like gnomes or monsters of the earth, and I
could not rid my mind of shrinking.

The emotion rose into terror when I heard sullen cries and shrieks rise on
every side from the petrified fragments of the past. Over the rim of the mountain cup shot another of their funeral sleds filled with figures that showed
sombre against the heaven beyond; and in the hand of each was a huge thong
with knotted end. My companion started, and seizing me by the elbow pulled
me in under the shadow of a tower that still rose gigantic out of the new rock.
I could see by the occasional flash from the upper cloud what consternation
had taken him. For a time he could scarcely command breath to speak—a
striking thing in this superfine master of language. I crouched with him for
a few minutes in the darkness, and at last he hoarsely whispered in my ear,
"It is the overseers, and we shall be caught!"

We skulked from pillar to wall, from wall to buried figure, ever in the
shadow, till we had reached a deep fissure in the hardened lava, out of which
streamed a sulphurous vapour. We were glad to lie there panting for a time;
and, as we looked out over the steaming abyss, we saw the visored slaves flying with groans and yells to their work. Some thrust bars into gleaming lava,
and then taking great hammers smote the metal into shape upon clanking

anvils. Some melted the snow from the rim of the crater and poured it into channels between beds of well-dug earth that showed green buds just shooting above the surface; others gathered fruit from plants that had matured in this immense forcing-house; whilst others laid mould deeply over the warm rocks and mixed with it the débris from below. Here it was that the lazzaroni of Tirralaria had their luxuries produced; this was the huge workshop of the island; without it the lapses of nature left to herself would long before this have let the race fall into the inane. It was slave labour, and that under the most cruel *régime*, that kept this anarchic society alive. Here the rigours of the law had gathered into one great clot of blood, leaving the masters in idleness and lawlessness.

We were not long left to conjecture how the thongs stimulated the products of nature. Across the abyss I heard a wild shriek, and a stalwart overseer stood in the glow of the red-hot lava with lash again uplifted. But the slave had evaded it before it fell. We saw the wretch speed to the lip of the fire-lake, the knout-holder following, though at a distance. Something exceptional was about to occur, for all the rest, slaves as well as overseers, raised their heads and let their instruments fall to the ground. Their gaze followed the swift feet of the refugee. Nearer and nearer he came to the crag that overlooked the lake of fire. Still the pursuer shouted to him threats. A flash from the hidden fires lit up the cracked and seamed edges of the chasm, whilst a wind moved aside the curtain of steam and let the canopy above gleam luridly. When the sulphurous cliffs and the upper clouds seemed to glow with the light, the hurrying figure came to the edge of a yellow precipice, and with the impetus of the rush hurled itself far over the molten lake; we saw it turn head over heels and then vanish. It was the work of a moment, and my guide clutched me and drew me on with a whisper hoarsened by alarm: "Flee for your life." I rushed after him as he made for the lip of the crater towards the eye of the wind, for I heard a low thunder beneath our feet, and a louder rumbling behind us. Wearied though I had been by my night's climb I felt my limbs light as thistledown. The wind was rising against us, yet we seemed to leap from fragment to fragment, from rock to rock heedless of its force. The thunder grew behind us, and seemed to quicken the pace of my guide. We reached the rim in safety and crouched in the snow underneath it. And looking up we saw the whole heavens lit, and away in the direction of the ruined city a fire outlined on sepulchral black. It was the passion of the mountain finding new vent. We crept down over the snow, sometimes sliding hundreds of feet in a moment over its smooth and glistering surfaces, till we reached the vegetation. The morning had begun to break, so my guide quickened his pace and hid in the densest of the thicket.

Once safely covered, he seemed to get the command of his terror. He lay for a time panting and unable to speak. But, when his throat had recovered enough from its parched state to be the channel of sound, he whispered: "We must get out of this; they know that we are on the crater, and they will pursue us as soon as the eruption is over; they will track us in the snow with ease. We must double back through the forest and then downwards to the shore. We must defeat their scent." He fell again panting to the ground, his face pallid and drawn. It must have been exceptional consternation that had so dread an effect. I let him recover again, and then asked him what it all meant. In a low, hoarse tone he whispered: "It was the slave's vengeance. They know that if they plunge a body of some mass into a certain boiling caldron of liquid lava, the mountain will regurgitate it. This wretch knew in any case that he would die in taking revenge for the lash, and he felt perhaps that a plunge into the boiling fire would be the quickest and the fullest vengeance. His pursuer would perish before he turned and reached the rim of the crater. The rest who were nearer it would run the risk of being overwhelmed, for the wind would carry the ash cloud directly over their heads."

But Sneekape did not care to waste time over talk. He knew from the experience of former deputies from his island how prompt and complete was the punishment for being caught in the workshop of Tirralaria. So we set out again and doubled on our path; he kept his eye on the cloud over the peak, and ever and again put aside the foliage to have a look at the sea. He clearly knew every district of the island. Once or twice he stopped and listened intently. He thought he heard the far-off cry of the pursuers. He seemed satisfied, and took advantage of the pause to search for wild fruit; we both ate eagerly from several trees and bushes. But he was not at ease. The success of the pursuit depended on whether they knew that his falla lay off shore for him. He had kept the fact from them, but they might have seen her from the mountain. He had also a canoe from her lying in the shelter of a cave on the least frequented shore. If he could put his pursuers on a false trail and then gain this means of escape, there would be no danger for us. All day we lay in a thicket some hundreds of feet above the beach waiting the protection of twilight and night. We sated our appetites with the berries and nuts around us and put a small store away in one of our loose and unnecessary rags. He kept his eye on the sea through a crevice in the foliage, and once as the sun began to wester he started with alarm; he saw the blistered track of some boat that had crept close to the shore bronzing in the yellow light. Whether it was the enemy or his own men it was difficult to say. He crept, still under cover, to the point of a promontory that shot sheer down into the ocean; and looking over he saw the rags of the Tirralarians flutter in the wind as they bent to the oars. Almost at the same moment he noticed his own falla tacking far on the horizon, evidently waiting some emergency.

He returned and told me the result of his reconnaissance. He conjectured that the overseers had communicated with the capital and that a boat had been immediately dispatched along shore to cut off our embarkation on the falla. Our best chance lay in its keeping on its course to his usual place of departure. It was likely that his falla would lie off that spot and that the Tirralarian boat would remain all night between it and the shore. We would then make for the canoe which lay farther to the west, if the night favoured us.

Happily the gloom was profound, for the sky was moonless, and the starlight was drenched with moisture and shone with lustreless and dull edge. As soon as twilight had shuttled its pall for the dead sun we took our little store of fruits and started down the hill with extreme caution. If either of us snapped a twig or dry stick, we stood with beating hearts, all ears. Then on again with slow pacing. It must have been midnight when we reached the rocky shore. Sneekape felt his way till he found a tree of singular growth, all bent and gnarled by the beat of the waves and the salt spray. Then he doffed his rags and dived from the edge of the rock. Within a few minutes he had found his canoe in the cave, unmoored it, and paddled his way to an easy descent. I carried down his rags and our stores, and embarked.

Cautiously we stole out from the shelter of the cliffs; he shot his paddle into the water with such care that not a ripple could be heard, and I aided with my hands over the side. About three or four hundred yards from the shore we opened out a bay behind a far out-jutting promontory; and as I looked back I saw a dark object close inshore break the faint gleam of starlight on the water. Sneekape raised his eyes and fell into his former panic. His paddle would have fallen into the sea had I not caught it. The movement seemed to awaken the distant shadow, and the sound of oars soon broke the still night air. Our pursuers were on our track.

Sneekape immediately recovered his presence of mind. Our only chance of escape lay in what he took to be the position of the falla. We were quite two miles away from our would-be captors. We strained every nerve. Yet they gained on us. The two miles were rapidly reducing to one. We could hear the muffled beat of their oars.

My companion seemed, however, less excited than he had been. He even seemed to relieve the tension of his paddle in its stroke. Was he losing his senses? I dared not break in upon his work lest it should lapse altogether. I felt a shiver run through me as if a cold wind had blown. I looked behind, and the island had vanished in mist. And even as I gazed, the dim veil enveloped the dark shadow on the water that was straining after us. I could feel our canoe jerk into another direction, almost at right angles to our previous path. The beat of the pursuing oars was swallowed up in silence. In about half an hour my companion laid his paddle down and threw himself down on the bottom of our canoe and laughed a long, low laugh. The fog had outwitted the revenge of the advisers of the people.

We were so wearied with the long strain that in spite of our rags and the chill of the night we stretched ourselves and fell asleep. When morning broke the thick veil was still over the sea, and where we were we knew not. We relieved the pangs of hunger and waited. It seemed as if we had got into some current, for either we were moving with considerable swiftness through the mist, or the mist was driving over us.

As the sun rose towards the zenith the dense veil grew more transparent, and then rent in twain. We saw the blue sky above; and soon the whole envelopment of the world had melted into the azure. Klimarol was a white phantom on the horizon with a thin blossom of cloud above it. Nothing else broke the outlook in that direction; but in the opposite, whither we were rapidly drifting, a low coast lay like a thin nebulous stratum.

Sneekape, when he looked round at my gesture, gave a cry of surprise. He had expected to be near his falla. But it was not to be seen; and he had not yet made out what island it was that we were bearing down on. This consolation we had, that we had enough fruit with us to serve the day's wants, and the new land seemed less than a day's journey from where we were.

CHAPTER XVIII
MEDDLA

IT WAS NOT FAR in the afternoon when my companion, taking a look ahead, gave a long, low whistle and laughed. He had recognised some feature of the land we were now approaching. "You will have some fun here," he said. "We shall have to bridge our way over the lunatic asylum of the archipelago. It is a series of islets on which we have classified and quarantined our cranks for many ages. Anyone ridden by a fixed idea or habit is shipped off to those of his own kin. So we keep our communities clear of quixotism and crazy eccentricity. You will see each for yourself, for we cannot get to Figlefia unless by passing over every one of these islets in order to provision our canoe for each voyage across the passages between them. We call the group Loonarie; but each has its own special and grandiloquent name to distinguish it, for they have a supreme contempt for one another."

We paddled and drifted with considerable rapidity, and the features of an island grew more and more distinct; for the current which bore us evidently ran close inshore. The beach swarmed with people as we approached; their fantastic dresses made a brilliant but grotesque scene; everyone seemed to have tried to produce as loud and individual an effect as possible by the colour and shape of his garments and the slovenly way in which he had pitchforked them on. It was not the colours of the rainbow, but a complete diapason of discordant colours. As we got nearer they seemed to have chosen garments by lottery. Their lean, lank forms showed like May-poles in the loose finery; and their sharp faces and small red heads almost disappeared in the enormous beribboned turbans they wore. They all looked preternaturally solemn and wise. There was much buttonholing amongst them, and most confidential communications were evidently passing from lip to ear.

I feared some sinister purpose with regard to ourselves. But Sneekape laughed when I mentioned the idea. "They only wish to convert you to their way of thinking, and each is getting ready for the assault. One soul gained to their side, they say, is one soul saved. Propaganda is their passion."

We beached our canoe amid much dignified fussing that really delayed us instead of helping us. I thought the efforts they made to do us a service would have landed us all in the surf—a matter of little consequence to us in our rags, but somewhat serious to them and their ill-harmonised finery. We were like to be torn into fragments by the candidates for our friendship when we had got our feet on the sand. They were all eager to clothe us. Sneekape rescued me from a dozen who clutched at my rags; and we followed the most dignified personage in the crowd and got re-clothed. I had imagined that it was in pure charity they had been eager to substitute something better for our rags. But it turned out that we had to pay most handsomely for our new and gorgeous garments, and that they were the uniform of a party. The benevolence lay in taking the custom to a shop owned by one of the party, and perhaps in saving our souls by giving us the badge of that party.

The majestic ribbon-pole who had captured us entered into conversation with me in Aleofanian. He had seen me in Aleofane when he was there on a mission to the heathen; and he had yearned to save my soul from the baneful influence of men who had not the true faith—faith in altruism. He asked me if I knew that I had landed in one of the noblest countries in the universe, Meddla, the Isle of Philanthropy. Here was the true centre of the universal fire of love. Here lived those who yearned to save the souls of their neighbours, who cared not what became of themselves, if only other men were saved. Had I thought over the momentous question of the true harmony of colours? Of course a man of experience such as I was had thought it out and decided that green and blue were the divine mixture, were indicative of the noblest qualities that God had conferred on human character. I looked down and saw that my new garments were a motley of green and blue; and of course I knew that black and yellow were the colours of the principle of evil. Ah, if only men knew how much the difference meant to their souls and to the destiny of the world, they would not trifle with the question! It was the deadliest poison, the rankest sin to wear black and yellow. All moral evils went with this mixture. And if I knew how serious a thing life was, I would join them in their crusade against this diabolism in colour, would put forth every effort to suppress it and prevent the world being lost.

I would have burst into a roar of laughter, but that I caught a warning glance in Sneekape's eye. I kept serious and he helped to rescue me from the enthusiast and devotee of green and blue, by whispering something in his ear that spread a radiant smile over the meagre face.

He had not left us many minutes, when I was pounced upon by another May-pole, who thrust his little head into my face and addressing me in Aleofanian wished to know what I thought of Meddla. Was it not the greatest community on the globe? Had it not reached the acme of civilisation? Did not its fundamental principle of anxiety for the souls of others make it the centre of the universe?

I told him that I was afraid that I had not had time or opportunity for forming a judgment. I had just landed and had never seen the island before. He must excuse me if I did not answer his questions.

But I had spoken with Wispra, one of their leaders; what did I think of him? What were his faults? The speaker had the deepest love for his fellow-men as all Meddlarians must have, but he must exercise that love in sweeping all faults and vices out of their civilisation. Foreigners were the most apt critics; they could see flaws, which home eyes passed over from long custom.

Well, if he would insist, I thought that Wispra was a little dogmatic. At the word, the little head shook with excitement and wagged with stifled wisdom. Was that his fault? Of course it was. And it was the fault of all Meddlarian human nature. Oh, he was delighted to have found it out! And he would cure it straightway. The legislature was just sitting. He would call a meeting and get a resolution passed in favour of the complete abolition of dogmatism. He would send large posters and tracts all over the island urging immediate action. His agents and supporters would get up public meetings in every village and settlement; and mile-long petitions would soon roll in to the assembly, asking it to suppress this vice. A law would be passed, I should see, within a week prohibiting the use of dogmatism in conversation, or in any form of speech under the most rigorous penalties. He would be the saviour of his country.

Away bustled the lank agitator, oscillating his wise head in excitement; he must set the crusade afoot that very minute. Before I left the island I found him and his disciples persecuting the dissentients from his views and calling them by the most opprobrious epithets; they would have no conditioning of their dogmas, and no questioning of their assertions; they would listen to no argument, but howled down in their meetings everyone who dared to advise caution and consideration before venturing on a crusade against so widespread and delightful a method of speech. Such mild protest was taken up and used as a missile for wounding the protester and his sympathisers. It showed, the speakers from the platform said, how necessary the reform was when a man would have the hardihood to stand up in a respectable audience and declare in the same breath that the habit was universal and yet that it should be approached with caution. Before the week was out, I had to leave; but I saw that the agitation was working its way through the island and splitting up parties into new and surprising sections; households were rent asunder, old friendships broken, old loyalties dissolved; I began to regret that I had ever uttered the word to my buttonholer. And so did Sneekape; for he knew that they would send out missionaries to the adjacent islands to disturb and harass the souls of their inhabitants in order to achieve their salvation.

Some of the greatest popular movements of their past had had, I ascertained, marvellous results. One of them had been for the spread of the custom of wiping the nose with a handkerchief; a section of the community had been satisfied for centuries with their sleeve or their fingers. After two or three ages of wild political agitation, a law was passed making it penal to accomplish the act without an officially marked piece of cloth; and there was a large charity organisation which spent all its days and nights in making and distributing amongst the poor patent attachments that would keep the government handkerchiefs hung close to the nose; and it had a paid staff of teachers and preachers who went around educating the people how to save their souls by wiping their noses in the proper way.

Another great reform that had come about after long searchings of the national spirit and untold sufferings on the part of its advocates and martyrs was the abolition of the practice of thrusting the hands in the pockets. The reformers saw that this introduced indolence and its attendant maladies and vices, and this imperilled the salvation of thousands of innocent victims to the habit, who began it in childhood when they did not know what to do with their hands, or in cold seasons, when they needed warmth; the practice was most insidious; it had generally mastered a man before he knew that he had begun it; and no preaching, no demonstration of its awful consequences could break him of it. After heroic efforts, a law was passed prohibiting the habit under the severest penalties. Yet it was by no means eradicated; men preferred being imprisoned to giving it up. So there was a great society, chiefly of women, who busied themselves in watching offences against the laws and prosecuting the offenders. But they were too philanthropic to confine themselves to such negative proceedings; they distributed gloves gratis in winter and the members went about with needle and thread sewing up the openings of trousers pockets. They were the busiest of all the citizens yet; for gloves had a trick of getting lost and sewing a trick of coming undone; and the kind-hearted women found themselves worn to shadows in their unselfish endeavours to make the law a reality.

Another law had been passed after great commotion to compel the people to wear table napkins when feeding; slovenliness and uncleanliness were two of the most soul-destroying vices; and, if the meals were taken in order and without soil, all other virtues would follow. Another huge organisation busied itself in distributing tracts on the nobleness of the practice that the law commanded and in supplying napkins to those who could not afford them; recently they had, on the suggestion of one whom they revered as a genius, combined their two functions and printed their tracts on the napkins they gave gratis. The members all felt that the eyes of mankind were upon them, as they went round the various villages seeing that their napkins were tied on properly.

They had a multitude of prohibitory laws for the cure of every habit that anyone had considered evil or worked up a movement for the suppression of. One forbade the raising of the little finger in drinking, another the wearing of hats so large as to occupy too much space in the streets, another the use of expletives, another the mutilation of a guttural sound that was apt to pass into a palatal, another the habit of boys standing on their heads in public places, another the use of worms in fishing, another the following of any business on certain hours of certain days.

The statute-book was an enormous one, and was filled with such laws as these. A considerable number clashed with others, and yet there were societies founded to see the carrying out of each of the conflicting statutes, and their agents and supporters often came into fierce collision, reaping on each side a full harvest of bloody noses and cracked crowns. But this only made the devotees more devoted. Most of the prohibitions ended in rooting the habit more deeply, by sending it underground. One instance was the law for the suppression of winking except on the approach of sleep; prosecutions always failed because the culprit generally contrived to fall asleep on the way to court or prison and so destroyed the case against him. I never saw so much winking in any community of the same size; I thought at first that they were all in the incipient stage of eye disease or of paralysis; but an arrest by an agent of the anti-winking society cleared up the mystery for me.

Of course I soon saw that the greater matters of the law had to be neglected in order to join in these quixotic crusades. The population had fallen into drunkenness, lying, thieving, slandering, fornication, and even murder. Every man and woman had some one or more of these vices; and all were accomplished hypocrites, I discovered before I left. Yet they all spent as much time as they could save from business or amusement in the pursuit of the salvation of their neighbours. Every citizen of either sex was a member and spy of one or more of these philanthropic societies, and was ever joining in some movement for getting the legislature to make the prohibition more rigorous and detailed; and none of them but thought that the gaze of creation was upon them as they followed their crusade. They were the true saviours of the world; they had the salt of love and altruism that would never lose its savour; they had reached the secret of true happiness. In spite of their philanthropy, they were eaten up with envy, jealousy, malice, and all the minor evil feelings that sting men and make men sting each other.

I was quite prepared to believe Sneekape when he said that the archipelago translated the name of the island differently from the inhabitants; it was the Isle of Busybodies. The gradual discovery of the true nature of the people made me glad to escape. We went off without notice one midnight in our canoe, which we had well provisioned some days before.

CHAPTER XIX
WOTNEKST

THERE WAS AN ISLAND near that carried the belief in the potency of law to a still more insane pitch. I had heard of people with new-born legislative functions thinking that they could accomplish anything they desired by merely passing a law. Revolutionary fervour even in the West had worked wonders with the human power of self-delusion. But the story of the isle of Wotnekst or Godlaw, as it might be translated, roused my curiosity. I could not believe that there existed outside of lunatic asylums a people so far gone in hallucination.

Much against the will of Sneekape we were driven by the current and the wind right upon a lonely beach of the island. As it was evening, I persuaded him to camp on the shore for the night. Before we were fully awake in the morning we were surrounded by a crowd of the most tattered and slovenly men and women I had ever seen, and this after I had been in Tirralaria. There was a wild, fanatic light in their eyes that warned us to humour their fondest freak. They stood between us and the margin of the sea where our boat was beached, and we saw that they meant to shepherd us inland, whether as prey or guests we could not tell. Sneekape made the best of a bad bargain and, after taking a slender meal of what we had left from supper, he marched away from the shore and I followed. The tatterdemalions began to move too.

It was one of our pieces of good fortune that my companion, though he had never made an expedition to the island, because of its lack of attractive quarry, had amongst his many accomplishments acquired a smattering of its language from some of the descendants of those who had escaped from it. For they had not long before passed a law that their language should be and was the universal language of the world; they had long enough suffered from having to learn the languages of barbarians and foreigners, in order to have intercourse with them; they would suffer the indignity no longer; other men must learn Wotnekstian; and in fact it was their true, natural, or mother tongue, and they had forgotten it only through their negligence; it was time that they picked it up again, and they would have no trouble in doing so, once the auxiliary series of laws was passed for enabling foreigners to learn the language in a day. They should like to know how any man could fail to learn it once the legislature of Wotnekst had taken the matter in hand and passed the necessary laws. They should like to know what Nature had been doing all these centuries in letting the native tongue of the earth fall into desuetude in so many nations. Nature knew well that Wotnekst was the primitive source of all mankind and had remained the leading country of the earth and the model for men to follow. It had been foremost in legislation and had shown the way to the whole world; for legislation was the supreme factor of life.

I heard the loud and threatening eloquence, and though I did not understand the import of it I knew from its tone that I had better keep silence. I sheltered under the knowledge of Sneekape, and watched him negotiate and cringe and flatter. I afterwards discovered that it was his knowledge of the language, meagre though it was, that saved us from terrors they did not attempt to define. Sneekape knew their general reputation in the archipelago as a feeble folk too loquacious to do any harm. Yet he showed by his cowering and fawning look that he was not quite sure what might occur; and the more he spanielled them the louder and more arrogant they grew. It was then I knew by instinct that they were cowards, attempting to hide their cowardice and drive courage and boldness out of the hearts of possible assailants. Once Sneekape took in the situation, he changed his attitude and adopted their loud voice and swaggering gait. He was, as I had seen, a master of effrontery and fanfaronade. But his change of rôle was too sudden to impress them; and they had gathered confidence and impetus from the torrent of their own blustering and rhodomontade and from their growing numbers as they approached the town. They outbrassed the insolence and swagger of Sneekape, and he cut but a poor figure for the rest of the march to our destination.

We could not see the houses for a long time; and when we came amongst them we still looked for the town ahead of us. The hovels were so squat and mean and filthy that we could not imagine human beings living in them; but we soon stopped before one that was conspicuous for having been built as a penthouse to the ruin of what had once been a considerable edifice. We were informed that this was the capital, the very centre of the civilisation and power of the world, and that what we saw around us was the greatest city on the face of the earth. The filthy kennels were the town, and this pigsty was the residence of the government.

We were led to the door, and one examined the contents of my pockets and handed them over to an official within. Another took his place and examined my hat and grubbed in my hair. A third stepped forward and ransacked the inner places of my garments. And so on the investigation proceeded over the whole of my person till every crevice and opening was examined. Then marched up another group, and through Sneekape made sundry inquiries as to our origin, past history, means of subsistence, ultimate destination, race, religion, political tenets, attitude towards the existing government, views on the exciting questions of the island and the day, and endless details that were of no consequence to any but ourselves and of little consequence to ourselves. A third set pursued an investigation into our health; and a fourth into the health of the island we had last visited. In fact our examination continued all through the day; and my belief is that it would have gone on for weeks till we had dropped from emaciation and fatigue, but that the leading politician had been disturbed in his attempt at sleeping inside, and had rushed out in a frenzy and dispersed the crowd.

Left to our own resources, Sneekape and I foraged about till we found a few scraps to eat; for we were famishing; and from sheer fatigue we lay down under the shelter of a tree, and without troubling to find an elevation or even a stone for a pillow we were dead asleep at once. We awoke in broad daylight to find ourselves again the centre of a tattered and inquisitive crowd. I heard Sneekape mutter under his breath: "God help us! another plague of inspectors!" Then I realised what we had gone through and what we might have still to go through. Every person in that mob which had shepherded us up from our boat was a government inspector of immigration and importation, and had to show his zeal for administration whenever a stranger landed. They had several thousand acts relating to aliens who approached their shores, and every act had necessitated the appointment of so many officials to see its provisions carried out. There had been in former ages considerable commerce centring in the island; but the minute regulations for its conduct had frightened every merchant and sailor from its shores. There was nothing left of its olden trade but the countless laws passed for its administration and development and the mob of inspectors to see them enforced. There were inspectors of tides, of harbours, of fore-shores, of weather, of clouds, of shoals, of rocks, of captains, of crews, of native sailors, of foreign sailors, of native passengers, of aliens, of goods, of native and foreign clothing, of native and alien epidermis, of native and alien vermin, of native and alien diseases; the list proceeds through a whole encyclopedia of detail. Yet all the imports they were able to inspect were the planks and nails and bolts of an occasional shipwreck, and all the human beings were strangers driven by stress of weather or current on to their inhospitable beaches. Our arrival was an era in the existence of this host of inspectors.

But the legislators were as eager to have a foreign audience, and rescued us from the tender mercies of the inspectorate. A special act was passed relieving us from the jurisdiction of the thousand alien laws that were to be found on the statute-book and of the ten thousand inspectors who were to enforce them. We were fêted and banquetted and made so much of that we could not get a moment to ourselves or sufficient hours for sleep. The worst of it was that all their feasts were of the Barmecide order. We were urged to help ourselves; but there was never anything to help ourselves to. The speeches were most grandiloquent, and often laudatory; but we should have been better satisfied with a crust of bread. Nor dared we hint that we were starving; for that would have reflected on their hospitality, and perhaps led to unpleasant consequences. Now and again we tried to get away from our eulogists amongst the fruit trees that Nature provided on the island; but on our escapades we generally found every branch rifled; and we were generally captured before we went far, they were so eager to induce foreigners to settle on their island or traffic with them. If only we would return and bring others with us, they would pass innumerable laws for our benefit. They had not yet realised that it was too much legislation that had isolated them; for it was now the only thing they had to lavish. But Sneekape saw his opportunity and seized it. He promised that he would flood their shores with merchants and traders; and he effected his purpose. We were allowed to depart before emaciation made us incapable of leaving; and we were accorded on the beach the most fervent of farewells.

When we had drawn out of sight of the land, the wind favouring us, Sneekape pulled from underneath the planking of the boat some of the fruits we were familiar with on these islands. Without my stopping to inquire how he had got them, we ravenously ate them. Feeling appeased, I tried to find out what ingenuity of his had extracted food from an island that seemed to be without it. He had managed to get into one of their households and to flatter the women and they had provided him. I suspected from his look and his reluctance that there was some baseness or intrigue that even his mean spirit had become ashamed of, and I pressed him no further.

He was quick to recover from such an unusual emotion; and after a few hours' sleep in the bottom of the boat, his vanity came uppermost. He awoke in the best of humour with himself and his achievements and discernment, and I had a full account of his past knowledge of the island and his immediate observations on it.

It was the most fertile in the archipelago and the richest in the precious metals and the common minerals; and it had at one time bidden fair to be the most opulent. The people, though too fond of politics, had been industrious and thrifty. There were several large cities in the island full of splendid buildings public and private. The coast was studded with excellent harbours constantly filled with ships loading for other parts of the archipelago. They kept a strong fleet for the protection of themselves and their commerce. Wotnekst was the envy of the other islands.

What had brought most of its population together was the belief that if only they could each get his pet political theory put into practice, the world would be saved and the millennium would be here. Every leisure moment they had they spent in discussion with each other on their favourite topic. They had started as a republic with complete freedom of meeting and speech; and so there was no bridle to their dominant passion. Politics was talked of every hour of the day and dreamed of every hour of the night; and their dreams were perhaps less mad than their daylight projects. Every man tried to outvie his neighbour in the eccentricity of his theories and suggestions; and they were gauged and promoted not in proportion to their wisdom and practicability, but in proportion to their departure from the beaten paths of tradition. Every one was, of course, intended to order the world as it ought to be ordered; it professed universal prosperity and happiness as the certain goal. There would be no more poverty, no more evil, no more misery in the universe, if only it were adopted; and the electors, feeling the annoyances and woes pointed out to be real enough, and recognising the objects aimed at as excellent and quite in harmony with their own yearnings, eagerly adopted every such proposal. They did not stop to inquire whether the means were adequate to the ends, or whether they would not introduce evils greater than those to be remedied. The actual existence of the woes and the magnanimous motive were enough to secure their sympathy, and anyone who offered to criticise was howled down as the enemy of mankind and of all progress.

And, as always happens, there arose a set of politicians who pandered to this passion with a view to their own advantage and glory. If a scheme, however utopian, seemed likely to be acceptable to the majority they would trick it out with one or two special features of their own and proclaim it as their own discovery; and all their energies would be bent towards having it put in the form of a law on the statute-book. Statesman after statesman rose on such stepping-stones to power and fame; and at last it was recognised that the only way to success in Wotnekst was a brand-new project for the cure of all human ills.

The first stage of those panaceas was based on the idea, natural to a republic, that the suffrage was the noblest thing a man could wish for. What floods of eloquence were turned on to the theme! What pictures of the happy state that would ensue on each new expansion of the electorate proposed! How cruel and inhuman those who opposed it! The toughest struggle was the first for the removal of the most irrational of all the political disabilities and anomalies that had grown up with the growth of the community. If any human system remains untouched for a generation or two without any automatic power of self-adaptation, it becomes a caricature of justice and wisdom through the growth of the commonweal to which it is intended to apply. The Wotnekstians suddenly awoke to find the electorate, consecrated by long tradition, a nest of absurdities and wrongs; but it took the eloquence and ridicule of two generations of reformers to put it right and to get the franchise extended to all holders of a certain amount of property. The abolition of the property qualification was a struggle only second to this in its violence. Then the flood came. Every new statesman had to rise to power on some new suffrage scheme. From residence for a year it was brought down to residence for a month in the community. How irrational it seemed to place any time limit to the acquisition of political interest and insight and wisdom! Every limit, indeed, could be proved to be arbitrary and illogical; and the final step was easily taken to manhood suffrage.

Then they waited to see the effect; and there grew upon the people, first surprise, and then indignation that all human ills had not vanished from the island. There were poverty and crime and disease with them still in all their virulence. Who could be at the bottom of this failure? It could not be the patriots at home. It must be the foreigner who frequented their shores and marts. Then the second stage of panacea legislation began. This was occupied with taxing the foreign commerce of the island. Tariff after tariff was passed for the purpose of drawing as much blood as possible from the alien who came to their harbours, without actually killing him. He was getting fat on the trade with their island. Increase the revenues out of him, was ever the cry. For more and more was needed for the army of guardians and inspectors of the trade and for the statesmen who passed the tariffs and their followers; all the needy and the indolent amongst the middle classes looked to the new services for their sustenance. As commerce dwindled under the burden of inspectors and tariffs and regulations, the demand for revenue increased; till at last the harbours were empty, and the marts inhabited only by the government officers. No politician, however, dared to propose the reduction of this army of idle inspectors.

An ambitious young statesman who could not oust his opponents or get himself into office bethought himself of a new scheme. He knew what it was that had annihilated the commerce; but the electorate would not listen to him if he told them the truth; they thought that it was malignant envy that had driven foreign nations into withdrawing from the ports of the island; how could it be Wotnekstian legislation, when it had all been meant for the good of the human race? But let them go; they could do very well without foreigners. The youth saw it was vain to attempt to persuade them that their own laws and tariffs and inspectors had made commerce impossible; and he turned his attention to a new stepping-stone to power. In their anxiety to please and conciliate the middle classes who had achieved all the recent reforms, statesmen had forgotten the artisans and labourers; and everybody assumed that in passing laws for the benefit of employers, they were conferring benefits on the employees too; their interests were bound together. But this new candidate for power saw that the lion's share went to the middle classes and that the interests of the two divisions of the community were by no means completely identical.

He sent his lieutenants and agents out amongst the workingmen and wooed their confidence by urging their grievances, which they suddenly awoke to find they had. His emissaries made the artisans pick quarrels with their masters, and he stepped in to settle them; but he settled them in such a way that they should be chronic ulcers. He encouraged their discontent and promised them a position in the commonwealth as good as their masters. At intervals the strife he provoked blazed out into open warfare; and he led the crusade. He was execrated by the middle classes; but he did not care for that; for, as soon as he had inspired the mass of the workingmen to act independently of their employers, he knew he would carry the day.

And after ten years of uphill struggle he came out victorious. He had rent the state in two; but he had the larger part behind him; and he took every precaution to bind it to him with all the bonds of self-interest and fear. There followed a long period of legislation in favour of the artisan and labourer. He drew his revenues from a new source, the penalisation of capital. Every man who employed others with profit, or who had any surplus from his earnings, was forced step by step to hand over his profits or his surplus to the state or in the form of wages to the employees. Industry after industry grew waterlogged and sank. All who were thrown out of employment had to be provided for by the state; those vile employers, through hatred of labour, had in their malignity withdrawn their capital from the industries, and many of them had gone abroad with it to escape taxation and the just laws that had been passed to guide them in the employment of their capital.

The new army of government inspectors and employees who had come into being in order to see the labour laws carried out could not be dismissed; and the government had to take over most of the industrial enterprises that had been abandoned. The labourers learned with facility the art of seeming to work when idling; and, as they were the masters through the ballot-box, it was no one's interest to see that they did what they were paid to do. Things drifted from bad to worse; but the statesman put the best face upon them.

Borrowings from abroad at huge rates and crooked accounts concealed the deficit for many years.

At last his rival, a younger and as unscrupulous a politician, advertised the disaster that was about to befall the state, and, though denounced as a liar and slanderer, persuaded half the electorate that he was not far from the truth, especially as the administration was driven to all kinds of dubious shifts to pay their employees; and a considerable section of the labouring class looked to them for work and support. But in the crusade against industrial capital and foreign trade the landlords and mine-owners had been forgotten. Agricultural work and mining had not been to the taste of the Wotnekstians, and they had allowed these employments to drift into the hands of introduced labourers, contracted, or, in other words, enslaved, for a number of years. The owners kept as silent as they could and shut the mouths of their foreign workmen by learning their language and allowing them no opportunity of learning Wotnekstian. It was assumed that they were contented and happy, as no one heard them complain, and all outsiders who could understand them were carefully kept out of their way. They cost little beyond their sustenance to their masters, who avoided any show of the wealth they were laying by, and even kept up the appearance of being poor.

The new candidate for power was an outcast from their ranks, and knew the enormous profits that came to them from their lands and mines. He spoke with authority when he declared that he could pay all the expenses of administration without laying any more burden on the existing taxpayers; he could in fact remove many of their taxes, enrich the state coffers, and give a higher rate of wages to all the employees of the government. His long-successful rival made a bold stroke for the retention of power. He knew that his own special party, the artisans, had the largest families, and had therefore the largest number of women and young men in their ranks; and he brought in a bill extending the suffrage to women and to youths of sixteen years and upwards. His opponent was suspiciously eager to help him in passing it; but he could not draw back; and it became law. The result was a still more overwhelming defeat for him and his followers. His rival had honeycombed the labour party with disloyalty by means of promised bribes.

Then began the new system of taxation, which was to draw all revenues from lands and mines. From time to time the taxes had to be increased in order to fill the gulf that was made by a new addition to the inspectorate. The owners had to resort to a lower and lower stratum of workers, who would work for nothing and whose food would cost less. The proletariate raised a cry against the introduction of such savages; and the artisans and labourers took it up, and insisted on native labour being substituted for the aliens. Stringent laws were passed excluding all aliens from the island; and real poverty began to take the place of seeming poverty amongst the landlords and mine-owners. A few generations of laws against foreigners and of taxation of natural products ruined this milch-cow of the state; and the end was that all lands and all mines had to be taken over from private owners.

Still there were new stepping-stones for youthful ambitions in politics to rise. One who thought that too many years were passing without the due recognition of his genius saw that his only chance lay in an utterly neglected section of the electorate. The paupers and the unimprisoned criminals, though long enfranchised, had been too unimportant to appeal to. But state employment, state doles, and state impecuniosity had by this time pauperised half the population, and the half-developed criminals had begun to recognise in the statesmen and politicians brothers-in-arms, whilst the constant torrent of legislation had induced utter contempt of all laws and made most of the people lawbreakers.

Our young political leader saw his opportunity, and knew that if he propounded a scheme that would appeal to both pauper and criminal he would seduce Wotnekstian human nature and rise into power. He proposed to give a competency to every man and woman above fifty who was poor enough or idle enough to appeal to the state for sustenance or employment. He did not reveal whence he would get his revenues to carry out his scheme, but assured the electorate with great confidence that he would find them. The semi-criminal was astute enough to see that it was out of his quiver that the new scheme must find its weapons. The pauper did not care whence the means came; and the two combined put the budding statesman into office. The financial scheme was of course to take from those who had saved and to give to those who had spent their all or had never earned. Anticipating the effect of his measures, he passed a law prohibiting emigration from the island; and he made the semi-criminal inspectors to see its provisions enforced. In spite of increasing deficits and increasing inability to borrow from the islands around even at exorbitant rates, statesman after statesman climbed to power by reducing the age at which a competency would be granted, and the age at which a boy or girl could begin to claim electoral rights.

Notwithstanding the army of inspectors and the precautions taken, the thrifty section of the people who did not care to abandon work dribbled away one by one clandestinely to neighbouring islands, along with their thrift. The wealthy had taken care to escape long before; and the state bank, which had gradually absorbed all other banks, had begun to feel the limit of its paper. Its chief reserve and plant had been for many years a printing-press. One ambitious youth of meagre intellectual capacity had leapt into power on the preaching of the doctrine that the only essentials of great wealth in a country were a good supply of paper and a good printing-press; the credit of the community did the rest. So thoroughly did the people come to believe in this that the precious metals and the movables of value were allowed to drift out of the island along with the rich or thrifty escapees. They were chary of accepting any piece of government paper in payment for anything they did or sold, and still the people believed in the inexhaustibility of the wealth of the state. Did not the whole of the industries and mines and lands of the island belong to it? Issue of paper followed issue of paper to meet the increasing deficit, each growing of less value and of less acceptance than the last. More than half the population were government inspectors, and the rest were government pensioners; and they had to be paid. At last there was nothing to pay them with but the state bank paper. Then there was indignant protest. Statesman after statesman in whom the electorate trusted to pay them in goods or the cash of other islands was hurled from power. Hundreds of laws were passed asserting the value of the paper money and refixing it at its original face value. Yet neither electors nor politicians would acknowledge the facts of the case, that as long as there was no one to work, there was nothing to be got to pay the inspectors and pensioners. There were the mines and lands as rich as ever they were; but there were none to dig or cultivate them. The alien labourers who used to work them had been thrust out, and the natives had worked in such a way that they did not earn their wages. There were the factories and industries; but they were silent and their buildings were falling into ruin.

Yet the electors were convinced that it was the politicians that were at fault; and the politicians had each his theory, which, if put into practice, he was sure would set everything to rights. Every new statesman had a new panacea, and when it failed to pay the state wages and pensions in goods, down he went. Another statesman rose into power and another political nostrum was tried. Fortunately for us the last favourite theory had been the encouragement of foreigners. A politician had shown that, if commerce were encouraged and aliens invited to settle in their midst, everything would be right again; and his brief term of office covered our compulsory visit to Wotnekst. That he would fail was as certain as that night would follow day. Yet none the less would the whole people believe that salvation was to be found in passing laws; and they would continue to spend their days and their energies in arguing out new political schemes for the return of prosperity, just as they and their ancestors had done for generations. Nature, meanwhile, was kind enough to save them from actual starvation; her wild roots and fruits were free to all, and in ordinary seasons gave them bare subsistence the year round. But when in one of her violent or barren moods she refused them food, then famine and ultimately plague blotted out by the thousand the less vigorous amongst these believers in the omnipotence of legislation. The survivors, as soon as they gathered strength to talk and argue, began to hammer out a new scheme for putting the state and the state bank and the state industries and state lands and mines on a sound footing. If the passing of laws did not bring them prosperity and happiness, then they were certain that nothing would.

Such was the outline that Sneekape gave me of the history and character of the Wotnekstians; but it seemed such a caricature of human nature that I half suspected he was playing off a jest on me. He saw my hesitation and he assured me on oath that he was speaking the truth. His oaths had never impressed me much, and I tell you his story for what it is worth. That a whole people should so insanely believe in the omnipotence of legislation is beyond credit. That a whole people should adopt such foolish schemes, and on their failure continue to forge and put into practice similar schemes would strain the most primitive credulity. But that any nation could bring themselves to think that the encouragement of idleness and unthrift would lead to anything else than leaving them to the mercy of the moods of Nature was indeed a jest too patent to impose on me.

CHAPTER XX
FOOLGAR

THE ADJACENT ISLAND OVER which we had to pass made me almost regret our departure from Wotnekst. It was a low, marshy, rich-soiled island that did not bulk into the appearance of land till we were almost half-way across the straits. A few knolls, like a row of buttons, ran across it and gave it the appearance at first of a thread of minute islets strung rosary fashion. They were each topped with either a house or a group of houses that as we approached stood out amid groves of trees against the sky. A nearer view made the island even picturesque; streams and brooks flashed in and out across the low terraces that, meadowed and treed, broke the slope downwards to the shore.

When we reached the surf, there was no one to be seen; but for the cultivated aspects of the centre, we should have said that the island was uninhabited. We shot through the broken water at the mouth of a stream, and ran up its channel as far as the shallows would permit. We moored our boat and made for a little village that nestled at the foot of one of the hills; but we could not get anyone to speak to us. I thought that they were all deaf, till Sneekape demonstrated the contrary; one to whom we spoke went like the others past us, his nose turned skywards; my companion at once imitated with his tongue the twanging of a bowstring and the whizz and cloop of an arrow that enters wood; the figure first cowered and then ran, and when at a safe distance glanced furtively round.

We left the islander to recover from his fright and turned into what seemed a shop in the long street. Here we experienced wholly different treatment. We made extensive purchases of personal clothing and exchanged our absurd Meddlarian guise for this. Our appearance was now less like that of circus clowns. And something in our gait and manner, something perhaps imperious, changed the sullen irresponsiveness of the shopman into the most obsequious attention. He rubbed his hands and bowed before us and anticipated our every wish. He grew servile and cringing; and Sneekape fooled him to the top of his bent. He got the whole of the goods of the shop turned out upon the tables; he objected to everything, or showed the loftiest contempt for the services and eagerness of the capering, bowing salesman; he ordered this or that in the loudest and vulgarest of tones, and the man danced attendance on him all the more abjectly. I stood by and wondered at the change from the haughty churlishness to the supple servility. It came about after and not before we had made our purchases and donned them. In spite of the trouble that Sneekape had given to the clothier, he bought nothing more, and yet was bowed out of the shop with the most fawning of smiles.

We entered another at the upper end of the street; and our reputation, or rather Sneekape's, had preceded us; for we experienced the same sycophantic court. The attendants bowed us in and offered us seats with bent eyes and gracious smiles. We wished something to eat and drink, and my guide gave his orders with the same insolent parade and pompous voice that he had assumed in the garment store. It was indeed amusing to see how the shopmen bustled about and smirked and bowed to his every command. I knew that there must be another section of the islanders who indulged freely in the manner Sneekape had assumed—loud, overbearing tones, inflated contempt, and supercilious swagger.

I had not long to wait for a specimen. A female islander sailed into the eating-shop with an elevation of her nose and chin that would have annihilated a less impudent man than my fellow-traveller. I sat in my corner and watched. She assumed the most complete oblivion of our existence, although we sat right in front of her. A minute had elapsed before any one of the attendants had perceived her entrance. She answered his eager and servile inquiries as to her wishes by freezing silence; she still held her nose in the air far above mere terrene interests. He offered her a seat, and after a time she bent her rigid frame and majestically rested. He then retired into the background crushed. When she had settled her dress and airs, a trumpet note of the loudest, most contemptuous kind recalled him to her side, and he knelt down before her and apparently begged her pardon and the knowledge of her wishes; she ordered like a drill sergeant. When the food and drink came, there was a comparative lull; nothing but the sound of her instruments and jaws for five minutes.

Sneekape outswaggered her; he paraded with proud strut from side to side of the shop and trumpeted his orders into general space till the whole of the attendants buzzed round him like a swarm of bees, leaving the high-toned engulfer of viands in solitary state. Even the clatter of her plate and spoon seemed to subside. It was as when a rooster in full crow in the middle of the barnyard on a sudden hears another crow more lustily within a few yards of him; with wings depressed and feeble strut he collapses and seeks a safe corner; whilst the partlets range around the newcomer. He knew the human nature he had to deal with, that coarse, swaggering fibre of would-be aristocracies that is on one side bully and on the other craven. There was an almost subdued tone of appeal in the lady's voice when she next addressed the shopman; and she sidled out worsted and crestfallen.

There was a buzz of interest around us as we inquired our way to the main town, and traversed it. The story of Sneekape's lordly airs and voice had preceded us. Great court was paid us by those who were evidently members of the trading class, whilst the labourers assumed a peculiar rigidity of body, their usual method of showing respect to a superior. The few of the lordly class we came across passed us by with a prolonged stare that seemed as if it would investigate the internal machinery of our bodies.

We had not got far into the streets of the town, when an elaborately arrayed flunkey gleaming in purple and gold stopped us with a servile genuflection and besought us in the name of Soma and Sama Deloorna, the latter of whom had met us in the eating-shop, to do them the honour of resting at their house. We had nothing else to do, and Sneekape in his most lordly manner bade the lackey lead the way.

We entered a fortified courtyard, surrounded by low houses, evidently the dwelling-places of the menials of the household. Across it, we reached a showy portal whose doors opened with a suddenness that was overawing. We were bowed in from lackey to lackey through a gloomy and pompous hall, and were at last ushered into a great room that was almost grotesque in its equipment. Everywhere were sculptured or painted forms of men and women in their burial-dress, the ghastly, lustreless gaze of the dead upon their faces. Around each were gathered what were evidently the favourite relics of the original, here a hunting-whip, there the skins or feathers of wild animals, here a skull mounted as a drinking cup, there the mummified feature of some animal or human being. It was a great museum of the dead, perhaps the ancestry of the household. Above each figure was stuck what seemed a heraldic emblem, wreathed in the folds of some white cloth, brocaded with gold; and in front of it what might be a little altar, a shallow cup on it that steamed and smoked with smouldering fragrance.

After a delay of an hour or more our hostess entered with great bustle and retinue. She apologised, so I was afterwards told, for not having shown in the shop the courtesies of Foolgar to so distinguished strangers. It was Sneekape she meant; for she turned to him and bowed and smirked and acted most graciously to him in her majesty. She was not massive; yet the performance was like that of an elephant condescending to a minuet. My companion was equal to the occasion, and trumpeted forth as lordly apologies, bowing as graciously. He began with distant references to his far-back ancestry, astutely introducing some of the most distinguished names of Riallaro; he made large draughts on his imagination, he afterwards acknowledged to me, when he was elevating himself at the expense of the Foolgarians by showing me how he laughed at them. For she too had entered on the imaginative task of out-ancestoring him. The contest was evidently a very keen one; for the two bridled up to new hauteur at intervals. I did not understand the conversation; yet I could see the drift of it in the gestures and interplay of emotion on the faces.

It ended in another victory for my guide, as I could see by the obsequious manner in which she now treated him, in spite of the presence of her menials who had come to announce the approach of her lord. This great red-headed lout bent himself low before each of the funereal figures on the one side of the room as he came up. I afterwards learned that these were his ancestors. Then with a stiff majesty that ill suited his swollen pompous figure he approached us and bowed. He was the coarsest specimen of humanity I had ever seen. If he was proud of his ancestry it was difficult to understand how there could be any reciprocity in the feeling, should their spirits be conscious. He had a huge, ill-cut chasm for a mouth, even larger than Sneekape's, and the thick lips would never fulfil their original purpose of concealing the amorphous, unsightly teeth and the processes of salivation and speech,—two processes that were ever in foamy, spluttering contest. He would insist on stretching the slit to its full elasticity by wearing a sickly, patronising smile; and the rusty-red hair sprawled over various sections of his face, and failed to conceal what it might have concealed with advantage. The sections it left exposed to view were measly with freckles and new artistic patterns in terra-cotta.

Still he held himself with the personal vanity of an Adonis; and it would not be hard to conceive him dying of love of his own reflection, like Narcissus in the myth. Yet he was so substantial that the process would have to be spread over years, if not centuries.

He knew Aleofanian, and he prelected to me with the condescension of a god on the greatness of his ancestors. It was the dreariest infliction I had ever borne; but he would allow no interruption, and with considerable diplomacy he turned the flank of Sneekape's endeavours to try a fall with him. He had me all to himself; whilst his wife abased herself before my companion, he made up for the abasement by a truly pavonine strut and spread of his feathers.

Amongst the few items of fact that floated on the torrent of his imagination were these: the name of the island was, translated, the Land of Lofty Lineage, and there were none amongst them whose ancestry did not trace back to some god; their history covered myriads of centuries; and no race on the face of the earth or even in the heavens above could compare with them in ancientness or nobility; ah, they were the most unfortunate of men, so lonely in their majestic isolation, there being none in the universe with whom they could deal on an equal footing.

The thought took him up into regions whither ordinary mortals evidently could not follow. The gross features were as near transfiguration as they could ever be. I was glad to be ignored or, at least, unaddressed, during his reverie on the solemn grandeur of his solitude in the universe, glad to feel I was too insignificant for his lofty notice. He strutted with a low, cooing chuckle as if he were superintending the hatching of a world.

Sneekape jerked him out of his trance as with a lasso. He used an epithet which, he afterwards told me, implied in these islands the obliteration of ancestry, what would be considered nihilism in Foolgar. It was like a whip-stroke to the bovine frame. He writhed as if stung. His persecutor followed up the interjection with a stream of eulogy of his own ancestors, piling in heroes and gods, till the lineage overshadowed all mortal heraldry. The keeper of the great ancestral museum and saint-shop, in which we were, fell at the feet of his braggart visitor, prostrate. He had been outboasted, and grovelled before this surpassing artist in heraldic imagination and in the vulgarities on which he so prided himself.

He gave us a retinue wherever we went throughout the islands, and fêted us every day, till we grew sick of his unwholesome attentions. He looked as if he would lick the ground over which Sneekape walked. A man with so great a lineage and such lordly airs and voice must be made much of.

Sneekape had still a wicked twinkle in his eye. He gave the gorgeous servants of our host a high-sounding embassy to return with, and then led me away through by-lanes into an unpretentious, if not squalid, section of the town. We stopped before what I would have called an ancient temple; it looked outside as if worn by the weather of centuries, and it was clothed with their filth too. It had upon its pediment a huge inscription in letters of gold, and this, according to Sneekape's interpretation, meant: "Honour thy forefathers; they circulate in thy veins and guide thy life; there is no godhead equal to theirs." A feeling of solemnity crept over me, as we stepped into the antique portico of what was the oldest shrine of ancestry worship in the archipelago. All round there were evidences of primitive customs and relics of olden times; and, in spite of the filth and dust of ages, worshippers in rich robes knelt or moved about with anxious looks upon their faces. I supposed that they were waiting for admission to the inner temple, though they had a skulking gait, seemed to try to avoid recognition, and had their hoods drawn over their faces. Every few minutes men with villainous low brows, whom I took from their official robes to be attendant priests, came out of the great folding-doors and had conference with one or other of the hooded figures in confidential whispers.

My curiosity was deeply excited; for the service was evidently proceeding; even in the street as I approached the building I could hear the hubbub of adoration, and when the door opened the babel of voices suppliant or hortative burst upon our ears in deafening tumult. Sneekape approached an attendant and after much haggling, during which I saw several times the half-concealed passage of coin from palm to palm, he seemed to succeed in his requests. We were soon threading our way along devious and dark passages; I stumbled frequently; but, after escaping many risks of accident, we found ourselves again outside of a door that smothered the devotional riot within; and in another moment we had plunged into the tempestuous ocean of devotees.

It was some time before I collected my wits sufficiently to observe the centre of the scene; it was a huge priest in official robes standing in a raised pulpit with two subordinates seated beside him writing in books and a bevy of acolytes buzzing hither and thither around the dais. He was shouting almost continuously with stentorian lungs that must have needed the full capacity of his huge chest to contain. He had a hammer in his hand and with this he pointed in various directions throughout the congregation as he exhorted or chided, besought or encouraged; and ever and anon a sounding blow of the mallet on his desk would still the babel for a moment, while the buzzing acolytes rushed hither and thither bearing new documents or inscriptions that were evidently portions of the sacred writings.

I looked round at the sea of faces upturned in worship, and I thought I had never seen such a villainous collection outside of a criminal court. It was little wonder that the priest had to exert himself so frantically, if he were to make any religious impression on such a crowd. Their countenances belied them if they did not stand sorely in need of his exhortations. The officiant was now ready with another portion of scripture, an inordinately long scroll; and around in niches behind him had been placed by the acolytes a row of mild-faced images that I took to be a collection of minor deities, evidently of one family; for there was a strong likeness in the countenances of all of them. Again the tumult of devotion rose; I felt scared by its importunacy and reflected that no god would dare to disregard such a deafening invocation; but the priest's voice rose above it like thunder in a tempest. He appealed to them in bovine tones and with postulant gestures; he exhibited his script and read portions aloud for their benefit; he turned back to the images and seemed to laud them to heaven; and ever and again he jerked out some appeal to the assembly, gesturing wildly with his mallet; and responses to his litany came now from one worshipper and now from another. As the scene proceeded, the service seemed to narrow itself to three officiants, the priest in his pulpit and two somewhat lordly-looking worshippers, whose faces I could not at first see. The interchange of appeal and reply was like a fusilade, so rapid and sharp was it; and ever and anon the acolytes held up an image, or raised the long strip of manuscript in the air. The suppressed excitement in the assembly grew intense. Not a sound was heard but the voices of the three officiants, that of the priest in the pulpit predominating.

A crisis was evidently approaching, the threefold litany crackling out upon the blank silence like thunder on the depth of midnight. I was conjecturing what would be the climax, when the mallet rapped with a sharp click on the desk, and the acolytes bore off the images and the manuscript. One of the response-givers turned around and his face was dark and troubled as a tumultuous sea under the shadow of a cloud. With excited gestures and rising intonations the worshippers bustled out; a fierce quarrel was manifestly on foot, there being, I could see, two contending sects present; face turned to face with darkening scowl and arrested threat. Religious fervour had changed into virulent bigotry; and the narrow space within the temple seemed to accentuate the suppressed volcanic fire, to judge by the fierce, dark faces all hieroglyphed by the passions of a murderous past; there was bloodshed in store for the two divisions of the church. We did not follow them; but before long we could hear in the neighbourhood the furious cries of a sanguinary contest with a fringe of feminine wailing and screeching.

Sneekape drew me aside, and, when the crowd had thinned off, we went into what seemed a huge warehouse in the rear of the temple. Here were great rows of images and countless rolls of manuscript; and the attendants were taking from the hands of hooded figures other images and rolls. My guide took me into a still corner, and told me that this was a pedigree pawnshop we had entered, and that the scene we had just witnessed was an auction of ancestors. The great temple of ancestral worship had been poverty-stricken till it had recognised the signs of the times and ceased to prohibit with its ban the secret but long-established traffic in lineage throughout the island and archipelago. The ever-progressive extravagance and impoverishment of old families had led to its necessary consequence, an ancestry exchange, where for a consideration a new favourite of fortune could acquire an ancestry with its good name and titles and its resultant social position and prestige. It is true the commodity was encumbered with a few stones of human flesh in the shape of a daughter of the family whom the newly enriched or his son had to marry, or in the shape of a son to whom he had to give his daughter in marriage; but there was discount for that, and he could soon get clear of the encumbrance by divorcing it to some other island. There was generally a higgling of the market according as there was more supply or more demand all over the archipelago. The mothers and fathers of the old families prided themselves on their bargaining skill; they drew from the aspirant the more coin, the more they disparaged himself and his forefather; if they could make him out a blackguard, so much the better bargain could they drive. Most romantic stories were told of great fortunes being made out of such a sale through the employment of detectives, who found out the scoundrelism of the buyer's past.

The church had for centuries considered the traffic as a desecration of the ancestral worship that it cherished, and frowned upon it; and the consequence was that it was itself sunk in poverty and neglect. But a generation before, a great ecclesiastical genius arose, who saw the possibilities of the practice, and blessed it instead of cursing it. He organised it into a regular business over which the priests presided. He established the famous ancestral pawnshop behind the ancient temple and extended its operations through the whole archipelago. At first the priests kept the commerce semi-private so as to save the feelings of the old families; but most of these latter had no compunctions about the haggling for a price and pressed the church officials more and more eagerly and openly to make a good bargain for them. After a time the business became so large and open that an auction was established in the temple; and bidders gathered from all parts of the archipelago. The growth of commerce and the rise of new families to wealth at first overtook the supply and then out distanced it. An old family name and pedigree was one of the dearest of commodities and re-enriched impoverished households. Still some of them shrank from the publicity of the auction and pawnshop of ancestry and came thither with their proposals hooded and unrecognisable. The church and then the individual priests grew rapidly in wealth; and their increasing taste for luxury demanded larger and still larger income. They established agencies in the other islands, and at last, to meet the demand, set up a great pedigree factory.

Our next visit was to this. One department of it printed off the long strips of parchment with fictitious records of lineage, the earlier part of it in ancient letters and language and stained with the marks of age. Another department manufactured images, and artistically chipped, cracked, and sullied them into true relics of antiquity. It was indeed difficult to distinguish the old models from the new imitations; and I was not surprised to hear that the buyers of the brand-new pedigrees held their heads as high as those who had to pay ten times as much for a well-known ancestry and titles. The priests alone knew the difference, and it was their interest to keep it secret, and preserve the skill in distinguishing true from false as a trade mystery. Sneekape told me afterwards that it was the rarest of all privileges to get admission to the factory of lineage. He had great personal influence with one of the chief priests and considerable pecuniary influence over the subordinates. We were both sworn to secrecy over the sacred writings and by ceremonies that were meant to overawe us. I cannot say that I felt much inclined to reveal anything I saw, so ordinary did it seem to me.

What impressed me most deeply was the auction in the temple. I had never encountered any instance so bold and unconcealing of a practice, common to all peoples, yet usually hidden under a thousand different fine names and subterfuges. The scene engraved itself upon my memory, the priestly auctioneer crying up his goods, and the wild, dark-faced assembly of bidders, loudly competitive. I was soon led to understand that it had been an auction to be remembered even by a people accustomed to such scenes. The ancestry had been that of one of the most famous families in the archipelago, a family of statesmen, reformers, divines, and philanthropists, once of enormous wealth, now reduced to what was comparative poverty in that age of luxury. There was attached to the title and lineage the condition that the purchaser should marry the only female representative, a beautiful and gentle-hearted young girl; and the condition had this time given enhanced value to the pedigree. It drew bidders from all portions of the archipelago; but amongst them it soon came to be generally whispered about that no one had any chance against two notorious corsairs of Broolyi, who had lately retired from the overt pursuit of their profession with huge fortunes and bought great estates and castles in the island. The hooded figures in the portico had been the sellers hovering about, awaiting the result. At first the other bidders kept up the running; but the price soon overleapt the resources of all but the two pirates, who had each a force of his old sailors and followers ready to carry out what his purse might not be able to do. I had seen the conclusion of the matter as far as the temple was concerned; but the true conclusion had to be reached by the aid of knives in the open air. I protested against the fate of the young lady, who would have to pass her life with her piratical purchaser; but Sneekape and his friends on the islands only laughed at such a mistaken view of a provision of nature. Krokya (the successful corsair) had paid his full price; never had any lot had such a good market; the old family was set on its legs again; the girl was supremely happy; for she would have everything that money could purchase; and her husband, though he still had interests in several piratical craft that were doing a handsome business in the archipelago, had thoroughly reformed, and, having settled down to the life of a respectable citizen, was worthy of the best pedigree he could purchase. He would now move about with his head high in the most aristocratic circles of the best islands, and where could any girl find a better match? Her people, it seems, held high festival over the result of the auction; for, although they had bartered away the good name of the family, they had restored its fortunes. What nobler thing could religion have done for ancestors than to provide them with an organised and respectable means of raising the family out of the slough of poverty and misfortune, and attaching themselves to a new and successful family? The church had shown itself a true philanthropist in thus acting as intermediary between ancestried poverty and ignoble wealth.

After this explanation and defence of the system, I was anxious to return to the temple and watch another auction; and as a large number of small pedigrees were to be sold, the scene was sure to be interesting and varied. To me it was from one point ludicrous, from another sad. The officiant priest, evidently using phrases that he had used thousands of times before, stirred the competitive eagerness of the audience. "Here we have one of the finest commodities I have ever submitted in this temple; look at the length of the pedigree; roll it out before the gentlemen; show them the great names that occur in it; call out the lateral connections of the family with the greatest families of the archipelago. Now, gentlemen, let us have a bid; the opportunity will never recur; I have clients behind here in the pignorative warehouse who have been pressing me to submit it to private sale; why, I could have sold it twenty times over since the family put it into my hands; but I determined that the public, my old and faithful clients, should have the first offer. A hundred pounds! Come, come, you are joking. Let us begin with two hundred. You think this is a pedigree from the isle of socialists. I tell you it is from the greatest country in the archipelago, from Aleofane. Now look at the images of the ancestors. Here is one who alone is worth the money. He has got the lineaments of a god, and his life is written in the annals of the country. Just hold up this image to the gentlemen. This, you can see, is the face of a philosopher, thought in his every wrinkle, wisdom in the stoop of his shoulders, lofty meditation in the gaze of his brooding eyes. Pass on to the next in the row; who cannot see in his bold front, stern mouth and chin, and high cheek-bones the lines of a successful warrior? Victory is written over his face and mien; and, if you look into the features, you will see in the scars upon his face the map of his innumerable battlefields. Now, gentlemen, you can never be ashamed of a lineage like this. What! Only ten pounds more! No, no; I must have twenty-pound bids. And the lady who owns this lineage is a goddess in beauty and gait. Why, if I were not so old, I would unfrock me of my priesthood, and bid for the pedigree myself, so fair and so divine is she. No, no, it would be sacrilege to let it go for such a paltry sum." I could make out some of this now from his gestures, aided by my knowledge of the temple and its trade; and Sneekape eked out my conjectures by his running translation. The pedigree was knocked down for coin equivalent to our thousand pounds to a chimney-sweep who had made a fortune by extracting some valuable chemical from the soot. Now that he had a pedigree and an estate, he became a transmuter of fire-products, and he afterwards moved in the best social circles of the archipelago. My guide slily drew me up towards the images and manuscript as they passed out, and showed me that they had been amongst the most recent production of the factory. Where the priests got the divine lady attached to them, he said he could not explain. Perhaps this was their method of disposing of undowried, unancestored girls. It revealed at least the source of the vast and increasing wealth of the temple.

Up till this experience of mine, I had thought that they had no public religion; each household, it had seemed to me at first, had its own, and worshipped its ancestors with the usual outward devotion and inward freedom. They cared little for the character of those they worshipped, whether good or bad, and called only that divine in them which fitted their own desires and passions. There were amongst them all the evils of inbreeding, intensified by its being in the sphere of religion; they were tortured with morbidity and other diseases of the spirit, such as a sort of moral epilepsy, and spiritual anæmia. The worst malady amongst them was that which made them seem insane to the other inhabitants of the archipelago,—intellectual wry-neck and tip-nose; they could never look at any thing or person without getting their perspective twisted by a vision false or true of some far-back past; they were ever craning their necks back to an ancestry generally fictitious, or lifting their noses high above someone who did not trouble himself about whether he had any or not.

My guide had neither the conscience nor the honour to feel any scruples about taking advantage of their weakness. He trumpeted and strutted in a more and more lordly and vulgar way, till the Foolgarians, armoured though they were in genealogies that reached farther back than the creation, licked the dust off his feet. If they had not been such mean bullies and parasites themselves, I should have been sorry for them, so heartlessly did he trample upon their most sacred treasures and feelings. His ancestral references were as fictitious as most of theirs; but they were magnificent lies, brazened out irrespective of human weaknesses. Poor, lank body though he had, he managed to give it an appearance of volume by bulging his chest and raising his nose in the air and stamping his feet on the ground; and by some means I never discovered he changed his low nasal voice into a bovine trumpet-note, with which he outbullied the loudest lineage braggartry of the Foolgarians. The meaner side of human nature was gratified to see these pompous pretenders and bullies biting the dust before one of their own kin and revealing so plainly how natural to them was the other side of their nature, cowardice and fawning. He was their supreme god for a day or two.

Yet he knew that the charm would not work long, and that, when they discovered how like he was to themselves as an artist in genealogical fiction, they would turn and rend him. He chose the very top of the wave of devotion, and we made a triumphal exit, our canoe full of all manner of dainties and luxurious foods. To the last they kept their cringing attitude. Long after we had shot over the bar and put to sea, we could discern their bodies bending to the ground as in an act of worship.

Sneekape laughed loud, when we had got out of earshot and eyeshot. I did not join in the outburst; the spirit of coarse mockery and triumph by means of deceit was even worse than the mixture of bullying and grovelling we had just seen. He was evidently much surprised and tried to explain the jest to me. He said that these islanders were the butt of the archipelago; the meanest laughed at them for the lordly airs they assumed, and when his people were in lack of a good laugh or jest, they organised an expedition to Foolgar, taking with them some comedian, who would by his outlording their lordliness bring all to the dust-kissing stage of fawning. It was the happy hunting-ground of practical jokers, and they seldom failed to raise some good game, so mad were the islanders with the itch for ancestry. The usual translation of its name throughout the archipelago was the Isle of Snobs.

CHAPTER XXI
AWDYOO

HE SAW AT LAST that I had little sympathy with the part he had assumed; and with a wily insight and versatility he snaked himself round into a confidential conversation on our next step. He told me that he was glad we had come off so well-laden with provisions; for he wished to avoid the next islet in the chain, Awdyoo, or the isle of journalism; it was the foulest place on the earth, and no one ever landed there who could avoid it.

It was the quarantine station, whither all the scribo-maniacs were deported. Every island but Aleofane had used it as an asylum for those who were afflicted with the desire to address their neighbours in writing or type concerning their neighbours' affairs and characters. In Aleofane the government controlled and utilised the morbid state of mind for the advantage of the governors. In other islands it was lamented and guarded against as one of the foulest of contagious diseases; once it had taken root in a community, they knew there was no eradicating it except by the most wholesale exile. It generally caught the meanest and most malignant natures, too, and turned them into moral sewers. They would not let the affairs of their neighbours alone, and stirred up every mud pool until it became offensive; and, when they could not find anything in the shape of scandal or foible or quarrel, they had to manufacture; so they filled the citizens' minds with lies about each other, and with cues of attack or offence. They fomented bad blood, and infected the whole community with every spiritual disease that could possibly approach it. There was no lunacy that Riallaro so greatly feared as that of journalism, it was so disgusting and so swiftly spreading an epidemic of the mind. Every man who was touched with it came to fancy himself absolved from all laws of courtesy, honour, and morality; he assumed that he was practically omniscient, and whosoever dared to question this assumption had to be pursued to the death with his most envenomed and deadliest weapons, malice, slander, ridicule, misrepresentation, impudence, lies. They had all agreed at a conference many centuries before that there were no such dangerous madmen, and that their mental disease spread more quickly than a plague. They had therefore fixed on Awdyoo, one of the most isolated of the islets, as the hospital for this epidemic; and whoever showed any symptoms of it in any island was deported thither.

The place had become a complete pandemonium in these centuries. The inhabitants had substituted physical means of attack for their old spiritual weapons, for every one of them had grown so thick-hided from perpetual attack of the others that the foulest charges fell lightly on them. They laughed to scorn the most irritating slanders and lies and banter and mimicry, the favourite methods of their journalism. So, to relieve their feelings, they had to translate their moral and intellectual warfare into physical. And the weapons they used were the physical equivalents of their old journalistic methods of attack; they had great air-guns, from which they shot various mixtures more or less glutinous; if they found someone they wished to parasite, it was butter; if they had a rival or neighbour to quarrel with and blacken, it was ink; other preparations were paste variously coloured and stench-generative, filth highly granulated with pebbles, and the extract of cuttlefish mingled with the poisons of various plants and animals. Their missiles were not absolutely lethal; they were only noisome and inconvenient until washed off. They were made into minute pellets with a hard gelatine shell, so that they made no commotion in the olfactory nerves till broken. Even those they wished to honour were incommoded by the streams of butter that soon streaked their clothes and face. Honour, flattery, from them was almost as little desired as their hostile attacks; and it was one of the islands which no one visited unless under a stern sense of duty or the incitement of some heroic mood or from accident. Yet they were thoroughly convinced that they were the arbiters of all reputation in the world. If they laughed, mankind trembled and were sick. If they threatened, the orb shook. If they approved, posterity accepted their verdict and threw up their caps in applause. A nod or a frown from them had as great effect as a thunder-storm or an earthquake. Their fiat was immortal, even though they should immediately contradict it, as they generally did. Their respect for principles and facts and truths continued as long as these continued to support their conclusions and beliefs; and then the alliance was broken; they considered that no loyalty was due to things that were disloyal; it was a case, then, of internecine warfare; veiled in great professions of respect and devotion for the enemy, if only it would cease to be hostile. Their treatment of persons was based on the same ideal of rights; omnipotence was not to be trifled with; omniscience was not to be questioned.

What was their religion? It was the Veiled Ego. They believed that the only true way of making divine was by mystification. Hide the average personality under namelessness and mystery, and you give it the attributes of godhead; its utterances, however feeble, gather strength from the secrecy of their source, and seem to come from the mouth, if not from the heart, of mankind. The primary article of their creed was this: a voice from behind any veil, however tawdry or foul, becomes the voice of the people; and the voice of the people is the voice of God. Every man of them, therefore, had become a god; and it was his object to bring the rest of the world to worship at his shrine, or sheet, behind which he ever concealed himself. He believed it was only a matter of time, when the whole universe would fall at his feet. Meantime his fellows on his own island had to be subdued to the true faith; and his whole time was spent in warfare and the invention of new forms of attack, especially of ambush. He was filled with complete faith in the righteousness and ultimate triumph of his cause, and was ever asserting that truth will prevail, at the very moment that he was manufacturing fiction and stench pellets for the conversion of his neighbours and the salvation of their souls. By truth he meant his own deliverances. For the gist of his creed was this: "There is no god but I, veiled under We, the essence and sum of all created beings; and I, veiled under We, is his prophet."

I had become so deeply interested in his account of Awdyoo, and he in his narrative, that we had not noticed a dark band round the horizon broaden and gradually obliterate the islets. A cold effluence from it had crept over us to the effacement of our compass and landmarks. The mist soon closed and shut out the sun and sky, and then we knew not where we were or whither we headed. We dared not move lest we should drift far from both land and our course. We had only to throw ourselves passively into the bottom of the canoe and await a change. Sneekape was evidently much moved, and did not add to my cheerfulness by telling me that these mists were frequent and long around Awdyoo; and that they were brought about by the everlasting hail of gelatinous missiles that rayed forth stench when burst.

Two nights fell upon us starless, like the walls of a prison, and still the mist rose not. Our provisions would not last many days; but we felt that the boat and the sea were drifting under us, or that the mist was floating swiftly over us. It must have been about midday, when my companion started from his prostrate position, and put his hand to his nose. "It's Awdyoo," he exclaimed with bated breath. He knew it by the indescribable medley of smells that floated over the islet as from a thousand chemical factories, and he fancied that their repertory of missiles must have greatly enlarged since his last approach to it. There was a new variety in the fetid redolence of the atmosphere. If all the putrescent waters and heaps of the world, all its assafœtida and noisome plants, and all its polecats and skunks, had been gathered into one centre, and all the exhalations from them turned into one nozzle, the result would have been aromatic and balmy beside this mephitic stench. It was not alone the nose that it invaded, but every sense and pore of the body; the whole of our human system seemed to be mastered by the olfactory section of it. We longed for one sniff even of the crater of Klimarol.

Gradually the sense of smell got partially paralysed, and a smart grating sound shivering through the framework of our canoe recalled our mental force to eyes and ears. The current was bearing us over a sand-bank, and we could see a dim, low line as of land beyond. We rose in frenzy to our oars, and pushed off; and the current bore us past several tongues of land, and then, it seemed, out into deep water. We spent hours in the struggle before it succeeded. Happily the veil was close drawn over the whole scene. But it was now near noon, and the strength of the midday sun began to penetrate the thick gossamer of floating moisture. In a brief time the whole pall lifted, and we saw the island lying at a safe distance, yet near enough to show us the inhabitants and their occupations. It looked as if they had all hung out a very dirty washing to dry; for there flapped in the light wind, that had rent the veil of mist, hundreds of long sheets that had once been white. Out from behind them peeped the nozzles of air-guns and of men and women, and back and forward darted various forms of familiar animals, whose appropriate noises we could still hear in the distance. My companion explained, with a smile at my mistaken conjecture, that these sheets were their entrenchments, behind which they were nameless and secret, that on them they printed threats and challenges and abuse for the benefit of rivals and enemies; and when anyone approached they poured forth a shower of stench pellets upon him, or chased him in the disguise of some animal.

One by one they saw us; and a howl of execration rose from them and gathered force as they collected into a crowd. There was evidently great excitement; we had still one long spur of land to pass, though happily at a distance. They galloped with all their following and their artillery towards it. It was a narrow escape for us. We had just shot past it into deeper water, when they arrived at its point and set their guns in order. The pellets fell short; but as they struck the water they broke and infected the air with putrescence. One unfortunately touched the gunnel and bespattered Sneekape; and he acknowledged that they must have invented some new odours surpassing for their strength and noisomeness. Yet, as the current and wind drifted us out of the reach of the raining stenches, it was almost a pleasure to have only the offensive fetor of my companion's hair and clothes near me. We lowered the islet into a thin line by distance; then we could see them scatter like insects to their various sheets; and night sheltered us soon with its cool neutrality of perfume. My odorous mate had dipped himself again and again into the sea and wrung himself out, till at last only a faint reminiscence of the polecat hung about him. It was faint enough to let me listen to his diverting chatter as we drifted. He assured me that the current would bear us of itself to the next islet in the chain.

CHAPTER XXII
JABBEROO

BETWEEN IT AND AWDYOO, but farther to the north than the current was likely to carry us, lay a group of islands that Sneekape declared would have been as good as a play to see. He entertained me with an account of them as we drew away from the odours of Awdyoo. I listened with reserve of judgment; for his story, as usual, sounded like fiction; and I had no means of testing it. It was interesting enough, and drew my mental energy from my nose to my ears. I knew afterwards that there was a good deal of truth at the basis of it, even though the tricky, airy manner made me doubt the whole of it. The nearest of the group to Awdyoo was called Jabberoo, and seemed to be the inferno of talkers. Hither were banished all who had become insufferable for their loquacity. For a time it was said to have been the silentest island in the archipelago, such an effect had the encagement of so many praters in one place upon the disposition of each. They had all been so enamoured of the sound of their own voices that they could not bear to hear anyone else speak; that was the disease for which they had been quarantined; and it looked as if this drastic step of exile was about to be an effectual cure of it. Once the patients from the different islands realised that Jabberoo was nothing but a huge garrulity hospital, they howled with rage and found a certain distraction in airing their grievance to one another. Each tested the listening power of every other inhabitant of the island, and, finding that it was no greater than his own, settled down into sullen taciturnity. Not even the variety of dialects in which they spoke gave them any consolation; the babel only intensified their horror and disgust at being cooped up with men and women as passionately fond of babble as they were. Every talk they started became almost at once a competitive duologue; the two voices rose into a shout that made hearing the words an impossibility. Not one of them could bear to see his neighbour begin to talk; he knew he could not get a word in except by main force of lung, and he dared not risk the torrent of babble. The first few days on land left them hoarse and exhausted; and thereafter they muzzled their passion and went about mute as fish. Mariners and boatmen avoided the shores of the island after a time; for those that landed at first were almost torn to pieces by the

Jabberoon mob, each eager to secure a good listener; and even if any arrival had the good fortune to meet only one Jabbaroon and be monopolised by him in secret, he was glad to make his escape, lest he should turn into a pillar of salt under the infliction of fluency; the only successful means of flight was to bear the torrent till the darkness of night, slip out of his upper garments which his buttonholer held, and leave in his place a wooden substitute. The sullen silence had been no cure of the disease after all.

A benevolent Swoonarian took pity on the wretched islanders and invented an automatic listener. But, like all the inventions of his people, it came to nothing. In theory it seemed as if it would work. He made a figure in human form with a sensitive word-repeater inside it that at certain sounds could by internal mechanism set it swaying and gesticulating, as if in high nervous excitement. It could be wound up for a whole day, or in some of the more expensive specimens even for a whole week. As it heaved and swung about, one would have said that it was a real, human listener moved by the eloquence of a speaker; but the shipment failed. Superior though the automatic audience was to most human beings in responsiveness and emotional endurance, something was wanting; the look of suppressed despair on the face, the irritable attempts at interjection, and the unavailing efforts to escape. The inventor intended, if this venture had succeeded, to add those movements to his figures; but unfortunately the first purchasers lost their tempers over the monotonous acceptance of all they said and the repetition of the gestures and attitudes as they repeated their favourite phrases; they grew frantic with rage and smashed the whole consignment to pieces.

It looked, indeed, at one time as if the community of Jabberoons would go furiously mad for want of good listeners, and commit suicide in a body; but a missionary arrived from a neighbouring island, called Tubberythumpia, or the island of demagogues; and though his sufferings often rose to torture at first, he knew from experience in his own land how to endure them. In the end he conquered; he was able to get a word in now and again; and this occasional word won its way by slow degrees into the brains of the Jabberoons and bore fruit. They listened to the gospel of the newcomer once a week or so, and resolved to adopt the new evangel of alternation of eloquence. They organised themselves into councils, assemblies, senates, conferences, synods, mob meetings, boards, election meetings, parliaments, cabinets, conclaves, chambers, convocations, congresses, consistories, diets, juntas, comitias, directories, commissions, sanhedrims, and committees, so that every man and woman was a member of forty or fifty of these bodies and could attend the meetings of two or three dozen of them every day. They adopted it as a basis of their new constitution that only one was to speak at once in any sitting, and, whenever two began to speak together, it was thereby dissolved. It is quite true that there were dissolutions every hour of the day; but some speaker had had his say out, and those who were disappointed in getting an escape-valve for their tongue energy had plenty of other meetings to attend, where they might have a chance of evacuating their own particular section of the dictionary.

The plan was a miraculous success for a time. It saved the Jabberoons from universal frenzy and suicide. Every one of them was able to get off half a dozen eloquent speeches every day to an audience more or less unwilling, but that had by the constitution of the country to listen; and it was easier for them to keep the mouth shut when they knew that they too would have their chance before long. They worked just enough to keep the wolf from the door; and then all the rest of the time was given up to those delightful meetings and conferences, where each felt that he could make others hear the sweet sound of his voice. They never settled anything of any importance to anybody; but they felt that the existence of the universe depended on their oratory. To satisfy themselves they discussed every possible topic that had occurred or could ever occur to any human mind, and they passed resolutions upon it to send on to other meetings and conferences and assemblies. By the time these resolutions had got through the various bodies and come back to the originators, they had become so transformed as to be unrecognisable, and so bewildering in their labyrinth of clauses and amendments as to be beyond human intelligence; but they were recommitted and recreated and again sent on their career of transformation. They kept the jaws working and the tongues wagging. And every ambiguity introduced served the same national and benign purpose.

With all this development of eloquence and elaboration of counsel, it might have been expected that Jabberoo was the best governed country in the world. Every citizen worked the clack-mill night and day for the good government and guidance of every other citizen. Nothing could surpass the earnestness and enthusiasm of the whole community in pounding out the arguments for and against every possible course that any member or section of it might take in life. They were in danger of starving, so busy were they in deliberation over the questions, how every man should earn his food, how he should cook his food, how he should eat it, and how he should dispose of his surplus. They had not time to drink, so strenuous in their tongue exertions were they over what to drink and what not to drink. They left their children to run naked, and their own clothes to fall into rags, whilst they discussed the best kind of cloth for different weathers and climates, and the best form of garments for various ages, and the best way of wearing garments. No people in the world had ever held so many deliberations and consultations, or ever spent so much eloquence and wisdom over the proper way of bringing up a family; meantime every family was allowed to tumble up in the best way it could, till the momentous questions were settled. Never was there a nation that so strove to get at the highest ideal of government as the Jabberoons did in meeting and conference and assembly; and never was there a nation so devoid of all pure government or even co-operation for their own internal administration or their defence. There was nothing they would not do in their speeches on behalf of their country, so fiery were they in their patriotism; but when a pirate landed with a small boatload of men, there was not a Jabberoon to be seen within shooting distance, and once, when a mad dog was let loose on the beach, the silence and solitude of the island could be felt.

For himself, Sneekape asserted that, if the Jabberoo women were worth a thought, he would land and walk off with the whole of them; but they had such predominant and huge mouths and such pestilential tongues that no ordinary human nature could endure them. Their recent developments under the Tubbery-thumpian missionary had made their shores safe for strangers to visit; but for his part he would keep at a safe distance from such a nation of magpies. He could not endure the endless chatter of a prating, gossipy woman. He preferred her with a good stormy channel between him and her.

The latest development of their commonweal had again made landing dangerous. Their tongue-courage had grown too mild for the expression of all they felt. Argument and eloquence had given way to vituperation and insult, and their meetings now generally ended in free fights. Scratched noses and cracked crowns had become the natural accompaniment of political fervour.

CHAPTER XXIII
VULPIA

THE ONLY CHANCE OF restraining and correcting these furious scenes of debate, and preventing them from ending in complete annihilation of the Jabberoons, was to turn the inhabitants of a neighbouring island loose upon them. These were the Vulpians, exiles from the rest of the archipelago for over-astuteness in diplomacy. They were hated by the Jabberoons as the most deadly enemies they could encounter; for they exploited their loquacious neighbours in the most heartless and shameless way. For years they had been almost enraged at the simplicity with which these orators fell into their snares. They would go over in troops, and each fleece his man of all his goods, if not of his wife and daughters, without making him feel anything but gratitude at his friendship and patronage. Time after time these expeditions had gone unsuspected. These wily flatterers would insinuate themselves into the good-will of the Jabberoons and leave them naked, and yet with the sense of having received unmeasured favours and advantages. They fooled their victims to the top of their bent, applauding their feeblest gabble as matchless eloquence and persuading them by their attitude of admiration and their ambiguous phrases that they had only to go out into the world to have it at their feet. They had but to listen in silence or with an occasional cunning question or implication of reverence and enjoyment in order to get the orators to accede to all their requests or desires.

The game was laughably simple and unworthy of the great powers of the Vulpians. But, as years went on, a sense of being cheated of what they had earned by hard and repulsive work grew in the minds of the Jabberoons underneath the soothing flattery. They became uneasy and timid at first, and afterwards furiously hostile to Vulpian approaches. Though they were passionate for listeners and for flattering applause, whether loud or silent, they rose in a body whenever they saw a Vulpian expedition near their shores. Nothing so united them or so froze them into taciturnity and action as the appearance of boats from the neighbouring isle. Yet they were exploited and fleeced as much as they had been willing to be before. A stranger would land on the opposite side of Jabberoo, and rouse them into still greater fury against the Vulpians; he would head them in their attack on the expedition. In the enthusiasm of victory he would persuade them to provision their own fleet and sail out to the conquest of the other islands of the archipelago. As a preliminary they made first for Vulpia, which, they were convinced, would fall an easy prey to their prowess. It ended in their tumbling into the trap laid for them. Their fleet was piloted on to shallows, where it had to be abandoned, and their enemies kindly ferried them back to their homes. The supplies for the long voyage of conquest were secured by the Vulpians; and their temporary leader vanished, no one knew whither.

That was one of the Vulpian methods of warfare; but they had the astuteness never to use any one too often; and, as the Jabberoons began to feel dupe written broadly over their natures, their neighbours had to exercise to the full their mania for diplomacy. Their schemes for deceiving them were absurdly labyrinthine, till at last even the simplest of the Jabberoons could entangle them in their own deceits. They generally aimed so far ahead of their machinery that it was the easiest thing in the world to cut the connection and bring the scheme to naught; in fact, so far-seeing in their diplomacy did they become that the mere development of events often destroyed the interest in their aim.

Amongst themselves the Vulpians had long ago reached this point. They were so astute and so elaborate and far-seeing in their schemes for attaining even the most trivial object in life that they ceased to vex themselves about the lives of each other. No one ever thought of finding out the purpose of his neighbour's moling and undermining. They grew weary of the effort after so often discovering the paltry nothing that lay at the end of the machinations. They took it as their own natural habit of mind to follow out their aim by many a circumflexion and twist. At last, if a Vulpian wished to cheat his fellows he adopted the simplest and most direct way of getting at his object; and he had reached it whilst they were fumbling in the dark and floundering in a slough of conjecture and far-reaching guess. It came about that these born diplomatists acquired in dealing with one another the direct and simple methods of the most ingenuous people. The homœopathic cure of lunacy and eccentricity adopted by the archipelago worked its usual miracle. The caging of men of the same weakness or vice made them sick of it and resort to its opposite. It was only against a people who were off their guard that their old diplomacy became a passion in them again.

And Vulpia was one of the favourite hunting-grounds of the wags of the archipelago. They delighted in sending this nation of cunning diplomatists on a wrong scent or on a track that would lead them into a ridiculous position or in pursuit of something they detested. There was nothing in the world that so pleased the youths of the neighbouring island of Witlingen.

CHAPTER XXIV
WITLINGEN AND ADJACENT ISLANDS

THE ADJACENCY OF VULPIA was the only thing that saved the inhabitants of Witlingen from stark madness. They organised raids upon its shores in order to let off the accumulated wit of the weeks or months in which they had had to repress it. They could all join patriotically in such an expedition against the common enemies, the human foxes and tedium. For weeks they enjoyed the elaborate preparation for the brand-new practical jokelet; whilst its success-ful consummation saved their reason and gave them laughter for months.

At other times Witlingen was a hell upon earth for them. Here were they gathered together, the professional joculasters of the archipelago, exiled from their favourite hunting-grounds and condemned to the company of the men whom they detested most in the world. It was indeed the most lugubrious of the islands. Everyone knew as thoroughly as his own all the jests of the rest of his fellow-islanders. They had repeated them or heard them repeated till they fled from them like a plague. They knew the whole gamut through which human wit could play, and smiled dismally and sceptically at the idea of a new joke; they had gone back through the jest-books of past times, and seen how every age had merely revamped jests that must have been prehistoric. They were quite convinced (and so had been the fatherland of each before exiling him) that in no realm of human industry was there so close an approach to the automatic. And a Swoonarian, it was said, had once invented a human automaton that could supply any one of all the witticisms that the human brain had been able to hit upon, with a subsidiary movement for adapting it to the circumstances or dialect of any island. The Witlingenites were so enraged at his offer to equip the government of every country with as many as they needed at small cost that they waylaid the ships that carried them and sank them with their cargoes.

Theirs was one of the islands for the wayfarer to avoid; for on landing he was liable to be mobbed, every Witlingenite rushing to secure him for an audience, and if by any chance he was saved and became the personal perquisite of any one inhabitant or section of the inhabitants, he had not the life of a dog; he became the butt of their jests and, still worse, he had to be the appreciator of them. The only way in which he could survive or escape was to feign deafness or, still better, inability to understand their witticisms and so to compel them to explain them.

If any one of the Witlingenites managed to escape back to his fatherland, he was soon recognised by his mosquito-like buzzing round the market-place and his buttonholing of all and sundry, the confidential and sage wag of his head, and the strut of his demeanour after a series of successes; there was nothing in earth or out of it but he could make himself superior to by uttering one of his little jokes upon it; he could tread on the neck of omniscience and omnipotence itself, if only he was allowed to jest about it to his fellow-men. It was this peculiarity of the joculasters that made them the pariahs of the archipelago. When one was found to have escaped from Witlingen, it was the duty of every sane self-respecting man and woman to get him quarantined, like a leper, and sent back. It was only there that they got free and kept free of their terrible disease. Besides Vulpia the Witlingenites had now another recreation-ground, in which they could play off practical jokes much to their own satisfaction. It was the small island of Fanfaronia. The peoples of the archipelago had begun to be plagued with a new type of eccentric, the would-be world conqueror. The success of two or three on military expeditions and the great glory that they gathered to themselves thereby had sent an epidemic of militant brag amongst the youth of the various islands. The manner was most infectious; and, in order to stop the spread of the plague, the saner majorities had to adopt the usual homœopathic cure. Every youth who strutted with head on chest and arms folded, and assumed superiority of genius to his fellows, and to their moral rules and conventions, was exiled to Fanfaronia; and there proximity of likes kept the disease in abeyance. But as soon as a stranger landed, the Fanfaronians struck the stage attitudes of great conquerors and looked for adoration from him. It was on this weakness that the Witlingenites played, and thus found another escape-valve for their own mental malady.

They had rivals for the use of this new arena in the inhabitants of the large island of Simiola, that lay close to their coasts. The particular disease that had brought the Simiolans together was an irresistible tendency to act the shadow or echo of those whom they saw or heard, and especially of those whom others admired. The best and feeblest of them had been useless to the communities in which they had lived; for, though innocent of any malignant purpose, they were mere parrots that depreciated the currency of good words or manners or acts or wisdom by the wear of too frequent repetition. But most of them had been mischievous or even dangerous in their habits. They were by nature backbiters and malicious, with a passion for depreciating

and trampling in the mud whatsoever had stirred the praise or admiration
of other people or their own envy or jealousy. These had become foul or
ape-like in their habit of life and even in their forms. There was nothing
they would not condescend to in order to bring down to their level all that
seemed to be above them. Their island was seldom approached by voyagers,
so dangerous was it to land on it. Yet waggish expeditions frequently made it
their hunting-ground; for looked at from a distance their conduct was often
laughable, and their growing likeness to apes gave zest to the comedy. But
they became violent if the strangers ever attempted to mimic them or laugh
at them; and the favourite method of teasing them was to bring an ape and set
it beside them; they hated the mere sight of the beast, for in it, it was thought,
they discovered their own certain destiny. Yet their chief deity in their central
shrine, it was found by a daring traveller who penetrated its mystery, was
the representation of an ape, gigantic and monstrous yet man-like. They did
their best to put that traveller to death; but he had taken all precautions
and escaped. They thought that they worshipped the noblest being in the
universe, and seemed quite unconscious that they had made his image in
the likeness of an ape. It was only a foreigner and alien who could see the
resemblance.

Close by the shores of Simiola, and as like it as isle could be to isle, lay
Polaria, a still more favoured hunting-ground for the waggish youth of the
archipelago. This was where they fleshed their first intellectual weapons; for
the Polarians fell into the traps set for them with exceptional ease. They had
been exiled and brought together here on account of a strange but common
malady, that of guiding their words and conduct by the rule of contraries;
finding themselves with a passion for independence of action, and without
the power of origination, they tried to attain the appearance of it by contradicting all they heard and making their actions the opposite of those they saw.
They, so to speak, enjoyed each other's society more than the inhabitants of
the adjacent islands; for it made their hearts leap to hear a flat contradiction
of what they said; their blood was up, and they had a good run by the rule of
contraries. They hated each other most heartily, and would put themselves
to infinite trouble to find out what their neighbours or friends did or loved
in order to do the very opposite. It was their daily feast to go abroad and
especially to wander in the market-place; for, if they met a man who seemed
to know something about a subject, they could contradict him to their heart's
content, and make him feel how little he knew of it. They cultivated ignorance
of the favourite topics of the day so that they might have a free hand in saying
the opposite of anyone who had studied them. Knowledge would shut their
mouths and deprive them of the rapture of a good long wrangle.

It was amusing to see one of the wags lay his traps for them. He would find out from neighbours or friends what were their pet opinions, beliefs, or principles, and being fully equipped he would approach and announce in a loud and assertive voice one or other of them; at once would come the recantation; and through the whole range of their creed he would pass and get them to deny all they believed. But it needed some adroitness to escape ultimate detection, and he had to make arrangements for avoiding the tempest of rage that was sure to follow the process of making them eat their own words.

They had the greatest contempt for the inhabitants of Simiola, and hated them even more heartily than they hated each other. The very sight of them on their distant shore drove them into a violent passion. Yet a Simiolan would as naturally contradict a Polarian as if he had been a Polarian himself. The two were too much alike in their principles of action to have any chance of common sympathy.

Farther away in the direction of Tirralaria, but nearer Wotnekst on the side of Feneralia, lay another group of islets inhabited by those who were crazy on the subject of thrift. The Grabawlians were the misers of the archipelago; they had developed such a faculty for the concealment of money and possessions that you would have thought them as stricken with poverty as their greatest enemies and nearest neighbours, the Iconoclasts. These last counted capital the unpardonable sin. They refused to cultivate the soil lest they should have to harvest its fruits and store them up. Thrift they considered the greatest of vices. Trade and commerce they abhorred, and money, wherever they found it, they threw into the sea; it was their devil. Tools and houses they eschewed as the outcome of providence, and a form of capital. The only accumulation that they looked on with tolerance was that of filth and the refuse of Nature and man. Clothing they would have none of; it was the result of industry and the sign and symbol of hated forethought; they ignored and tolerated the kindly services of Nature in trying by means of her winds and dust and various forms of decay to mould them a substitute; for they refused to assist her in her ablutional attempts to undo her work.

No one ever saw them eat; but this was no proof that they never ate. The fruits disappeared off the trees; and there were many holes in the earth to show where roots had been dug. If ever they felt the pangs of hunger or thirst they vanished from the neighbourhood of their fellow-men; they would rather die than acknowledge to either; for to satisfy it meant the indulgence in industry; and industry was the sure sign of a nature degenerating into thrift and capital. Their meals were, everybody knew, nocturnal; they kept up the farce to each other of professing to be above both meat and drink.

If they were ever seen to bustle about, you might be sure that they were exterminating a nest of ants or chasing a bee off the island; these were in their view the criminals of the animal kingdom, the economisers and capitalists. One of their favourite maxims was this: "Go to the ant, thou thriftling and idiot; consider her ways and be wise; see how she toils and stores unceasingly from birth to death, enslaved to a despotic instinct, brutally fettered to the future."

The wonder was that they did not follow out the logic of their creed and crusade against thrift in Nature's own camp. There was she treasuring up the carbon of the falling leaves to make the fruits of the coming summer. There was she storing up sap during her idle months that she might make her trees and plants blossom in spring. Nay, in their own systems was she at work from infancy onwards carefully providing for later periods of life. They did their best, it is true, to defeat her in her providence and thrift; for they were walking skeletons and hospitals. But after all their efforts they failed to eradicate her thrift from their own systems. It was their unhappiness that every new turn in their lives revealed to them some form of it in themselves, that they had either to attempt to get rid of or pretend to each other that they had not got. They refused to see that the only avoidance of thrift was suicide, and that even that was a form of thrift. Nature, their foe, had perhaps generously blinded them.

A singular group of islets was situated beyond these and collectively called Paranomia. Their inhabitants had all been exiled for some craze they had developed on the subject of law. They respected it either too much or too little. Some were so devoted to it that they spent their time in litigation and missed approach to the spirit of equity; others reached the same goal by snapping their fingers at all law.

One of the group, called Palindicia, was colonised by justitiomaniacs, who were not happy unless engaged in dealing out justice. They did not object to acting the part of prosecutor or counsel; but their especial passion was judicial; they would have risen in rebellion, had not their administrators given them daily employment on the bench or in the jury-box.

How to supply the people with cases and criminals was the difficulty that beset the government, and drove them to their wits' ends. Once they had proposed to put in the dock a dummy or automatic criminal; but they nearly lost their lives in the brawl that resulted. It was an unpardonable insult to the humanity of the Palindicians to make them play at toy trials. They would not suffer such an outrage and caricature on the justice they so adored. They must have real flesh-and-blood criminals to try, cases with a vein of tragedy running through them, to whet their judicial skill upon. They would soon produce a good supply, if the government did not look out; the administrators would last a good while, if placed one after another in the dock.

In fact, they rather preferred an innocent man for their experiments in justice; for, they often said, where lay the talent or ability in sheeting a crime home to one who was guilty? There was something of true genius in convicting an innocent man, and in making his friends feel that there was something wrong about him. His defence was so earnest that his prosecution and trial had to be exhibitions of the greatest judicial talent in order to secure his condemnation. A real criminal was clogged and handicapped by the consciousness of his crime, and after a little struggle succumbed. The guiltless or his friends kept up the judicial battle for years, and the whole nation was drawn into the case, so that every citizen revelled in the exercise of his sense of justice.

One of the most successful methods for employing all the people in a trial for a long period was, when a crime actually occurred, to get the wronged in the dock and make the guilty try him. It relieved the government for years and years of anxiety about the supply of subjects for the judicial scalpel. The bench of criminals so enmeshed their victim in the toils that there was no escape for him, and yet there was the most exquisite exercise for the national passion. The labyrinth became almost too intricate for their sense of justice. Yet they were thankful for it; it was exactly what they wanted; for it meant appeal from court to court, and trial after trial with all the evidence and the details over again. In fact, they had manufactured so many tribunals, one above another in even gradation, that the simplest case might last them years, and every member of the community have his judicial skill whetted every day. The result was that, however guiltless the accused might seem when he first entered the dock, he was driven into false witness, or perjury, or treason before he had gone far, and by the close every Palindician was convinced that he only got his deserts, when condemned; their sense of justice was fully satisfied, as well as their passion for judgment; and those who had brought him into the meshes were panegyrised as true patriots. They were always deeply grieved at the condemnation of an accused by the last court of appeal; for the case was then finally disposed of, and ceased to afford an arena for their judicial talents. The only consolation in the misfortune was that the defence and its failure might possibly supply a new crop of traitors, whose cases might last for years.

Century after century they had had a splendid judicial preserve in the remnant of an aboriginal race that had developed a genius for finance and subtlety. Whatever laws the Palindicians might pass, these aliens were so astute that in all their financial triumphs they could avoid breaking them.

It was one of the patriotic amusements of the citizens to get up a periodical battue and hunt one or another of these unfortunates into the legal nest; self-defence or retaliation generally led him at last to commit some crime, treason or assault or slander, against a citizen; and thus a first-class criminal was manufactured for their unemployed law-courts, and, as he was baited by witnesses false or true from court to court, he fell deeper and deeper into genuine criminality; by developing new phases and working up new issues, they could husband the case for a long period.

But too frequent battues had thinned the game in this legal preserve, and the proclamation of a close season had not sufficed to restore the old numbers, or even make them commensurate with the Palindician passion for justice. They were driven at last to use up any strangers that landed on their shores. Unfortunately most of these were criminals from the other islands, and they had always made better material for the bench than for the dock. In fact, it had become the custom for the Palindicians to use them as judges; for who could dispense justice so well as the guilty? Who more experienced than the criminal in finding out crime? The culprits of the archipelago were so convinced of the rightness of Palindician judgment that they fled at once to the island, unless the cruel despotism of law retained them in their own. It was with regret then that these devotees of justice were driven by failure of the natural supply to change their policy and put them in the dock. There they were anything but satisfactory, and were convicted too easily and rapidly.

The Palindicians had grown sad as they reflected over the mysterious workings of Providence; for here were they with all this passion and genius for justice; and yet this new supply ran short. The criminals of the archipelago had ceased to believe in Palindician justice, and preferred in their blindness to take refuge in some other paradise; and it looked as if the inhabitants of this unfortunate island would either have to find subjects for their judicial talent in their own ranks or abandon its refinement and power through want of practice. Such a dilemma never had any people had to face.

And where would justice find a home, if they were driven to the latter alternative? Would not the world mourn the greatest of virtues perished, if once she were banished from her last refuge? No, rather would they resort to the trivial contests of civil litigation than permit such a catastrophe; rather would they manufacture their criminals out of the guiltless in their own ranks than let Palindicia cease to be the jewel of justice. Not one of them but would sacrifice his dearest friend rather than allow the genius for judgment to vanish from the earth.

It was prattle like this that made me forget the malodorous state of the narrator. Sneekape knew that he had to do something in order to withdraw my energies from my olfactory nerves; and he succeeded. His entertainment, when it ended, left me again a prey to the thought of the commanding odours that rayed out from him. But rest and freedom were near; for night fell and mesmerised our faculties.

CHAPTER XXV

KLORIOLE

THE GAUNTLET OF STENCHES that we had run stifled us into deep and long sleep. The sun was far up the sky when we awakened, and its heat seemed somehow to have subdued the traces of Awdyoo to a faint, though pungent and offensive, odour. We looked ahead and astern. The current was much slower; some undercurrent in the opposite direction must have been dragging it back. All trace of land had vanished behind us. But there was either a cloud or the top of some hill on the sky-rim to which the canoe was drifting. We fell into stupor again; and, when I stirred to life, the stars were keen as stiletto points above us. I lay staring at them till they became eyes that spoke to me of the deep night and the infinite abysses wherein they were moved to tears. A warm breath softened the distance between us and soothed my senses.

I must have been asleep again, dreaming that they had a language of their own full of intensity of meaning, and that they bade me approach them without fear; for the sunlight was around me, as I seemed to fall from them with prosaic suddenness into the still fetid reminiscences of Awdyoo.

At the moment of awakening there dropped upon me as I lay what seemed at first almost an emanation from the gleam of heaven. I raised my head and found that a white, bird-shaped float was lightly resting on the bottom of the canoe. I lifted it and saw that it was covered with written or printed characters. I handed it to my companion, who was also awake, and, as he read, he burst into a derisive laugh. It was a love-poem, he explained, written in the fulsome conventional language of Kloriole, as he called the island we were approaching. He translated a few lines into Aleofanian with a sneer:

> *Deity and sex combined,*
> *Godlike despot of the mind!*
> *Look on our eternal fate,*
> *Ere the ages antedate*
> *All that we shall be in death,*
> *Mingling souls in fleeting breath.*

God and woman, make me god;
With thy glances starlight-shod
Slay me; for I would be slain;
Slay me once and yet again;
Slay me with thy deadly kiss;
Sweet such apotheosis!

Let not mercy stay thy hand!
We shall never understand
All the god that in us lies
Till from death our spirits rise,
Never know what might we own
ill through space we wing alone
On from orb to orb of night,
Shedding our creative light;
Whilst our mortal worshippers
Watch from world to universe.
Free my spirit from afar,
Thou my love's own avatar!

I was bewildered by the strange medley of love and religion and mysticism. Sneekape saw the perplexity in my eyes, and with a gross laugh tore the kite of love to pieces and flung them into the sea. He expressed the greatest contempt for such feeble mystifications of the delights of the senses. I confessed that I had not much sympathy or admiration for such performances; they were, like buffoonery and wit, a mere trick of the mind; it was generally lame thought that needed such rhyme and verses as crutches; learn the hobbling gait early enough, and you could go on to infinity. It was not at his contempt, then, that I felt disgusted; it was perhaps at the petty sneer that accompanied its expression.

In order to cast out the loathing, I began to wonder whence the missive came. I looked back, and right above us loomed a great hill crowned with a massive building, and up to the gigantic porch climbed innumerable flights of steps cut into the living rock. Scattered over the balustrades and niches and recesses that ornamented the upward course of the stair stood or sat many beings fantastically dressed and looking up either to the sky or to the edifice that broke the azure. Some were floating what seemed paper kites; others were watching their flight, as they rushed before the wind or fell like falling stars into the sea or behind the hill, or vanished into the blue distance. I knew then whence had come the amatory lyric that had butterflied into our canoe.

It was the marvellous ascension of the steps that struck me most. They seemed to dwarf by their broad spacing and their number the enormous building that crowned the height up which they clambered. How puny seemed the men and women that moved about their upper flights. I could see that they were human beings; but that was all. Even half-way up it seemed a lark's flight into the blue. It wearied the imagination to count the gradings between; still more to think of the ascent, or the long years that must have passed in chiselling out this daring work of ambition.

The lowest flight had its knees in the ocean, and as we approached we could see the verdant sea-hair float and fall across the rising wave or shimmer in the ripple. For a hundred steps or more the sea in its tides or its passions claimed dominance and left the record of its conquests. We moored our canoe between two pillars cut in the rock, and attempted to ascend. But it was a work of extreme difficulty and danger. Each step had been smoothed into a slope by the feet of ages of climbers and by the action of the waters; and the lubricant green, wherewith the waves velveted them, made footing almost impossible. We slid and tumbled back into the sea a dozen times, and each time we made effort to scale the flight it became harder from the growing burden of water in our clothes. At last one of the native climbers farther up indicated the sides of the steps, where they were but roughly cut out of the rock. Swimming along to the right side, we found there was almost the sierraed roughness of nature. We could just catch some of the sharp points, and, by means of these, and at first almost prostrate, we hauled ourselves over the sleek garden of the tide. Then, finding the weed less silken and the rock less jagged, we crept on our knees up many steps; and when we looked back we saw traces of our own blood upon them. Then we looked into the notched rock before us and saw the dark bloodmark of generations that had gone before us stained deep into its texture. This lower portion of the marvellous staircase was indeed hieroglyphed and pictured with human lifeblood.

The thought made me shudder, as I looked back into the flood, for there doubtless had been the grave of myriads. How could any merely human fingers cling here when the waves were high, or the wind lashed them into fury? Out in the open I could see the fins of sea-monsters glance in the sun; there was the fate of the fallen climbers; there were the scavengers and mortuary vaults of the feebly ambitious dead that yielded to their destiny and fell; there was the reason why the sea around was not one vast gehenna.

We were strong with exposure and exercise, our cuticle hardened and thick; and yet we were wounded and torn by our upward efforts. We were now almost sea-creatures from our life in the briny air and the splash of the billows; and so, perhaps, it was that the man-eaters below let us alone when we fell back into the waters; at any rate they swam far off from us, as if they would have no dealings with such strangers.

At length we reached the upper margin of the sea's domain, and sat down, weary and faint, to let our blood harden on our wounds in the sun. Around us stood a crowd of pale and shadowy forms, their long hair matted or tressed over their shoulders, vague distance in their eyes, and something that looked like a pen in their right hands. They fingered our clothes and hair in a dreamy way, and sighed, and looked, and sighed again. Then one or another would retire into the background and seat himself on one of the steps, where others too, I now saw, were seated in an attitude of meditation. They gazed into the sky, and then looked intense; they ran their thin white fingers through their long hair; then they consulted slips of paper, on which were evidently printed rules for their guidance; they threw their heads wildly about; their eyes seemed ready to burst from their sockets; they rose and flung their arms aloft; they whirled around and danced at imminent risk of falling back into the sea. Then I saw them settle into a stupor; their lips moved and mumbled as if in sleep; they awoke, and over a sheet that they held in their left hands their pens flew. These performances went on for almost an hour till everyone around us had settled down to his pen and paper.

Sneekape whispered with a contemptuous smile that this was inspiration. They had been waiting, probably months, for a new subject, and our arrival had set them all poetically adrift. They had each hope of rising another flight up the steps of fame, borne on the pinions of a new ecstasy.

We rose to look at the frenzied bevy of poets. And now I saw that across the head of the flight, on which we were, ran a lofty arabesque fence of adamant with a narrow gate in the middle most elaborately bolted and padlocked. Inside it stood in an attitude of attack a serried array of lank forms, clothed in vestures that were splendidly formal, some holding scissors on the end of long poles, others bearing in one hand dirty, long-handled brushes, and, in the other, pots streaked with some black and greasy fluid, a third set swinging censers alight, and a fourth carrying huge inflated bags on their backs. They looked, a scowl or a sneer on their villainous low brows, upon the writhing romancers on the other side of the adamant scrollwork. Half of them were boys with a low type of face that indicated more bravado than intelligence, more flippancy than wit; of the others some had more years and more truculence, and a look of envy and malice in their eye; the rest were men bowed by years and despair of life, and on their faces was a look as of pity and reminiscence.

This was the lower ring of acolytes of the great temple of Literary Fame, Sneekape whispered to me; there were four divisions of them, as I could see by their implements, and these were the snippers, the defacers, the burners, and the windbaggers, as their Kloriolean names might be translated. They had a mean and somewhat soiled shrine of Fame on the left side of their rocky platform, and here relays of them kept up continual worship, burning on the altar imaginative productions that they caught.

My attention was drawn to the other side by negotiations going on there. Some of the wild-haired youths, who had evidently finished the result of their frenzy, had come up to the scroll-fence and were haggling and bargaining with one or other of a group of sleek business-like men within it. These were called the propagators, my companion said, and their function was to supply the means for floating any new product of the fancy towards the priests and the worshippers of the temple of Fame. I saw that most of the pale youths returned to their seats on the steps with a look of baffled eagerness in their eyes. They touched and retouched their sheets and wearily erased and inserted with their pens. A few succeeded in getting paper-floats with their complement of gossamer thread and other apparatus from the propagators. And with the gleam of proud achievement in their looks they prepared to attach their writings to them and set them afloat. But most of the literary kites refused to rise, and when thrown up into the air fell heavily back into the sea and either sank or were torn under by the devouring monsters. A few of more prosperous and cheerful appearance approached the windbaggers; I watched one of them: aided by his propagator, he got some coin or valuable transferred through the interstices of the fence into the hidden palm of one of the sack-bearing acolytes, and before long he had his kite afloat, dancing upon the puff of wind that issued from the nozzle of his ally's bag. The other acolytes made fierce lunges at it with their scissors, or brush, or censer. Amongst those that managed to float, one had its thread early snipped and fell over the parapet; another sank, heavy from the foul effacement from an ink-brush; another caught fire and was burned in a censer. Two succeeded in running the gauntlet and floating higher; but at the next enclosure they succumbed to the attacks from behind it. The owners of these were admitted within the fence by which we stood; and I saw the proud smile on their faces. One of them was persuaded to join the group of acolytes, and, when he donned the vestments, he seemed to lose his old and picturesque personality and take on the truculence of his new companions. The other turned away from them with a weary but ambitious face and climbed up the long flight towards the next barrier.

As I looked upwards I now perceived that there was a barrier, with a crowd of acolytes and propagators on the one side and a diminishing crowd of suppliants on the other, at the head of every flight. The strange thing was that, as the distance increased, the size and sleekness of each fence-divided bevy increased too, till up at the porch of the temple, priests, propagators, and poets looked fat and almost bloated; they reclined on rich couches, and were surrounded with the luxuries that would fit an outdoor tropical existence. It was little wonder that the thin, pale faces of the candidates below looked up with such longing to that Olympus and Elysium in one. Sneekape pointed out to me on each adamant barricade the meaning of the scrollwork; he translated the letters; the announcement ran: "None enter the mighty temple as gods but by this ascent."

In the middle of the explanation we were startled by a wild cry and a rush of the crowd around us to the right-hand parapet. We ran in the same direction, and, hearing a fierce, gruntling noise, looked over and saw one of the long-haired tribe being devoured by jackals. To keep candidates for fame back from the land approach to the great stairs, an iron-barred enclosure ran its whole length on both sides, and in this lived a number of wild beasts, fed upon young poets and other seekers of glory. The priests and propagators saw that the supply was kept up. It was not long before the victim had completely vanished and his comrades sat down with a new and stirring topic in this suicide for fame. Perchance their wild sympathy with him might produce such a poem as would open the gate for them. They were soon all absorbed in their new inspiration.

In looking from one to another bowed figure, I saw a sheet flutter near the parapet; I took it up and handed it to my companion. He laughed and said it was evidently the young suicide's bid for fame; the verses had rhythm and meaning like this:

> *Sea-borne strangers, whence are ye?*
> *We have nought but sorrow here;*
> *Fate hath made you fancy free;*
> *Fly this fame-envenomed sphere!*
> *Hell-born torture would be bliss,*
> *Soul-ecstatic, matched with this.*
>
> *Ye have never known the care*
> *Lives within a heart like mine;*
> *Spirit palsied with despair,*
> *Anguish past all anodyne,*
> *Follow me where'er I flee.*
> *Who can quench my agony?*

Through the dawn-flushed arch ye came;
Bright new worlds are shining there,
Worlds dispassionate of fame,
Gloryless as they are fair.
Oh! to tenant freshly born
Some new star beyond the morn!

Ah! new life is stale as old,
Outlook dull as memory,
Death an idiot's tale half-told,
Hell's own caravansary.
God, if thou hast in thy breast
Love or pity, let me rest!

Nothingness, I thee implore,
Rid me of this vacuous dream,
Let me fade and be no more,
Be the phantom that I seem!
Sweet Oblivion, let me light
In annihilative night!

There was a loud, coarse laugh behind the barrier over this pessimistic effusion and its baptism of blood, and what made it sound stranger was that it rose from the midst of pæans and hosannahs over the poem that had borne the other aspirant up to the second arabesque. The echo sounded even to the porch; for the priests seemed to move and listen as in a dream. I was eager to see the production that had stirred such a commotion in the ranks of the guardians of fame; and Sneekape managed to get a copy for me, and translated it into Aleofanian; it must have suffered in the change; for it was difficult to see the superiority. It ran in rhythm and sentiment thus:

Ye are only the van
Of the army of man
That is marching over the sea.
Ye would seek to attain
The immortal fane
Of the glory that is to be.

No mightier god
Has ever trod
The crust of the quaking earth.
He has come to assist
In dispelling the mist
That clings to thought at its birth.

Through a long series of such doggerel verses the composition proceeded; and I thought, how meaningless the pæans, if this were all that opened the gates of literary Fame! I turned away from the sight of this sordid injustice and looked for the first time out upon the level shores of the island that stretched on either side of these sanguinary stairs. And I was surprised to find them full of men and women of look and figure and dress nearer the normal; they were evidently toilers with the hands; for they were muscular in frame and tanned by the weather. They formed, indeed, a wholesome contrast to these priests and worshippers of fame.

A longing to be amongst them seized me, a kind of homesickness to be with the toilers of the field again. Sneekape could scarcely restrain me from trying to leap the parapet; he showed me the jackal-haunted chasm that I would fall into and the impossibility of crossing it. He got the canoe in to the lowest step; nor had we so far to slither down; for the tide had risen; and in a few minutes we were seeking a place to land. At the risk of our lives we managed to get on the beach and were soon in the midst of the crowd.

They were the slaves and artisans of Kloriole; and, as it was now evening, they had finished their day's labour and were engaged in the usual recreation of the country, listening to or making songs and ballads. It was a babel rippled with snatches of melody. I could catch no intelligible phrase, nor could Sneekape help me much; for they did not write or print their productions, and they composed them in the popular dialect.

Just as the westering sun was tinging the zenith with gold, one ballad seemed to run like wildfire through the clustering singers, and at last was caught up and chanted by the whole multitude. It had a fine symphonic oscillation, and the bodies of the group and the movements of the great sea of heads swayed with the waves of its sound. At last a cry rose above it and spread until it extinguished the fire of song: "To the temple!" and I saw raised on the shoulders of two stalwart artisans a feeble-looking child with an over-developed head and outstanding eyes. The multitude began to move round a cliff and then along a path that wound hither and thither up the hill. They kept chanting the song till they reached another and far greater porch of the temple on its landward side. With huge crowbars they pried open the doors and burst into the vast edifice. It was niched from floor to dome with innumerable shell-formed recesses, gaily painted and ornamented; and into most of these were thrust, often jammed, a dozen or more mummies with labels and printed sheets liberally stuck over them; peering to the back of them I could see that most of those behind the front row were falling to dust, their sheets all yellow with age. It was often difficult to distinguish mummy from mummy or dust from dust; and there was throughout the building, large though it was, a smell as of a charnel-house; the movements and breath of the crowd seemed to shake out the forgotten atoms of the famous dead.

These, Sneekape explained, were the embalmed bodies and productions of the successful worshippers of fame, preserved to immortality. I saw in some of the niches dusty forms of priests move, most of them greybeards, and read the yellow sheets in the dusk, or rake for them in the commingled dust. These, I was told, were the scholar-priests who tried to arrange and furbish the fretwork of dusty death. But it seemed to me that they helped even more than the trampling multitude to distribute the remains of mortality into the atmosphere and the lungs.

The priests and their followers shot scornful glances at the rudely surging mob; but without effect. Then they raised their paper lashes that had made the worshippers on the stairs writhe with pain; but they sounded feeble and childish against the noise of the chanting crowd; and their strokes seemed to have no more effect than if applied to the billows of the sea. The singing multitude swept on up the long aisles of the edifice, and with a crash the adamant arabesque that hedged in the shrine of the deity fell before it. The brawny arms of the bearers perched the child on the altar, and the priests, cowed and silent, had to accept him as one destined to be sustained at the expense of the temple and at death to be placed in the niches of immortality. Under the goad of fear, they had to leave their obeisances and fulsome adulation before their favourites who had been admitted up the flights from the sea into the precincts of the deity, and give all their ceremonial eulogy to this illegitimate bantling of fame. In comparing the new object of their adoration with those from whom they now turned, I could see little difference either in grace or intelligence. Those who had been admitted by the recognised ascent were most of them flabby boys or youths, fattened by luxury and robbed by vanity of the little native intelligence they had had; a few were old men in their dotage, whose every foolish word and act was caught up by acolytes and recorded.

I turned to Sneekape for an explanation. We had kept close together, lest the jostling crowd should do us harm in the worship of their bantling. His face was puckered up in a derisive smile. "This is the result of their devotion to what they think fame. Their literary art has become child's play, an exercise in what they call style. These priests and acolytes, who have wrung out of the anguished labour of the common people this gorgeous temple and its endowments, have gradually formulated into exact rule all the points of poem or prose that would admit a writer to the shrine as a sharer in its sustenance and glory. It can be almost automatically decided what is worthy of eternal fame and what is not. They pride themselves on this mathematical precision. Of course this means the exclusion of all idea or fact or utility from the literature; all that is required is the form, and if that comes up to the recognised standard and conforms to the rules which we saw the candidates at the bottom of the stairs continually consulting, then the writer is raised flight by flight to the shrine. The compositions have come to be empty and meaningless; their chief merit is that they have a kind of melody. They must be according to the received convention.

"Through the ages, then, the stage of life at which the talent for such work is found has been growing lower and lower; and now mothers watch anxiously in the cradles for the lisping of numbers; they record the most infantile chatterings and send them forth as mystic compositions; and these priests, who are also interpreters, profess to find in them the most profound wisdom. I have not heard yet of a babe in arms being admitted to full literary fame; but the day is evidently near when only sucklings and idiots will have any chance of success amongst guardians who adopt such ideals and such mechanical rules, and who profess to find depth of thought in what comes only from the lips. The truth is that the priests and propagators desire to keep the whole emoluments of the temple for their own benefit. Mere children will never interfere with their power or their allotment of fame. When they grow up into youth, they either vanish or are absorbed into the priestly ranks, and the guardians, those that have the fame of old age, vote themselves the most lucrative and elevated posts. For themselves they keep their loftiest eulogies, their wildest devotion; they form mutually admiring and advancing groups; they have no praise for those who will not praise them or be likely to praise them. This habit has spread as a contagion right down the flights of the ascent. No wind is lent to raise a float unless the service is sure to be repaid. All the middle-aged about the temple or the steps are priests, acolytes, or propagators. Children and old men are the subdeities of fame, almost as easily managed as unseen gods, and as easily disposed of. The literature has reached the level of first or second childhood; it is an exercise in the art of saying nothing in the most melodious or mystic way, and in the conventional form. Creation and criticism have both become ceremonial, automatic arts, that have been switched off from the influence of the imagination and every other faculty of the soul. Vacuity veiled in mystery is what those long-haired candidates we left on the sea-flight have not learned and cannot learn, and they must remain there or leave; unless they acquire the other great art, that of interflation or mutual windbagging.

"It is the natural development of a community in which one half are creators and the other half critics by profession. The latter absorb the reality of power and luxury and fame; the former get the shadow. The critics pretend to worship creation; they are the gods, for they have the omniscience; they give the rules and the ideals that are thought divine; to their fiat the others have to bow. They have enslaved the intelligence of the island and are gradually stifling it, that there may be as little chance of outbreak as might come from beasts. Such popular riots as we have seen to-day make them tremble for their power and privileges. The uneducated people, trained in nothing but to worship what the priests of fame profess to adore, feel at times the old musical and imaginative instincts surge up in them, and they rush in rhythmic passion to immortalise the singer who has resuscitated the old nature in them. They are supposed not to know what literature or song is; but they have caught the contagion from the singing in the temple and on the stairs, and they encourage their offspring to attempt ambitious literary flight from the cradle upwards; for is it not something to be the parent of a subdeity of Fame? Amongst them alone is the true sense of natural song unobliterated; and occasionally in their dialect some native, untaught genius gathers its music round an old memory or emotion, and the result is a lyric that sets their whole buried natures on fire; no priestly power can repress the volcanic outburst, and a new idol is set up in the temple."

We saw the people retire and find their way down to the lower levels as the night fell. We followed and found shelter till the morning. Not long after daybreak they filed away to their tasks in the fields and the workshops, and the incident of the previous day was evidently forgotten.

After a meal Sneekape led me over a spur of the hill to a rising ground that commanded a deep valley into which the sun never seemed to come, so filled with shadow and gloom was it, so walled off from the world of light.

We serpentined down half-way into it till our eyes grew accustomed to the obscurity; and then I could discern figures like the scholar-priests moving about at the bottom of a fissure filled with bones and yellow shreds of parchment or some other stuff that could withstand the weather. Some were turning over and raking this graveyard and some were intent upon yellow fragments they had found.

This was the valley of dead ambitions and dead literature. Into this the literary kites that had their threads cut by the snippers generally fell. Hither were brought the dusty remains of the mummies that had decayed with their writings past recognition in the niches of the temple. It was the charnel-house of the great sanctuary. Here were half the scholar-priests trying to find intelligible relics of the past, that they might by resuscitating them place their treasure and themselves in some higher niche.

And Sneekape closed his explanation with a sneer. "Here they toss most of the infants of fame who are not astute or worldly enough to enter the ranks of the ecclesiastics. The child we saw enthroned on the altar yesterday will be starved out, and, if he does not escape and return to his slave-mother to sink into happy obscurity, his bones will soon be found in this gehenna. The people, though they continue to sing his songs, will utterly forget him; and this the priests knew well, when they ceased their resistance yesterday."

I looked down to the ghouls that battened below us on the hideous past; I looked up to the great edifice that dominated the island; and I remembered the vaunting inscriptions that decorated its interior. "Here dwell the immortals"; "Who enter here never die"; "The gaze of all men is upon us"; "The centre of the universe." The valley of death and oblivion was the natural complement of this hill of arrogance and self-righteousness.

My companion laughed at the sharp antithesis, and wished to go down into the valley of dry bones to enjoy the folly of the rakers and the readers. In gloom and dejection I climbed the spur again and fled down to the beach. It was too ghastly a comment on the whole civilised world to linger over. If only I could wipe it from the mind! The mortal dust of the immortals clung to my nostrils and throat. Heedless of the danger I plunged into the sea, and was soon on board the canoe. Sneekape did not wish to lose me, and was beside me before I could raise the paddle. As we got into the current again and swept past and away from the islet, we could see the stairs still crowded with the candidates and the priests absorbed in their pursuit of fame; and not one of them turned to see us drifting away. It was almost the time of stars before we had our last glimpse of Kloriole. The cupolas of the temple still threw its glory back upon the sun from beneath the horizon till it was difficult to tell them from the golden light on the domed billows.

CHAPTER XXVI

SWOONARIE

MY FELLOW-VOYAGER LAY DOWN to sleep as soon as the field of night above us broke into its myriad flowers. I could not sleep for the thought of that wretched miniature of the great world; I could not forget the suicide and his poem, the wild ecstasies of the neophytes, the poor little dropsical-headed poet of the people left to weep and starve in the gorgeous temple, or the murky fissure of the dead with its mortuary vultures. Wearied out at last with the sombre thoughts, and in spite of the heaving of the canoe, I fell asleep at the paddle; and chaotic medleys of all I had just seen made new visions that wakened me in terror to feel ostracised and forlorn under the eyes of infinity; and it was as cheerless to sleep as to wake with this nightmare of the world and its ambitions pressing in upon me.

The long night span itself out into a thread of dreams and reveries; at times it was hard to distinguish between the vision of sleep and the vision of waking, so closely did they twilight into each other. Even when the cold gleam of daybreak shimmered over the waves it was difficult to unravel the tangle of dream and thought; pictures, half real, half unreal, filmed over my senses; the very air, as the sun languished into sight from behind his sultry curtains, became dreamful, the wind and sea fell, and a trance-like silence filled the dome of sky. We had passed into a charmed sphere. Languor welled through me till I dropped my paddle and stretched along the bottom of the canoe, floating on the surface of sleep.

My companion I found trying to waken me. He was steeped in drowsiness himself; but the grating of the boat on some bank had roused him; he could not get to land without help. In a sluggish, half-vegetative state I got up, and we seemed to paddle through an unending series of shallows that entangled the canoe. The exercise at last broke our torpor, and with a few vigorous strokes we reached land.

It lay so low, as far as eye could reach, that the sea in tempest must take possession. Yet we saw human beings move in the distance. At first we thought that they were cattle grazing, so slowly and spasmodically did they trail along and so low did they bend their heads.

We got on shore. Only vigorous movement kept us out of the comatose state that threatened us every moment. We saw men and women stretched on the sand; but we could not get them to take any notice of us, and we had strong desires to drowse prostrate too. We struggled on over the opiate plain, till at last we found the ground rise gently. Our limbs quickened, our senses began to grow nimble, and when we were high enough to look out over the island and the sea, we had completely recovered from our lethargy.

We reached a cluster of dilapidated huts, that turned out to be mere roofings of pits dug in the earth. Men and women were working here and there, but paid little attention to us when we spoke to them. Sneekape at last found one who looked up, as he was addressed in Aleofanian; and, after a long series of vigorous efforts and questionings, he left off his slumberous style of digging and answered in droning, far-off tones that sounded like the echo of muffled bells. There was a somnolent look in his great cow-like eyes, covering what might have been depths of intelligence and emotion, or what might have been nothing at all. We followed him to a bench outside of his rooftree, and we sank down on it with a sense of seeming collapse.

After a space our senses shook off their torpor and drew themselves together, and we found in slow and measured question and answer that he had no desire to know us or be known by us; he was too busy upon a vital problem to feel any interest in other matters. It was this we discovered on much inquiry: whether worms could be taught to do all the agricultural operations of a farm; they were the ploughers, manurers, sowers, and harvesters; but they were all these at once; he had been experimenting for years to get them to divide their various operations over the appropriate seasons. He seemed harassed that we had interrupted him in attempting to fence off his ploughing worms from his harvesters. There was just one link wanting, and when he found it he would reform the agriculture of the world.

We had to leave him to his problem; he sank into it as into a pit of sleep. We noticed as we passed along his domain that there was not a green blade or shoot to be seen anywhere; his workers had evidently harvested the estate.

The next man we came across was too busy hedging round his shadow to attend to us. It gave him infinite trouble. If only he could fix it down and get it secured in a net, he could make his fortune by exporting it to equatorial climates, to cool down the temperature and reduce the glare.

Everyone we met was absorbed in some problem, and had no time to spare for idle questions like ours. They were ready enough to talk about their experiments and discoveries; but anything else was futile; they at once dropped from consciousness, and no effort could awaken them. We always tried to get at their favourite project in order to lead them on to the information we

required. We laid siege to dozens without avail; any divergence from their
great scheme at once hypnotised them.

One was engaged in an attempt to exhaust the atmosphere in order that the
pure ether might descend upon the world and make them capable of flight.
Another was busy upon a rope-making machine that would twist light into
strands so that men might draw the sun nearer when they needed more heat
and light, or make out of the beams of any star a rope ladder whereby they
might climb to it. A neighbour of his was just on the point of discovering a
crucible that would extract silver from the lustre of the stars. One had invented a shovel that could level all the mountains into plains, if only he had the
force for it, and he was attempting to organise a company to supply the force.
Another had made a machine that would tunnel to the centre of the earth;
and he was about to form an association for working it; he said that one result
alone would enrich them beyond dreams: they could make a market for the
precious metals near the centre of the earth, where they would have greatly
increased weight. His neighbour was in the way to discover antigravitation,
by which they might be able to do what they liked with the stars and the
universes. The next man we met had a scheme for the annihilation of all
intoxicants throughout the world; and to induce men to agree to it he would
supply ailool, their favourite narcotic, instead; the world needed sleep, not
excitement.

Other projects and inventions that were in hand, we found, were: to teach
spiders to make all the garments men needed, and ants to be providers for
the human race; to mass insect-power in order to drive engines; to yoke birds
together for aërial navigation and carriage; to utilise the waste breath of men
for turning windmills; to run a road back through time as through space, that
we might eject our worst faults from our ancestors; to distil the divine essence
out of the ether in order to supply it in bottles to religionists all the world over
for ceremonies and miracles; and to drive a conduit back into the age when
the gods were present in the world, so as to deliver direct inspiration from
them at a few pence a gallon.

We got weary of attempting to extract any piece of information available for our purpose. There was not a scheme but had only one link wanting to make it a success. I had been at first inclined to pity these men and
women,—their lives seemed so pathetically futile,—but I changed my emotion when I saw that, however long they had been at their project, they never
lost the brightest hopes of it; they were the happiest of mortals, so absorbed
in their one thought, that care and sorrow could not approach them. Nature
gave them enough in most years to support them; and when famine came

they ate their opiate, ailool, and stretched themselves upon their narcotic plain. The vultures were their sextons and did the rest.

Sneekape never ceased to sneer at them or find food for petty laughter in their enthusiasms and absorption. Before we left them I felt the keenest envy of their happy unconsciousness of the stings of time.

CHAPTER XXVII
FENERALIA

WE GOT AT LAST to the highest point of the island, and thence we saw on the other shore a large falla at anchor. Sneekape came as close to ecstasy as such a petty nature could; he recognised her as one from his own island; at this period of the year they were able to bargain for the best females from Swoonarie for use in his country; now was the time when they were most hypnotised by their narcotic atmosphere or their problems; and it was easy to take the most beautiful, healthy, and dreamy-natured. These sleepy denizens of Swoonarie were great breeders, and their women when young had a dreamy grace that made them especially attractive to a race of active, marauding disposition; away from their opiate plain and atmosphere and the seductions of their ailool, the blood in their veins grew almost active and touched their peachy cheeks with bloom; their dark eyes languished with slumberous light; their limbs moved as in a dream-dance; their voices grew as sweet and far-off as the scarce-caught echo of lapsing rivers, or the low sigh of wind through grass; their thoughts and passions would rise at times out of the dim abyss of dreams in wild, consuming tempests. This falla-load, if it had been well selected, would fetch an enormous price and fill the treasury of the state.

We posted as quickly as our sleep-viscous limbs and faculties would permit down towards the beach; and soon we were on board of a luxuriously fitted galleon, the largest I had ever seen in the archipelago. Off shore the glutinous lethargy that had clogged every pore of our being seemed to melt and move with the blood. Sneekape was soon closeted with the leaders of the enterprise; and after the interview I was admitted to their fulsome salutations and oppressively eager acquaintanceship. The women were in the middle of the ship; for I could hear a faint, confused hum that rose at times into the muffled sounds of feminine voices. Towards evening the swish of paddles was heard, and going on deck I saw through the thickening gossamer of twilight a canoe approach. It grated against the bulwarks, and the men leaped on board and drew up after them some mantled and swathed figures that must have been another instalment of women. There was a hurried consultation, and the anchors were lifted. The great paddles were set in motion; but before the sails bellied with the wind that blew outside the shelter of the island the whizz of an arrow struck on my ear; the missile sliced the water not many yards astern. Towards the shore dark objects moved in the dim light, but the wind had now given the keel and helm firm grip, and no paddles could overtake us. The expedition had just escaped its greatest danger,—an attack from the fierce Feneralians for poaching on their preserves. Most of these voyages to Swoonarie ended in bloodshed, and it often happened that neither falla nor crew ever returned.

I had full opportunity on the voyage of hearing about these neighbours of the dreamers; for it fell calm, when we had got out of sight of land, and the paddles propelled the ship at but a slow pace. Feneralia was an island to which had been deported for centuries all the habitual bankrupts of the archipelago. It will scarcely be believed in the communities of Christendom, and it was long before I could be brought to credit the story. But Sneekape asserted again and again that a species of financial madness often seizes some of the more luxurious of the peoples on the islands; they imagine that they have been specially commissioned by heaven to spend; they have a fixed idea that mankind is naturally portioned off into the earners and the spenders, and the latter are as rare as creative genius upon earth; they are angelic spirits that have abandoned their birthright to the infinite, and wandered down into a world condemned to labour and acquisition; they are beams of heavenly light let in upon the darkness of a race given over to wage-earning. In some communities their story of divine mission is accepted; they are made politicians and statesmen, and the public treasury is handed over to them to do with as they please; some new tax or loan is ever demanding their powers of expenditure; and how to turn the plus into a minus almost wears them to a shadow. In other communities they have been smiled at as harmless madmen till they have grown subtly skilful and ingenious in inventing new methods of getting command of the surplus earnings of their neighbours; to gratify the moral weakness of their fellow-citizens they become periodically bankrupt, and start again on their virtuous mission to turn the needless plus of some other plutocratic locality into a minus. When their divine mission has thus come to be considered harmless lunacy, they are given the alternative of joining the altruists on Tirralaria or being deported to Feneralia. This was an island originally of great fertility and natural powers, but nothing would now grow on it, and the inhabitants in order to live had to become the buccaneers of the archipelago. They called themselves philanthropists; for they loved their fellow-men so much that they were ever relieving them of unnecessary burdens and spending for them that which they had never learned to spend for themselves. Another favourite name that they adopted was financiers;

they were ever sailing out on great loan expeditions; they would land in force on an island, advertise a huge loan with the attraction of a large percentage, pay the first interest out of the capital and vanish forever with the rest. If they went back there, they had some other scheme to cover their philanthropy: for example, a company to extract gold from sea-water or silver from starlight, destined to make all the shareholders rich. Sneekape held that they were nothing but freebooters.

On these financial raids they generally employed some of the mild-eyed dreamers of Swoonarie to mask their batteries. These had always some fine scheme on hand that needed money to make it coin gold, and by their simplicity they easily drew a community into belief in their dream; when the money was secured, a Feneralian force was ready to make off with it and repel any attempt to reclaim it; and when any people tried to retaliate on Swoonarie, or make reprisals, or injure it in any way, they swooped down on the invaders with their bloodthirsty manners and cheerful arrogance.

They were the spenders of the world; the rest of mankind were the earners. They would not hear of joining with the Tirralarians. Socialists! Not they. They did not believe in the equality of men; there were at least two levels, that of themselves and that of all other men; they had the appetites and the appreciation of enjoyment; the rest of the world was their purse; what did Heaven mean by such specialisation but that the one set was to serve the other? It was only the lack of numbers that prevented their carrying out the scheme of nature in its entirety. It was this that made them starve for months on their now barren island, whilst their harvest was preparing in the rest of the world. Ignorance blinded the wage-earners to the true object of their earning and made them fight to retain the result; if only they could open their eyes and look at things as they are in reality, they would see that it was meant for the appetite-bearers, the Feneralians. So these latter were often kept out of their rights, and had to fight to the death for them. They were often cooped up in their island by the stupid savages, who would not listen to the voice of nature and justice. Periodical raids were made upon them by way of retaliation; but it had been impossible to clear out this nest of pirates, as other men called it; this home of philanthropy, their own name for it. It was ever being recruited by the unearning spenders who had failed to make the people in their own islands believe in their divine mission. They were a cheerful, active race that never abandoned hope even in the midst of starvation, and never lost their patronising manners even when clad in rags. They were the natural lords of creation, dethroned by their slaves, the earners and fortune-makers. Some communities were wise enough to recognise their genius and make them their statesmen. The millennium would never arrive till all communities did the same.

CHAPTER XXVIII
THE VOYAGE AND THE WRECK

WHETHER THIS WAS A mere fable I was never able to verify by personal experience. Christendom will doubtless take it as wholly the creation of Sneekape's brain, so unlike nature does it seem. The only feature that I could vouch for as fact was the warlike attack as we weighed anchor from Swoonarie. I was awakened from my meditation over the question by a low murmur from the women's section; I listened, and was certain that it was a sleep-song they were chanting. Sneekape gave me the drift of each verse, and I tried to turn it into the same metre as they used:

> *Snowflakes of starlight*
> *Drift on us for ever.*
> *Suns lend their far light,*
> *Transmuter of river*
> *And slumberous ocean*
> *To shimmer of gold.*
> *Eyes dim with emotion,*
> *Eyes infinite-souled,*
> *With magic diaphanous*
> *Our spirits entrance;*
> *In our hearts, as they coffin us,*
> *Dreams quiver and dance.*
> *Dead to our kin we lie;*
> *Only the worlds of night,*
> *Wizards that charm the sky,*
> *See our unbodied flight.*
> *Dream-winged we hover,*
> *Death-drawn from birth;*
> *As lover to lover,*
> *Soul to its earth.*
> *Break we the bond at last,*

Breasting the infinite;
Future is clear as past,
Chaos as light.
Afloat on the stellar deep
Rest, rest, we crave,
Cradled to eyeless sleep,
Dream we from wave to wave.
Sleep, sleep, let us slumber!
Oh, we have lived and fought,
Borne pains without number.
Waken, Oh, waken us not.

It is impossible to give the drowsy sound of the melody in a language, like English, that has been forged in unflagging struggle, in the stress of battle with the forces of nature. Generations of ailooled nerves and lips had saturated every word with languorous music. No cradle-song that I had ever heard approached it in soporific power. All who sat within sound of it dropped their eyelids; the voices began to seem distant and stifled. At times the music died away, and again it rose in dim yet growing echo, at first like the murmur of bees in the still summer air, then like a wail swept fitfully by a breath that comes we know not whence and vanishes in a moment; out of unknown depths the lullaby threw its charm and then slowly withdrew it; the scarce-felt gradation of the cadence was as strong in its hypnotic fascination as the breeze-flung note. The singers seemed to fall into a dream as they sang. The words melted into one liquid rill of song. Faint and muffled its melody floated up as out of a dream. The falla lagged and dallied upon the gleaming levels of the sea; it was the barge of sleep, and we seemed to have been a thousand years fettered in trance. The sound of the paddles came only at intervals, and then it ceased, and the whole skyey vault and the weary sea and the specks of being that traversed it vanished. I fell countless fathoms through space. And then the existence snapped short; a crash rounded me up into the confines of life again. It was the fusillade of the boatswain's whip. And before we were rightly awake the ship was swinging along to this loud chant sung at full lung-pitch by the paddlers:

We beat with our paddles the passionless sea;
The flush of our wounding dies out on her face;
We dance free as gods on her billowy lea;
The trail of our feet no mortal can trace.

The life in our veins
Outgallops all pains.
Allanamoulin, Allanamoulin.

We slake our fierce thirst from the cup of the sky;
Its azure hath fathomless depths to exhaust;
Translucent within it worlds numberless lie;
With the gold of the dawn its rim is embossed.
The life is divine,
We drink with such wine.
Allanamoulin, Allanamoulin.

Our blood beats in time with the palpitant stars,
Our paddles in harmony rise and fall;
We cease from our labour, and life is a farce;
We rest, and our hearts grow weary of all.
For life, it is toil,
And happiness moil.
Allanamoulin, Allanamoulin.

The grave is the only repose for our being;
Thou 'rt welcome, Oh, death! When thou wilt, we are thine.
There's nought on this earth that's worth thinking or seeing,
And life's fitful fever has no anodyne.
To work is to rest;
To die is the best.
Allanamoulin, Allanamoulin.

The refrain is untranslatable; it was as old as the race, I was told; it had been used from generation to generation in paddle-songs, till it had grown rounded and smooth in the stream of time and lost all trace of its inner grain and force. An approach to the meaning would be, "Farewell, Rest! There is none upon earth." Sneekape and his friends were unwilling to taint their lips with it; for it had been a slave-word for centuries and they considered it beneath contempt. It was difficult even to get some translation of the paddle-song; but verse by verse and line by line I dragged it out of the haughty Figlefians.

Yet when they talked of their slaves, they spoke of them with leniency and even with kindness. Pressing questions home, I found that they considered the lash one of the most benevolent of institutions; it softened the asperities of slave-nature; for slaves were children, and had to be dealt with as children;

they did not know what was good for them; and their masters had to find out and insist; their best welfare was obedience to law and routine, and the whip administered with judicious severity induced obedience and prevented too large doses of this wholesome physic.

It was the first outrunner of a breeze that had awakened the master of the paddles, a cool breeze that seemed to come off distant snows. Soon the falla was all bustle, and the great square sails that stretched beyond the bulwarks twice the breadth of the ship were taut before the wind. We spun along at a merry rate, and the paddles disappeared from the sides. But it was only a catspaw, and died away. The sails fell heavily against the masts, and had to be run down. The slaves again took their place at the paddles, and we lounged along the sultry leaden floor of the sea.

But suddenly there fell upon us like the stroke of a hammer a wandering gust; the masts creaked, the loose cordage lashed the ship in their fury till she staggered. Then all was still. The old leaden dulness came upon the waters; it had been like the gleam of gnashing teeth in the sullen monotony of enslaved work. A yell from the slaves' quarters punctured the silence; it was partly from the whip of the boatswain, partly from the breaking of their paddles by the ridge of water that swept athwart us. In five minutes we were helpless between the surly rancour of the hurricane and the truculent floundering of the billows. On we rushed, staggering, drunken, with horror and frenzy. The slaves would not rise to the lash; the officers muttered curses between their teeth, and did what they could to guide her course. The daylight was blind with the angry dust of showers; the circle of grey film caged the ship, and eyes were futile and weary in their frantic eagerness to pierce it. Down in the women's quarters I could see Sneekape and his fellows lying prostrate, their faces in their hands on the planks; the women were huddled together in apathetic limpness.

Out of the wreck that drowned so many of the Figlefians I was rescued by one of the slaves, who canoed me with his bride to the base of a great cliff. The tide was low: as high as we could reach, the surface was rough with living shells that moved to our touch, and streamers of seaweed rose and fell with the ripple. At last he forced the boat back from the rocky wall: there was strong suction inwards. He bade us with a gesture lie down flat in the bottom, whilst he at the bow grovelled with a hand raised to the low-valuted rock. We shot in underneath into darkness, but in a few minutes we were out of the torrent, moored in a peaceful bay.

CHAPTER XXIX
NOOKOO

WE GOT ON SHORE in a sandy corner of a great cave; and we were soon asleep from our great exertions and endurance. When I awoke, I saw that the dome underneath which we slept was covered with myriads of glowworms. Before long my eyes grew accustomed to the twilight of our abode, and I could see pillars of gleaming white stretch from floor to roof, as if hewn out of marble by the workmen of some great sculptor and then abandoned before the capitals and bases could be carved into floral symmetry. Pendent masses waited for some architect to hollow them into forms of grace. Vaultings and domings of countless variety were there, needing only the skilled hand to make them harmonise into marvellous beauty. I could hear the rush and bustle of the current that had borne us in, as it swept I knew not whither. I looked to see the direction, and was for the first time struck by the wondrous azure of the light that was around us. Untroubled depths lay close to our resting-place; and the sunlight that shot through the waters of the low archway bore up the mingled colour of the sea and the sky into the half-darkness of this undercliff cathedral; all the mouldings and groinings of the vault were bathed in a deep violet light such as we see in rare skies when the sun has long set, and the thin moon stands sicklewise beside the harvest of the stars. Only in our own shelving niche were there marks of the discolouring hand of man; the débris of former fires lay scattered, and dark shading ran up the marble of the roof; it had been used, I could see, for generations as a camping-ground of recurrent dwellers in the cave.

Our guide soon had a fire lit, and the meal he cooked was welcome. As we ate, he told me his story. He had with the aid of the father of his fiancée followed up a wonderful invention of his father's, who had died from an accident in his researches. It was a method of utilising the germs of disease in warfare. Millions of the most destructive and most prolific plague-scattering microbes were inclosed in minute globules for arrow-points and in huge bombs for catapults. To prevent the plague spreading amongst friends, they had also found a powerful disinfectant, that could impregnate the air for miles in a few minutes and destroy all the pestiferous germs.

A Figlefian, having heard of the invention, lured him into their island with the promise of making a hero of him, but had enslaved him instead; and he had lived like all the Swoonarian slaves, nursing the hope of independence and revenge. He had been taken by his master on the last voyage, and had discovered during the shipwreck that his bride was included in the human cargo. He burst out into loud invectives against the licentious tyrants; and he justified his determination to revenge by a description of their devilish lechery and intrigue.

When the story was finished, his bride had disappeared; and we followed her along the gallery that edged the torrent. We came across her seated upon a broken stalagmite, but as we sat down near her on a shelf that had once been the tidemark of the water a wild shriek pierced our ears; it shot through the gorge we had just passed, and, peering into the darkness through which it was sliding, we saw two men like Sneekape clutching fiercely at the slippery walls of the ravine as their canoe swept onwards. It was the shriek of despair and helplessness. Away into the unknown it sped, and the agonised voices were swallowed up by the darkness on the other side. The yell grew muffled and far-off, and then suddenly sank. Our guide laid his ear to the azure depths of the indwelling ocean, but he heard no more than I did,—the suck and splash of the waters in their undercliff passage and the boom of the waves as they struck on the wall of rock without.

We returned to our sleeping-place. We watched the twilight of our cave die out and the glowworms glimmer and flash on the roof; and I fell into a dream of starflights in space and the intricate dance of worlds across the face of night. I was oppressed to agony, and awoke. The violet light was rippling along the vault and paling the steely glimmer of our living lamps. I heard the rush of the torrent; but there was no breathing or rustle of mortals. I looked around. My companions were gone.

Here was I, alone, buried in this underground hiding-place of the waters. Frenzy seized my mind, and I rushed to the edge of the torrent, only to find the canoe gone and the traces of the feet of my guide and his betrothed upon the sand, where they had embarked.

After a time I roused myself from my despair. I noted that the inrushing waters had a downward flow. If I followed them, I should be certain to find human beings. I made torches of the garments that lay in the nooks, and stumbled along the marvellous cave, for how many days I know not, guided by the hiss of the tortuous waters. To the right I often lost the wall that I crept along. There were deep subcaves branching off. At last I sank down in weariness and nausea of life. My torches had given out. I had long before eaten the last of my food. I fell into a swoon, and I seemed to dream. I saw Sneekape tempted by beautiful women and agonised to find them phantoms. He was whipped and lashed as he and his countrymen had whipped and lashed the Swoonarian slaves. Phantom after phantom drew him into love-passages, till at last I saw him sink in death upon the earth. He had died of his own special passion.

It was no dream at all, for my rescuer appeared and interpreted to me the scenes I had just witnessed. They never killed any of these cruel tyrants who had done them so many wrongs; they only let them feel what they had been, and allowed them to die of surfeit of their own passions. It was worth the trouble, to make them agonise through the dreary fate of their victims and meet the natural result of their own vices. To kill them off would be too merciful. The method of nature was more just, to make their own sins punish them.

They were about to apply a quicker solvent to these obstructives of the progress of man. They had the germs of all the diseases that attacked their vices, and every Swoonarian woman was to be armed with capsules of them, and whenever any one of the licentious tyrants approached her with unjust or salacious intent in his mind, a capsule was, with its sharp point, to effect a slight scratch on his body and, broken, to pour its contents into the wound. The Swoonarian men were escaping by means of seeming suicide. They plunged into what the Figlefians thought a boiling caldron in their burning mountain Nookoo. But there was a cool space in it, and it was into this that they dived and came up in the cave.

My rescuer had pleaded with his fellow-conspirators for my life and on oath that I would never divulge their secret I was given up to him. He blindfolded me and led me by a rough and devious path, that zigzagged and circled round in the most bewildering way. Then was I conscious of being enclosed in something that seemed a coffin. I dared not rebel; and in fact I fully trusted the good faith of my rescuer. I soon felt myself hurled as if through the air and my strange enclosure plunge as if into water. For a few moments I had the sensation of stifling, and then I felt a rush of briny air into my lungs; there was buoyancy about my cell, and before long it moved along the surface of water and struck land. I heard the voice of my guide again; the lid of my coffin was unlocked, and I knew that I was standing on the earth in the sweet air of heaven once more. Many a mile, it seemed to me, was I led up and down, but at last we sat, and food was supplied to me. Again we started forth on our rough journey. I was led down to a sandy beach; I knew by the sound of the rippling waves and by the soft pliancy of that on which I walked. I heard men's voices and the sound of paddles. I was lifted into a canoe, and my rescuer whispered in my ear farewell. I sought his hand, and pressed it in token of gratitude.

When the band was removed from my eyes, I was on board my own yacht, and the dawn was breaking in the east.

CHAPTER XXX
THE VOYAGE TO BROOLYI

OH, THE ECSTASY OF that first day! To hear the accents of my native tongue around me, to see the features of the men I loved, after the long months of sojourn amongst strange peoples! It seemed years since I had used English, or spoken soul to soul with any human being. I dared not laugh or express my joy; I feared lest my utterance should be so overdone that I would seem mad. I sat and reined in my passion of reminiscence, waiting for the ebb of its inundating waters. My whole being was flooded with the intoxication of the familiar thoughts and moods of the past. I asked my old comrades to let me lie and meditate a while, and as soon as a meal was prepared, they might call me. As I lay I felt the memories of my boyhood and youth play upon me like the sweet sunshine of my old home in summer. I could have lived thus for ever. No utterance could have measured the happiness of my soul. Then the last touch to the overbalancing of my emotion was given by Sandy Macrae, my steward. As he moved about below preparing the table, he burst out into "Ye Banks and Braes o' Bonny Doon." The tears rolled down my cheeks, nor could I tell whether they came from sadness over the graves of the past or joy flooding every pore of my existence. He had a fine voice that tided with waves of emotion; and as he wailed forth, "And I sae weary, fu' o' care," I broke into low sobbing. It was as if the spirits of my loved dead were speaking to me across the years and bidding me come to them, as if the voice of lament rang out of the unseen. Every nerve in my being quivered on the edge of song; I was shaken like a harp in the wind. Oh, if only I could have found utterance for this music of the infinite that was thrilling athwart my heartstrings! Nothing would come but tears.

The song ceased, and I fell back into the dull and joyless lethargy that follows great excitement. Life was a grey mist without vision beyond the immediate sensation. Annihilation—any change from this blank existence—would have been a delight. A shiver ran through my frame, as if some enemy had crossed my grave.

Again the pathos of the voice found full expression in "The Flowers of the Forest," that beautiful threnody over the graveyards of dead ages; and the sense of the swift oblivion that overtakes even the greatest of the past came upon me. This earth was but a funeral orb of vanished pomp and ambition, a vast God's-acre, wherein a few years or ages mingled the epitaph and the graven tombstone with the forgotten dust. The whole of life was but a burial procession into a nameless past, a series of everlasting farewells on the brink of an infinite oblivion. That all this passion and sadness and weeping should vanish without effect! That the singer should lie in the same unremembered dissolution as the sung! That the sighs and groans and cruel rendings of the heart that make up so much of the tale of life should be, within a few decades, as much forgotten as to-day's zephyr or yesterday's storm! That even this funeral orb should itself within a brief period of the life of our universe blacken and shrivel into death! The shrilling "a' wede away" pierced the very heart as it sent these thoughts through my brain.

The ringing of the breakfast bell threw me with almost volcanic impetus out into the commonplace world of working and sleeping and feeding. I was soon replenishing the exhausted fires of energy, and the close of the meal found me rid of sentiment and settled into everyday feelings and purposes. We put out to sea that we might escape any hue and cry that might arise from the disappearance of Sneekape or the outbreak of the revolution of the slaves of Figlefia. It was not long till we had left that island a speck on the horizon scarce distinguishable from our smoke that lounged cloudlike across our wake, and we were deep in the history of our adventures.

The sailing-captain of the *Daydream*, Alick Burns, acted as spokesman, with a court of appeal in my old guide through Aleofane, Blastemo, and my steward, Sandy Macrae. After seeing me safe aboard the Tirralarian falla, they set out for Broolyi; but they had not reached it, for they were driven off by a great storm, and, in battling against it so as to prevent drifting into the circle of mist, they had exhausted their fuel, and had to make for the nearest islands of the archipelago they could find. Blastemo thought they were approaching a group of islands that was inhabited by the fiercest and most quarrelsome savages to be found within the rim of fog. Nothing could tame them or reduce their vanity and belief in their greatness and invincibility. When exiled from their respective communities, their ancestors had been of the ordinary size and usual proportions of men. But in the process of the generations they had gradually grown into pigmies with increasingly venomous dispositions. Their shores were the most inhospitable for all strangers, and no falla would approach them except under dire necessity. Stories of their inhumanity and towering conceit were told all over the archipelago. If they had as much ability to unite and as much power as they had venom and inflated self-esteem, they would dominate the whole earth. Happily, they were a feeble folk, still more enfeebled by their mutual envies and jealousies and dissensions. Yet they did all the harm they could, and especially delighted in getting the weak or invalid or sensitive amongst them to whom to apply their tortures.

CHAPTER XXXI
MESKEETA

BLASTEMO, WARLIKE THOUGH HE was, was greatly alarmed at seeing the wind fall and the *Daydream* drift towards one of the lowest of the group. He knew it was Meskeeta, which he translated the isle of Book-butchers; the people themselves translated it the isle of the Discerners of Good and Evil. But it was the evil, our friend explained, that they especially loved and indulged in; and it was not difficult for them, with their venomous habit of anatomising the quivering tissues, to find evil in the best of good. The ship was drifting so fast on the low shore that he got Captain Burns to anchor; and soon after the great chains clanked and whizzed she had stopped in her course. The crew began to feel their faces and hands smart as if stung with nettles; and before long they discovered that minute darts were sticking in their skin, feathered and pointed and adhesive with some poisonous acid. As a rule a good vigorous rub brushed off the microscopic barbs and prevented the venom searching the blood. But those who had sensitive skins suffered keenly from the volleys that came sweeping down the light puffs of wind now beginning to set out from the shore. The captain would have heaved anchor and sailed, had he not found that their provisions were running short. So he ordered the thinner-skinned below, and with the others he watched the beach to see if he could find the dart-throwers. Only by aid of the ship's telescope could he discover them, so diminutive were they and so masked were their batteries. Blastemo had not much hope; but they might try whether the islanders had any stores. Meanwhile, to reduce the virulence of the pigmies, on his advice they lit all the lamps they had and crowded them together on the point that would produce most effect on the shore. At once the volleys ceased, and through the glass could be seen the little beings falling in the dust. The effect was still more pronounced when blank cartridges of gunpowder were fired and showers of rockets and squibs. The creatures grovelled towards the ship, then bit the dust, and scattered it with their hands upon their hair and bodies. Blastemo told them that these pigmies were worshippers of anything that flashed or dazzled, but whenever even the sun got obscured or clouded they began to shoot at it. Into this island had been exiled all who were bitten with the mania of criticism, and, however stalwart their proportions when cast on its shores, their microscopic fault-finding within a few generations reduced their descendants to the size of this puny race of dart-throwers. For lack of books and authors to dissect and torture, they resorted to this petty internecine warfare. They never did much harm, it is true, except to one another and to oversensitive targets, their missiles had grown so minute and their vision so oblique and so marred by the habit of wearing varieties of spectacles. These spectacles were all spotted and cracked and twisted, in order to produce blemishes to be criticised and attacked in every object gazed at; they had been originally assumed, it was said, to permit them to stare at the sun and other luminaries without blenching, but, as they were never cleaned or mended or renewed, they became invaluable in their daily business of fault-finding; they discovered stains on the purest white, and defects in the most perfect thing ever created; and that was a great comfort. It was also a comfort to their victims; for they could not distinguish the vulnerable parts from the invulnerable or even see to shoot straight; they were as good as purblind. The worst the venomous little creatures could do was to send their poisoned barbs down the wind in volleys and thus obscure the vision of their foes or of those who looked on; they even thought that they thus obscured the sun at times, and they were sorry for this, for they adored everything that flashed with brilliancy.

"When we saw them lie on their stomachs in the dust," continued Burns, "we struck out in our boats for the shore, expecting peace at least. But, as we got out of range of our lamps, the dwarfs leaped up and began pouring their paltry missiles into the air. We landed with some inconvenience but no real harm; for we were all thick-skinned. They crowded round us in groups, busy with their petty bows and slings. Their missiles flew like dust. But they did more harm to one another than to us, they missed us so often, and we spread our handkerchiefs over our faces and hands. This last resort was necessary, for we noticed that one group made the face their target, another the neck, and a third the hands; their functions were, we could see, carefully specialised. One feature that perplexed us was that they had their upper parts concealed in such enormous masks as, if we had not seen their legs, would have made them seem giants; each man's mask was large enough to cover a whole group; and the masks in each group were all exactly alike; but, as they shifted from group to group, they interchanged masks. The only thing that seemed to distinguish one from another was that a few of the masks had names on them.

"We were much puzzled about all this till Blastemo, here, showed us that it was a ruse to hide their identity in their internecine warfare; no one could tell which of his enemies had dealt him any blow or poisonous wound; and the size of the masks was to deceive as to the numbers and force, when the foe could not see the legs. The gigantic heads had huge brows, and beneath these protruded eyes that added a more truculent expression to the already truculent face. These eyes were the spectacles which were intended to give especial protection to the living eyes behind and to distort and mar the objects looked at; they were an especial mark for the missiles of enemies; and so they were cracked and scratched in all directions. Blastemo also explained to us the sudden change of attitude towards us after we had left the ship; it was the dazzle that they adored and not the sources of it. We would not have minded the artillery of the pigmies, but that, after seeing how futile it was, they began to squirt water as well, and we were soon covered with fetid mud from head to foot; the minute missiles mingled with the water, and the poison on them gave the disgusting smell.

"We sent off to the ship for lamps, and we bore them, each of us one, gleaming on our heads. We were at once safe, except for guerilla warriors, who might be for the moment behind any one of us. They did not now grovel in the dust; the light was not strong enough to produce this effect. They approached and patted us with most patronising familiarity, minute though they were. They seemed to draw infinite courage from their numbers and the masking of their faces; for if we caught any one of them alone and lifted him in our hands and took off his head-gear, he shivered with fear and lay down flat on the palm of our hands with imploring gestures; and when we let him down on the ground he scampered off to the shelter of some group as if for dear life. We were glad to be rid of the wretched little creatures; for when held close to us they stank abominably, reminding us of certain bed-lurking insects of Christendom. Without their masks they seemed to lose their self-confidence and braggart airs, and yet there were a few who wore none, and stood off from us in haughty isolation that almost made us laugh, so incongruous was it with their stature. Blastemo tells us that these were the great men amongst them, who thought they had the power of conferring godhead and everlasting fame; they called themselves, in fact, Todes, or the godmakers of mankind. Sandy Macrae thought of bringing off one or two of them in his pocket, so useful would they be to people without a religion, and to title-beggars and popularity-hunters in the old country. Sandy's waistcoat would have held enough to serve all Europe. But the thought of the proximity of the dirty little imps to his nose made him rob Christendom of such a reinforcement of its courts and centres.

"We watched them for a time, and observed that all of them had a squint in their eyes, so that we could never tell which way they were looking. And their noses extended right across their lips into a sharp point. They were, in fact, a most treacherous looking crew; and treacherous they were, too, as any one of us soon found when his lamp went out or when he turned his back on a group of them. We soon discovered, too, how innumerable were the dissensions and divisions amongst them. When they were all in front of us and all our lamps were shining brightly, group would turn against group; but if that was not possible the members of a group would turn and embrace, or adore, or brush the clothes of one another. Blastemo explained to us that mutual flattery was the only alternative they knew for malicious hatred or envy or jealousy. They build their temples over the graves of those whom they call great men and whom they have persecuted to death, and each worshipper expects a temple to be erected over his grave when he dies. So you can imagine the number of sacred buildings in the island. No stranger is admitted to any of them; but it is said that each of them is a vast mirror within; only one worshipper enters at a time; and he sees on all sides of him nothing but glorified editions of himself. Without, they are of a jaundiced colour, broken only by the light of green lamps that are ever kept alight, in order, they say, to ward off the evil eye. There are no priests, for every devotee is his own priest; but each has a doorkeeper who is dressed up to represent Envy. His chief duty is to see that only one enters at a time and that he adds his quota to the fire on the altar. This consists of some book that he has criticised and shown to be full of faults. They keep a feeble folk in slavery, dwarfs like themselves, to produce books on which to exercise their critical powers. These poor creatures have highly sensitive skins and feelings, and they writhe under the attacks of their critics; it is their agony that gives the keenest pleasure to their masters and makes the sweetest incense in their offerings to the gods. The Meskeetans, indeed, would have lost the end of their existence and died out but for this diversion. Occasionally they get mad over a book of real power; they dance with rage and afterwards with delight, for it piques their best faculties to energy; and the joy they afterwards get out of its petty faults is tenfold because their rage did not lead them to burn it at once or tear it into fragments. Every comma or letter or word misplaced makes them inordinately proud of their acumen; they strut and crow as if they had found the source of original sin. The overseers of the slaves make them insert mistakes in the books in order that their discovery may gratify the venomous little masters. The lot of no people in the whole archipelago arouses so much pity as that of these book-makers, so utterly hopeless is it. They are kept alive that their anguish may be enjoyed; they are carefully watched lest they commit suicide, all to gratify the inhuman desire of the little monsters, their owners.

"This we knew afterwards from our friend here," continued our captain. "But we went up into their town to see if we could get food or fuel. We saw their yellow, green-lanterned temples, and came upon some of the poor scholars in chains bent over their books. The houses were made of glass like their temples, and it was somewhat painful for our eyes to look at them in the sun; but inside they were all mirror; every little man could contemplate his own self, whatever he did within his own household; outside he could see nothing to adore but the sun and its reflection; inside he took the place of that luminary and god. Every house bore evidence of having stood siege: it was cracked and splashed with mud in almost every part; there were some spaces that were left intact, and on these I saw something engraved; it was, Blastemo interpreted, the chief maxim of their adored book: 'God has given us to know all things, and to say all things without error; let the world worship us, His prophets and vicegerents upon earth.' Where this was written, the glass was thin and transparent, so that it could be read both without and within; all the rest was fortified to stand a siege by any one group.

"We could find no supplies. They had no food but a flour obtained by pounding up the bones of those whom they considered the great dead, or a kind of chalky paste obtained from reducing statues of themselves and of the gods whom they worshipped. Their only drink was a black fluid that tasted like vinegar, and no fuel could we get but a few of the books produced by the enslaved people.

"The oil in our lamps began to give out, and we had to beat a hasty retreat, for they had found that we did not bow before them as omniscient or divine, or treat their sayings and life with any great adoration. They began to concentrate their sharpest and most poisonous darts upon us, as we turned to make off, and yet when we arrived on board and massed our newly lighted lamps, we could see the little creatures down on their faces again in the dust."

CHAPTER XXXII
COXURIA

"THE WIND HAD RISEN offshore; but, not long after we weighed anchor, it fell and we began to drift. When the morning came, we saw that a current was rapidly bearing us down upon another low island that closely resembled in its outline the land we had left; but it was evidently very productive, and here we seemed certain of obtaining supplies. Blastemo thought it was Coxuria. If it were and if the pigmies that inhabited it were able to lay aside their everlasting hostilities, there was plenty to get on the island. We cast anchor therefore and pulled to the shore.

"It was yet early, and on the beach there were but few pigmies, who were greatly excited at our arrival. Each of the wizened little atomies laid himself alongside of one of our party when we jumped out of our boats, and began to prove to him the superiority of some dogma he held. We did not understand them, and listened in bewildered silence. But the friendly fervour died out of their manner as soon as it dawned on them that not a word of their eloquence was understood by us. A shade fell upon their faces and turned them, with their restless malice and cruel hate, into miniature maps of hell. They were like little demons as they consulted together. They chose a representative, who addressed us in Aleofanian, and Blastemo interpreted. But the faces of the silent Coxurians grew darker and more scowling; suspicion and hatred gave their expression to every feature.

"The stuff we listened to was the most absurd jumble of doctrines and arguments. The orator began by asserting as the first truth of religion that the gods were between two and three feet in height, and had shapes exactly like the Coxurians: that needed no proof, so he did not stop to prove it; the world was agreed upon that. They had never appeared upon earth except to the saints of Coxuria. With their saliva they had moistened and leavened a cake that grew in all its essential ingredients like the bodies they had assumed when they had come amongst men. A little of this cake was enough to transform everything it touched into divine material, and there was none of it except in Coxuria. The true belief was that everything that it touched had this miraculous power of transformation; only vile heretics could assert the opposite. Yet some still worse heretics affirmed that only their high-priests who had been touched by the hands of high-priests who had touched the original saliva had the true divinising faculty in their hands. Another fanatical sect held the damning doctrine that it was neither the original saliva nor the cake that gave the power of miracle, but the words that had come out of the mouths of the gods when the saliva sputtered on to the cake. He cursed these heretics with wild vituperation, evidently selected from their sacred books, and threatened them with everlasting damnation. He was still more furious in his damnatory eloquence when he came to those who held that the essence of religion lay in turning the face to the rising sun in all ceremonies, and clipping all the hair off round the left ear. All true reverence consisted in modesty towards the gods, who lived in the sun; and their dazzling brilliance there was intended to make the worshippers turn away their faces from them. The direction in which they vanished in the evening in their car of light was that towards which the reverent face ever should be turned; for by their fading away and letting the curtain of night be drawn they meant to encourage the worshipper to look sadly after them. Then, every man knew that it was the right ear that heard most distinctly; it was this that was meant by the gods to be uncovered of its natural veil in order to hear the divine harmonies of the universe. It was appalling to hear any human lips utter such blasphemy as that the face should be turned to the east or that the left ear should be unmuffled. No torture was too great for such heresy.

"He proceeded with other damnatory classifications of Coxurian religionists, and bit by bit showed how he and his fellow-worshippers beside him alone were to be saved. He implored us to turn to the true faith and not be lost for ever. We managed to suppress the smile that was ever rising to our faces. Then, with a look round, he warned us to be careful of error even within the true faith. There were mistakes made even by the best of men. He besought us to avoid the belief that it was only over the tip of the right ear that the hair was to be cut, or that the body was not to be bent quite to the ground in worship towards the west. The whole sense of hearing was meant by the gods to be unbared; and it was the main part of the body that was to be turned up to the rising of the sun; reverence could be shown only by turning the eyes completely away from the dazzling beams of the gods. He was getting more and more fervid in his denunciations of such errors and others like them that his fellow-sectarians had fallen into. He and he alone was the pillar of true religion upon earth; he and he alone would reach the sphere of the gods; alas for the solitary grandeur of his position in the universe!

"Suspicion more and more filled the faces of his pigmy supporters. Nor could we longer keep down the amusement that was pressing upwards within us. We had just burst into a roar of laughter when there crept down upon us in his rear a cloud of pigmies armed with the most jagged of lances and arrows. The effect was magical. Our theological rooster who had crowed so lustily and his band of our would-be converters turned tail and fled, yet not without bravado or menacing gestures. The newcomers went through the same performance as their predecessors, except that they insisted on the special points of doctrine that marked them off from all other sects. We could not understand the difference between the two claimants of our souls. The leader of the second crowd put the distinction into a single word and pounded the meaning of it into us. He scowled and explained, preached and exhorted. Not a gleam of intelligence passed over any of our faces. Their inappeasable hatred of the sect that had just disappeared over the horizon had no other basis, it seemed to us, than the unmeaning syllable 'buzz.' Their gods when they appeared on earth had, according to our furious orator, proclaimed 'fuzz' as the name of the saving cake; it was a damning error in the fugitive schismatics to hold that it was 'buzz-fuzz.' It looked as if we were not going to be converted to this saving syllable. The ugly weapons of conversion were raised more threateningly, but thanks to Blastemo the awkwardness of the situation was got over. Without consulting us, he rose and accepted all their statements as the everlasting truths of the universe, and expressed for us the profoundest loathing of the doctrines that had before been vented upon us. The scene was turned into one of jubilation. The ugly weapons were lowered, and the loathsome little imps ran forward to embrace their converts, as far, at least, as the minuteness of their bodies would allow. Never at one sweep of their doctrinal net had so large a haul been made. It seemed to be our size as much as our numbers that gave them joy; every cubic inch of us freed from the damning error told in the ultimate sum of salvation. We did not understand it all till we got on board."

Here Blastemo broke in with a loud but somewhat awkward laugh. He seemed to understand something of what was being told.

"We followed them bewildered, as they led us inland with shouts of joy. But we had not gone far towards their city when a larger troop was encountered, evidently still more formidable in their doctrinal dislikes and means of conversion, for our conductors slunk away. Again were we flooded with oratory, and again Blastemo managed the affair with delicacy and success, as it seemed to us at the time. The same type of incident occurred half a dozen times before we reached the town gates. Our last troop of soul-captors was the largest of all, but dissension broke out in their midst. It seemed that several understood Aleofanian, and each of these declared that their orator misstated their creed and gave us only his special shade of it. They kept whispering to one another, till at last discontent broke out into a general mêlée. To make matters worse, most of the bands that had been forced to steal off and let their convertites slip from their grasp had evidently come to an understanding and discovered that they had all been deceived by Blastemo. They united their forces and came down upon us and our convoy, just at the moment that they were rent with dissensions and ready to come to blows. In the confusion Blastemo smuggled us into the city, and out again by another gate, leaving the two parties to fight it out. When we had got near to our boats he saved us again. We saw the whole mob of pigmies hurrying over the beach. A few minutes were all we needed to embark and escape. He uttered words that seemed to paralyse them. It was a curse upon the most fundamental and sacred part of their creed, a point on which they had agreed to sink differences. But it was only a momentary paralysis. They recovered and rushed on again. Again he hurled amongst them words that we did not understand. The effect was as strange. They divided up into two hostile groups that set upon each other with the greatest violence. Before they had seen that it was a ruse of his and had checked their dissentient fury, we had got far enough from the shore to be out of reach of their missiles, which now began to rain into the sea.

"The phrase that had saved us was one on which the island was equally divided; one set accepted it as the saving part of their creed; the other abhorred it as the very poison of the soul. Blastemo explained to us the fundamental difference between the two forces of 'babbyclootsy'; but none of us could grasp it, or, if we did, we forgot it at once; it was far too fine for translation through two languages. We abandoned the effort. So did we the other niceties of creed that split the Coxurians up into units. At various stages in their history they had succeeded in attaining unanimity of opinion for a short time; one party through greater procreative power or missionary zeal got the upper hand in numbers and annihilated the minority by what they called "acts of faith," processes of slow torture that ended in most cases in death, but it was only for a short time. They divided up again into two main sects; within, each was rent almost into units by fierce differences of opinions; but the differences were sunk in hatred of the opposition. This same history repeated itself every second generation. Every decade or so the majority wiped out the dissentient few by the usual process of faith, and then split up, only to re-coalesce into two almost equal bodies for temporary belligerent purposes.

"They are very lazy except with their tongues; and so they are very prolific, as nature almost unaided supplies them with plenty of food. Their numbers are constantly recruited, too, with outcasts from the other islands, exiled on account of their passion for religious dogmatism. But through the ages the

Coxurians had gradually grown smaller and smaller in size, more wizened in countenance, and more venomous in feelings. Their perpetual internecine feuds would soon have wiped the miserable imps off the face of the earth but for two provisions of nature; the arrival of new immigrants made them at times quicksilver into two masses in order to save the souls of the newcomers; at other times the exceptional force of will in one or more individuals produced militant organisation that obliterated minor hatreds. It was a good thing for the archipelago that there were ever a surviving few, amongst whom might be placed all the doctrinomaniacs of their various communities, in order to give issue to the poisonous theological blood. These exiles would never remain if the island were deserted; as it was they were welcomed and made much of by the two parties, that their souls might be saved."

CHAPTER XXXIII
HACIOCRAM

"ONE GROUP OF ISLANDS we were warned to avoid was that of the Rasolola, or theomaniacs. Hither had been deported from the chief countries all who allowed their peculiar religious ideas to outrun common-sense or the permissible limits of worship or theological belief. A storm, however, drove us close to the small archipelago, and we had to anchor off Haciocram, or the Isle of Prophets. We had no sooner come to rest than there was raised on a signal-board above a lofty tower on the island an inscription in enormous letters. We got our guide to translate it. It did not remove our perplexity to learn that it was only a number, 1999. What could it mean? He could not enlighten us; but there was a provoking smile on his face. Before we could question him further, we saw a canoe put off from shore. Its occupant reaching us bounced on board, with fiery eyes standing out of his head, and his long hair on end like a mop. He was the inspired messenger of the inspired high-priest of the island, and he came to ask us if we accepted that (and he pointed to the sign-board) as the true number of the beast; if we did not, we might just as well be gone at once; for we would not be allowed to land. I wanted to know what beast it was; I knew a good many beasts, both human and inhuman; and I should like to know which one it was he meant. What! Did I not know what the beast was? the man of sin? the foul creature that was to creep forth and pollute the world at its end? The true number of him had but that day been revealed, and the whole world must accept it. For the sake of peace, I indicated my acceptance of it, though I was no more clear as to its meaning than before.

"Blastemo explained how the Haciocrammers had taken the sacred books of the islands with them as the sole consolation of their exile, and had worked out from them the most extraordinary theories of the constitution, history, and fate of the world. But, as they took, some of them the words, and others the letters of the words, of the book as inspired, whilst one section accepted its Thribbaty form and another its Slapyak form as the true, there had been the bitterest dissension amongst them. At one time the dominant section converted the others by great physical pressure brought to bear on the thumb,

then considered the seat of the soul; at another it was the great toe that was
the point of attack in conversion crusades; if the conversion could not be accomplished thus, then were the recalcitrants purified by fire as the only means
left of saving their souls. Sometimes the dissentients pretended to give up the
errors of their way, and when strong enough rose in rebellion and overturned
the dominant set. This had occurred again and again, till it was difficult to
tell from month to month, or now even week to week, which sect was in
power. There were as many sects as there were symmetrical combinations of
numbers, and they were all, when in power, equally fierce in persecution of
the others. Their experience as victims taught them no lesson of tolerance, but
only filled their hearts with a furious passion for revenge, that was ultimately
blended and confused with a passion for conversion.

"But had not the long series of mutual persecutions cleared out most of
the population? No; not one in a generation suffered the purification by fire.
Either the thumb or the great-toe persuasion was usually quite sufficient.
What had resulted from the perpetual conversions by pressure was one of
the most treacherous dispositions in the whole archipelago. Cunning had become an ingrained instinct as strong as their fanaticism in these numeroma-
niacs. When they were not dragooning and oppressing, they were busy pro-
tecting themselves from persecution by pretending to assume the colour of
the persecutors. Alternately victim and fanatic oppressor, the Haciocrammer
had become one of the most singular mongrels in creation. He was bold as a
lion to-day, and confident in his own inspiration and infallibility; to-morrow
he was cringing and supple and obsequious as the veriest slave. This creature
who had just brought the order from the ruling high-priest, whose eye was
all fire and fanaticism, would, after the next revolution to-morrow or the
following day, be ready to lick the dust beneath your feet, whilst his eye would
be full of mute and stupid appeal; you would not believe him to be the same
being, his nature would be so thoroughly turned inside out.

"We tried to persuade the ambassador to sell us provisions, but he was so
eager to persuade us of his infallibility and the finality of the new number of
the beast that he could not listen to our requests. The world had been waiting
for this number so long that it could not afford time for anything now but
the contemplation of it, and if only we would consider the method by which
the high-priest had come at it, we would see that the universe was saved.
He had counted all the words in the Thribbaty version of the sacred book,
and all in the Slapyak version, and added them together for a divisor; and
for a dividend he had counted all their letters and added them together and
multiplied the sum by the number of divisions in the book; what he got he
divided by the number of words, and thus he found the new number. What

was more important was that he had prophesied this before he had reached the result by arithmetic.

"Having got at the number, he had interpreted it in as original and infallible a way. He had taken the number of strokes needed to make any one letter of their alphabet as the numerical rendering of it, and in this manner he had translated the whole alphabet into numbers. He thus found that the new number stood for the name of his chief antagonist; if taken numerically, it indicated that this enemy of his and of the sect he represented would descend into Hades at the end of the world, whilst the high-priest himself and his sect would ascend into heaven; and the end of the world, he announced from other signs in the lettering of the sacred book, was next year.

"Blastemo told us that every time he had approached the island the world was to come to an end the following week or month or year; so, in order to test the high-priest, we sent off a message by his envoy offering to buy the surplus provisions of the island that would not be needed after the date he gave for the collapse of all things. A negative answer came back; and, as the storm had moderated, we lifted our anchor and left."

CHAPTER XXXIV
SPECTRALIA

"AS WE SAILED OFF, Blastemo entertained us with stories of the groups of islands that lay near at hand, and especially of one that lay away off to the north nearer the sunset than Coxuria and the other islands of religion. It was the place of ghosts, where the supernatural can have things to itself without the intrusion of sceptical worldliness and common-sense. It lies almost within the ring of mist that encircles the archipelago, and it is dominated by twilight when it is not midnight. The inhabitants have an invincible fear and hatred of the sun, and especially the rising sun; and if he ever dares to show his shameless face without a cloud they raise a dust that makes him like the eye of a drunkard. In order to avoid the impudence of his glances most of them used to live, and one section of them still lives, in cellars underground, sleeping there by day, and following their avocations out-of-doors by night. Mariners in that region land fearlessly when the sun shines, but avoid its shores during times of cloud and darkness, lest they should be taken for spirits and bodily enshrined for the purposes of worship. To be retained either as a resident or as an object of investigation or reverence was a fate to be shuddered at, for it was considered one of the worst wards for lunatic exiles. Hither were deported all who were incurably persuaded that they and they alone had direct communication with the other world. There was something uncanny about the conduct of everyone who found his way thither; in his eye shone the gleam of insanity, a reflection from the baleful light of hell.

"Another feature of the island, as of all the theopathic group, was its rank sectarianism. Almost every man was his own sect. There was a rough classification of them by travellers into 'antiquated ghost-seers' and 'modern ghost-seers'; but none would acknowledge allegiance to any classification. They all believed in spirits, or disembodied beings, who visited their island; beyond that resemblance ceased. Most of the older Spectralians, however, believed only in ghosts of ancient lineage, who had the stately ways of olden times, who seldom condescended to speak or communicate their thoughts, and who looked mutely piteous or minatory on their appearance for a few seconds and then vanished. The more recent exiles, having had a tinge of modern science, laughed at these fantastic monstrosities of a primitive age and insisted on the logical outcome of supernaturalism. Every human being had a ghost, and when death thrust it out of its body it hung about its old locality and tried to make itself manifest, now to one sense, again to another, but most frequently to hearing. It had been a custom of former spirits to address themselves chiefly to the eye; but that was in the silent old times when men preferred striking and acting to speaking. Now that the tongue had become the chief organ of action, it would be obviously absurd for the world of spirits not to adapt itself to the new ways; and so it was now to the ear that they addressed themselves, and seldom to the eye. And, whereas they had been ridiculously limited by ghostly conventions and could appear only in solemn guise at midnight by tombs and in abandoned chambers of castles or in rooms where murder had been done, now they were free to make themselves heard when and where they pleased, or rather when and where their corporeal clients and patrons pleased. There had evidently been a great war of liberation in the region of ghosts, a sort of French Revolution, that had thrown off the shackles of old and absurd convention from their limbs, if such a mode of speech were permissible. Now there was infinite variety in the world of the disembodied as in the world of common things. They all kept shop, as it were, and were ready to serve any who approached them in the due and proper way.

"There was in fact a small section of these modernists who prided themselves on their superior modernity and held that they could take a spirit out of its living body as easily as a pea out of its pod; for, they said, there are really two spirits in every human body, the detachable and the undetachable; the former it is that expatiates, the world over, in dreams and holds communion with worlds whereof the senses know nothing; the other is the workaday spirit that with observation and reason carries out the practical functions of daily life. They plumed themselves upon having thus solved all the problems of existence, that have puzzled mankind so long, by this simple device of two labels or classifications for the contents of the human body or vessel. They were even proud that the rest of the archipelago counted them no less mad than the other Spectralians, whom they scorned; it was the true sign of superiority in mental power, wisdom, and modernity to be called mad by other men.

"They despise the ancient ghost-seers for their old-fashioned ways and the funny old castles and rickety houses they build for their friends and clients from the other world. To think of going to the expense of putting up tumble-down buildings in order to woo spirits into them, a kind of ghost-trap, is to them the most laughable of proceedings; but the old fellows never lose faith in their creaky ghost eelpots, and go about as solemnly as ever they did making the walls of their castles chinky, the passages draughty, the rooms full of dark corners, and the halls like vaults for the dead. It is amusing to see them loosening the footboards of the corridors and stairs in order that they may creak and start and flap as soon as the shadows fall. They always hang old tapestries and sheets at odd draughty corners to rustle and lift in the blackness of the night; and they put a rooster handy outside of every cobwebby old castle they erect to give the word when their clients should be off. For themselves, they spend most of their nights there. The early part they pass in reading the most ghostly and blood-curdling books they can find in the archipelago and stuff into the dirty old libraries. These are the religious literature and litanies of the ghosts. It is a proper rule in every faith that the worshipper should get his mind into the due receptive and inspired attitude before attempting to approach the shrine; only thus can they see and hear the objects of their worship. Hours do they consume in reading the pious literature of ghosts, and then every nerve is on the alert, and every sense awake for the footfalls of their friends from the other world. The passages begin to creak, the tapestries to flop and rustle, the doors, that they have left ajar for their clients, to slam. They know that the spirits of the mighty dead are then approaching them; their eyes flame out of their heads; and with a gleam like lightning the expected apparition flashes over the line of their vision.

"The modernists smile at these preparations and precautions, and declare that nothing of these manifest themselves, but only the shadow of the watcher himself in some passing starlit or moonlit space. They know that the true modern spirit cares for none of these things; he has been brought up in the midst of the best medical science, and avoids draughty old buildings as bad for colds and rheumatism and full of the microbes of countless diseases; he has advanced with the ages, and asks for nothing better than the simplest modern appliances; he has learned, as a modern should, telegraphy and telepathy, and all he needs is a table to rap on, or a planchette or slate to write on; that is his whole outfit, as becomes an occupant of an immaterial world; he has the electricity in his own system to work the thing; but if he has got to materialise, he does like the lights turned down; for modern gas and oil lamps are very trying for a poor old spirit's eyes, that have been accustomed to the dim, ethereal spaces. It is all right when he can remain unseen and merely let his mind out in rap language, though that is a rather slow way of communication for beings that move and act as quickly as thought; but to doff his old habits and his invisible form makes a ghost as shy as for a human being to appear naked in broad daylight. It is no wonder that spirits insist that the lights be down, when they are asked to appear to the eyes of the initiated.

As for the worldly and sceptical, they will never have the privilege of seeing anyone or even hearing anyone from the world of spirits till they abandon their scoffing, faithless ways. Faith is a prime essential of all communion with the immaterial world. The gross senses of the worldling can never see or hear what his more refined neighbours catch from the spirit-sphere. It is only Spectralia that ghosts will ever favour with their countenance. Now and again they appear to men and women of peculiar natures in other islands in order to have them deported to their favourite isle; they are heard of no more after the exile, having followed their clients. But, if those they address lose faith in them and remain with their fellow-countrymen, the ghosts cease to appear to them.

Even the modernists acknowledge that spirits have but limited means of communication; they prefer two or three methods and will have no others. A story is told over the archipelago of a Swoonarian inventor who had no-ticed this and had thought out plans for opening a clear highway into the spirit-world. One was to erect a vacuum tube up through the atmosphere of the earth and to catch the ghosts in gossamer nets at the bottom of it as they were sucked down. Another was to have a megaphone with an enormous mouth stretching above the clouds and its terrestrial end in a vast magnifying hall that would turn the poor ghost whispers into clear, intelligible sounds. A third was to utilise their rapping propensities; he proposed to have a great musical instrument with keys placed in position underneath their favourite tables, where the spirits loved to rap out their answers to questions; a little training would soon develop in them the power of earthly harmony, and, as they struck the keys, the Spectralians would have the most divine ghost music. A modification of this would provide a method for spirits to express applause when they approved of earthly performers and speakers; a series of fans or clapboards were to work round a freely moving axle and to come in contact with the soft, flat surface as they spun round, so that they would produce a sound like the clapping of hands; as the spirits rapped on the keyboard, the vanes whirled round, and the effect of tumultuous applause was produced. Still another modification was intended to use spirit force for human purposes; their rapping power was to be concentrated on engines that would drives mills and looms and the other machines of Spectralian factories. He had a great windmill too that was to be blown round by the breath of spirits; and an automatic spirit reporter that would record whatever was done or said in spirit-land. Another line his inventions took was to provide bodies that would invite wandering souls into them. A third set of inventions was in-tended to relieve the over-population of the Spectralian atmosphere; he was convinced that the region was uncomfortably crowded, because all the ghosts of the archipelago flocked thither, and there were no sanitary arrangements for making ghost life endurable; so he proposed by one of his new machines to take a census of the spirits in and around Spectralia, and then to send his automatic spirit-emigration Propaganda amongst them in order to induce large numbers of them to seek other and more wholesome spheres.

"After long years of work on these, he came across a wealthy and enthusiastic Spectralian, whom he convinced of the fortune that lay in his machines. The two shipped the cargo of notions and landed safely in Spectralia. But before they could be put out on the market there was a ghost riot one night; what were the poor spirits to do for a living if all their functions were to be appropriated or concentrated by these vile inventions? Half of them would be thrown out of the employment they had been accustomed to, and how were they to learn all these new-fangled notions? It was too much for ghost nature to bear, and the machinery was smashed to pieces in a single night; and the spirits formed themselves into a trades-union for keeping such agitators and inventors far from the shores of Spectralia; it was said that the Swoonarian and his patron fled before the indignation of the mob of ghosts that pursued them, and the last that was seen of them they were on their knees uttering mad cries of alternate prayer and threat to their unseen tormentors.

"Another story told the adventures of a missionary from Aleofane, who was sent to convert Spectralians to the true faith. After long and enthusiastic labour in preaching and praying he found on examination that he was no further forward than when he landed. The Spectralians were as unconvinced as before; and on inquiry he was told that as long as the spirits were unconverted their clients would adhere to their old faith. So the missionary set himself to the work of converting the ghosts, promising himself that, this done, the whole island would go over to his religion. At first they could not understand a word that he said; and he learned their rap language. Then they refused to listen patiently to his homilies and litanies; he had no sooner called them up and launched into his eloquence than they had dispersed like leaves before a gale. He tried to get at the bottom of this universal reluctance on their part to hear him out; and he discovered that they were a good deal more primitive than savages or children; their education had been completely neglected; they could never tell anybody anything that was not known to everybody before; they indulged in the dreariest platitudes and the most obvious truisms, and they thought that it was more than spirit could bear to hear lengthy sermons on the obvious poured broadside into them. He assumed that his truths were too high for them to understand, and never realised that he was doing nothing more than pouring water into the ocean. It was true that their education had been wretchedly neglected; the most elementary truths of science were unknown to them. He set himself first to their tuition in the use of reason before attempting to convert them again. Alas! his task was an endless one. As with savages, after teaching any simple and primal principle, he found he had to begin teaching it to them over again. He did not weary of his burden; for he knew that he had the great prize before him of converting a whole nation. He grew a white-haired old man before he could get them beyond such elementary truths as two and two are four, and he died at his task, a martyr to the platitudinarianism of spirits.

"We were steaming along under the lee of Spectralia, the night fast lowering upon us, as Blastemo held us spellbound by these stories. A crash and a quiver of the ship cut short his narrative, and we rushed on deck. The engines stopped, and peering over the side in the struggling moonlight we could see one or two dark objects rise and fall on the gleaming wake. We lowered a boat, and soon had two dripping figures upon the deck. We anchored and attended to their necessities; and by the morning they had so far recovered as to be able to give an account of themselves.

"They were the superintendents or presidents of the Spectralian ghost markets; so Blastemo interpreted for us. There had been reported to them, as the sun set, a strange appearance on the horizon. It had become too dim for them to make it out by the time they had reached the beach; but as its mass of lights grew in size and brilliancy and a singular throb seemed to come through the air from it, they could form no other conclusion than that it was an influx of emigrants from the more distant regions of spirits. As it approached, they could see it move on the face of the waters, and they knew that it was a ghost ship; for they could perceive dark flights of spirits gleam in its lights and hurry it on as they spun through the night behind it, and they could hear the multitudinous beat of their wings in the air. None but they were officially authorised to welcome ghostly immigrants into the island; it was their duty to meet the spectral fleet before it touched the land, and they rushed for fallas, as they seemed to see it about to pass their island. From a promontory that would most easily intercept it they swung their paddles towards it; and their hearts were gladdened as they found themselves right across the track it was making. The next they knew was that they were floundering in the water and it had passed them. They shouted; but, faint as they were, they thought that their cries would make little impression. The elfin ship stopped, however; the throb of the winged host ceased; and they were hoisted by the strange spirits on board.

"We asked them what they wanted to do with the new arrival of ghosts when they got them. The answer came; they would dispose of them in the market of souls. Each division of the people, the antiques and the moderns, had a market of its own, and that was why the two officials rushed, each to his own boat, to secure the cargo of ghosts, and why each ventured into such danger to secure his prize. They did not know for certain whether the new arrivals were spirits of the olden time or modern spirits; but each had good reason to think that they were ghosts of his own special affinity. The man of the dead-soul market was pretty sure that the cargo was for him; for none but ancient spirits would arrive at midnight with such appalling sounds, in such sable robes, and with such flash of lightnings. The president of the living-soul market was as sure that they were for him; for only modern ghosts could arrive in such novel circumstances, and in all the panoply of modern science. It was with difficulty that we could keep the two from blows; they wrangled furiously, and hurled insult and vituperation at each other with manifest effect. At last we had to get them into separate compartments that they might not do each other bodily harm.

"Alone with us each calmed down into comparative tranquillity, and we were able to get a fair and rational account of the two markets out of the chaos of their mutual misrepresentation. After collating notes of the scene with each we came to the conclusion that the two markets were at opposite ends of the island, and that they belonged to the two great sects of the people, the antiques and the modernists. At stated times there were great ghost fairs to which the inhabitants crowded that they might be able to exchange familiars or traffic the spirit that had become too commonplace to them for one that might give them more exquisite shocks of supernatural surprise and alarm.

"The goblin-shop, as the modernist called the market of dead souls, was evidently the place where ghosts of the olden type were bought and sold. It was situated, like the catacombs, underground, and above it lay old grave-yards, ancient ruins, castles, chapels, and shrines where the goods trad-ed in might squeak and gibber and disport themselves for the edification of the purchasing public; these dilapidated old cages were a kind of ghost menagerie, or, as the modernist sneered, the goblin kennels; in them the spirits were penned during the ghost fairs, and the intending purchasers wandered round and listened to the whistling, moaning winds through the crevices and tried to get the sensation of being startled by the ghost rustle and speech or by the apparitions that came and went within the dark pens. The traffickers went in twos and threes around; for they dared not trust them-selves alone in the presence of these uneasy supernatural beings. Every one of these strange creatures had either committed murder or suicide or been present at such a deed; nor could he ever find rest night or day. It was only in the deepest darkness that he was able to make himself manifest to his clients; as soon as the first streak of dawn touched the horizon he vanished like a dream, and not even the faintest smell of sulphur remained during the day where he had paced by night.

"The antiquist expressed the greatest scorn of the new-fangled rubbish traded off on poor humanity in the demon pigsty, as he usually called the market of living souls. But the modernist waxed eloquent on the miracles wrought by the spirits bought in his institution. His goods were not the frequenters of tombs or mouldy fragments of buildings; they were willing to talk to their clients by the light of day and in the most comfortable surroundings; they were human and humane in every respect; they liked the society of living men and women, especially if these were commonplace and preferred information on topics that had no mystery about them; they delighted in communications on the obvious, and would rather talk to clients who wanted to hear of what they knew already; they did not care for tombs and ghostly surroundings; though, if people insisted on getting a sight of them, they preferred a dim light; they were shy; for they were unable to procure in spirit-land the phantasms of the garments that they had worn upon earth to clothe their nakedness. Still better, they sold in their market many a phantasm of the living which could tell its clients their own thoughts, and communicate facts that they were certain to find out by common observation within a few minutes or hours. They sold dream-stuff that would supply the sleeping client with warnings as to the future so that when the future arrived he would recognise it. In their market they had practitioners who could draw souls like teeth, and, after polishing them clean of diseases, put them back again. They had others, each of whom could send his detachable soul down the throat of a patient like a chimney-sweep, and, after cleaning the system, draw it back again. There was not a disease in man but had its origin in the imagination or detachable soul; and what was the use of medicine or surgery, when all a man had to do in order to be cured was to get this free soul taken out of him and sent to the practitioners in the market or to borrow the free soul of a practitioner for a few hours or days as the case might need? He could go on for years, if we liked, telling us the miracles and wonders done by their spirit-therapeutics in their market of living souls. No less marvellous was the consolation afforded to the bereaved when they were able to come and converse with the souls of the departed. For a small fee they could call up any spirit they pleased, and get it to write on slates or give in rap language answers to any questions they might ask, provided the questions did not touch on its actual state or destiny and related to facts well known to all present. The spirits they dealt in would give no satisfaction to the profanely curious or impertinent.

"We suggested that most of these phenomena could be explained by natural causes; and in each case the Spectralian broke into rage at the suggestion, and when he had calmed down told us of the fate of a missionary from Figlefia, who had come to convert them to naturalism. They found that he addressed himself especially to the women, and most of all to the good-looking women; but when he began to smile at their creed and covertly sneer at it and attack it the women waited for a dark night and, aided by the spirits of their dead ancestors, they spoiled his smirking beauty for him and gave him such a scare that in his madness and terror he ran into the waves and drowned himself. Each of them pointed out to us a rocky islet off the coast, and told us the story of it, evidently as a warning to us against our unseemly unbelief. It was called Astralia, and contained a miserable sect that had attempted to explain all the phenomena of their markets by the swarming-off of astral bodies like invisible hoops from them. They also professed to have found a new means of consulting the souls of distant wise men; they could write their questions on any slip of common paper and put it in a cupboard, and down from the ceiling would flutter the answer, which was so unintelligibly wise as to puzzle men for years. These poor creatures were at once exiled and were dying of starvation; for, though they were eager for material food, they professed to subsist on nothing but spiritual sustenance, and were wasting away in this pretended astral-exhalation process.

"After the two rivals had been put on shore and we were steaming off on our course, two packets were found in the bunks they had occupied. Moist and limp, they were dried; and when opened they were found to contain placards and advertisements of the goods to be traded off in their respective markets at the next great ghost-fair. Blastemo translated a few for us, both from the dead-soul packet and from the live-soul packet. 'For sale, the ghost of a knight walled up in the bastion of an old castle four hundred years ago; warranted to walk in armour every stormy night that has not too much moon, and to produce the most appalling clank as he moves along the corridors or through the locked doors.' 'For immediate sale on the lowest terms, a genuine old-fashioned spirit, that cannot bear the crowing of a cock or the least streak of light on the horizon; supposed to be the perpetrator of a mysterious murder that took place some centuries ago; the sound of gnashing teeth and of the drawing of swords is distinctly heard as he paces along, and the echo of a loud sigh as he vanishes.... The owner is clearing out of his present premises, because his physicians have recommended him a more bracing alpine climate that is quite unsuited to his family ghost.' 'To be sold by auction without reserve, one of the finest collections of antique spirits ever made in this island; they belong to a splendid ruin in one of the most picturesque and dismal localities of the country; every one of them has either perpetrated a murder or been the victim of cruel assassination; the rooms to which they are confined have the marks of bloody footsteps all over them, and, where these are dim, they can be easily renewed at small expense; one of them is headless and carries in his arms something that has been identified by the best experts as a head; another bears the form of a young girl, all covered with blood, the supposed victim, and vanishes with a heart-breaking sigh. The late owner died childless, and has joined his own collection of midnight walkers. The heirs live in a distant part of the island in a castle already well provided with spirits, and are willing to treat with intending purchasers on easy terms extending over a number of years. Cards of midnight inspection to be obtained from the auctioneer in the market.' 'Wanted, for a dilapidated mansion newly built, a ghost of harmless propensities but awe-striking habits. He must be at least three centuries old, and have all the favourite traits of blood-curdling apparitions. No upstarts of recent introduction need apply.'

"The live-soul-market advertisements were as definite in their terms; the few that Blastemo translated were these: 'For sale, the spirit of a wise man just deceased, accustomed to daylight seances, and highly trained in rap language and slate-writing. He would be a valuable adjunct to a household that has no library, or one that from want of education or eyepower is unable to consult a library. His knowledge is encyclopedic, although his powers of observation are limited. The daily intercourse with his spirit would be an education in itself. His children and heirs have no further need of his instructions.' 'Offered for sale, the spirit of a successful thought-therapeutist, who when alive could cure any disease without the intervention of any material medium or medicine or even the proximity of the patient. He had simply to think the disease away, and it was gone. His spirit, now being free of all bodily trammels, is even more potent than before. In fact, it is more than likely that the possessor of it will secure immunity from all sickness, if not from death itself. It would be a perfect mine of wealth for a medical practitioner. Terms easy.' 'Wanted, to hire out for short periods, the detachable spirit of a great sage who lives in a distant part of the world; well accustomed to sending occult answers to occult messages, and to all the recognised methods of occult communication and intercourse; would be especially suited for the entertainment and instruction of select companies in the evening; terms on application; a reduction for a series of parties or entertainments.' 'To sell by auction at the great fair, a famous troupe of table-tipping spirits, the finest collection ever offered to the community. Have been employed in drawing-room entertainments. Might be utilised in large hotels or mansions in removing large tables from room to room, or in large factories instead of elevators.' 'Wanted, immediately, for a bed-rid invalid, a spirit-companion, who can enter into all his tastes and humour all his fancies, converse with him without irritability or caprice, and materialise in the cold hours of the night and dematerialise when the patient is too hot. A high salary for a thoroughly competent spirit.' 'Wanted, by a genius, a spirit-amanuensis, who could inspire his hand when it lags on the paper, and fire his imagination at all times. One accustomed to dream suggestion preferred. No eccentrics need apply.' 'To be auctioned without reserve, the finest collection of detachable spirits that this island has ever seen. For Spectralians who wish to study human nature in all its variety this affords a grand opportunity of acquiring specimens of every kind and type of spirit. A guarantee given with every individual sold that he will stand by the purchaser for any fixed period agreed on and allow him to look microscopically into his inner mechanism.' 'Wanted, for a small and unhealthy country village, a thought-therapeutic, who could, if he wished, reside at a distance and project his spirit whenever a patient needed his power. One who has had much practice in hysterics and hypochondria, the prevailing diseases of the village, preferred.'

"Whether it was from inadvertence or design that our Spectralians left their packets we were unable to discover. We counted them of so little value that we never thought of putting ourselves to any trouble to send them after their owners. Besides, we inclined to the belief that they had been abandoned on board deliberately and for missionary purposes. The twinkle in Blastemo's eye as he read them seemed to us to imply that this was not the first time he had had the experience; that, in fact, it was a policy of the Spectralians to litter the archipelago with their placards and advertisements. At any rate, we took no trouble to return them; they were, on the contrary, used for menial purposes that did not fulfil their high mission."

CHAPTER XXXV
THE VOYAGE CONTINUED

"A NEIGHBOURING ISLAND, WHICH Blastemo called Fanattia, he would not hear of our visiting; for there were gathered all the mad quixotists of the archipelago; any who thought that some special kind of food, or drink, or clothing, or gesture, or ceremony, or manner was ruinous to both body and soul, and sacrificed all the other interests of life to its destruction or abolition, were landed here and allowed to fight it out like scorpions in a bottle. God pity any poor shipwrecked stranger who fell into their hands! it was seldom that he was not torn limb from limb by rival charlatans or the parties of conflicting shibboleths. They were all threatened with famine; for what one grew or manufactured from the fruits of the earth another detested as bad for the human system and did his best to destroy; one thought tubers poisonous and fruits good; another held the reverse opinion; and the violence of their enthusiasm would not let either rest till he had destroyed his neighbour's crops, all for the good of that neighbour's soul; one thought a solid food, made out of any products of the earth, destroyed the sense of duty; another thought that liquid food made from them dulled the senses, the portals to the soul; impelled by his zeal neither could stop short of destroying all that his neighbour manufactured. The result was that there was never any food, either liquid or solid, to be found, and the miserable creatures had to subsist on anything they could pick up on the beach. It was the same with garments and gestures, with attitudes and manners and tones of voice. There was not anything that could not find a hostile critic, and the critic had at once to show his hostility in the most violent crusade, that could not cease till the thing or the believer in it was driven out of existence.

"There were other groups of islands near, on which Blastemo advised us not to land; one was a group occupied by exiles who cultivated religion apart from morality; another was occupied by exiles who devoted themselves to imagination and let conscience decay; the inhabitants of a third sank all human methods and thoughts in the interests of political party. This was the worst class of monomaniacs in the whole archipelago. They were in the most degraded condition, and were constantly burning or torturing out some wretched minority, just as the Meskeetans and Coxurians did. They paid little attention to the amenities of life. As long as they still had islets to which they could exile their dissenters they had not been so venomous as these two peoples. But recently they had become unbearably offensive in their manners and their attacks on strangers, and everyone now avoided their shores. The God-wise, as the religious monomaniacs called themselves, had grown licentious and even obscene; they had developed the most disgusting and beastly habits from the idea that they knew the will of God and could dispense with the common rules of morality and decency, those 'badges of mere earth-born natures.' The worshippers of beauty had grown callous in their cruelty. Squeamishly sensitive about their own feelings, they condemned any dissentient amongst them, or any alien whom they found, to the most excruciating tortures; every man who had anything abnormal in his face or features or gait was given to the death-men. The federators of humanity were the most dishonest and corrupt and quarrelsome of all; they held that other considerations, moral, political, religious, were as nothing compared with party organisation; and they had ultimately come to feel all bonds dissolved but those of party, and to hound down everyone who advocated anything, however noble or great or even decent, that was outside of the party programme; no wonder they had grown so offensive in their personal habits, so cruel in their relations to the rest of mankind. It was useless asking any of these peoples for supplies, they were so improvident; nay, it was dangerous approaching their shores with such a property as the *Daydream*.

"There were other groups of islands that were too small and barren or too much out of our course to think of visiting. There was the art-religion group with Calocosm or the isle of art-popes in the centre of it; their inhabitants were most intolerant and quarrelsome. Not far from it is the isle of Cryptia, where the dwellers spend most of their time in mystic ceremonies and parades, dressed in the most fantastic garments, and carrying the most ludicrous paraphernalia of office; their ceremonies are performed in dark caves dimly lit, and, in order to impress the imagination, mimic in absurd fashion the wild feasts and rites of savages; they believe in a religion without a god, without the religious or moral spirit; a religion that is nothing but ceremonial. In an opposite direction lies a group that is given up to medicomaniacs; its central island, called Fidikyoor, has all the ailments of humanity in full force; and yet the islanders can, if they will, cure any disease they like by the mere act of belief. The other islands in the group have each its system of therapeutics: one cures by blowing in the face, another by spitting in the face, a third by striking on the cheek.

"Nearer to Coxuria lay two groups that were the natural complements of each other. One group had as its centre Theophane, and the inhabitants all believed that they had but to elect one of their number by ballot in secret meeting in order to make him a god, who whilst he lived could converse with the gods and get from them the absolute truth of all existence. The president of each island might be the most consummate liar in the archipelago, and yet all he said whilst president was taken as divine revelation of the truth; and everyone who believed or professed to believe in anything that disagreed with it was promptly brought to his bearings by the most effective and summary punishments. So there was perfect unanimity of belief in these communities. But the numbers in each isle had become so small that every man expected some day to have his most manifest fiction accepted during his period of office as the most undeniable truth. Over against them lay another group that had as its centre Antidea; its islands agreed in vehemently denying the existence of all gods; but each had its own particularly unpleasant way of affirming its creed. The people were virulently intolerant, hating most of mankind because most believed in some deity or other. They asserted so firmly and confidently that they had found absolute truth on this matter of gods that, had a theopath landed on their shores, they would have burned him in order to save his soul from the grovelling superstition.

"Between the medicomaniacs and the theopaths lay a mediating group called Dirtethos; here lived the exiles that counted sin and crime as a mere aberration of intellect or of digestion; their religion was a matter of food and medicine. If a man stole from his neighbour, then all the rest of his neighbours came to sympathise with him in his misfortune whilst the victim was left in deserved neglect. If anyone got into the habit of telling lies, then, poor fellow, he had to go to bed and be nursed; his stomach was out of order. If anyone murdered his mother or his wife or his friend, he had to go to a hospital and get soothed, and his relations and acquaintances rushed to console him in his temporary sickness; it was sad indeed to have such an overflow of blood to the head. If one should outrage all recognised traditions and rules of morality and legality, then his friends spent their days and nights with him reasoning him out of his sad mistake; he was the hero of the hour; his victims were forgotten. An incorrigible criminal was sent to the university, where, by sympathy and lectures, he had his chance of recovering his tone. There he held receptions, to which the most important people of the island were honoured in being invited; here he discoursed with them on the methods of his crimes and lapses, and spoke of his past as if it were a piece of ancient history of a foreign nation; everybody conversed with him on it with the impartiality of philosophers or the whispered consolations of bosom friends; his teachers mourned with him over the hard lot of humanity which condemned poor mortals like him to such mental aberrations. This group Blastemo considered the worst of the lunatic settlements of the archipelago; no locality was so dangerous for the stranger or the shipwrecked mariner.

"By his advice we steered for the island of Grabawlia, where those who had a mania for finance dwelt. When we landed, the people did not crowd around us as they had done in the other islands; they hovered off like vultures waiting a solitary swoop. But we soon discovered, as one after another approached us and explained his benevolent intentions, that we were about to be exploited. Pilot-financiers always preceded the great man who wished to make the negotiation. They brought no goods for us to see; they only spoke of them as procurable, showing us samples that were very attractive in their appearance. They stirred our appetite or our curiosity in the most astute way. When any transaction was about to be completed, in would come some bustling islander, offering a better price for the goods and loudly declaring that he was being robbed in not getting his opportunity; it was no genuine market that gave special favours to special buyers, and gradually the price was raised till we had to give an enormous sum for everything we bought. We had also to buy by samples; for it was asserted that the mass of goods could not be brought down to the beach till they were bought. Some of the superfluities that we had on board they decried, but said that they would be glad to sell for us. They did not care for them; but if they were offered very cheap they might take them off our hands to oblige those who had bought so much from them. When they had beaten our price down to little or nothing, some newcomer would press forward and offer similar goods at a lower price. At last they got our surplus practically as a gift.

"When we had completed our negotiations and thought we had bought enough stores and fuel to last several months, we went off to the ship, and the goods began to arrive in fallas. They were in boxes or well-covered bundles. Not till we had sailed did we find on opening our purchases that half of them were rotten or worthless, and that in the boxes that contained the fuel, stones filled half the space.

"These Grabawlians had the foundations of their houses of gold. They would not let one coin of the precious metal pass out of their hands if they could help it. They were the great barterers of the archipelago, and took the goods of one island to trade off for the goods of another, and wherever they could they got gold as the net result, till their island was filled with the metal. We had seen that they were half-starved, the only flourishing feature of their faces being their nose, which protruded over their lips, and gave a foxy appearance to their faces. They starved themselves to get more gold. They lied and cheated that they might add even one coin to their heap. Again and again were they found by their neighbours famishing; nor would they give any of the treasures, on which they lay dying, to pay for the food that was brought to them. They were always in dread of pirates and freebooters, for ever and again through the centuries some warlike people bore down on them and carried off the accumulations of ages. Blastemo himself acknowledged that it was no infrequent thing for his island to pick a quarrel with them and rob them in war of their savings. They were the milch-cows of the archipelago. Their gold was a mere encumbrance to them. It was better to be distributed again.

"After all the useless stores and the stones out of the fuel had been thrown overboard, we calculated that we had remaining enough to last for a month or six weeks. We were about to make again for Broolyi, when a boat from Tirralaria informed us that you were intending to reach Figlefia and embark there. When off that island awaiting orders, a slave in a canoe came off in the darkness and bade us sail for the uninhabited side of the island if we would save you from destruction; and he indicated the bay where we ought to anchor that night. We were doubtful; but we carried out his instructions. And the result is that we have you now with us."

Burns showed considerable agitation over their adventures and over my return. I had interrupted him with many a question which had broken the even flow of his narrative and lessened his emotion as he proceeded. He and the others evidently expected an account of my wanderings; but I was too much excited, too rent with conflicting melancholy and joy, to accede fully to their request; and I gave them but a rough outline of all I had done and suffered. The scars had not yet healed in my spirit; the thoughts over life that my experiences had stirred in my breast were too crude and sorrowful to find consolation in utterance; so I paced the deck for days in solitary meditation.

Nothing could keep me long from the problem of problems, the central mystery of the archipelago. What was that land which the inhabitants of the various islands never had long out of their thoughts, but which they so carefully avoided in speech? When forced to mention it, they pretended to shudder at it as an island of devils. None of them seemed to have visited it or to have had any personal knowledge of it for many centuries. Their fear of it had crystallised into myths of horror. For ages they had made fitful attempts to approach it, and failed, and at last a fence of impenetrable darkness and terror held them far off from it; and the fear that paralysed every energy, if ever their ships came within sight of its shining peak on the far horizon, had taken permanent shape in their traditions and stories of the isle of devils. What it really was had faded into twilight, and the veil of the supernatural had finally shut it out from human view. It was useless to attempt analysis of the pictured curtain of tradition. The fabric would vanish in the process instead of revealing its original texture. Once and once only had I seen the pure sheen of its highest snow-clad mountain above the rim of the sea; and at the sight I resolved to reach it, cost what it would. I looked forward to our visit to Broolyi with no special interest except as preparatory for the great expedition. I would say nothing of it to Blastemo or his countrymen, lest they should discourage my men or otherwise stand in my way. Nor would I confide at first in my comrades, not indeed till I had seen my way clearly, and got all my methods of preparation mapped out. They set my absorption down to my past adventures, and I kept my own counsel whilst I inquired into the conditions of my problem and found the possibility of a solution.

CHAPTER XXXVI

BROOLYI

DURING THE LATTER PART of our conferences Blastemo had fallen silent; his oaths and wild exclamations had first grown less frequent and then ceased. When I looked to find the cause of the break in the torrent, I laughed to see the rubicund face blanched, and instead of the usual militant boldness of the expression a tremulous light in the eye. Sandy Macrae at a gesture from me helped him below and we saw no more of him for days, and heard nothing either but long-intervalled groans of agony. For the wind had freshened ahead, and, as something or other had disturbed the compasses, we could not tell whether we were keeping our course or not. We steered by the sun; and, as we had not our pilot to correct us, we had gradually shot far past our destination, and a current had carried us away to the east.

Before daybreak on the third day our lookout called our attention to a strange object on the horizon all gleaming white. At first the captain thought it was an iceberg wandered into these tropical regions, but as the sun forged up towards the rim of sky the ever-shifting tints that it threw over the vault revealed to him that it was a snow-peak on whose top lay a wreath of white filmy wool like a cloud. As the sunlight strengthened, they saw the wool-festoon float out like a pennon, tinged with the scarlet and gold of the dawn. The stars grew dim and winked out. The day broadened into a glare, and still the peak stood firm with its pennant of steam.

I was called, and I knew what it was they had been watching. It was the mystery of mysteries, the Isle of Devils, that was thrusting up its snow-peak into the sky. I bade Burns steer straight for it, and the wind that still blew fresh from the north-west was with us. The gleaming cone grew loftier and more beautiful in its outline, and past noon we could see the cloud-turbaned peaks that flanked it begin to show beneath its radiance. Still we pushed on, and, as the sun shot his western shuttle through his great web of rays, and we could see the land darken at the roots of the peak of snow, a strange circumstance occurred. There came over the heavens a glossy look as if we were moving under a dome of crystal closer to us than the azure of the sky. It was an occurrence I had noticed once or twice before, but I could get no

satisfactory explanation of the phenomenon. It was like the glitter of the sky
on a morning of keen frost, that is just about to be followed by a tempest of
rain; and what made it stranger was that the crystalline dome vanished as
suddenly as it had come. The stars came out with a precipitance that alarmed
us. We had not time to recover from our terror when a shout rose from the
bow, "Breakers ahead." We had but a few moments to bring her round and
lower the sails, and together the sea and the wind struck us with a thud and
made the ship stagger. I thought she would go to the bottom, she heeled with
such suddenness and shipped such a mass of water. The masts broke like
reeds, and the yards thundered down upon the deck.

In the midst of the commotion I saw Blastemo rush towards me over the
wreckage, the pallor gone from his face. It was now livid with terror. He
looked for a moment to the horizon, and then to the smooth sea that lay on
either side of the tornado. He seized me by the arm and in a hoarse whisper
begged me to hurry away from the accursed peak that still shone clear over
our stern. Within half an hour we were in as peaceful an atmosphere and sea
as we had had; not a trace of the storm or of the troubled water was to be seen.
Even the long roll of billows with which we had run so long had vanished. As
we cleared away the wreckage, our guest lay down exhausted on the deck.
In a whisper of terror he told me the same story as I had heard from other
islanders. None of them had ever been able to approach the Isle of Devils;
every ship that had made the attempt had been disabled and blown off. This
had been the case for long centuries, although there was a dim tradition that
their ancestors had come from it in vessels. The shock seemed to have driven
out his sea-sickness to some extent, and he kept by the man at the wheel till
we were out of sight of the snow-peak. Before he left the deck he gave such
instructions as to the route that no mistake could be made again.

Even this would not satisfy him, and in spite of his recurrent pallidity he
returned to his post in the morning and watched every point on the horizon
to see that we should not deviate as we did before. In three more days of
light winds and calms we came in sight of a land that filled him with almost
uncontrollable delight. He recognised its first dim outline upon the horizon as
his own. As we approached it, its sierra rose boldly into the heavens, though
rarely to the line of perpetual snow. Great ranges of mountains seemed to
divide it into isolated corners, and jutted into the ocean in beetling precipices
that forbade too close approach to the angry snarl of their surf. It was in every
feature of it the home of warlike tribes bastioned against mutual peace and
intercourse. I was much amused, therefore, to hear Blastemo break into an
invocation to his fatherland as the home of all that was noble and peace-loving. He repeated its name again and again with eulogistic epithets, "noble,

pacific Broolyi"; and, seeing us stand by unenthusiastic, he tried to rouse us by explaining that the name meant Isle of Peace, for the inhabitants were engaged in converting the whole archipelago to its doctrine of peace; they were the great missionaries of the gospel of peace to a world given over to war and mutual hatred. The confused swell near the iron-bound coast relieved us of the need of reply; for he quietly collapsed and sought a recumbent posture below.

We ran north along the wild scene of sheer cliffs. Solitary bird haunts waist-deep in the sullen billows, monstrous toothed jaws angrily churning the waters that ebbed and flowed across them, hollow-sounding caves that echoed to the splash and boom of the sea and to the screams of disturbed flashes of winged life, varied the monotony of the adamant bulwark of nature. A note of everlasting war between land and sea sounded hoarse along the shore, and ever as we approached there rang out the wild challenge of the torn and recoiling waves. The marks of the unending warfare of centuries lay in the reefs and outlying fragments of rock that chafed the waters as they flowed. It was indeed a conflict of Titans, whose chief ally and source of power was Time. Round great headlands we swept that mocked and baffled the high-flashing onslaught of the immortal enemy. How many generations of men had wailed into life, grown, fought tooth and nail, and lapsed into the grave, since these browbeaten cliffs had begun to outface the passions of their restless foe!

We rounded one foreland more colossal and overhanging than any; but its fantastic shapes held us only a moment, for beyond, the land rapidly fell into a broad valley, and there two embattled bodies of men were busy hacking and hewing each other. Their armour clashed under the strokes, fierce shouts issued from those that were hurrying from the rear, and a minor undercurrent of sound was a medley of wails and groans. The crew were soon all on deck absorbed in the new spectacle. Even Blastemo had recovered and ascended. He looked on from a modest hiding-place in the rear; but, as soon as we saw him, we burst into a roar of laughter, remembering his recent eulogies of peace and of the pacific nature of his countrymen. He knew what we meant, and slunk below again.

I had occasion to go soon after to my cabin, and I found him pacing the floor in wild agitation. The sound of the clashing arms and the shouts and groans reached him even here, and he saw, though dimly, through the thick glass of the port-hole the swaying masses and the give-and-take of the combat. His blood was in ferment, and he pleaded with me to put him on shore, that he might join in the struggle. It maddened him to hear the clangour and not be in the midst of the fray. He confessed that he had not looked closely or long enough to know who were the combatants or what was the right or wrong for which they fought. All he knew was that it was near the capital and his own district, and his desire to keep the peace was overwhelming everything else in him. I refused to listen to his petitions, fearing that by landing him we might draw the fury of either side or perhaps of both upon us. We sped on and soon melted the uproar into a confused hum and shut out the sight that so fevered his blood.

Our next experience was as exciting. We shot past the cape that like a sheltering arm curled round the great harbour of the island, and a city spread upwards from it bastioned to the roofs. And what a commotion filled every parapet and wall and street! Never had such a craft been seen in these waters; and our fame had spread before us. Every movement of the *Daydream*, since she had approached the island, had been messengered to the city. Banners and trophies swung in the breeze. Wild music made the air a hoarse discordant pæan. Bells rung, gongs sounded, shrill pipes shot skirling blasts into the ear of heaven. Marchings and countermarchings of squares and rectangles of blue and green and scarlet humanity made a moving tartan of the shore. The chromatropic effect was as harassing to the eye as the clangour to the ear. Puffs of acrid smoke obscured the air at intervals. At a distance it was alarming. What would it be near at our hand? The whole armed population was evidently in motion. Our guest, mad though he was with excitement, managed to reassure us, and, taking from his cabin a small blue-green and red pennon, flung it out from our poop. The effect was instantaneous. The commotion ceased. The troops wheeled and marched inland, and soon only the ununiformed crowd were left to watch us as we swept up to an anchorage within a breastwork of the harbour.

The night fell, and silence shed its sleep upon the many-coloured, myriad-noted world. With the morning returned the bustle and skirl and brazen echo of a warlike community. Everything, as we looked out to the shore, seemed to move to disciplinary rhythm. I went to the royal levee with Blastemo and, after he had prelected to the courtiers and the king in a language that I did not understand, I was addressed from the throne in Aleofanian. I could see from the speech that my fireship had deeply impressed the community and especially the governors of Broolyi, but their warlike purpose and employments were veiled in eulogies of their mission of peace. Peace was the ideal and prayer of their inmost souls, and this fireship of mine would enable them to fulfil it the sooner. It was difficult to disentangle this from the labyrinth of ceremonies and gestures, verbiage and oaths, that seemed to form the very heart of Broolyian civilisation. Every climax reached by the monarchic eloquence we heard echoed outside of the palace by the roll of drums and the air-splitting shrill of pipes. The whole life of the community seemed to move to machinery that centred in the court.

This I afterwards found was no mere metaphor or fancy. The next day was their great festival of the week, and the people crowded into the temples to worship the gods. None worked or were supposed to work. I went with Blastemo first to one sacred building and then to another; and I was struck with the fact that everything seemed to proceed as by clockwork, the music, the sermon, the genuflections of the priest. "You are right," said my guide. "And I will show you how the whole thing is worked."

He took me to an enormous hall behind the palace. It was like a huge factory, so full was it of machinery, all in motion. It was, indeed, he assured me, a religion factory, one of the grandest institutions in the world. This controlled all the services in the temples of the island. He took me to one great machine that had on a capacious barrel all the litanies of the year. At the moment we came up it was started by the controller of religious services, who sat in a recess of the inner hall of the king's palace. We heard a prayer to the god of peace most painfully and articulately intoned. I did not understand the words, but I could make out from the tones in which they were uttered the changes of meaning and spiritual attitude. It was marvellous, the solemnity of the effect, provided we shut our eyes; there was such majesty in the volume of the sound and in the elocutionary variations of the tone; one might have imagined a vast assembly pouring forth in unison a submissive appeal to heaven. In the temple the clack and shuttling of the machinery were not heard; instead of it there was an automatic priest magnificently clothed, bowing and posturing to suit the word. It was only a wax figure containing clockwork controlled by this great litany machine, but the effect was like life, or rather much more impressive. There was none of the hawking and hemming of the human priest, none of his awkward pauses and blowings of the nose, none of the clumsy gestures or inability to dispose of the hands; and the voice rang out through the great buildings with a bell-like clearness and naturalness that would have made the human voice seem bathos. How feeble and tremulous, I remembered, buzzed the voices of the priests I had heard intoning in the cathedrals of Europe! I felt almost ashamed of the memory.

With a whirr and a click the litany machine stopped, and the processional machine took up the tale. There was more noise and clang in this, for more force had to be applied; a hundred or more processions of marionette acolytes and priests through the various temples of the island were impelled by it. There was a manifest rhythm in its motions, almost like the sound of a stately minuet. I saw these processions afterwards; and nothing could exceed the solemnity of the motions of the man-like fantoccini. I never saw such an impressive ceremonial; every step, every gesture was in harmony; there was no unseemly merriment in the eyes or conversation on the lips of the youthful figures; and the chanting was so noble and beautiful, filling as it did the whole vast edifice with its mournful, or jubilant sound. The service was well through before I had come into the religion factory, and the only other machine I saw at work was that which produced the music. It was in an adjoining hall, which was filled with thousands of pipes of the most varied size and construction. There sat the musician, and the whole building trembled as the keys were struck. It was intolerable; the groaning and thunder it produced made the very tips of our ears to shake. But when delivered by tubes or wires into the vast temples of the country, nothing could surpass the softness and harmony of the volume of sound.

One large edifice served for the central section of the town; it was spacious enough to contain every man, woman, and child that lived in the district. Each suburb had a smaller temple, yet large enough to dwarf the cathedrals of England. I was deeply interested in them, and every weekly festival I visited one or more of them. I was especially anxious to hear the sermon or prelection. The lay-figure rose and moved his eyes and lips and his arms and body to suit the words that were uttered. The whole of the audience was too distant from it to distinguish the movements; and the wax lifelessness of the face, which I made out when, after the service, I approached it, could not have been seen by any of the worshippers, so far aloft was it perched in a pulpit on the farthest wall. The tones reached every ear in the huge edifice, and their modulation and expression were perfect. I conjectured that the sermon had been spoken into some recorder before, and that this reproduced it by machinery on some diaphragm in each church, and that over the diaphragm was fixed some instrument inside the lay-figure for multiplying many times the volume of the sound.

The illusion was complete. I never heard oratory so impressive, or religious service so solemnly performed. The sermon was, Blastemo told me, a discourse on peace as the aim of all mankind. It painted the horrors of war, and brought out in contrast a portrait of the man of the millennium, who would have his passions so under control that nothing would rouse him to anger or strife. It closed with a vindication of the warlike policy for reaching this great ideal. Nothing but continual and effective warfare would make men afraid to quarrel or bring their quarrel to issue. The ebullience of the passions of the world was to be mastered by fear. When they had brought warfare to the perfection of destructiveness, all wars would cease; terror of death would be the universal guiding motive of communities and individuals. Then would the god of peace have voice through the whole world, for he would have his mentor in every human breast in every assembly, the knowledge that any strife must end in the annihilation of all those who take part in it. The peroration was fervid in its appeal to the worshippers to pursue warfare till it should be absolute in its annihilative power.

I was deeply impressed by the whole performance; never did it approach to that bathos which, I remembered, had so often marred the services in even the greatest cathedrals and churches of the various divisions of Christianity. There was no halting in the oratory, no feebleness of voice, no ridiculous straining of the nervous or muscular power. There was no hitch in the processions or ceremonies, nothing pinchbeck or tawdry or mean. The music was noble, and in its softening and shading as fine as the massing of tens of thousands of human voices, there was no discord, no jar. The effect of the whole was uniform, deep, and abiding.

Yet I could not get out of mind the cogs and wheels and keys of the religion factory, the workmen moving about seeing that the machinery was well oiled and that it worked without chance of breakdown, the solitary performer sitting at the keyboard, and the king's minister in the royal recess grinding out the service. I expressed my feelings to Blastemo as we walked away, and he warmly defended the method of his country. They had had in the past a priesthood attached to the various temples, but it had been found that their lives so differed from their teachings that the people laughed at the whole of religion as a farce. The performances and discourses were so feeble or extravagant or grotesque that the buildings were deserted as a rule, or, if one was frequented, it was by a wild crowd of enthusiasts stirred by some mad preacher to a crusade against law, order, or progress. The church and religion had grown a scandal. Women were the only regular worshippers, and they were in the hands of unscrupulous priests, who used them against the aims and ideals of the government and the community. The state tried for a time the effect of adding to the creed a dogma that the religious efficacy of the services was quite independent of the character of the priests; it came direct from heaven, and the pollution of the vessel or channel did not mar the divine influence. It was all in vain. It did not bring the men to church; and it only hurried on the degeneracy of the priesthood. The church became the nest of all the unclean and revolutionary characters in the community. Again and again it threatened the safety of the state by instilling a rebellious spirit into the women, and through them into the youths of the nation during a serious war with a neighbour. Something had to be done. There were the grand old temples; there was the litany of the state religion consecrated by long generations of worshippers; and yet the institution was but a lurking-place for the indolent and voluptuous and hypocritical and rebellious in masculine breasts. The endowments had fallen into a hopeless state. The finances were quite inadequate. The worshippers would not support their own services.

There was a great statesman at the helm of affairs, the ablest monarch that had ever been selected by the council of wise warriors. He saw his opportunity. He happened to have one of the most original and inventive engineers as his right-hand man for the manufacture and superintendence of war material. This latter had landed on the shores of Broolyi they knew not whence. In these islands they ask no questions but accept what the gods send them. The two together elaborated the existing religious system. The dogma that the divine influence was altogether irrespective of the channel or priest had thoroughly soaked into the natures of the worshippers from the sermons of the preachers; and it was easy to turn the flank of the doctrine by showing that automatic priests would have least effect of all upon the religious elements that came through them. They would be completely neutral like the air or the ether through which the gods influenced the minds of men.

There was some talk of rebellion when the system was changed; but most of the priests were too manifestly disreputable or characterless to bring much influence to bear. They were banished to the islands that were occupied by the non-moral religionists, and were never heard of more. The women were only too glad to see the services conducted in order and decency, whilst the men saw with pleasure the rotten finances taken up by the state. It was one of the most peaceful and natural changes that ever occurred; and now the temples were filled with men as well as women. The music was splendid, the ceremonies solemn, the discourses worth listening to. It cost far less. It was absolutely controlled by the state, and all throughout the island had the same spiritual fare.

I suggested to Blastemo that there was surely great monotony in having the same thing year in, year out, every festival. He laughed at my simplicity. The monarch and the engineer had fully provided for that feature of human nature which makes it weary of mere repetition. The finest imaginations of the country were employed in writing discourses; the best musicians spent most of their time in composing the hymns and songs; the finest theatrical talent and the most devout minds combined to make new ceremonies and services. That was the reason there was not standing room in most of the temples of the country. Everything was under the eye of the king and his wise warriors. It was one of the most effective disciplines that ever state had had in its hands; the state-organised church of Aleofane was not to be compared to it. The souls of the community were regimented like their bodies.

I was silenced; but any doubt of the efficacy of the institution was not dissipated when I heard that it was still comparatively new. The monarch had not long since died, and the engineer was still living. It had still to be tested by time, and the attraction of novelty had not yet worn off. Yet I had to acknowledge that it was a most effective method of ridding a state church of irregularities and keeping a strong hand over the minds of the community. Whether it would allow the civilisation to advance was another question. Originality would soon be a thing inconceivable in the island, if it were not already completely dead. Peace in the spiritual world had been reached, but at the expense of all new thought or individuality of character.

When I heard that the inventor of this automatic worship was still alive, I felt eager to see him, certain as I was that he must be a man of remarkable powers; but I found great difficulty in getting Blastemo or anyone else to tell me about him. Since the election of the new monarch, I ascertained by sundry hints, he had been in exile. Where he was imprisoned I could not find out. His great capacity and his ever-advancing thought had manifestly aroused the jealousy of the new occupant of the throne. Hence, I conjectured, it was that the new arts of war had grown abortive, promise though they once did to go far towards the ideal of absolute destructiveness which would lead to universal peace. I saw that he or someone else had introduced an explosive, which might, with improvements, have made as effective a means of war as European gunpowder. It had enabled the last king to batter down the fortress-mansions of his nobles in the country and drive them to settle round the court and abandon their continual little internecine wars. Under his successor, the makers of the explosive had lost its true secret; and the baronial castles were rebuilding, in spite of the threats of royal displeasure. This was the meaning of the battle we had seen before arriving at the harbour; two nobles were settling a quarrel in the old way, heedless of royal power or judicial courts. Whilst I was in Broolyi I saw hundreds of quarrels that were settled by duels. The Broolyians had no control over their tempers, and during the reign of the explosive they had given free play to them, as they knew that the result would be no risk of life, but only to property in settlement before the law-courts. It was like living over a gunpowder magazine, and I avoided intercourse with these spitfires. Indeed, it was difficult to conduct without hitch the commonest conversation with Blastemo, now he had returned to his native fire-damp of an atmosphere. Nothing but isolated residence in fortified keeps with miles of morass or mountain or forest between them could ever insure peace amongst such a people. To think that the name of their country was "Isle of Peace," and that the great object of their worship was the god of peace!

One day I heard of another community off the farther coast of Broolyi; it was said to exist without government or institutions of any kind. My curiosity was excited, and, though on inquiry I found that it was the exile asylum of the archipelago for all who were plagued with the craze of anarchism, I resolved to see the island for myself. They could not laugh me out of my determination, and I at last procured a royal passport that would pass me over the intervening districts in safety. For the rest I was to look after myself if I ventured over the channel that lay between the islands. None of the Broolyians would ever risk their lives in that den of wild beasts, Kayoss. It had been chosen because of its proximity to the most warlike people in the archipelago; and, if any of the inhabitants attempted to leave it, the Broolyians were authorised to shoot them down. A garrison was regularly established over against it for the purpose.

I set out, glad to be free from the harassing ceremonial of a military, machine-like, and yet most capricious-tempered community; but it was a long and difficult journey, from castle to castle, over mountain and through forest, often delayed by some local imbroglio or the jealousy of neighbouring barons. Nothing but the magnificence of the scenery could compensate for the petty annoyances that retarded my passage. Everywhere I could see that the military commonweal was founded on slave labour. The ground was tilled and the operations of common life were conducted by men of a different race and climate from the oath-compelling fire-eaters that ruled the island; and over them stood overseers with whips to urge their industry. It was a sorry sight; and when I looked into the faces of the workers, I could distinguish the wreckage of nobler natures than were to be found in Broolyian breasts. The foreheads were larger, the skulls more capacious; the eyes were full of a shy melancholy that seemed to shrink from investigation; they had not the huge lower jaws of their masters, or the cavernous mouths, or the red hair. They were now but beasts of burden, and their limbs were muscular and heavy and their footsteps dragging and torpid; but there was romance lurking in the refined lineaments and the occasional grace that shone out here and there amongst them. Whence they had come and what was their fate I could not ascertain. That they were not natives I could see; and that it was inferiority of will rather than inferiority of intellect or imagination or civilisation that had led to their enslavement to the fiery-willed Broolyians I could easily conjecture from the ruins of their past that peeped out through the labour-clotted masks of their rustic or artisan life.

I had to disguise my interest in them in order to get through the country. Any sympathy or pity would have roused the savage wills of their masters and sacrificed my hopes of the future, if not myself, to the exaggerated Broolyian ideas of rebellion and the punishment it demanded. Whenever I could, I lay in the shelter of some tree or coppice, and watched the movements of these interesting relics of a subjugated civilisation. Perhaps I might be able to do something for them when I gained a higher platform of vantage.

CHAPTER XXXVII
NOOLA

AFTER MANY DIFFICULTIES AND delays I reached the garrison on the western shore of Broolyi, where it faced Kayoss. I delivered my pass to the commandant, and was accommodated with shelter and food. The soldiers were not communicative; but after a few days I encountered in my wanderings on the beach one of the strangest men that I had ever seen, and he opened up vistas into the history of the islands. He was short in stature, but so light and springy was he in his gait and tread, I almost thought that he never touched the earth; he seemed to skim along its surface. He had a broad chest and great muscular development of the shoulders that singularly contrasted with his bird-like progress. His head was large for the body, but finely proportioned. It was the face, however, that most attracted me. It seemed almost to speak to me as I passed; it carried the soul in the depths of the eyes and in the whole expression. This soul, I felt after one glance, was a beautiful thing, marred only by some deep sorrow that draped it in everlasting melancholy. There was a heaven of pity and regret doming the nature, one could see in the sheen of the eyes and the strange translucence of the features. I was drawn magnetically to this new type of manhood; and yet I shrank from speech with him, his nature seemed so majestic and overawing.

I asked in the garrison concerning him, but all I could find out was that he was an exile from the city, and that he was kept under surveillance. It had been at his own request that he had been settled opposite the Isle of Anarchy. Finding that there would be nothing done to prevent my speaking to him and that he knew Aleofanian, I addressed him in reverent words the next time I met him, and we were soon fast friends. We met daily and wandered on the shore, and both of us seemed to find unfailing consolation in the ever-varying music of the sea, as it tided along the beach, and answered to the moods of sky and wind and current like a sensitive instrument. To me it had ever been a thing of life that sang and quivered to my every impulse and change of spirit. To be away from it was to be forlorn and widowed, and out of the reach of pity and sympathy. To him it seemed to fill the same large space in life. His thoughts were stimulated and made sublime by its rhythm; his whole existence was fuller and more musical in that wider sense of the word which applies it to the movements of the worlds on the face of night. I soon discovered that he was the engineer who had centralised and mechanised their religion for the Broolyians, and set them on the way of fulfilling the object of their existence and of establishing universal peace by universally annihilative war. He confessed that he had not been sorry to leave the capital and give up the petty ambitions with which he had been fired for a time. It would have meant but little effort on his part to perfect his explosive and master the whole island for his own purposes; but a look into the future had shown him how absurd was the ideal the Broolyians pretended to hold up to themselves, how impossible it would be by any homœopathic means, such as they proposed, to cure humanity of its everlasting feuds. He fell into despair and let the new king do as he would; and now in his solitude and meditation the love of his older past had come back on him, and he longed to see his native land, his paradise, again.

He had asked to be exiled to the garrison that watched Kayoss, in order that the sight of that wretched community might keep his ambitions down. There on the island opposite (and he pointed across the strait) lived the anarchic exiles from the islands of the archipelago. As he uttered the word "live" he smiled wearily. They lived but a few days after they were landed, for they came to violent feud, and strife and bloodshed ended the tragedy of trying to exist without government before the animal was dead in man. He raised his eyes suddenly, and he pointed to the opposite shore. On it moved a human being. That was the survivor of the last shipment to Kayoss. The garrison had never had any trouble. Within twenty-four hours after the anarchists were out of their fetters and free on shore they had found weapons against one another. They divided up into conspiracies and fought, and before many days were over, two or three remained too maimed and wounded to fight. When they recovered, they fought for the mastery, and one remained sorely stricken, often to die, sometimes to recover only to become a maniac. Such was the state of the wretch whom we now saw gesticulating on the beach. There never could be anarchism on this earth till the wild beast had died out of the human breast, and man was ready for flight to purer spheres. It was but poison in the existing state of mankind. A little of it did not do much harm. Its best cure was to give it full scope, for it soon killed off all existences within its reach and itself with them.

As he rose to this climax, his transparent face began to cloud and grow turbid. There was not that clearness of depth in the eyes which had so drawn me to him. His nature seemed to become shallow and tempestuous, more like the men of Broolyi and those I had known in the old western world. But it was not for long; he drew himself up with a sharp gesture of self-scorn, and then there settled upon him a silence and a melancholy that resisted my efforts to overcome. He grew quite unconscious of what I said, and, walking back towards his hut, left me. It was useless to attempt intercourse with such self-inwrapt thoughts.

For days I saw how purposeless would be all speech; his figure was bowed, his face was bent with grief, his eyes were fixed on the earth. I had never witnessed such tearless sorrow in human form. I persevered in my silent reverence for him, and at last the cloud lifted. He stood erect one day in the sunshine, and on my approach, he smiled answer to my greeting. All the dark and troubled appearance of his face had vanished, and his eyes and his complexion seemed to show the depths of his nature again with perfect limpidity. I was soon in sympathetic converse with him. There still rang through his utterances a note of sadness and regret. It reminded me of the undertones of so many folk-songs that wail with the reminiscence of lost ideals. How wearily it sounded, as it echoed through the depths of his meaning! It was as if his words fell from the stars quivering with the emotion and thought of the spheres in their everlasting rhythm. Out of infinity into infinity their wisdom seemed to pass. There was no limit to their depth of suggestion.

From his words there gradually developed the story of his life, with reservations that I could by no questioning or interest penetrate.

"Many leaden-footed years ago,—brief in the tale of my own life, long and slow taken by themselves,—I drifted on to the eastern shores of Broolyi, and fell into the hands of Nunaresha, one of the most powerful and ambitious nobles in the country, who was then endeavouring to get the ruling monarch dethroned and to have himself elected in his place. He saw before many moons had fruited and died that he had in me a godsend for his designs. Oh, the misery of it! I listened to his flattering proposals, and supplied him with the instruments to carry them out." The thought overcame him; the words died away on his lips, and his consciousness seemed to ebb into unknown depths of sorrow. I kept a reverent silence, and the thought of his broken story tided upwards again into words. "Ah me! the memory of my atavistic folly weighs my whole being down, when it comes upon me. Out of my warlike forefathers of hundreds of generations before had come into my nature some taint of their military passions and ambitions. For several hundreds of years it lay dormant. The wise observers of my country had seen it in me from my birth, and had surrounded me with such conditions as would keep it in abeyance, if not deprive it of all living force. Unhappily the profession of chemist and engineer, for which I was found on examination of all my faculties to be best fitted, opened up to me a vista into the destructive forces that permeate the universe, and the marvellous power over them that our own chemical knowledge gave. This and my growing acquaintance with the myriads that inhabit the earth and with the consequent scope for military ambition roused the sleeping devil in me. I passed my time in the analysis of the destructive elements in nature, in the manufacture of explosives, and in devising plans for their concentration against an enemy, although it was a fundamental maxim of our commonwealth that no member of it should ever harbour evil thought against the life of a fellow-being. Innumerable gentle and indirect methods were applied for my cure; but it was all in vain. My ancestral passion was roused like an unquenchable fire. I could see the sorrow over me in the faces of the community. At last, without their ever having come to formal resolve, I was placed in a boat with my share of the wealth of the island in precious metals, and blown far out to sea in the direction of Broolyi.

"Doubtless by the help of the forces my countrymen have control of, I drifted towards this island, and came to be received by Nunaresha. He almost at once raised me to the position of trusted adviser. He accepted every device I invented for his purposes, and supplied me with the material I required. I gave him such power over explosives that he felt himself almost invincible. He subdued his quarrelsome baronial neighbours with the greatest ease, and by the help of his explosive catapults made his friends throughout the island supreme over their districts. His influence was soon predominant, and the feeble intriguing monarch was deposed and Nunaresha chosen in his stead. He spared neither friend nor foe in order to attain to unquestioned despotism. The baronial castles were demolished by the new force, and all were drawn into his court by its attractions and its concentration of power. The barons became the mere parasites and flatterers of the new king.

"Yet did he feel unhappy in that the ecclesiasts could still wage secret war against him in the hearts of the women and thus in every household. At any moment the rebellion might break out, and, though he could crush it, once it became open, he never felt safe from the weapon of the assassin or fanatic. I, the still-degenerate Noola, came to his aid, when he pleaded with me; and I manufactured the spiritual mechanism of the country for him to control as he pleased. He banished the priests and substituted an automatic priesthood and service such as might be completely at his beck. It was an easy matter for me to invent the various machines, musical, ceremonial, marionettic, and locutory. I saw that some such spiritual control over men was needed, if universal peace were to be attained on the earth. I still believed that peace was the true aim of human civilisation, and that this could be reached only by such warlike forces and such spiritual authority in the hands of a single governor or council of governors as would make rebellion seem an impossibility and a farce to every reasoning mind.

"I have been utterly disabused of all such thoughts. Such peace can mean nothing but universal stagnancy of mankind. There is no advance, no life without struggle and competition. I could have invented after years of work such a weapon of war as would have enabled a man to master the world and keep it cowering in fear. I could have extended my mechanical religion so as to control the thoughts and beliefs of all men. But what was the advantage, if the ruler grew worse? It was only to connect all the spiritual fountains of the earth with this tainted source, and thus to keep them for ever impure. I saw his unbounded power gradually sap the will and the morality of the monarch. He sank into dissipation and debauchery. He made the whole of Broolyian art and religion and morality coarse and vulgar. The women grew more pampered and fat and licentious; the men became hypocrites and laggards. In the court there was nothing but display, vulgar accretions of gaudy uniforms and of jewels of all kinds. In the country there was increasing degradation and misery. It was patent to the eyes of those who were not blinded by the possession of power or the shadow of power. The only thing that saved the nation from collapse was its frequent war expeditions. They hated the water passage to other islands, but they delighted in the excitement of conflict, and they came back fewer in numbers, slimmer in figure, and more active in habit. You might have expected the women to preponderate in the population, because of the war drain on the men. But perhaps you have noticed that amongst the children and youth, it is our own sex that has the best of it in numbers; whilst fat old women are seen everywhere, old men are seldom seen. A warlike community ever recuperates by means of the physiological fact that, where only young and vigorous soldiers are the fathers competing for the love of the young women, who are few and somewhat pampered, there is a predominance of male births. It is this prevention of old age amongst men by the sharp sickle of war along with the seclusion and delicacy of the women that keeps the community from complete effeminacy and ultimate extinction. Broolyi is the exile asylum of all the passion for militarism in the archipelago, and the internecine wars of the exiles reduce their numbers and yet keep them active; their hatred of the sea saves the other islands from conquest by them. Their great heroic age was the reign of a woman who had been expelled from my own land for her warlike passions. She overcame their nausea for oceanic expeditions by training most of the boys like a coast population to take delight in boats and ships, and it was only the jealousy of the other women that prevented Broolyi from mastering the whole of the archipelago. She ever fostered her desire of revenge on her original country, and at last led an army of vengeance against it; but she was again and again repulsed with ease. In the disfavour of defeat the Broolyian women accused her of witchcraft in drawing away the affections of the young men from them, and had her put to death. Degenerate though I have grown, I never nurtured one thought of retaliation for my exile; and even had I, I should never have been so foolish as to imagine that I could have carried it out. She must have been mad or drunk with passion to attempt such a thing. When she died Broolyi sank back into the even tenor of quarrel and civil war. Alas, that I should have been the means of stirring it again to warlike ambition for mastery! It was my mistaken ideal of universal peace by means of universal and omnipotent authority. I have come to the conclusion that all government is but giving the monopoly of opportunity to one set of robbers in order to save the nation from the ravages of most others. It is worse for the higher natures of the governing than for those of the governed; and I have recanted my heresies.

"How weary I grew of the pomp and show of the court, of the dreary round of war and dissipation! I would have given the world for exile into solitude; and yet I dared not secede from the monarch and his following. I had shown myself too resourceful to be allowed to go free in the island. The king never would have believed that I was at rest and only desirous of rest.

"But the inevitable conclusion came. Lapped in the luxurious security of unquestioned power, he grew careless; thinking that every mind in the island was tuned to his key, hatred to him had grown silently in the hearts of many. At the most unexpected place and moment it blazed out, and he fell by the hand of an assassin. He had meant to establish a dynasty, but his children all fell with him; and the nobility elected his successor from amongst themselves, one of the mildest and most characterless. I saw that this was my opportunity, and I pleaded with him that I might be sent into exile and solitude; and, in order to make him feel sure that I could not be plotting against him, I asked that I should be near the garrison that watches the island of anarchists. Here I have rested these many years, working out my spiritual purification in sorrow and regret. I have climbed higher in soul than I had ever thought to reach; and yet clouds of anger at times float across my nature and mar my power of vision. I am not worthy to return to my own land. Ah, that I were! And what hope is there of any such return for me, the outcast, the degenerate?"

He fell again into self-inwrapt reverie. His thoughts had gone back to that land of mystery whence he had come, and vain was it for me to attempt to follow them. I must wait. And I thought I saw my way to bring about my purpose.

One day we had again grown intimate in our conversation, and he had become familiar enough to ask me whence I came. I told him how I had crossed the circle of fog with my yacht, and he asked me how I had resisted the magnetic forces and sea currents that so effectually fence in this sub-tropical archipelago. I described the *Daydream*. At first he could not realise that she could move swiftly without the help of wind or current or oar; but, when the thought of steam power propelling her came on his mind, it took full possession of it. He made sure that I could force her right in the teeth of a storm, and then his face was illumined with joy and hope.

The next day he was all eagerness to know the construction of her engines and her mode of propulsion; and, having satisfied himself that she had ten times the power of the largest falla driven by oars, he surrendered his inner thoughts to me. He now saw a way by which he might return to his dear native land, and he described to me the singular means his countrymen employed for hedging off intrusion and expelling members of their community that are alien to its main purpose. Round the shoulders of their central peak, Lilaroma, runs, on an enormous scaffolding, what they call the storm-cone; it is a huge trumpet-shaped instrument with its wide end turned on the horizon, and out of it is blown from the centre of force in the island a blast that, when concentrated on any point, has the power of a tornado; nothing propelled by oars or sails has hitherto been able to resist the artificial hurricane. By night it moves slowly around the horizon, and, if its blast encounters any object floating on the surface of the ocean, however small, it brings all its force to bear on it till the resistant material flees before it. It produces a local tempest, and the intruder either sinks or escapes before the blast. There is no record in the archipelago of any falla or human being having ever reached the shore of Limanora by sea; and though the long tradition of this tornado barrier-to-all has ended in a more complete, because a spiritual, barrier, that of superstitious fear, the storm-cone never ceases its vigilant blast.

I saw the source of his hope and told him of our encounter with the storm-cone and the result, fearing that he did not understand all the conditions; but, after ascertaining that we had sail set, and that the tornado caught us broadside, his face bore a smile that implied complete mastery of the problem. He showed me that, if the sails had been down and the bow had been pointed right to the storm-cone, the ship could have easily held her own against the blast; but, that we might not be too sure of the result and might not introduce a whole shipload of intruders into the island, he would invent a method by which we two alone should reach its shore. It was this. He intended to make two wooden, water-tight shells in the shape of a fish with sharp snout and directing tail; into these, as we got close to a shelving beach, we two would enter. The lids would be sealed so as to let no water in; and then the sailors of the *Daydream* would shoot them from two huge catapults of his, so that they would plunge into the sea, and speeding through the water, would rise to the surface, and float into the shallows close to the sand.

I could see the feasibility of the plan, and entered gladly into it, for at last I perceived a chance of reaching his mysterious fatherland. As he had agreed to take me for his comrade, he began to teach me his native language. He told me he could not give me more than the rudiments and framework. The niceties of it and the great vocabulary come only in long years of familiarity. It was constructed on the principle of assigning the easiest words to the commonest and easiest things and ideas. It grew in difficulty and perplexity in the higher spheres of thought and investigation. The names for the familiar objects and needs of human beings were monosyllabic, and each expressed some essential or striking quality or feature of the thing either by means of the nature of the sound or by resemblance to some other but abstract word. The verb, or as he called it, the energy-word, and the adjective or quality-word, were generally dissyllabic, the former by means of the affixing, the other by means of the prefixing, of one of many different sounds or letters. Half of each of these sets of extension elements were vowels, the other half consonants. They were phonetic alternatives; the consonantal was meant as neighbour to a vowel sound, and the vowel as neighbour to a consonantal. For example: "kar" meant "dust"; "karo" meant "to reduce to dust"; "okar," "having the essential qualities of dust." "Tri" meant "sea-water"; "trim," "to use sea-water"; "atri," "salt and liquid like sea-water"; "trik," "to plunge into sea-water"; "itri," "dipped in sea-water." There was no difference in form between the adjective and the adverb, and there were only two kinds of relational words or words that showed the connection between ideas or things or energies or qualities that we brought into relation. Our prepositions and conjunctions would be included under the one type; the same particle or kin-word might be used to express the affinity between two of the simplest words for concrete objects and two such complex ideas as are given in sentences. The other kind of relational word was what they called their pointer and seemed to stand for our pronoun. It pointed out some object or idea already mentioned or to be mentioned, in order to show its relation to other objects or ideas, or pointed out the relation of the energy-word or of the quality or of the object to some personality. These kin-words or pointers consisted each of two letters; there were some hundreds of them, and their number was ever growing as new relationships grew out of a more complex civilisation or out of advancing investigation and discovery. There were no separate words of one letter, all the letters being monopolised by the prefixes or affixes.

The subtones or slight variations of the common sounds were utilised to express various shades of meaning; as for example, time was expressed in the verb by a modification of the sound of the affix, whether consonantal or vocalic. "Lo karō ti rak" meant "I reduce this rock to dust"; "Lo karō ti rak," "I shall reduce this rock to dust"; "Lo karōō ti rak," "I reduced this rock to dust." Accent on the affix was used to express stage of action, beginning, in process, or complete; or rather lack of accent expressed the second, sharp accent the first, and full accent the last. Pitch was employed to express attitude of mind to the action; the higher tones giving various shades of determination or order, the lower, various kinds of uncertainty or question, and the full, ordinary tones expressing the different phases of assertion or surety.

Transferred or metaphorical meaning was indicated by the use of a variation in the vowel sound of the noun. "Kăr" with long, broad vowel is "dust"; "Kăr" with short vowel implies the sporadic ideas that float in a civilisation or community or period or mind; and all the various grammatical and sense modifications of the original concrete noun were applicable to the new noun with the transferred sense.

The grammatical framework of the language was so simple that I mastered it in a few days. A few more days sufficed to get familiar with what they called the infant's vocabulary, all the concrete words for common things, like earth, rock, sea, sky, food, arm, hand, head, light, fire, smoke, cloud. What made this easier was that words for things that had a close resemblance or connection in action had the same consonantal sound but different vowels, or the same vowel and one consonantal variation; "foresight" was "lum"; "fore-energy" was "lim"; "rum" was "gravitation," "rim," "force"; "lul," "smoke," "lil," "cloud." When I passed to the youth's vocabulary of less concrete words or words with metaphorical applications, it was more difficult, partly because the vocabulary was larger, partly because the differences were subtler; but I was greatly aided by the universal and primary law of their tongue, that the same sound should not stand for more than one meaning or shade of meaning; whenever a word tended to acquire a new sense, a new modification of the form was deliberately invented and adopted. Thus there were none of the ambiguities and shifting senses that make all other languages and especially the European like a quagmire or quicksand. One of the more important annual functions of the community as a whole was language sanitation.

It is one of the greatest mistakes of European civilisation to let words take their own course, the most dangerous source of spiritual epidemics. In them lurk foul thoughts and suggestions that spread their moral contagion as soon as the child comes into contact with their inner meanings. Nothing is so pernicious, so obstructive of progress, as the virus of uncleansed words. They

let out on new ages moral diseases that have been forgotten. In them contagious germs adhere to the nooks and corners for generations as in old houses.
Even the fallacies that cling to the human mind from the many and shifting
senses of words are bad enough, but worse is the opportunity they give for
villains to palter with them. Nothing is easier than in our old civilisations to
betray the innocent; language with its chameleon nature can fit itself to every
atmosphere and light; it gives the readiest shelter to dishonesty and error.
Unpurified, undefined, it is the quaking bog in which half the souls that are
born into the world are irrecoverably lost.

Ages ago his countrymen had taken their language in hand, and swept out
of it all foul suggestion. Now their chief task was to prevent ambiguities and
double or shifting meanings from creeping into words and making them the
cloaks of dishonest purpose, the stumbling-blocks of the still feeble human
soul. There were linguistic specialists whose duties were to watch the use
of words by the community and note down those that were changing their
signification. They had also to invent new words to fit the new meanings,
and to lay the results of their investigations before the meeting of the whole
nation. Whatever were unanimously adopted became at once a part of the
language; and for those that were rejected the experts had to bring forward
other suggestions.

The result was that their language was as limpid as their own thoughts;
and it was kept musical too. After the linguists had made out lists of suggested
substitutes, they submitted them to the imaginative men and the musicians;
through this ordeal, and that of the meeting of the people, none but noble
words could pass; and for words that had to cover new ideas in some department of science or art the linguists had to consult with the scientists or
artists. This people thought no trouble lost that was spent on ennobling the
garment of thought and the master-element of music and imaginative work.
"All is false, if words are uncertain," "Language is the ether of thought; it
interpenetrates all existence," were two of their favourite maxims. Another
that was often on the lips of Noola was: "Take care of the words, and the
thoughts will take care of themselves."

It was little wonder then that I found it easy to master the primary stages
of this most translucent language. The stage of full manhood and the stage
of the wise, I could see from a few illustrations he gave me, had difficulties
and subtleties that could be mastered only by long acquaintance; and it was
not till I had been many years in Limanora that I came to understand them;
for, though the vocabularies were constructed on the most symmetrical and
clear plan, they had as many words as all the languages of Europe put together. Most of them stood for ideas or elements that were beyond European

thought or discovery, or for ideas that were, many of them, fagoted together under a single word in our Western languages. No idea, no shade of an idea was without its own word. Half the false starts of European civilisation or science or philosophy were due to misunderstandings caused by the number of meanings that attach to single words. European controversies and discussions are interminable owing to this fertile source of fallacy and of shifting ground. I was not surprised at the small progress made by both old and modern civilisations after I saw the trouble the Limanorans took to purify and define their words, and the ease with which one could master the most difficult thought expressed in their limpid language. As I tell you my story now in your own and my native tongue, I feel as if I wandered in a dream through a land of mists that are ever shifting and deceiving. I have often to abandon the attempt to explain to you the noblest of the Limanoran ideas. At other times I have to translate clear expressions into muddy, uncertain words, or to resort to makeshifts that, I fear, give you but little notion of the originals. As I talk with you in your English tongue, I seem to be moving amid illusions and phantoms. How unmelodious it all sounds! A language like the Limanoran needed no poets; it was poetry itself, so musical was every word and every combination of words, so bright and strong, so suggestive and harmonious every idea that needed expression in it. When an Englishman is able to choose the musical words of his language and put them together with rhythmic harmony expressive of the inner harmony of the ideas, he is canonised as a linguistic saint, a poet. The Limanorans were poets by virtue of their language and their nature and training, and it is like passing into the most commonplace of prose to express even their commonest words and ideas in the most poetical English.

Little though Noola taught me, I was enamoured of it, and could scarcely keep from crooning the words to myself, like the lilt of an old song. And every sentence seemed to be as melodious as the separate words. I tried to form discordant combinations, but, on presenting them to my tutor, I found that they bore no sense; they were impossible combinations of ideas. Especially was the harmony of sound predominant in the higher stages of the language. The commonest description of even the most difficult scientific investigation sounded like a noble blank verse poem. To speak in English again, much though it brings back out of my oldest past, is to walk in fetters.

Before Noola was satisfied that I could make myself understood in Limanoran, and just as he had perfected his plan for our projection into the beach waters of his native land, we had aroused suspicion in the garrison by our long colloquies. They watched our every movement. Nor did I allay their fears by my assurance that we were about to attempt a landing on Kayoss by sea. We were seized and sent to the capital to be dealt with by the king and his council. Long debate and threatening civil war delayed the decision, but I am certain that the result would have been condemnation to death in the end, for the whole country was honeycombed with suspicions and fears of plots; and executions of suspects occurred every day.

But the unexpected rescued us. We lay in our prison cells, weary, half expectant, half wishing more delay. Our food was thrust in to us day after day through a small aperture in the iron doors of our pitiless stone-walled dungeons. At first we heard through the narrow iron-railed slit that served as a window the hurry and bustle of the city, like the sound of a distant torrent. One day it seemed to grow less and less, and at last it ceased. The silence was oppressive and ominous. Next morning the wicket aperture in our door did not open. All day we were without food. We wondered what had occurred. Four days threw their twilight into our cells, and not a sound of human voice approached us. I felt my hunger pass from the gnawing stage into languor and collapse. I sank on my reed pallet unable longer to pace my floor. I swooned rather than slept when twilight thickened into gloom. I knew that a few days at most must end the alternations of collapse and consciousness. I dreamt that I was back in the old fishing village in my mother's hut on the cliff; and her voice sounded sweet in my ears, as she welcomed me home at night. I thought that I fell asleep in it and that the morning had come. I remembered that my comrades were to call me and that we were to start early on a long fishing excursion. I moved uneasily, half conscious that I ought to rise and see if the dawn had broken; and then it seemed to me that the hum of voices sounded in the distance. "It is my friends," I said; a loud rattle and clang, I thought, must be their volley of stones on the roof and windows to waken me. Then I heard their Scotch accents beside me. I must awaken. With an effort I rose and jumped from my bed. The cold of the prison floor brought me to consciousness. There beside me was my captain, Alec Burns, with some of his men. I sank back on my pallet in a swoon after a sign of recognition. They applied restoratives, and in half an hour, though faint and weak, I was able to totter out on the arms of two of my sailors into the passage and thence into the sunshine. Under an awning I lay panting back into life, and nursing and liquid sustenance gave me appetite, and made me strong enough to walk alone.

I asked Burns for an explanation of all that had occurred. The royal officers were about to seize the *Daydream*, he discovered, and he was intending to put out to sea in the night. He had got up steam and was about to heave the anchors, but he found that she had grounded, as it was low tide. As her screw moved, the water gave forth an unbearable stench. He stopped her and the fetid odour disappeared. In the morning he looked out to the city, and saw the streets and the ramparts completely deserted. Not a being moved anywhere. All day the same death-like stillness prevailed. No boat moved in the harbour; no soldier appeared on the battlements; not a sound of marching or of military music was heard. It might have been a city of the dead. The following day opened with the same experience. They pulled on shore, and the streets echoed empty to their step, as they walked up from the beach. They knocked at doors, but received no answer. They entered houses, and passed through them unmolested, unchallenged. At last the explanation forced itself upon their senses. In one house they could not proceed for the fetor that met them at their entrance; and in the next lane they saw dead bodies strewn, as if cast from the windows, in some places heaped high above the earth. It was a city of the unburied dead, and no living creature was to be seen to bury them.

The next day, on landing again, they encountered some of the slaves, who were plundering the houses, and who fled as the sailors approached. They followed one up, and saw him enter the huge building, which they found to be the prison. They saw him take the keys and open the various cells; and out poured his imprisoned fellows. They heard from one prisoner of my incarceration, and then discovered my dungeon and led me out into the sunshine.

As Burns came to this point in his narrative, I remembered my fellow-prisoner, Noola, and I hurried them off to look for him. They returned with him none the worse for his long fast. He did not complain of hunger. He had, I could see, a fund of sustenance to draw upon unusual in the human bodies I had been accustomed to. We persuaded him to try some of our restorers; but he took them with none of the eager appetite that I had shown. It was manifest that he had a physical constitution altogether different from ours.

He asked us how it was that Burns had been allowed to set us free. He listened with equanimity to the explanation, but, when he heard of the slaves, he started in alarm, and bade us hurry to our ship. It was not long before we were on board, and, as it was full tide, the *Daydream* was now able to get from her anchorage and make out into the open sea.

When he saw us safe out of the harbour, he settled down and told me the meaning of his sudden fear and advice. "These slaves inhabit the interior of the island in myriads, and, under the whips of their overseers, do all the work that this military community needs. They are so shamefully treated that, if ever the bonds break and they rise in rebellion, they show no mercy, and make no distinction in their fury. The opening of the prison doors meant that the slave population was about to revel in crime and bloodshed. They will crowd down uncontrolled from all parts of the country, and fill the city with a ravaging, plundering mob. Had we remained till they were in force, we should have had no chance of escape; we should have perished in the general hate of all but their own kin.

"You ask me why so powerful and so military a people should ever permit such an outbreak. It is because they are cowed by a greater fear, that of the plague. You have perceived how low the tide has been, and how hot the sun. The mud upon the shore of the harbours, when it is laid bare by the waters and exposed to an exceptionally hot summer, breeds a plague that sweeps through the ranks of the Broolyians. There is no means known of stopping its ravages, no cure for it. Once seized by it no man can last more than one day; and once dead the body putrefies and spreads the contagion far and near. All the citizens flee to the heights, to be out of reach of the pestilence. There and there alone can they have any chance of survival, and then only if no one bears with him the seeds of the terrible disease. It is piteous to see the cowardly stampede of these bold warriors. The slaves know the meaning of the flight; it is their carnival; they are untouched by the plague; they can move with impunity amongst the rotting dead bodies or the putrid mud.

"It is a strange example of the revenge that a law of nature takes upon those who outrage it. Long ages ago the war-loving exiles, who were landed upon Broolyi, subdued its gentle inhabitants, but so wore them down by driving them as slaves that they almost died out. Their place had to be supplied; for the masters had become accustomed to freedom from manual and sordid employments, and nothing could persuade them to give up their weapons and swaggering military employments and put their hand to the plough or the hatchet. They had to send emissaries out in all directions to steal, borrow, or buy slaves. Peaceful and often highly civilised islanders were kidnapped and battened down in the holds of the fallas in order that they might not resort to mutiny or attempts at escape. In these foul dens oftentimes men and women who had been accustomed to the delicacies of civilisation were penned; and they suffered the horrors of an unclean, putrid dungeon and of a rough sea passage. By the close of the voyage half the captives had to be thrown overboard dead or next door to death. Those that survived were proof against the diseases that originated in such nests of contagion. When the shipload had been disembarked, the filth of the voyage was washed into the harbour, and the germs of a new plague took up their abode in the mud at the bottom, dormant for long years, and then, when the favouring conditions came, a hot summer and a series of low tides, rising into the air and filling the neighbourhood of the shore. It is one of these plagues that has emptied the city.

"The strange thing about this Broolyian fever is that its symptoms and horrible effects are those that the slaves experienced in the loathsome sea passage. The fever-smitten feel a sinking of the heart as in homesickness; this alternates with wild fury against wrongs that are in their case purely imaginary. They think that they are in darkness and filth and chains, unable to escape, in utter despair of life. They cherish a madness for liberty, which wears out their bodies and brings such exhaustion that they sink rapidly. Their faces and bodies grow red as with rage, then pale as with sea-sickness, then yellow with loathing. They come to nauseate living, and would gladly put an end to their tortures by suicide; yet their hearts again beat wildly as if clutching at life. Before the passion has collapsed and their energy has sunk, they become putrid in their limbs, till they shudder at the sight of their hands and feet. The microscopic life, that sprang into being in the holds of the slaving fallas, and that festers in the mud of the fore-shores, having drawn all the sufferings and feelings of the captives into it, communicates them to the people that wronged them. The survivors of the enslaved and their descendants are for ever inoculated against it. At every outbreak of the epidemic the slaves escape and hold high festival in the city, all the fiercer and more degraded in their orgies from the state in which they and their ancestry have been kept. In their drunken carousals they come to blows, though many escape back to their native land. When the summer has passed, some of the soldiers venture into the suburbs, and with threatening missiles force those that have remained alive to bury the dead, and to cleanse the city and prepare it for their masters. All settles back into its old state. New slave raids are organised to fill the places of those that have vanished; new horrors take place, and new germs are deposited in the mud."

There was the light of pity in the eyes of the narrator. I could hear his voice quiver and sound plaintive, although he gave but the barest outline of the history. He was filled with the vision, I thought, of the vanity of human life and its pursuits. I could see from some words that fell from him soon after that memory had brought up to him the dire chimeras that had led him from his native paradise; he saw the bootlessness of war, and the awful vengeance it works out upon the combatants; he realised the monstrous nature of tyranny and its recoil upon the tyrants; he felt how illusory, how mocking was the human ideal of luxurious ease. The faults that had banished him from Limanora had been burned out of him by caustic experience; his nature had grown purified by that long solitude which had brought wisdom again. He hoped the evil in him had been long subdued; but would his native land take him back? He despaired; he knew of no precedent; all who had been exiled had finally vanished. He hoped, for he felt how drastic his purification had been, how bitter his repentance. Yet the rapid advance of their thought and civilisation threw him back again into fear; he felt like a man put on shore at the head of a rapid and having to find his way on land and through jungle after the boat, as he saw it speed down the torrent.

I tried to draw him from the harassing turmoil of his emotions and thoughts by questions on the meaning of phrases that he had used to me. He had often spoken of the practice of banishment for moral or constitutional weaknesses. Would he explain to me its character and extent? I showed great anxiety to know how it worked.

After a time my eager interrogations drew him from the painful inner conflict, and, with one of his comprehensive and benignant smiles, that seemed to light up his whole being, he began: "It is a matter of very ancient history. It is indeed thousands, I might almost say, tens of thousands of years since it was first adopted; for it was a deliberate adoption on the part of our ancestors in Limanora. Long generations before, the idea of progress had fixed itself into our civilisation as its true aim. How to make the human system, both spiritual and physical, advance rapidly was the problem discussed year after year, age after age by our wisest men and women. All others were counted trivial or auxiliary. It seemed mere folly to look after the progress of our domestic animals with so much care and science as we did, and leave the human species to the assistance of accident. Our diseased kine and horses and fowls had to die off without transmission of their weakness to posterity. Only the finest breeds were paired or allowed to hand on their frames and powers. Every care was spent on the study of their anatomy and on the development of their best and most useful qualities. Whatsoever the Limanorans desired to do with these animals they did. If any feature of their bodies or natures or characters seemed worthy of development, it was soon developed, and a new species was established. What gross disloyalty to the destiny of man to let him drift when he was doing so much for his humble servitors in the animal world! A generation or two of discussion awakened our ancestors to the folly of their inaction. The cry of reform arose, and the feelings of the whole nation were aroused by the enthusiasts for progress in human breeding. Hereditary disease and the tortures it inflicted on the innocent were used to wing their arrows of eloquence. At last there grew up in the community an instinct as peremptory as conscience, condemning the marriage of men and women who had transmissible diseases. Public opinion passed into a moral sense in one or two generations, and, before a century had gone, all the diseases that tended to pass from parent to child had disappeared from every class but the poorest.

"Then did it begin to dawn upon the consciousness of our ancestry that the worst of all diseases had, though mitigated in virulence, been still left to fester in the human system. What was the use of curing the body, if the spirit were left to gather to it and transmit foul thought and emotion? The educated and responsible classes came to feel that the true problem was yet unsolved; nay, that, though they had purified their systems of hereditary diseases, the poor and neglected and improvident still nursed them and propagated them in the meaner suburbs of the town and in the poverty-stricken districts and villages of the country. Reformers applied their enthusiasm to educating the proletariat, and it seemed at first as if Limanora were about to be transformed. The annual bill of criminality was reduced, and many of the artisans and labourers learned the lesson of providence, and rose into the class of the well-to-do. Most of these soon admitted the physiological truths of heredity into their system as part of their conscience, and if they had disease of the lungs or heart or brain or nerve, they kept from marriage and generation, lest it should be transmitted.

"But there still remained the foul social fringe of the community, dabbled in the mire of improvidence, pauperism, hereditary disease, and criminality, and this was the part of the population that increased most rapidly still. It was an eating cancer in the body of the state. Its members refused education for themselves and their children, or, if they took it, used it as a new and refined weapon against their self-restraining, law-abiding neighbours, or against the commonweal as a whole. The true source of all the infection of the state was still uncleansed. The medical rulers who had managed affairs so well for several generations were unable to come at this incurable plague-spot. What was to be done? The most drastic remedies were proposed, and had their various advocates. The exterminators were never anything but a small party, because of the general sense of humanity in the people. The mutilators became more influential, especially amongst the party that attached them-selves to the doctors; but they never approached the really practical sphere of politics. Both continued mere parties of theorists, ridiculed and sometimes abhorred and execrated.

"At last there came a great religious reformer who spent his whole energies on the pauper and criminal skirts of society. He took up the altruistic motive and element in human nature, and set it in complete antagonism to the egoistic and individualistic. He connected it with the idea of God, and taught it as the utterance of the Deity. At first he implied that the utterance was given through all nature, but, forced on by his more superstitious followers, he had finally to announce himself as the special mouthpiece of this divine doctrine. The whole country was soon in a blaze, and great was the fervour of the proletariat. Their millennium seemed to have come. They marched about in great bands celebrating his praises. Many of them had their dormant powers stirred to eloquence. Even the ruling classes looked with favour on the movement, and some of the well-to-do joined in it.

"Then came the inevitable demand for practical doctrine that arises in the career of every successful prophet. What was he going to do for the poor and oppressed? What was to be the permanent solution of the problems of pauperism and criminality? The state, it was true, allowed a pittance to all who were completely stranded and appealed to its officers; but there was the brand of disgrace on the dole; every man or woman who took it slunk away from the sight of others. How was the world to be regenerated, if the horror of charitable mechanism was not to be removed? There could be no millennium without stern facing of this problem.

"He took the plunge. He declared for equal division of the wealth of the country. His mission soon became a crusade against, not merely the wealthy, but the well-to-do. All goods were to be held in common. No more was there to be inequality of position or possession. Property was a sin, to be prosperous and provident a crime, the crime of theft from the poor. The only possessions they should allow to be treasured up were the spiritual wealth in the garner of God. Beyond death there lay the only property that was worth having, happiness and serenity in the divine dwelling-place. No man should be allowed to appropriate or lay up other treasure. God would look after His own here; and none should want. It was the rankest folly, if not blasphemy, to save or hoard worldly treasure against the needs of the future.

"One or two of the prosperous amongst his followers came and laid their money at his feet; but most turned away from him, when they heard him shatter at a word all they had toiled for night and day during their weary lifetime. He denounced them as faithless and worldlings, unworthy to have followed in his footsteps.

"The governing classes took alarm and watched his movements with every precaution against outbreak; but the *posse* of converted highwaymen and brigands guarded him; and it was said that not a few secret murderers were in the band. They feared that he might be assassinated, and that his followers might then be left to the tender mercies of the law. He elevated their lives for the time by the religious fervour he infused into them. Whosoever saw them spoke of them as new men. It is true that he had adopted their own practical creed, antagonism to property, and had thus attached them to him by bonds of community; but he sublimated it, and, as long as the throb and transport lasted, raised them to something that seemed his own religious platform.

"There were symptoms of dissension in some, when they came to see that the world was not transfigured, whilst others, who had low, vulpine natures to begin with, sneaked round his camp to see where they could betray to their own profit. These latter, the rich hypocrites and machiavellis hired as assassins. The fall of their saviour under the blow of a midnight dagger at first paralysed the new enthusiasts; but soon there came the full revenge of all martyrdoms. The doctrine that had to be met by the knife of the assassin was surely strong. Many of the ardent youth of the governing classes looked into it and found it noble. They and some who had been secret followers of the popular leader openly espoused his faith, and put themselves at the head of the bewildered proletariat.

"The nation was suddenly involved in civil war. It was clear that the one side had nothing and the other everything to lose. If the new socialists won, then the rich and the governors would be reduced to the ranks; all they had gained through long generations would have to be surrendered for division. It was worth a struggle. Indeed, it must be a struggle for very life. Their worldly cunning came to their aid. Most of them were above the mean resources of treachery, were noble in every sense of the word, and refused to listen to anything but open combat. But the foxy diplomats suborned one of the youthful leaders and made him their agent in the camp of the enthusiasts; they sent their hirelings in to join the enemy. There was in the first battle a bold front offered by the socialists; but the traitors deliberately gave way and fled, and soon the raw half-disciplined artisans and labourers were in rout. The converted thieves returned to their plunder, and the poverty-stricken to their misery.

"Then a strange thing happened. To turn the flank of the new religion the gilded classes adopted it, and began to worship the martyr as divine. The more sincere of his followers were satisfied with the change, and settled down to their old life of discontent or content. The world took shelter under the beliefs of this hater of the world. His creed was emasculated of its socialism and altruism in deed, but was accepted in word. It became the symbol of all that was gorgeous and tyrannical. Magnificent temples rose for its worship; and in them haughty priests officiated. He who had been the apostle and prophet of the poor became the god of the rich and powerful. The new religion had left the nation not much better than it had been.

"One good thing, however, came from it by accident. It was long discussed what was to be done with the enemies of property, theoretical and practical, the socialists and the thieves. A solution was furnished by one of the most machiavellian of the diplomats; it was to give them as much as would be their share were the wealth of the state divided, and to deport them to one of the largest and most fertile islands of the archipelago, Tirralaria. It was hailed as the salvation of the state. Many ships, therefore, were prepared, and the enthusiastic believers in socialism and the thieves were put on board, and safely disembarked in their new domain, with the threat that, if any of them attempted to land again in Limanora, they would be at once put to death.

Two attempts were made to return; but they were beaten off. The expeditions in each case consisted of the better class of socialists, who felt the grinding tyranny of socialism, in which the bad are put on the same footing as the honest and conscientious. They were each too small to force a landing on any other island; nor would their fellow-islanders allow them to come back to Tirralaria. They could not live always in fallas; and they vanished from the archipelago. It is the current tradition, whence it comes I know not, that they burst through the circle of fog into the outer ocean, and sailing eastwards got footing on the western shores of America; but it is so many centuries ago when either secession occurred that the story is as dim as a dream of our infancy.

"The experiment was successful for Limanora, and supplied the new political formula of all reform. The state was well rid of knaves without doing them any wrong. Some of the worst blood of the community had been drawn, and yet the system had not been weakened to any great extent. The worst of the criminal and improvident part of the population had been expelled; and it seemed to optimists as if the Limanoran millennium were about to appear. Alas for human hopes! Though the virtuous section of the people had had their hands greatly strengthened, there were still the more gilded forms of vice to cope with. Ambition and love of war, sensuality and falsehood, were rooted in the hearts of the nation that had seemed to be purified. In order to gain their ends the ambitious were ever appealing to force and stirring up civil war, till at last it became unbearable by the peace-loving majority, who put into office sympathisers with their view of life and demanded expurgation of the loathed pugnacity. All who were warlike or ambitious in their nature or who had come of warlike or ambitious ancestry were deported to Broolyi; and you have seen the result of their civilisation.

"The hypocrites and the sensual were as eager as any to see the appeal to force finally extruded. They thought they would have it their own way when the swaggering, hectoring, military men were gone; but the licentious soon found themselves isolated. Their sins more readily found them out. Their outrages on what was honest in domestic life roused more sweeping and clamorous condemnation. The soldiers and bullies had had in their natures a side that was close to their own vice, and indulged in the amorous passion to licence, when their combativeness or ambition did not occupy the stage of their minds. They had had a sympathy for the lechers, and often protected them when public opinion had risen against them, knowing that they themselves at times stood in need of similar protection; and, though the lechers felt more kin to the hypocrites in their often demure or sly and crawling temptation of women, they found these anything but allies. In fact the machiavellis joined the hue and cry against them, and had them all carefully picked out of the community and deported with their share of the wealth of the state to Figlefia.

"The net was drawing round the hypocrites and liars, though they thought they were making themselves supreme in the nation. The honest and loyal and true element had grown predominant; and before a century had passed, the false had followed after the lechers; they were exiled with their belongings to Aleofane. Unlike the socialists and thieves, these last three sets of exiles made no attempts to return, or to enter into alliance against their old island. They found too great scope for their respective vices in their new countries to desire to leave them. They have prospered according to their own lights, and delude themselves into the belief that they have ideals far beyond those of their original land; Broolyi, as we have seen, sets up peace as its motive and religion, Figlefia matrimony and domestic life, and Aleofane truth. They each carried away with them so large a share of the wealth of Limanora that they long believed her too poor to be worth robbing. So they let her alone. Individuals for a time made efforts to land; but they were taught a severe lesson; and, since the invention of the storm-cone, all such attempts have been abandoned, and the central island is usually spoken of as the Land of Devils. Each of these now ancient nations adopted the principle that had led to their independence, and deport alien elements to other and smaller islands of the archipelago. One large group they call their lunatic asylum; thither they send everyone who is so fanatical in his enthusiasm for an idea or social theory, so extreme in his development of any alien vice or virtue as to be a danger to the state or to the peace of the community. Each island is given up to one type of monomaniacs; and it is an agreement on the part of the three great commonwealths to adhere to the classification of crazes. It is thus that they have been able to remain stable and united. The deportation policy has been their salvation, for it is the quixotic enthusiasts and crotchety extremists that constitute the greatest danger to the solidarity of a state; but in spite of their great advantages and the adoption of this method of state expurgation, they have not advanced in these thousands of years, during which they have occupied their islands.

"In after ages it was a matter of regret to the advancing Limanorans that they had not monasticised the exiles. It was useless, they knew, to adopt what you are thinking of, a missionary system. No propaganda, however successful, ever did more than send the old beliefs and habits below the surface to reappear in the new generations. Conversion through the intellect or the feelings is only skin deep. By no known process can the century-long growth of civilisation or virtue be abbreviated into a few days or months or years.

Selection in breeding and complete change in environment are the only true missionaries, and with many races even these are powerless, so deep has the virus of moral retrogression sunk into their natures. The best propagandist for them would be complete monasticism. The men of my day felt deep sorrow for the world that their ancestors had not sent the sexes of the deported to different islands, and guarded against the mutual approach by keeping three or four navies in the seas between, till the socialists, the warlike, the sensual, and the false had died out. It would have meant the greatest vigilance and the devotion of a large section of the people to naval pursuits for almost a century; but it would also have meant the disappearance of this obstacle to the progress of the world, this element of danger in the archipelago. The evil was irremediable by my time, for any attempt to remove it would mean conquest and bloodshed. And it had become not merely a maxim of state but an instinct born in every Limanoran that conquest and bloodshed are more than futile, are ruinous, that they destroy the higher nature of the conqueror or destroyer. To enter on such a course as would lead to the extermination of these vicious communities would be to sow again in our own the seeds of still greater evils. Nothing but the silent obliterative process of nature could justify itself to my countrymen.

"There was another reason that will perhaps seem to you more practical. It was that they had by no means finished their process of expurgation. No longer had great bodies to be deported. But from age to age an individual nature even in the most carefully bred and trained showed atavistic vice or weakness; and, when every means had failed to cure it, the individual had to be exiled; and one of these islands was his natural home, to which it would be no inhumanity to carry him; for there would he find choice spirits and natures akin to his own.

"This was my case. I had an ancestry that had in long ages gone by shown warlike proclivities, but in so subordinate and unobtrusive a way that they had not been banished. In the intervening generations their pugnacity had by means of selection and environment wholly disappeared; but, by some accident of nature or miscalculation on the part of the Limanoran sages who had chosen my parents and surroundings, the taint, that had seemed dead, reappeared. In spite of all remedies and care, I grew more pugnacious, more eager to excite my neighbours to war. I devoted my talents to the invention of weapons and war material. I made myself at last so obnoxious that no alternative was left. I was exiled to Broolyi, and there have I spent the long years since in efforts to burn the tainted spot from my nature."

The cloud had fallen upon him again, as he approached this part of his story. He persevered to the end; but so heavy lay the sorrow over his past upon him that it was keen anguish to speak further of it. I left him to his thoughts and went on deck.

I was surprised to find that we were close to the shore, and that on it stretched out a large and handsome city. I looked up to the great mountain that overbrowed it, and I seemed to recognise an outline with which I was familiar; could it be Nookoo? The name brought back my subterranean agony. The light streamer of mist that floated over its top showed it to have inner fires. The memory seemed almost dreamlike, and perhaps the unfamiliarity of some of the details was owing to our being on the other side of Figlefia, the side I had not seen.

Noola followed me on deck, and I conjectured that a subject like this might distract his thoughts and dispel his cloud. I called his attention to the land, and asked him if he knew it. It was Figlefia; but he seemed to be astonished at something in the scene. His eye was fixed on the city. I had never seen it before, and noticed nothing unusual in its appearance; but he saw with his keener and farther power of vision that no life was stirring in it. Another city of the dead was here. The dwellers could not be buried in sleep under the flashing scrutiny of noon. The ship's glasses could not help him to solve the difficulty; nor could his recollection of the history of the island; he had never heard of such devastating plagues in Figlefia as he had witnessed in Broolyi. It had slavery; but the slaves did not come such a distance, and were used as sailors and oarsmen in the passage over-sea. It was women that the lechers had mainly kidnapped, and it was these would have their revenge; but he had never heard of any efficient retaliation on the part of their seraglios.

It could not be an ambuscade to seize the *Daydream*? He alone would venture on shore; he would not hear of my joining him on his first excursion. When he got to land, I could see him move cautiously about the streets and then return still alone to the beach. He rowed off, and invited me to return with him.

It was one of the strangest scenes I had ever witnessed; for I had, because of my illness and haste of embarkation, seen little of the plague-stricken streets of the capital of Broolyi. The magnificence of the buildings and the luxury of the interiors of the houses contrasted with the loathsomeness of the rotting corpses. In every house lay some dead, generally in the midst of the most splendid tapestries and the most luxurious couches and seats; the spraying fountains of scent were now unable to overcome the stench of the dead hands that had set them flowing; but Noola observed that it was only in the houses of the lawful wives that the dead lay, men, women, and children. The seraglios were empty, except for here and there the stripped corpse of a man. The beautiful slave-women had all vanished; and there was not one of the male slaves amongst the dead.

When he had mentioned this to me, in a flash there came upon me the remembrance of my saviour from the wreck of the falla and my guide into the subterranean depths of Nookoo. It was, I saw in a moment, the ingenious missile he had told me of that had accomplished this carnage of the lecherous tyrants. The microbic globule in the hands of the women of Swoonarie had swept the Figlefians from the face of the earth. The infection had spread from each adulterer to his wife and household. How and whither the slaves had escaped it was impossible to find out. There was not a sign of life in the whole plague-stricken city. Doubtless his antiseptic armour and antidote had been found a success. Whether he and his people would follow up the victory by advancing with his death-dealing missiles against the other islands of the archipelago remained to be seen. That their old lethargy would overcome them when they returned to Swoonarie was the more probable result. They would be satisfied to have completed the revenge for the wrongs of ages, and to have freed their women who had been kidnapped, and the narcotic atmosphere of their native island would make them rest and postpone the dream of universal conquest. It was unlikely that they would occupy the island of Figlefia or the caverns of Nookoo, that had been their salvation by giving them energy; for there were too many agonised memories to lead them to rest there. Their own lotos-eating isle would draw the slave exiles back irresistibly, and hold them within it for ever as with bonds of iron.

Noola would not let me remain to speculate over the tragedy that had taken place or the romance of conquest that might follow it. There was danger for us in the pestilential atmosphere of the luxurious city. He hurried me back to the beach; but in passing one of the ramparts he saw some of the catapults that he had made for the Broolyians, capable of throwing enormous weights to great distances. He had intended to return to the Isle of Peace for two of them, as soon as he had allowed sufficient time for the slaves to reach incapacity by intoxication and sanguinary quarrels. This discovery obviated the expedition. He took two of the huge machines to pieces, and sent the sailors to carry them piecemeal to the boats. He had looked at our cannon and seen that they would be dangerous instruments for carrying out our experiment; he had got me to fire one of them, and decided that, though they had the power to carry the distance he desired, they had not large enough bore to admit of our enclosures, and to attach our cases to their balls might lead to failure of aim, or perhaps fatal injury to the two passengers in the missiles. When he had the catapults on board, he put them together; then he made two cases, filled them with material equal to the weight of a man, and shot them towards the shallower surf on the beach. They plunged into the waters and emerged in the ripple along the shore. He had them brought back, and found them intact. He went into one himself, and fastened its door securely within so that no water could enter. Then he instructed us to fire the man-missile in the same direction as the previous shots. The result was the same, and we saw him open the lid and walk out on the beach. Similar experiments with myself and with both of us convinced him at last that everything was safe, and that he could trust to the sailors to manage the affair with success.

We set out again in bright sunshine, and left behind us the deserted city of the plague. The next day the sun suddenly clouded, and looking up we saw that the cloud was rapidly moving over us and that it consisted of birds. We could distinguish the flash of the individual wings as they flickered in the sunbeams that broke through the ranks of the great army. We could hear far off the harsh or musical cries of the scouts and leaders, or the answering murmur of the embattled masses. At times we could see battalions form and reform in their flight, the van open its ranks and stretch out in long advancing line, and the rear ease their pace in order to cover the laggards. It was a marvellous sight, and the longer we listened the more distinctly could we hear the clang and whizz and creak of the myriads of wings. It was the annual migration northwards of the antarctic birds along the line of the submerged continent; so Noola explained. A large contingent for long ages had been inclined to settle each year on Limanora; but the storm-cone blew them onwards till they rejoined the main body. It was the storm-cone that was directing their flight now. He showed us how agitated were the rear battalions, how uncertain the beat of their wings, how irregular and shifting their formation. There we could see the strength of the blast bear stragglers out of their course, as they jerked their wings and uttered harsh cries; the spasmodic flash of the sunshine upon them was enough to show that they were bearing the brunt of some propelling storm. It took hours to clear the sky of this agitated cloud; but we set our course by its streaming flight, knowing that whence they were blown was our destination.

My heart bounded as I saw the face of our guide after instructing the man at the helm. It was set with strong resolution, and the eye blazed with the prayerful inspiration of a saint fixed upon his deity. He gazed into the shimmering light ahead with an intensity that seemed to imply some object dimly descried. We could see nothing, nor could we disturb him with question. We had surrendered the whole guidance of the ship to his discretion. On the morning after, we saw what had magnetised his gaze; the gleaming peak of Lilaroma with its streamer of cloud upon the distant rim of sky. He knew every inch of the shore; for, when it came clearly into sight, he turned the ship's

head directly east, leaving the fleckless white of the mountain on our starboard. We seemed indeed to be steaming away from Limanora; but he knew
his own purpose, and we let him alone. Night fell, and then we veered round
to the south, and faced the still gleaming point of purity upon the horizon. Up
and up it rose into the sky as we sped on; and yet the storm had not yet burst
upon us. He evidently knew the side of the island that was least open to attack
and therefore least watched. In the dim underlight of the dark moonless night
we could discern cliffs rise and snowless levels stretch dim and mysterious.
Still no sign of the storm-cone, though we could see the line of its passage
black round the snowy shoulders of the giant peak. On we forged as swiftly
as steam could make the *Daydream* fly. Noola paced anxiously from bow to
stern, from the look-out man to the wheel, never relaxing his gaze into the
darkness. It was a race with the quickest thoughts upon the earth. It seemed
as if we were about to impinge upon merciless crags, we seemed so near.
Still we held on with unabated speed. We were almost under the lee of the
threatening cliffs; and I thought that in a few minutes we should shut out
the sight of the cone-path round the mountain. With the suddenness of a
thunderbolt the tornado struck us. It made the ship stagger; but everything
was in readiness, every rope and sail tied up, every surface that would impede
our progress stowed below or turned so that it should not meet the force of
the wind. We seemed to stand still; I thought that we were even receding; but
she was cutting into the storm, for the cliff in front of us broke part of the
force of it. Still the cone roared; still the yacht made a few paces, we could
see as we threw anything overboard. He knew the conditions of the problem;
he knew that the people were certain to be long occupied with directing the
flight of birds away from the island; and he knew the section of the coast that
rose highest and would give us smooth water, blow the cone its fiercest. We
took some hours to get inside the ring of broken water; and it was still dark.
He then turned her head to the north, and soon we saw a shelving beach open
out beyond the cliff. He had the catapults ready. We were still protected by the
crags; but in a few minutes we would be out in the open, subject to the full fury
of the cone-storm. He gave direction to Burns to turn her head inshore full
speed as soon as we had run out of the shelter, and shoot off the man-missiles.
We entered our cases and fastened the lids securely. I felt myself moved and
laid in a groove that held the missile firm. I heard the word of command from
Burns; and that was almost the last thing I was conscious of from the old
world of my boyhood and youth. My heart leapt into my mouth as I felt the
concussion in starting through the air. I seemed to be dashed with great force
against something that was cushiony, and at that moment my sense of the
outer world and of myself lapsed.

POSTSCRIPT

OUR NARRATOR VANISHED AS abruptly as his story broke off here. Just when our curiosity had been whetted to its keenest we were left with the broken thread. We had noticed him hanging back from the account of his intercourse with Noola. His tissues had grown less transparent as he had proceeded with his description of the various islands. He had become accustomed to our food, and seemed to approach nearer to our common humanity. We came to take greater liberties with him, and even urged him to proceed with his narrative. We had become so interested in it that we would willingly have abandoned our pursuit of gold for days, if only he could have been induced to continue by daylight. The glimmer of our lamp or the dancing glow of our fire threw his face into shadow, and seemed to give him confidence; and even when storm and rain drove him in from the bush he resisted our persuasions as long as daylight lingered. He would lie so still that we were often afraid that he had died or fallen into a trance.

As he came to his story of Noola's exile, this reluctance increased even when the flickering shadows of the lamp or fire sheltered him. Our rough methods of trying to bring him to book only made him shrink farther into himself, and had it not been for the prolonged and stormy spring I fear that we should never have reached the natural close of his story, his exit from Riallaro. With his last word came bright sunshine and clear weather; and he disappeared as abruptly as he had come.